Love's Journey Home

KELLY IRVIN

HARVEST HOUSE PUBLISHERS
EUGENE, OREGON

Scriptures are taken from the Holy Bible, New International Version®, NIV®. Copyright © 1973, 1978, 1984, 2011, by Biblica, Inc.™ Used by permission of Zondervan. All rights reserved worldwide. www.zondervan.com

Cover by Garborg Design Works, Savage, Minnesota

Cover photos © Chris Garborg; Cathy Yeulet / 123rf.com

LOVE'S JOURNEY HOME
Copyright © 2013 by Kelly Irvin
Published by Harvest House Publishers
Eugene, Oregon 97402
www.harvesthousepublishers.com

Library of Congress Cataloging-in-Publication Data
Irvin, Kelly.
Love's journey home / Kelly Irvin.
    p. cm. — (The Bliss Creek Amish ; bk. 3)
ISBN 978-0-7369-5318-4 (pbk.)
ISBN 978-0-7369-5319-1 (eBook)
1. Widows—Fiction. 2. Widowers—Fiction. 3. Sons—Fiction. 4. Amish—Fiction. 5. Domestic fiction. I. Title.
PS3609.R82L68 2013
813'.6--dc23
                                                               2012026968

Printed in the United States of America

        13 14 15 16 17 18 19 20 21 / LB-JH / 10 9 8 7 6 5 4 3 2 1

Be still before the Lord *and wait patiently for him.*

Psalm 37:7

We also glory in our sufferings, because we know that suffering
produces perseverance; perseverance, character; and character, hope.
And hope does not put us to shame, because God's love has been poured
out into our hearts through the Holy Spirit, who has been given to us.

Romans 5:3-5

ACKNOWLEDGMENTS

To be given the opportunity to write this third story in the Bliss Creek series is a gift from God, but it's also the result of the hard work and faithfulness of the folks at Harvest House Publishers. I want to give a special shout-out to the sales and marketing staff. Thanks to Brad Moses and all the behind-the-scenes movers and shakers who get these books into the stores and online sales venues so that readers may be entertained, encouraged, and edified by them. I'm in awe of the personal attention and caring these folks have shown for the Bliss Creek series. As always, I owe a debt of gratitude to my editor, Kathleen Kerr, and to my agent, Mary Sue Seymour. None of this would be possible without the support of my family and friends—you know who you are. It goes without saying—but I'll say it anyway for the record—I owe everything to my Lord and Savior, who writes these stories on my heart.

Chapter 1

Helen Crouch squeezed by a couple busy scolding a small boy who appeared to have a green lollipop stuck in his golden curls. Smiling, she angled her way through the growing crowd along the parade route. She could remember when Edmond had been that age. He'd been so sweet and anxious to please as he rummaged for eggs in the chicken coop or helped her pluck weeds in the garden. Ten years and a *rumspringa* later she could see little of that child in her only son. Inhaling the mingled aromas of popcorn and cotton candy, she held her hand to her damp forehead to block out a July sun that peeked through glowering clouds overhead. Maybe Edmond had slipped into the crowd to find Emma and Thomas for her.

Not likely, given a recent spate of disappearing acts by a sixteen-year-old apparently bent on squeezing every last drop from his running around.

"*Mudder*, look, funnel cakes." The note of entreaty in Naomi's voice told Helen her oldest daughter wanted to ask, but knew better. Their egg and jelly money wouldn't stretch to treats—not this month. "They smell so good."

"Not as good as chocolate-marshmallow cookies." Helen patted her daughter's shoulder. The cookies were Naomi's favorite, which was why Helen had thought to pack them in the basket along with the sausage, cheese, and biscuits. "Let's find Emma and Thomas. They'll have saved a space for us."

"Helen, over here!" As if she'd heard Helen's words, Emma Brennaman's high voice carried over the many citizens of Bliss Creek who'd gathered, despite the threat of an impending thunderstorm, to see the Fourth of July parade of area high school marching bands, cowboys on decked-out horses, John Deere farm implements, and fancy cars from the dealership on I-35. "It's getting crowded already. We managed to save a shady spot!"

"We're coming."

After glancing back to make sure her two younger daughters were keeping up with Naomi, Helen dodged a knot of *Englisch* teenagers who crowded Bliss Creek Park's edge. They were busy examining a bag of firecrackers, looks of delight on their acne-dotted faces. She stubbed her toe in the crack of the sidewalk and stumbled. One of them grinned, his braces glinting in the sun. She forced a return smile. "So sorry. Can we get around you?"

The sea parted and they trotted through.

Why did she apologize? Habit? In another habit she'd never been able to break, Helen looked beyond Emma to make sure Thomas accompanied his wife. Her friend's husband stood in the shade of a stout elm, his back turned. He talked to another man, equally tall and lean. Helen picked up her pace and narrowly missed colliding with a double stroller and its occupants—rosy-cheeked twins dressed in matching red, white, and blue sundresses and bonnets. "Sorry. So sorry."

Her daughters tried to hide their giggles behind their hands, as they tended to do when she made a blunder. "Mudder!"

"Hush, girls." She turned to Emma, glad Thomas hadn't seen her latest misstep. As if it mattered. He seemed engrossed in a conversation that held words like *harvest* and *wheat* and *rain* and something about a well having gone dry. Indeed, Thomas had his hands full, it seemed. Helen focused on Emma. "Have you seen Edmond?"

"He's not with you?" Emma ran one hand over a crisp apron that did little to hide her swollen belly while she grabbed little Caleb with the other to keep him from escaping into the street. "Don't worry. Knowing Edmond, he won't want to miss the fried chicken, homemade potato chips, and pecan-chocolate-chip cookies we brought to share with y'all. How's your mudder doing? It's too bad she couldn't have come along."

"She's doing better, but crowds don't suit her. What about Annie? Didn't she come?" Helen glanced at the quilts strewn in the grassy strip between the sidewalk and the street. No Annie. "When I dropped off my jams and jellies at the bakery yesterday, she promised me she would come—that she would try to come."

"*Ach*, if only it were so." The customary happiness in Emma's face since her marriage to Thomas and Caleb's arrival fled for a second. "She isn't ready. She decided at the last minute she didn't want to come. Couldn't come, I reckon. She can't seem to bring herself to celebrate anything yet."

"She'll get out when she's ready." Helen knew this from experience. The deep wound of loss took time to heal and could be ripped open by the simplest thing. A smell or a taste that reminded one of a person forever gone. "With time, she'll find her way."

"It's been a year. It's time for her to begin again." Emma's tone was kind, but firm. "She's young and she should marry again. Noah needs a father. She needs a husband."

"A year isn't so long."

Helen said the words at the same time as the man who stood next to Thomas, one hand propped on the tree's trunk. He'd turned at Emma's statement and his gaze met Helen's. In his expression, she saw a fellow sojourner, someone who'd experienced the rocky, meandering road that follows the death of a loved one. Who had he lost?

"Not so long at all," the man added, his dark eyes filled with a sadness that quickly fled, replaced with a polite blankness. "All things considered."

Helen intended to agree, but instead she remained mute. The man had been cut from the same cloth as Thomas, sewn with the same careful stitch. He could've been a twin, except older, at least forty. Threads of silver and gray shot through his dark beard and the unruly hair that escaped from under his straw hat. His eyes were large and the color of tea allowed to brew all afternoon in Kansas's summer heat. His leathery bronze skin spoke of years spent working outdoors. Crow's feet around his eyes told the story of squinting against the broiling afternoon sun. Or laughing.

"Helen? Helen." Emma's insistent tone jerked Helen from her inventory of this stranger who seemed so familiar. "This is Gabriel Gless, Thomas's cousin."

Feeling as awkward as a child on the first day of school, Helen scrambled for a simple salutation. She opened her mouth and nothing came out.

Naomi nudged Helen with a sharp elbow. "Mudder?"

"Nice to meet you." She managed a nod. "Welcome to Bliss Creek."

Straightening, he moved toward her, a glint of laughter in his eyes. What was so funny?

"These are my daughters." She introduced the girls. "Are you and your *fraa* visiting long?"

"My fraa passed." No emotion visited those words but Helen saw the same expression in his eyes as before. He might be able to stifle the feelings in his speech, but not in his heart. "Been almost three years now."

"Gabriel's not visiting." Thomas spoke up as if to rescue his cousin. He too knew about this rocky road, even if his had diverged toward happier times. "He and his *kinner* moved here from Indiana. Making a new start of it."

Gabriel cleared his throat. "Meet the Gless clan." He swept his long arm toward the wiggling mass of youngsters engaged in all sorts of tomfoolery on the quilts. "Isaac, Daniel, Mary Elizabeth, Samuel, Abigail, Seth, Isabelle, and little Rachel."

They all chimed in with hellos that ranged from bellows to softly uttered words and ducked heads. Mary Elizabeth, whose blonde hair and blue eyes must've belonged to her mudder, shifted from one bare foot to another. "Some of us will be looking for work, if you know of any."

"Work...*jah, jah*, I'm sure you'll manage that around here. Annie, Emma's sister, have you met her?" Helen glanced at Emma, who shook her head as if to say not yet. "She's needing a hard worker who knows how to bake to help her out at Plank's Pastry and Pie Shop."

"Not now." Gabriel gave the girl a sharp look. "We'll have time for that later. For now, let's enjoy the parade."

Mary Elizabeth ducked her head, but she seemed pleased with Helen's tidbit of information. Helen studied the rest of the children. Rachel appeared to be about three, Isaac probably twenty-one or twenty-two. Quite an age spread. At least the older ones could care for the younger. As if to underscore the thought, little Isabelle, who might be about four, escaped from Mary Elizabeth's grasp and trundled toward Helen, arms up as if to offer a hug. Her sweet smile enveloped Helen, and she accepted the damp offering of a hug and a kiss.

"It's so nice to meet you, Isabelle." The hug warmed Helen's heart. Her own daughters were quick with affection, but this little girl didn't know her in the slightest, making her unconditional offering all the sweeter. "You are very welcome to Bliss Creek too."

"Wants cookie." Isabelle had a lisp. She patted Helen's cheek with a sticky hand that indicated she'd already had at least one dessert. "Hungry. Want cookie. Have cookie?"

Not only did Gabriel have his hands full with eight children, but this child would require extra care. Her almond-shaped eyes, round cheeks, and stubby fingers and arms were all signs that Isabelle was one of those special children who would forever be a child. Helen raised her gaze to Gabriel. She saw nothing in his bronzed face but a father's deep love for his child.

Isabelle wiggled from Helen's grasp.

"Pony!" Her hands flailed and she skipped in the direction of a wagon that had pulled into a parking lot on the other side of the street. "Pet pony."

"Not now," Gabriel called. "Don't go in the street, little one."

Isabelle looked up at Helen and smiled. "Pony."

"Jah, pony." Helen waved at Luke, Emma's oldest brother, and his wife, Leah, who were directing their flock as they hopped from the wagon Luke had outfitted with rows of wooden seats for his big family. "You made it. The route's almost full."

An unsmiling Leah returned her wave with a barely noticeable flick of a hand. "We're late as always," the other woman called as she hoisted baby Jebediah onto one hip and rousted her twin girls from the second-row seat. "I forgot the basket and we had to go back…"

The high, tight whinny of a horse interrupted Leah's words. Helen glanced east toward the beginning of the parade route. A buggy, swaying from side to side, raced down the middle of the street, the horse pounding in a frantic gallop.

"What is…who is…" Helen's questions were caught up in the murmurs of the crowd that immediately began to swell. Plain families didn't participate in the parade. They only came to watch in anticipation of the fireworks display to follow. "Whose buggy is that?"

The horse looked familiar. *Daed's* Morgan? She still thought of him as Daed's Morgan even though her daed had passed in April. She couldn't get a good look at the driver of the buggy. His hat covered his face. Then he stood and snapped the reins. One hand went to his hat and lifted it high. He whooped and yelled, "Yee haw! Ride 'em, cowboy!"

The voice. The face. The face so like George's. Her cheeks suddenly hot, hands shaking, Helen started forward into the road. "Edmond? Edmond! What are you—"

A hand grabbed her arm and jerked her back so hard she tumbled into the quilt and landed atop Abigail. A knee gouged her back. With a startled cry, the girl scooted to the left, causing the other children to scatter. Tangled in her long skirt, Helen scrambled onto her knees, fighting to see over Daniel, Isaac, Samuel, and the other boys who jumped to their feet.

Gabriel dashed into the street and swept Isabelle into his arms just as the horse and swaying buggy whipped past them, wheels rattling on the asphalt. His momentum carried him to the far curb. He stumbled, dropped to his knees, but kept the little girl securely wrapped in one long arm.

The buggy, still swaying wildly, disappeared down the street. Several folks in the crowd, their faces at first puzzled, and then amused, began to clap. From the looks of them, they were tourists. The teenagers hooted and hollered their appreciation. Others, older folks, shook their heads and muttered, disapproving looks on their faces.

Gabriel popped up, whirled, and marched back toward them, Isabelle still dangling from his arm like a stuffed doll.

"Who was that?" Despite his obvious anger, he kept his voice down to a low growl. He panted, furious red blotches on cheeks that had gone white. He seemed oblivious to his daughter's giggles. "He nearly ran over Isabelle. He could've killed her."

"I—"

"Police. Stop. Stop that buggy now!" Police chief Dylan Parker raced past them on foot, dodging people who had spilled into the street to watch the buggy continue its flight toward Bliss Creek's city limits. The police officer's hat blew from his head, but he didn't halt. "Edmond Crouch, stop now!"

Sirens wailed. Flashing blue and red lights came into view. One of Bliss Creek's three police cars gained on Chief Parker, swerved around him, slowed, and then halted long enough for Parker to jerk open a door and climb in before picking up speed again.

The noise of the crowd grew. Laughter mingled with questions and curious bystanders turned their gaze on the Plain families who had congregated in one spot along the parade route.

"You've met my daughters." Fighting the urge to cover her face, Helen rubbed the spot on her arm where Gabriel had jerked her aside and gazed up at him. "That was my son, Edmond."

Chapter 2

Isabelle squirmed in Gabriel's arms and wailed. The sound penetrated an anger born of fear. Laura had left him in charge of their children. He alone had the job of watching over them and raising them properly in their faith. In his wife's absence, he would do whatever necessary to care for them, keep them safe, and send them on their ways to start their own families of faith. Some days, like today, the promise proved to be a tall order. He deposited Isabelle on the sidewalk. She trotted back to Helen and again held up her arms.

"*Nee*, Isabelle, go to Abigail." He nodded to his older daughter. "Take her."

"But Daed, she's all sticky and dirty—"

"Then get her cleaned up and make sure she stays out of the street." The girls spent a great deal of time caring for Isabelle and little Rachel. They didn't complain, but Gabriel knew their burdens were heavy in a household without a mudder to oversee the cooking, laundry, sewing, canning, baking, and gardening. "The parade will begin any minute. Then we'll eat and later we'll watch the fireworks."

"We'll take care of her, Daed. Don't worry."

Abigail smiled up at him. With her curls, fair skin, and blue eyes, she was the spitting image of Laura at sixteen. Gabriel had known his wife from the time she was four. Secretly promised to marry her at twelve. Done so at eighteen. He swallowed the lump in his aching throat. Abigail hoisted Isabelle to her hip and snatched a rag doll from the crumpled quilt. Isabelle laughed and clapped her hands. Laura would be pleased with their children. This was Abigail's rumspringa and she spent it caring for the little ones, not running wild in the street in a runaway buggy.

New anger blew through him. He turned and bore down on Helen. "Does your son always race along parade routes acting like a cowboy?"

"Nee. Never. It's his rumspringa…" The woman's voice trailed away. "He's been…different."

Having been through three rumspringas already with his own kinner, and now Abigail in hers, Gabriel found not much surprised him. But this wild ride through the streets in broad daylight, this was a new one. What would possess the boy to do something so openly? Back home the teenagers wore Englisch clothes, smoked, carried cell phones, and even drove cars. They sneaked around, thinking no one saw. Parents turned their heads and pretended not to know. But this flaunting of it was different. Disrespectful. His hope that this move to Kansas would make it easier for him to protect his children from worldly influences drained away.

This boy, this Edmond, had been out of control. What kind of mudder raised a child to act like that? Helen looked so forlorn, he might have felt sorry for her were it not for the hairsbreadth he'd been away from being trampled by the horse. He'd felt the breeze of the buggy as it passed. For himself, he had no worries. But for his children. They had only one parent now.

"Edmond's a good boy." Thomas spoke as if reading Gabriel's thoughts on his face. His cousin stood next to Helen, towering nearly a foot over her, his arms crossed over his chest. "He's a hard worker. Works for me on the farm."

Thomas would never say something he didn't mean. He rarely spoke at all, but when he did, he meant it.

Still, the horse's whinnies sounded in Gabriel's ears. The feel of

Isabelle's body squirming against him as he hurled himself past the buggy caused the panic to rise again. Fighting for composure, he leaned over to examine the knees of his pants. Better they didn't see his face. One pant leg had been torn by his rapid descent to the asphalt.

"That was strange behavior for a good boy." He managed to sound calm. No judgment. "He seemed...crazed or drugged."

"He's embraced his rumspringa, as many of our youngsters do." Helen put her hands on her ample hips. Gone was the awkward woman who'd introduced herself earlier, replaced by a mother hen whose feathers were ruffled, her chick found wanting. "As I'm sure your older boys have done. That is the point of it. He should be forgiven for that."

"My boys didn't put a little girl in danger." Warmth flooded Gabriel's face and showered his neck. She ought not to speak back to a man such as himself. Yet he couldn't help but admire that she stood up for her son. "Forgiven, yes. But his actions—endangering others and flaunting it in public—must be corrected. Surely you'll talk to your bishop."

"Now your bishop as well." Thomas spoke again. Why did he defend this woman and her undisciplined son? "I'll talk to Edmond."

"So will I, being I'm his mudder and all." Helen dusted her hands together as if to wash them of the subject. "I'll go now. I reckon Chief Parker has caught up with him and given him a talking to. Emma, could the girls stay with you until I come back?"

"Of course."

"Rumspringa doesn't give him the right to put others in danger." Gabriel couldn't help himself. He kept talking even though she'd turned away, giving him her back. She was short and sturdy, very different from Laura with her long legs and thin build. The direction of his thoughts confounded him. "Does this community's Ordnung allow him to do that?"

"Nee." Thomas answered yet again. "He'll be dealt—"

"Mrs. Crouch!" A sweaty, heavy man in a uniform so tight the buttons looked as if they might burst wormed his way through the parade goers. His skin was burnt red from the sun and he wore shiny sunglasses that hid his eyes and reflected everything around him. "Mrs. Crouch, I need to talk to you."

Helen turned back. Her dimpled cheeks turned from red to an ashen gray. "What is it? Is he hurt, Officer Bingham?"

"No, ma'am." The officer removed his hat. He nodded at Gabriel and Thomas, then glanced at a notebook he clutched in his hand as if seeking guidance. "Chief Parker says to tell you, begging your pardon, ma'am, that your son is drunk. He's being arrested. For drinking and driving."

Drunk. Drinking and driving. An Englisch act. Plain folks didn't imbibe. Not those who followed the Ordnung. Gabriel had hoped for a strong, faithful community where he could raise the children and guide them with the help of that community. Instead this. The packing, the leaving of everything and everyone familiar. The endless drive across the Midwest. All of it had been for nothing.

"That can't be." Helen brushed past Gabriel and stood toe-to-toe with the officer. "Edmond wouldn't do that."

"We caught him, ma'am." The officer made a *hmmph* sound that was halfway between a cough and snort. "He was out there with a bunch of kids from the high school, out behind the Pizza Parlor where the trash bins are. When we pulled up, Edmond had the bottle in one hand and a red plastic cup in the other. Red plastic cup, ma'am. You know what that means."

Helen's face turned from white to red again. "You arrested him for having a red cup?"

"They use them at keggers and the like. You see a red cup, you're seeing alcohol, ma'am."

A kegger. The officer spoke a language Gabriel recognized from having worked in the Englisch world, but it was obvious Helen didn't comprehend. She glanced sideways at Gabriel, her round cheeks flaming. "Did you see him drink from the cup?"

"He threw it down. The bottle too. Then they scattered in all directions. Your son took off running to the buggy. We yelled for him to stop. He didn't."

"Likely you scared him," Thomas said. "We don't deal much with law enforcement, as you know."

"Helen." Emma touched her friend's arm. "You must go to him."

A look passed between Emma and Thomas. Thomas doffed his hat at Gabriel and without another word, motioned for Helen to follow him.

Gabriel shook his head. "I thought Dahlburg's community had fallen into sinful ways, but I don't know of any of the young men in that community being charged with something like this."

Emma didn't answer. Her gaze followed her husband's back until he disappeared into the crowd. She seemed thoughtful.

"What's going on?" Gabriel asked, curious at the mix of emotions on her face. "Has this happened before?"

"Not with Edmond. He's a good boy who's a little out of hand." Emma turned to him. "Has Thomas not told you of my brother Josiah's misadventures during his rumspringa?"

Not likely. Thomas didn't do much storytelling, unless it was for the children's pleasure. "Nee."

Emma glanced at the children sprawled on the quilt. They were already getting to know the flock brought by Emma's brother and sister-in-law, Leah, a dour-looking woman who frowned at them and continued to berate her children for something. Gabriel had missed what they'd done.

"The parade's started. Finally." Emma sank into a plastic folding lawn chair next to the quilt—a concession to the fact that she could no longer sit on the ground, given her girth—and motioned for him to do the same in the chair next to her. He sat while Caleb clamored into what remained of his mudder's lap.

"Josiah ran away to Wichita, got drunk, asked a New Order Mennonite girl to marry him, and then jumped off or fell off—we're not sure which—a second-story balcony when she said no." Emma's expression and tone didn't change. Gabriel realized she didn't want the child on her lap to know of the seriousness of her words. "We almost lost him only a few months after my parents passed."

Gabriel had met Josiah the previous day. A broad-shouldered, burly man. Married—by the looks of him happily so—and a father of one child with another on the way. He was a hardworking blacksmith with big callused hands and an almost constant grin.

"How long has Edmond's father been gone?"

"You mean how long has Helen been a widow?"

"Jah."

"Seven years."

A man in the house would've had a handle on the discipline. A second thought chased the first: seven years of the kind of loneliness he had experienced for the last three. He never expected to be lonely with eight children in the house, but lonely he had been. Continued to be. Each night when he went to bed alone and each morning when he arose to face another day without Laura. He didn't wish that on anyone.

"Seven years is a long time. Why didn't she remarry?"

"You said it yourself. Everyone comes through that darkness on their own time." Emma fanned herself with a handkerchief and then used it to pat the sweat from her shiny cheeks. "There have been a few who've tried to court her, but it seems she hasn't found the right person."

"Maybe it's because she's so *doplich.*"

"She's clumsy because people—men like you—make her nervous."

"Not a sign that she would make a good fraa."

"She was a good fraa."

"Spoken like a true *freind.*"

"I didn't know her very well then." Emma leaned forward, her gaze on the parade route. "I know her now. She is a simple, kind woman who works hard and prays hard. You'll like her."

"Again, you are a good friend." Her meaning sank in after a few seconds. He squirmed in his chair. "You…I…nee…I…her skills as a mother…"

"You've only met her once."

"I have eight kinner, one of whom will need special attention for a lifetime. If I were to marry again, I would need a fraa who can handle that."

"Are you looking for a fraa or a caregiver?" Emma's smile took the sting from the words. "My Aenti Louise says love overcomes many things. Only God knows why and in time, He reveals His plan. Until then, it's best to enjoy the good moments, like a parade, and leave the rest to Him."

Gabriel knew her words were true. Hard as he found it to understand why God would take his wife from him so soon after the birth of their eighth child, there had to be a reason for it. She'd mentioned a headache in the afternoon. By evening, she'd been gone from a blood clot in her brain. The shock of her sudden passing still took his breath away when he awoke in the morning, slowly coming to consciousness. Groggy. Drowsy. Then wide awake and the pain of it sucking the air from his lungs. What greater purpose did this turn of events serve? Not that it was his place to ask that question. *Forgive me.*

A fat drop of rain smacked Gabriel on the nose as if to punctuate the prayer. He glanced up at the sky. The clouds seethed overhead, black and heavy. As much as the region needed rain, Gabriel prayed it would hold off. *Just a few more days, God. A few more days until the wheat is in. Thomas needs that. The whole district needs it.* "We may not have the parade after all."

"As much as we need rain, the timing couldn't be worse." Emma gave voice to Gabriel's thoughts. "Thomas has worked so hard. All the men have."

"Nothing can be done about it."

"I know God will provide even if we lose the harvest." Her steady voice told him she truly meant those words. Thomas had married a stout believer. "But it hurts my heart to see him work so hard to provide for us only to have the fruits of his labor wash away in a rain that we truly need. God's timing…well, it's God's timing, I guess."

She held up both hands, palms up as if to ask a question she dare not put into words. Gabriel had no answer. Caleb mimicked her moves and giggled when raindrops splashed in his chubby hands. Emma smiled and Gabriel joined her. Some questions didn't have answers.

Like why he'd moved to this community to escape the world that invaded his old district only to find it overtaking the new one. Had he been wrong to uproot his family? Would he have to do it again?

Chapter 3

Finally.

Blessed silence.

With one last gentle pat on the baby's back, Annie eased away from the crib. She gazed at his flushed cheek, wet with tears, and inhaled the sweet scent of baby. She saw David in the curve of Noah's face and the tip of his upturned nose. In the thatch of dark, fine hair that covered his head and fanned out on his chubby neck.

Thank You, God, for blessing me with Noah.

Annie said this prayer every night standing in this exact spot.

Every night, she also went through this bedtime routine. Little Noah didn't want to sleep. He fought it with every ounce of being in his tiny fourteen-month-old body. Like his daed, he wouldn't give up. Not until his body gave out.

In the late afternoon, when Annie came home from the bakery, Noah played, he laughed, he ate with such gusto he made her smile and laugh too, even as tired as she always was. Every night she carried him to his crib, thinking he had to be tuckered out, ready to sleep. Instead, the same tug-of-war ensued. Crying, wailing, kicking, wiggling, and screaming, he managed to prolong the evening ritual well past the point in which she had the patience to deal with it. How could it be that the moment Leah's little Jeb hit the crib, his eyes slid shut, and a second later he slept? It didn't seem fair.

Not that anything about life could be called fair. Far from it. With a soft touch, she turned the knob on the floor pole lantern and it ceased to glow. Then she stepped back, her bare feet noiseless on the piecemeal rug that covered the wooden floor between the crib, Noah's cousins' bed, and baby Jebediah's crib. They were crammed together, but the bedrooms were stuffed to the brim since Annie and Noah moved back into her childhood home. She didn't allow herself to dwell on this. She and David had agreed. Their house would be sold to another young couple in need of a place to start a family. Margaret and John Miller had a baby on the way.

She eased through the doorway. With infinite care, she inched the door toward its frame until it closed. Sighing a sigh so gusty it lifted her prayer *kapp* strings, she leaned against the solid wood of the door and closed her eyes. They burned with fatigue and tears she refused to let fall. The rain beat on the roof overhead, an unfamiliar sound after months of drought. Months without rain and now on the eve of the wheat harvest, it came down in a deluge that assured her that no one would be getting into the fields anytime soon.

She leaned her head down and prayed with a ferocity that surprised even her. *Danki for bringing me through this day. Give me the strength I'll need tomorrow. Give Luke and Thomas and all the men the strength they will need to do what must be done in the days ahead. Show us the path You would have us take.*

She opened her eyes and rested for a beat longer against the door. She'd made it through another day. Just as she would tomorrow. She would put one foot in front of the other. Day by day.

Taking a deep breath, she started down the hallway. Luke and Leah and the kinner must be getting drenched at the Fourth of July celebration. Knowing Luke, he'd remembered to stack tarps in the back of the wagon to cover the children on the ride home.

A banging sound pierced the quiet. *Rap, rap, rap.* Someone was knocking on the door, the sound loud against the patter of the rain.

"Nee, nee! *Ach!*"

Annie flew down the stairs and hustled to the front door. Who would knock at this hour? Family would come in. She jerked the door open. "I just got the baby—"

A woman dressed in a white blouse tucked into a dark blue skirt stood on the porch, a brown leather bag clutched in one hand, a dripping umbrella dangling from the other. Her blonde hair was braided in a plait that hung below her shoulders, and her hazel eyes were just like Annie's.

"Annie!" The woman's lips turned up in a tremulous smile that belied the tears in her eyes. "*Ach,* Annie. It's so good to see you, *schweschder.*"

"Catherine?" It couldn't be. After four years. It couldn't be. "Is that you?"

"It's me." Her expression hesitant, Catherine took a half step forward. "I know I can't come in, but I thought maybe you would come out."

Without thought, Annie hurled herself at her sister and enveloped her in a hug. She smelled like flowers. Lilacs. "I can't believe you're here. You're here!"

"I'm here." Catherine dropped the bag and the umbrella. Her arms came up and returned the hug in a quick, hard embrace. Then she extricated herself from Annie's grip and took a step back. "I'm visiting."

"After four years? You're visiting?" Annie looked beyond Catherine and saw a mud-splattered dark blue car sitting in the gravel driveway. "You drove here in that? From where? Where have you been? Why are you back? Are you staying in Bliss Creek?"

Catherine laughed, the sound soft, and held up her hand. "Hold on, schweschder. I'll tell all. First, how are you? How's the baby, little

Noah? I'm sorry I didn't come sooner, when I learned of your loss. Of David's death."

Darkness crept in. Annie pushed it back. She'd promised David to move on quickly. Not to dwell. To accept God's will for her life, as well as his. "Thank you, but there was no need for you to come. I'm fine. The *bobbeli* is fine." She cocked her head, puzzled. "How did you know? About Noah and about David?"

"Aenti Louise. She's written me regularly. Of course now her handwriting has gotten so shaky I can barely decipher it." Catherine glanced around, then nodded toward the four hickory rockers that dotted the porch. "Can we sit?"

Aenti Louise never said a word. Not once. If anyone could keep a secret, it would be Aenti. Barely able to comprehend the magnitude of the secret, Annie hesitated in the doorway, the humid night air pressing heavy against her face like a wet blanket, the pounding rain on the porch's roof loud in her ears. A gust of wind tossed the drops against her hands and face. She wanted to know more, but she shouldn't invite her sister in. Catherine had been shunned. Of necessity, but still, it hurt. Even after four years it hurt in a fierce, open wound way. "I can't. I don't want to leave Noah alone inside."

"For a few minutes. I promise I won't stay too long. Only a few moments."

A few moments. She hadn't seen Catherine in four years. God would forgive her. So would Luke. Annie held open the screen door. "The rocking chairs are wet. Come in."

She ushered Catherine into the living area as if she were a guest and not a sister who'd grown up in this house, scrubbed these very floors, and dusted the fireplace mantel and made quilts with all their friends and aunts and cousins. "Would you like some tea? We have ice."

"No, thank you. I want to talk to you, and I know I don't have much time. It's getting late and you get up so early." Catherine looked around, her curiosity bright in her face. "Everything is exactly the same. I thought maybe Leah would change things up a bit."

"She's been too busy with babies."

"Jah, Aenti mentioned that. Jebediah, right?"

"Yes, little Jeb. A sweet baby boy."

Annie took a seat on the sofa, letting Catherine have the hickory rocking chair Luke favored. She looked well, much better than she had after Mudder and Daed's deaths. Better than she had after she'd left her groom on her wedding day. Better than she had the last Christmas they'd spent together before she'd run away without saying goodbye. Annie studied her sister, younger by one year but looking far older in her damp, drooping Englischer clothes. She even wore pointy leather shoes and sheer stockings. She must be warm in that getup.

"And Josiah and Miriam. Our brother and your best friend." She smiled. "It must've made you very happy when he finally settled down. No more running around."

"Jah, and with Miriam. They're so happy together."

"Not surprising. She's a strong, faithful girl. You must have fun spending time together with the little ones."

"We try." She hesitated, not wanting to tell a lie, however inconsequential. Seeing Miriam so happy made her happy too, and sad. She tried not to compare. Another baby on the way already. Annie might never have that. "It's hard…she has little Hazel Grace and she's expecting another bobbeli soon. Her mudder and daed need a lot of attention now. She helped at first…after David…but she has so much morning sickness and Hazel Grace has colic so she has her hands full."

"So you don't spend as much time together as you used to. Don't worry, she'll be back. Miriam is a faithful friend."

"I know." Annie wanted to move the conversation away from painful topics, but everywhere she turned there were more to be had. "You don't want to see Luke and Mark?"

"Not tonight. I can't. Not tonight." Catherine plucked at the seam of her skirt, her fingers worrying a loose thread. "I think it'll be easier for me to do this a little at a time. Besides, I don't think Luke will be pleased when he finds you've allowed me into the house. The bishop won't be pleased."

"You're family, still. Luke will understand." Annie stopped. Family or not, Catherine had been shunned. She no longer had the right to share a roof with her brothers and sisters. "You've been gone forever. They'll want to at least see you—"

"They might want to, but I don't want to get anyone in trouble with the bishop."

"Why are you here? Why did you come now?"

"You first. How are you really, Annie?"

Annie had to swallow against the same rising tide of emotion that threatened to drown her in the dark of night when she rolled over and found the bed empty next to her. She inhaled and let the fragrance of wet earth that wafted through the open door calm her. "I'm fine."

Catherine leaned across the narrow space that separated them and squeezed Annie's hand. "Liar."

"I never lie."

"Wanting something to be so is not the same as it being so. If anybody knows that, I do."

"Why are you here?"

"I'm starting my senior year. I'm getting my bachelor's degree." Her answer proved to be no answer at all. Catherine leaned back in the chair, which squeaked softly as if in protest, and gazed into the space over Annie's shoulder. "I've missed you and Emma and the little ones. Not so little anymore, I imagine."

"If you missed us so much, why didn't you come back?" Annie regretted her tart tone, but only a little. "You only have to tell the bishop you are ready to return and embrace our faith. The community will welcome you with wide open arms."

"You're such an optimist. You always were." Catherine hugged her bag in her lap as if someone might grab it away from her. "I don't want to come back—not that way—the way you're thinking of. I'm visiting, and I'm thinking about the topic of the thesis I'll write when I start my master's degree next year."

"Thesis?"

"Yes, thesis. It's a paper you write when you get your master's degree."

"Master's degree?" Neither term meant anything to Annie, and that fact made her sad. She and Catherine lived in different worlds now. It wasn't the clothes or the car or the way she talked with fancy, educated words. Annie had known that, but it had only taken a minute or two to establish these facts in plain view for both of them to see. "This is important to you. Tell me more. But first tell me how you survived out there."

Catherine spoke quickly, as if she knew their time together could end at any moment. She described living in the home of her mentor, a psychologist who had treated her after she witnessed Mudder and Daed dying when their buggy was hit by a wheat truck. She recalled the weeks and months it had taken her to adjust to a new way of life, new clothes, new surroundings, new people. The one place she had fit in, she said, was in school. Her mentor had been right. Education suited her. Studying suited her. She soaked up every morsel of fact, equation, and data thrown at her by her teachers.

"Next spring I'll have a bachelor's degree in psychology with a minor in sociology," she said, her face lighting up with a smile. "Then I'll work on an advanced degree, a master's they call it. I'll work as a graduate assistant while I earn it."

"This is good for you?" Annie really wanted to know. She never had wanted more book learning. Her cooking utensils and her ovens and sugar and flour—these were the tools of her trade, and they gave her a sense of accomplishment grounded in the knowledge that she served others with nourishment to their bodies. "The nervousness you had before, the sadness...it's gone?"

"I take a medicine for it and the medicine helps." Catherine rubbed her hands on the chair's wooden arms. "What I'm doing makes me happy, and it's possible someday I won't need the medicine."

"You're happy?"

"Very. I have a passion for research."

"But you haven't married?"

"I know that's how you gauge happiness, and I'm so sorry for your loss." Catherine hugged her bag to her chest again. "But for me, it's different. That's not to say I don't understand love. There's a man—"

"An Englischer?" Annie tried to keep the disappointment from her voice. Catherine's path had long ago diverged from her family's. This shouldn't surprise her. "You plan to marry?"

"I don't know. Maybe. We're talking." The momentary happiness had seeped from her voice. "There are issues. He's a medical resident. He's studying to be a doctor."

"A smart man, then. Someone who helps others." This was good. Different, but a man who served others was good. "What stands in the way?"

"I found I can't have children."

The flat way she said the words spoke to Annie of how long and how hard her sister had worked to accept the truth behind them. Tears pricked Annie's eyes. She blinked them away. *You took David home before I was ready, but You gave me the gift of his love and You gave me his son. I am blessed.* "Are you sure? How can you know?"

"Doctors know these things. There are tests."

"And this man doesn't want you because you can't give him children?"

"Annie! No! Dean's a good man. He loves me. He says we'll adopt."

"So then, what?"

"I don't know. It's the same old thing. The thing I went through with Melvin. Poor Melvin. Did he ever marry?"

So all those words, that psychology Catherine sought when she ran away from her family and her community had not given her the peace she sought. Some lessening of her pain and sadness, but not peace.

Annie chose not to throw it in her sister's face for surely a woman of such learning had reached this conclusion on her own. "He did. He and Elizabeth have two children."

"Wow." Catherine sniffed and smiled a watery smile. "Good for him. He deserves such bounty."

None of them deserved bounty. God gave them these things because of His grace, not because of anything they did. Catherine had forgotten much in the outside world. They sat silent for a few minutes, listening to the rumble of thunder in the distance that reflected unspoken thoughts and feelings and words.

"You never did say." Annie studied the tense way her sister held her bag, then followed her gaze out the windows to the black curtain of clouds that made it seem later than it was. "Why did you come now?"

"I'm planning for my thesis."

"Jah." Something about her words told Annie there was more. Something that made Catherine even more nervous than the mere fact of the visit itself. Which was plenty. "Something you'll do next year. What brings you now?"

"It's about the effects of living in a closed community." Catherine opened the bag and pulled a chunky black thing from it. In the fading light, Annie struggled to make it out. "Also the effects of living in an Amish community and then leaving it."

"What is that?"

Annie leaned forward.

A camera. Her sister held a camera.

"I want permission from the family to take photos. I want to illustrate my thesis with the photos. And then publish it." Catherine held out the camera. "Touch it. It won't bite."

"I don't think...you'll have to..." Annie shrank back, letting the camera dangle between them. "Luke will want to talk with the bishop."

"I know. That's fine. I understand." Catherine laid the camera on top of the bag. "In my spare time, I take photographs. It's become my hobby, I guess you'd say. I want to be able to capture something here."

"Capture the memories you've missed and will miss."

"I've made my own memories. Don't be sorry for me. Be happy. It was meant to be."

"What do you mean it was meant to be?"

"Don't you see? If I'd stayed here and married, some Plain man would be forced to stay with a fraa who could bear him no sons, no daughters. God had a plan for me too, and it couldn't have been to stay here and doom some good man to a miserable, childless marriage. Don't look so sad. I'm fine. And there's more."

Annie shifted in her seat, wishing Emma were here. Emma would know how to handle this. More. More than the master's degree and the doctor and the not being able to have children. It seemed impossible that there could be more.

"I'm writing a memoir. It was Sheila—Doctor Baker's—idea. She says it'll help me to resolve unresolved issues. It's already been accepted for publication. I wanted you and the family to know since it involves you."

"A memoir? What is a memoir?"

"You don't know? Of course, you don't know." Catherine laughed, but the sound had no joy in it. "There's so much. A memoir is stories from a person's life. His or her memories."

"Your memories?"

"And by extension, your memories."

"You're telling people about my life?" So this was it. Catherine had come not for the thesis, still a year away, but for this memoir. This sharing of their private lives. Who would care or find interest in her life? Who out there in the world cared? "About me?"

"Yes. And Luke and Emma and Josiah and Mark and the twins."

Annie couldn't fathom it. She felt stupid, but still she asked, "You're telling the whole world, the Englisch world, about our family?"

"Yes. Well, anyone who decides to buy a hardback book for twenty-four-ninety-five." Catherine leaned forward in the chair, her gaze lifted as if searching for something. A crack of lightning sent a sliver of light zigzagging across the sky, brightening the room for a few seconds. Thunder rolled, a deep rumble that seemed to ripple from one horizon to the other. "And given the current fascination with the Amish way of life, I'm thinking that will be quite a lot of people."

A wail sounded from above. Loud and clear. Noah. Already. Annie despaired of him ever sleeping through the night.

Annie rose. Catherine stood too.

"I have to go up."

"I know." Catherine touched Annie's sleeve. "I'm sorry I was gone so long."

"Me too. I'm sorry you won't be staying."

"I can't."

"No, you can't."

The sound of a horse whinnying mingled with the pounding of the rain. Annie turned to look toward the door. A sharp intake of air from Catherine told Annie her sister knew. She'd stayed too long.

"I could still go." Catherine's voice quivered. "I could wave at them on my way out."

"No. Greet them. Don't run away like you did before."

Catherine walked toward the door, as if drawn there by her dread and her fascination with the painful moments that would surely follow.

Luke held the door open. Leah dashed in, a sleeping baby in her arms, the twins and their older boys, William and Joseph, trotting along behind her. They were all sopping wet. "Run upstairs, boys, get out of those wet clothes and into bed. Annie, whose car is that…?"

She stopped, her gaze fixed on Catherine.

"Look who's come for a visit." Annie tried to keep her voice light.

"I was just leaving." Catherine's gaze flitted over the children. "Where's Mark? I wondered…how tall he must be now."

"William, Joseph, take the twins upstairs." Luke's deep voice reverberated around them. "Now."

Their eyes wide with curiosity at this stranger in their house, the boys herded little Esther and Ruth up the stairs, their wet feet making squelching sounds on the wood.

Luke tromped past Leah and halted in front of Annie. He didn't offer any words of welcome to their sister.

"You know better." Finally, he spoke. He didn't look at Catherine, directing the words squarely at Annie. "Why would you let her in the house?"

"I wanted to talk—"

"You shouldn't be talking to her. You should've turned her away."

"She's my sister. Your sister."

Luke's stony façade cracked a little, and Annie saw the misery in his eyes. His Adam's apple bobbed. "Not anymore."

"Luke!"

"It's all right. I'll go." Catherine's voice held steady. "I don't want to cause any trouble."

"If that were the case, she would never have left Bliss Creek." His gaze swung to Catherine, then dropped to the floor. "But what's done is done."

"I'll go now."

"She can't." Luke spoke to Annie as if she'd been the one to utter the words. "Not now."

"What?"

"It's raining so hard, the creek is up over its banks. We barely made it over the bridge." He wiped rain from his face with the back of his sleeve. Water dripped from his hat brim, making the motion useless. "No one can get into town tonight—not unless it stops raining for a spell. The ground's packed so hard from the drought that the water is running off as fast as the rain falls."

Annie couldn't stand it. She couldn't stand by and let Catherine think her return had no import to Luke. She knew it did. She knew from the tight line around his mouth and the way his pulse pounded in his temple.

"Luke, Catherine is—"

"Catherine best stay in the *dawdi haus* for the night." Leah handed Jebediah to Luke. "She can get back to town in the morning. I'll make sure there are fresh sheets on the bed. Annie, you best check on Noah; I hear him squalling. I'll fill the lamps out there."

Surprised at her sister-in-law's deft handling of the situation, Annie blew out a sigh of relief. The dawdi haus would be permissible. The bishop would not object to having a wayward member of the flock stay there. "Leah will get you settled." She took Catherine's cold hand in hers and squeezed. "I'll see you in the morning."

"See you in the morning." Catherine squeezed back. Her gaze went to Luke's stony face. "Unless the rain stops."

As if in response hail began to ping against the roof, the porch railings, and the ground around the house. Hard, white balls bounced and ricocheted against the windows.

"I'd better go help Mark. He's putting up the horse and wagon and checking on the livestock." Luke held out Jebediah. Annie took him. Her brother started toward the door without a backward glance. "Annie, get your sister an umbrella and then see to the babies. It's time everyone was in bed."

"I brought my own umbrella." Catherine continued to address Luke even though he'd turned his back on her. As she had done to him four years earlier. "Don't worry about me."

"I stopped worrying about her long ago."

Annie couldn't imagine how Luke could be so cold. It wasn't like him. Not one for showing much affection, true, but he'd never been mean.

"I'd like to see Mark, since I'm here." Catherine didn't seem to notice or she chose to ignore his tone. "I'm spending the night anyway."

Luke pushed through the screen door, letting his words flow back toward them. "Dawn comes early for those who work the land and have jobs in town."

Annie had never heard Luke acknowledge that Mark worked hard, harder than most. That was something, even if it was a jab at Catherine in her Englisch clothes and her fancy car. "See you in the morning," she said to Catherine again. "I'll bring you some of my biscuits and jam."

Catherine lifted her umbrella and slipped out the door. Like Luke, she didn't look back.

Catherine's journal
July 4

I'm here. In Bliss Creek. At the farm. Once my home. What a way to celebrate Independence Day. A homecoming to a place that is no longer home. A renewal of the sense that I am totally and completely independent. I have no family anymore. I suppose Dean counts as family now, although that could change if things don't work out between us. He insists they will, but nothing's certain. Family shouldn't change. I chose this, yet I somehow didn't feel it because I was somewhere else, in another world where I could just be a girl on a trip away from home. I could tell people my family was back home in Bliss Creek. They wouldn't know. Had no way of knowing that the family back home would no longer call me family.

Rain and hail are pounding on the roof of this small dawdi haus that hasn't been used in years. Sleep is unthinkable. So here I sit wondering how long before the battery gives out on my laptop. Every fiber of my being is humming with the sense that I've stepped back in time to a place that no longer exists for me. If I were at my apartment in Wichita, I'd put on an old movie on the movie channel, pop some popcorn, and enjoy the storm. Here, I'm vitally aware of every second as it ticks by, ticking away the moments until I get another glimpse of Annie and Luke and Mark, a glimpse of Emma and her new family, Josiah and his family. My not family, my un-family, my estranged family. It's surreal, being back here with them, but not really back. I knew it would be. I prepared myself for it, but still it hurts.

Luke acted as if I were a stranger. It's to be expected, of course. I keep telling myself that, but somehow it remains unexpected. He couldn't even look at me. That's how strongly the shunning is ingrained in them. They must keep themselves apart from the world and I am the world now.

Luke looked older—older than the four years that have passed. He has lines around his eyes and mouth and less hair

*sticking out from under his hat. He's a little stouter. He reminds
me of our father. In a few years, he will be a replica of him.
Leah, on the other hand, looks no different. The same thin line
that passes for a mouth. The same mousy brown hair peeking
from under her kapp. The same efficient stride. She couldn't
look me in the eye, either, but that doesn't bother me. I can
freely admit I didn't like her when she married Luke and I don't
expect that to change. Not a Christian attitude by any means,
but the truth is the truth. One thing I haven't done in my time
in the world is become a liar.*

*Only Annie hasn't changed toward me. As much as she
believes in the Ordnung, she finds it impossible to harden her
heart. She shimmers with light and sweetness. I see it in her
face, and looking at her fills me with a sense of light all my
own. Goodness flows out of her and on to me. It was painful to see her torn like that. Torn between them and me. The
look of puzzlement on her face when I talked about the memoir would be almost comical if it weren't so painful. She can't
understand my world, nor I hers. I can't understand the rejection of learning and knowledge. I can't understand living in a
world so small and colorless.*

*I do envy her a bit though, despite David's death and the
terrible loss it is for her. She actively seeks contentment with her
lot and she's determined to find it because that is what her faith
demands. She is determined to be, if not happy, at least content.
And that becomes a self-fulfilling prophecy. She will be content.
Her contentment seems like happiness to her. A simple life with
her bakery and her son and her family near her is all she needs
to be happy. I envy that kind of faith. I doubt I will ever be content. It's my fate to remember the day of my parents' death as
the day I stopped having faith that everything will be all right.*

*The rain is letting up. Time to sleep. They'll be at my door
before light. I don't want them to catch me sleeping in. Silly as
that sounds.*

Chapter 4

The Bliss Creek jail contained only four cells. Helen took a quick, curious look around. She'd never been in a jail before, hoped never to be again. Chief Parker had been kind enough to let her and Thomas have a peek at her son. Edmond had his own cell, away from the Englisch boys who lounged at the other end. One looked asleep. A second lay supine, staring at the ceiling, while the third chewed his fingernails. His hat missing and his blond hair a tousled mess, Edmond sat on his bunk, looking everywhere but at her.

The cells smelled of ripe teenage boy and worse, the *schtinck* of tobacco and beer and an odor that surely came from the bare commode in the corner. Helen put one hand to her mouth and with the other grasped the bars that separated her from Edmond. He hung his bare head. His thick blond curls put her in mind of his daed. George would have been so disappointed at this turn of events. More likely, things wouldn't have turned out this way if he were still here.

At least they hadn't made Edmond wear one of those orange jumpsuits. Chief Parker knew better. No bright colors for his Plain prisoner.

Prisoner.

Edmond a prisoner.

Helen's stomach rocked and she let go of the bar in fear that she would have to flee to the nearest sink or trash can.

"Where's your hat?" Why on earth she asked that question at a time like this she couldn't imagine. "You didn't lose it, did you?"

"We have his hat," Chief Parker broke in. "With his other things. He'll get it back."

"Edmond! How…why?" She managed to ask the important question without losing what was left of her supper. "What were you doing?"

Edmond slunk lower onto the bare mattress.

"He's still feeling the effects, I reckon." Chief Parker shook the ring of keys he held in one hand. "He hasn't said a word since I hauled him in here, but you can see he's fine."

"He doesn't look fine."

"Don't talk about me like I'm not here." Edmond's words slurred. He sounded surly. Neither fact did anything to endear him to Helen. He hunched his skinny shoulders. "My hearing's fine."

"Maybe so, but the rest of you is under the influence." Chief Parker tapped the bars with a key. "I suggest you show some respect to your mother and this man here who have come to try to help you. What ails you that you would put your mother through this, embarrassing her in front of your family and the entire Amish community, not to mention the rest of the town?"

Chief Parker had a good understanding of the Plain community, having grown up here in Bliss Creek. Having this understanding stated so baldly didn't help settle Helen's stomach. Which was worse? The Plain community, of course, because she would answer to the bishop and the deacons, as would Edmond. The Englischers had more experience with teenagers and alcohol. She had none at all.

"Why, Edmond, tell me that?"

He lifted his gaze, then ducked his head. "I didn't mean to do it."

"Didn't mean to do it? You picked up the alcohol, put it to your lips, and drank, didn't you? Or do you mean to say someone forced it down your throat?" Her voice rose of its own accord, sounding like a shriek in her ears. Thomas shifted next to her. She glanced at his face.

She brought her voice down. "Did they tie you up and wrench your mouth open so they could pour it in?"

"Nee."

"Nee."

"Then you meant to do it." Thomas spoke in a calm tone that settled like a comfortable shawl on Helen's tense shoulders. "Done is done. I suspect you'll learn a lesson or two in the days ahead."

Yes. Consequences. For them all.

Helen breathed, in and out, in and out. She turned to Chief Parker. "Do you have to press charges?"

"Edmond endangered many people when he drove the buggy into the parade route like that. Underage drinking, public intoxication, driving while intoxicated. Those are serious charges."

Indeed they were. "What do we do now?"

"Sign some paperwork with Craig Southerland. He's the only bondsman in Bliss Creek, but he's a fair man."

Chief Parker turned and led them from the jail into the offices.

"Wait! Mudder, wait."

The entreaty in Edmond's voice forced Helen to look back.

He motioned for her to come closer. Without looking at the two men, Helen slipped back to the bars. His eyes huge against pale skin, Edmond leaned toward her and whispered. "I'm sorry. They invited me to the party and I thought it would be fun, but I didn't mean to do this. I didn't."

"I accept your apology." Helen touched her son's hand. It was cold despite the warm heat of the cell. "I forgive you. But now you must face the consequences."

"There was a bottle and it smelled bad, but they were all laughing at me and looking at me when I didn't fill my cup. They called me stupid names. Like bowl-head and fuddy-duddy Eddy."

"Why would you spend time with boys who act and talk like that? You have your own friends, your own kind."

"I just wanted to feel better." He stared at his feet. They'd taken his boots so he wore only black socks, a fact that struck Helen as sad. "*Groossdaadi* is gone. He was out there planting and then he dropped to the ground and then he didn't breathe anymore."

Helen nodded. The cold, like a draught under the door on a winter night, pierced her skin. That feeling. That sinking, sinking, sinking sensation. She knew it. She'd felt it when George passed. Edmond had been ten when his father died. Old enough to feel his absence. An absence that had been filled in large part by his grandfather. His groossdaadi had been like his daed for almost seven years.

But that didn't excuse Edmond's actions.

"Your groossdaadi lived a good life. He worked hard. He took care of his family. It was his time to go; he went. That's how we live and that's how we die. According to God's plan and His time, not ours."

"I know."

"See that you don't forget it again."

"What'll happen to me?"

"I'll be back for you."

"I mean…after."

"That will be up to the bishop and the deacons."

Helen forced herself to turn away and not look back again.

She stared instead at Thomas's back. She allowed herself to bask in his steady calm for a few seconds. Steady. Calm. They moved through the door in a silent, single line.

Once on the other side, she turned to Chief Parker. "Tell me what a bondsman does."

"The magistrate—you know Jim Walker, that lawyer who lives over on Oak Street—he's the magistrate—he was nice enough to stop by and set bail for all these boys so their folks can take them home. The bondsman guarantees the bond." Chief Parker stalked over to a desk covered with paperwork in neat stacks and picked up a file. "You pay a percentage and Edmond can get out on bond until he has to appear in court. If he doesn't show, you have to pay the bondsman the full amount of his bond."

Pay a percentage. Appear in court. Helen's stomach flopped.

"We'll help," Thomas said, as if he knew what she was thinking. "Emma and I have money set aside."

"That's your emergency fund."

"This would qualify."

"But the bobbeli will be here soon."

"And the community will help. As always."

As always. Helen nodded and sank into the chair Chief Parker offered her. He slid papers across his desk and handed her a pen. She stared at it as if it might bite her. Chief Parker cleared his throat. "Take your time, Mrs. Crouch. Craig Southerland already filled out the bond papers. All I need from you is a cashier's check or cash."

She had neither.

She picked up the pen. It shook in her hand. She tried to focus on the words, but the strange dreamlike quality of this moment made everything around her shimmer. She glanced away. A silver picture frame sat on the corner of Chief Parker's desk. It held a photograph of Charisma Chiasson and her two kinner. Things must be going well with them if he had her picture on his desk. Helen sometimes wished she had a photo of George to remember him by. But she only had to look at her children to see him.

"Helen." Thomas towered over her. "Sign it. Everything will be fine."

The door slammed open so hard it smacked against the wall, making her jump and drop the pen. It rolled across the desk and disappeared on the other side. A sign on the wall that said visiting hours were from ten to noon on Monday through Friday shook and then slid to the floor with a tinkling of broken glass.

"Where he is? I demand to see him this instant!" An open umbrella in one hand, Mayor Gwendolyn Haag stomped across the office, smacked the swinging gate that separated the lobby area from the desks, and halted in front of Chief Parker. She leaned over and tapped the chief's chest with a long, pale pink fingernail. "Who do you think you are? Arresting my grandson?"

"Beg your pardon, Mayor Haag?" Chief Parker's tone remained even, his expression polite. He leaned back to avoid the rain dripping from the mayor's umbrella. "Did you need something?"

Mayor Haag whirled, and advanced on Helen's chair. "Helen Crouch. Your boy Edmond started this, didn't he? I heard people talking on the parade route. This is all your son's fault."

"My son will take responsibility for the things he has done." Helen stood and planted herself on both feet. Her stomach churned and her heart ached, but she stood firm. "As each boy should do."

"Christopher's never been in trouble before. Now he's been hanging around with your son, and look what happens."

"Likely, it's the other way around." Thomas stepped between them. "There's little history of Plain folks drinking, if you'll beg my pardon for saying so."

"There's no history of Christopher drinking—not until your son started coming around."

"Isn't Christopher staying with you because your son sent him to you to straighten out?" Chief Parker waded into the fray. "Got kicked out of school, didn't he?"

"He's a sensitive boy. Very smart. Got bored at school." Mayor Haag waved a hand as if waving away the question. "This Edmond boy encouraged him not to go to school. Said it wasn't necessary for real men."

"I see." Helen did see. Edmond simply shared the ways of Plain people. Boys Edmond's age learned a trade from their fathers. They prepared to become men and fathers themselves. Thomas and her own brothers had stepped in to help her with Edmond. Even then he'd stumbled. But the Englisch world was different. In that world, Christopher was still a young boy with years of schooling ahead of him. "I'll speak with Edmond. He won't bother Christopher again."

"Fat lot of good that'll do him with this underage drinking and public intoxication. I've hired an excellent lawyer for him." The mayor rooted around in a black leather bag that hung from her shoulder and produced a check. "Here's the cashier's check you requested, Chief Parker. I'll be taking him home now."

Chief Parker took the check, studied it, and then paper clipped it to a folder. He proceeded to write a receipt and hand it to the mayor in unhurried movements. "You'll receive notification when he's to appear in court."

Keys in hand, he rose. "Mrs. Crouch, if you want to work on getting together the cash, that's fine. I'll stay here as long as necessary. My officer doesn't come in to relieve me until midnight anyway. Come back as soon as you have it and we'll get Edmond home tonight."

The kindness in his voice nearly undid her. She nodded, afraid to speak for fear her voice would crack. Thomas saved her. "We'll be back."

As soon as they came up with five hundred dollars.

Chapter 5

Helen snatched the teakettle from the side cupboard and plopped it on the gas burner. A cup of tea—even in July—might calm her mind enough to let her sleep. Tugging her robe tightly over her nightgown, she stared out the window over the counter as jagged lightning split the sky and lit up the night. The wind howled and whistled through the eaves overhead. Tree branches dipped and bowed in a violent dance. Not even tea would get her to sleep in all this noise. As if to underline the truth of this statement, hail began to pound the roof again.

She sighed and pulled a brown ceramic mug from the shelf, then shook out a tea bag. Even after all these years, she hated sleeping alone during a thunderstorm. Silly thing for a grown woman. She couldn't help it. George loved a good storm. He'd sit in his rocking chair next to the bed, little Betsy in his arms, and hum. He didn't sing outright, although he had a strong baritone, but he hummed the tune of some old, familiar hymn that comforted not only the baby, but Helen.

Of course, it wasn't just the storm that kept her eyes open, gaze staring into the black night in her empty bedroom. The memory of her brother Tobias's face when she'd arrived at his door to ask for his help with the bond looped round and round inside her head. It had woven itself together with the other memories: Thomas handing her half the money to match Tobias's. Edmond's pale face behind bars. Gabriel Gless's headlong flight across the street to save his small daughter from being crushed under the hooves of an out-of-control horse. Gabriel Gless, period. In the dark of night, she turned this memory over in her head. Something about Gabriel. His dark, sad eyes, his lined face, his callused hands, his broad shoulders still thrust back despite the heavy burdens he carried.

George had been short and stout, like herself, eyes blue, hair blond, a perpetual smile on his face. He'd never minded her social lapses or her awkward moments. He seemed to like them, in fact. He said she made him laugh and life should be full of laughter in between the tears. And there would be tears, so why not laugh whenever possible?

She'd liked that idea. She loved her family, but they were a somber lot. Work hard, obey the Ordnung, go to bed early, get up early, she had no problem with that. But to laugh a little each day. She liked that. Liked it a lot. Enough to marry a man who lived and breathed it.

Until he didn't anymore. Until the day he went on without her. It had been his time to go, but not hers.

"Helen? Helen, is that you?"

Helen started and dropped the tea bag on the floor. "Mudder, what are you doing up?" She knelt to pick up the bag and bumped her head on the shelf. "Ouch."

"I was about to ask you the same question."

Rubbing her forehead, Helen swiveled. Her mudder wandered into the kitchen. She didn't have her cane, but she did well, all things considered. As long as Helen didn't move the furniture around or leave a chair pulled out.

"Where's your cane?" Helen took another cup from the shelf. If her mother were up now, she'd probably be up the rest of the night. She hadn't slept much since Daed's passing. "You can't be wandering around in the middle of the night like this."

"What difference does it make if it's night, silly girl?" Mudder reached until her outstretched hand landed on a chair at the prep table, then moved forward until she could slide into the seat. "It's mostly dark all day long for me."

No self-pity lingered in those words. She sounded what qualified as cheerful for her. With her hair still neatly hidden behind her kapp, and a shawl over her robe, she looked as proper as she did in broad daylight.

Even the day Helen had taken her to the doctor and he'd explained the strange tricks her eyes had been playing on her, her mother had simply nodded and said, "Well, then, take me home."

Loss of sight in the middle, while the edges remained. Helen had the doctor write the name of the disease on a piece of paper, sure she wouldn't remember it long enough to share it with her brothers and write about it in letters to her sisters.

Macular degeneration. Words from some foreign language that translated to mean her mother could no longer sew or cook or even take herself into town in the buggy. Her vision hadn't completely disappeared yet, but so little remained that she'd taken to using a cane to tap her way about the house and the yard.

"Will you have a cup of tea with me? The water's hot." Pleased she'd managed to sound equally cheerful, Helen picked up a hot pad and poured the water into the two mugs. "Chamomile for you. Black tea for me."

"Black tea will only keep you awake."

"I'll add lots of milk and a dollop of honey." She knew she wouldn't be sleeping anyway, tea or not. "Honey for you?"

"Naomi told me about Edmond."

The muscles in her arm seemed too weary to hold up the teakettle. Helen set it on the stove.

"I know it must grieve you so." The gentleness of her mother's tone caused tears to well in Helen's eyes. For one split second, she welcomed the fact that Mudder couldn't see her weakness. "You've done everything you can to raise the children right. Your daed helped as best he could. The boys and your sisters, they helped. Whatever Edmond does now, he has to own. He chooses his path. You can't do it for him."

"I feel I failed." Helen wiped at her eyes with the back of her hand. No tears. She'd come this far on her own. "I think if George had been here…"

"You feel? You think? Edmond will not be able to use his father-lessness as an excuse for wrong behavior. He is approaching manhood. It is time he act like it. He has to step into the shoes left empty by his father and his grandfather. That's his job now."

"He's so young." Helen set the tea on the table a bit to the left of where her mother sat, hoping she'd be able to see it. "I've added the honey already. It's there to your right."

"He's your son, but you do him no favors by babying him. You only allow him to become weaker." Without hesitation, Mudder wrapped her fingers around the mug as if to warm them. "Your actions will show him what he can get away with in the future. Can you see that?"

Helen dropped into the chair across from her mother and sipped her tea. Scalding hot but still a little weak. She hadn't given it time to properly steep before adding the milk and honey. Like always, she tried to do things too quickly. "He must be punished."

"He must."

"The bishop will guide us."

"He will."

They sat in silence and sipped their tea, not speaking for long moments. Finally her mudder rose and, with a grace Helen longed to possess, glided to the large tub where they washed the dishes and set the cup in it. "We'll wash these with the breakfast dishes. It's late. Dawn will be here soon."

Swallowing against the ache in her throat, Helen straightened and took a last sip of the tea before repeating her mother's actions.

She followed Mudder through the doorway and slipped past her. "Let me help you up the stairs."

A roaring, screaming sound drowned out her mother's response. A second later, the living room wall ripped apart. Windows shattered. The enormous oak tree that had shaded Helen's childhood home since before her birth crashed through. The sheer surprise of it made Helen scream.

"What? What is it?" Mudder cried. "Helen? Helen! Where are you?"

"Right here! I'm right here," Helen gasped when she had enough air in her lungs to shout. She threw an arm across her face and looked up. All she could see were massive tree branches crashing down. "Hang on to me."

Branches smashed into furniture and sent glass, wood, leaves, and debris hurtling in all directions. Heart pounding so hard it might punch through her rib cage and free itself, Helen whirled, grabbed her mother, and thrust her to the floor. Her mother let out an *oomph* sound and tried to wiggle away. "Stop, Mudder, stay down!" Helen screamed over the continuous thunder. "Stay down!"

Ach, God, not her too. Please God, not her too. I already lost Daed.

Cowering from the flailing branches, she covered her mother with her body. Rain soaked her. Tree branches slapped to the floor all around them in a *bam, bam, bam* that made her jump each time.

Finally, the terrible crashing, tearing sounds abated, leaving behind the steady pounding of the rain and an occasional rumble of thunder. The noise was all the more ominous. Nothing separated Helen and her mother from the elements. The jagged hole in the roof and the wall stood open like a gaping wound.

"What was it? What happened?" Mudder struggled to rise. "Are you all right?"

"The oak tree." Helen sucked in air, but she couldn't get relief. No oxygen seemed to fill her lungs. She panted. *Please God, don't let me have a heart attack. Mudder and the children need me.* She tried again. "The storm felled the oak tree."

Another pillar in her life knocked down.

Chapter 6

Gabriel paused at the foot of the stairs, doing a mental recount. Mary Elizabeth and Abigail washed breakfast dishes with Rebecca, Thomas's oldest girl, while Mary and Lillie played with the little girls and kept them out from underfoot. Seth, Samuel, and Isaac had tromped out immediately after breakfast to survey the storm damage with Thomas. That left Daniel. The boy—hardly a boy at nineteen—spoke little but his unrelenting morose stare said it all. Gabriel sucked in a breath and prepared to do his fatherly duty despite a weariness born of a sleepless night and guilt and despair that lingered like cobwebs hanging low in a dark, dusty, unused room. They'd come to this place for a new start, only to find the same problems staring them in the face.

"Daniel? Daniel! Get down here. Time's wasting."

No answer. "Daniel!"

Nothing.

Gritting his teeth, Gabriel stomped up the stairs and down the hallway to the bedroom his four boys shared with Thomas's sons Eli and little Caleb. The narrow, stacked bunk beds lined the room, blocking his view. He ducked and peered under the top row of bunks. Daniel sat on the last one, facing the crib and squeezed up against the tall east windows, his back to the door.

"Son."

Still, Daniel didn't turn. Anger ripped through Gabriel like a grass-fire fueled by kerosene. "Answer me when I speak to you." He forced himself to tap down the flames. "Turn around and look at me."

Daniel turned, then stood with the deliberate air of appeasement. He gripped a pencil in one hand, his long fingers white at the knuckles, and a sheaf of paper in the other.

"We've chores to do and repairs to make." Gabriel managed to keep his tone even. "We need to earn our keep around here. Help out in exchange for such generous hospitality."

"I know." Daniel ducked his head, his dark, shaggy hair falling into his walnut-colored eyes. He needed a haircut. Laura would've cut it for him. "I'm on my way."

"Doesn't look like it. What are you doing?"

Daniel stuffed the papers under his pillow and tugged in a jerky motion at the green and blue quilt until it covered the white pillow-case. "Writing a letter."

"To Phoebe. You've heard from her, then?"

"Jah. A letter came yesterday."

Gabriel shifted his feet. He lifted his hat and settled it back on his head. They'd talked about this back in Dahlburg. They'd talked some more on the long drive to Kansas and Bliss Creek. The family needed to stay together. Phoebe's parents didn't wish her to leave home. Not at such a young age. If they were meant to be together, two more years wouldn't hurt. Separation would make their relationship stronger. It would make Daniel stronger. He had a softer, more sensitive nature than his brothers. At least that's what Laura had always said. Give him room to be himself, she'd said. He wasn't Isaac and Samuel. No, because Isaac and Samuel were like Gabriel, and Daniel more like his mother. "She'll be happy to hear how well things are going here."

"She misses me. She stays home all the time."

"I know this is hard, son, but you will see Phoebe again."

Daniel's head came up. His Adam's apple bobbed. "Jah."

"We best get out to the corral. The storm knocked down some of the fence and damaged the barn roof. It looks like some shingles are missing from the house's roof too. There's work to be done."

His face still glum, Daniel nodded. He grabbed his hat from the hook on the wall and strode past Gabriel without looking at him. He'd grown two or three inches in the last few months, such that he was taller than Gabriel now, but he had the scrawny arms and legs of a boy whose body couldn't keep up with the growth spurt. He kept his gaze glued to the floor. Gabriel started to pat his shoulder, but thought better of it. His son was a man now, not one needing comfort from his father. His hand hung in the air for a second, then he let it drop to his side. Daniel wouldn't appreciate being treated like a child. Even though Gabriel could still see him rolling around on the back of the hay wagon, so short the hay bales towered over him. A little helper, he'd been. The first to whistle, the last to whine.

Daniel studied the staircase banister. "You coming?"

"Coming."

Outside, without speaking, Daniel veered toward the barn, and Gabriel trudged to the corral where Isaac replaced a frayed harness so he could hitch the wagon. Gabriel inhaled the cool, slightly damp morning air, reminding himself to count this blessing. Once the sun came up, the heat would blister his skin and lungs. The rain of the previous evening had increased in fury throughout the night, bringing with it high winds and hail. It had cleared the air of the stifling humidity, but left behind downed branches, debris, and muck. Shingles scattered on the gravel road in front of Thomas's house suggested his roof had not fared well in the onslaught of rain and hail. Even if they couldn't get into the fields to harvest the wheat—if there was anything left to harvest—they would still have plenty of work to do.

"Daed, I want to go into town later this morning. I need to take a look at the shop. I imagine it will need work before we can open. Remodeling and such." Isaac took a step back from the gray Percheron that whined and snorted as if anxious to get started. Isaac stretched his arms over his head and then bent at the waist in a deep stretch. "I also heard Emma's brother might need help at the blacksmith shop. I was thinking the extra money might be needed until we get the shop open."

"You're needed here. There will be storm cleanup on every farm in the area. Levi Stubbs passed by and said some of the farm roads are blocked by fallen trees and debris."

"Every farm comes with a family and men who will do the work." Isaac crossed his arms, a frown marring his expression. Gabriel couldn't see any of Laura in his oldest son's face; he saw a reflection of himself. Unlike Daniel, Isaac had his personality, which made for frequent head butting. "If we're to make it here, we need to find work quickly or get the shop open."

"In God's time, son, not yours."

"Doesn't God expect us to make an effort?"

"Only God knows what His plan is."

Isaac blew out air in an exaggerated sigh. "I should've stayed in Dahlburg. Nothing will be different here."

"You had your chance."

His son didn't answer and Gabriel regretted his words. Isaac had intended to stay in Indiana, until the girl he'd courted for more than two years had decided to choose another man—his closest friend from childhood. Unlike Daniel he and the girl had been old enough to start their own life. The girl's father had been agreeable. The girl had been the one to change her mind. Isaac hadn't said a word about it, but tongues wagged in the small community, and a father could read much into a son's furious, insistent refusal to mention it. Instead, he chose to be the joker in the family. Acting silly. Acting lighthearted. As if that would make it so.

"I'll help with the cleanup, but at least let me take Mary Elizabeth to the bakery this morning." Isaac squatted and picked up a rake that had fallen to the ground. He stuck it on the back of the wagon with shovels, saws, and brooms. "That would be a fine job for her. She's a good cook and she'll be among Plain folks."

"And who will watch the girls, cook, sew, and clean?"

"Abigail is capable. You know she is. She's been doing it since—"

"Jah." Gabriel couldn't help himself. He cut his son off. He didn't need to be reminded of what the girls had done every day for the past three years. At first his sisters and cousins had taken turns helping with the baby and the household chores. They'd taught Abigail and Mary Elizabeth what they still needed to know to care for the two younger girls. It wasn't that much, considering what a good job Laura had done with them. Gradually they had taken over, growing up quickly in the absence of their mother. "There's Thomas. Where are Seth and Samuel?"

"Seth and Samuel are slopping the pigs for Thomas and helping Eli with the other chores. I haven't seen Daniel since breakfast, though. I suppose he's still mooning over Phoebe."

"Be kind to your brother. He's not like you."

Isaac whipped around so he faced Gabriel. "Not hard-hearted, you mean?"

"Nee. Just that you are different. You get through life in different ways."

"He moons around, I move on."

"Phoebe was too young to come with us."

"And you refused to stay in Dahlburg, on our farm, in our home."

"Jah." These recriminations weren't new. "I did what was best for all of us."

Gabriel held his son's gaze until Isaac's dropped.

The horse whinnied and stamped, eyes rolling. Using the interruption as an excuse, Gabriel turned to examine the horse. His sons would understand someday. Until then, they would have to trust his judgment.

"Easy, there, easy." He peered at the horse's hindquarters. One leg seemed swollen. A bite of some kind? Gabriel wiped sweat from his eyes with the back of his shirtsleeve and took a closer look. "Are you always so skittish?"

"That he is." Thomas strode toward them, his boots squelching in the mud. He didn't look happy. "Best leave him in the corral. We'll take the Morgan and the sorrel. Let this horse rest. He's my best horse for harvest. The wheat is battered and the fields are full of mud and standing water. By the time it dries out, it will be too late. We've lost it—again."

"I'm sorry, Thomas." Gabriel felt the loss as his own. As a farmer, he knew nothing hurt more then the loss of a cash crop. Thomas depended on the proceeds to support his family. "A total loss?"

"Yep." Thomas tugged at his hat, then shoved it back. "But we'll be fine. We always are. We'll use this time to clean up and then take a look at the well. If it's going dry, we must dig for another one. Soon. This week."

"You ever consider doing something else?" Isaac posed the question. "Everybody I talk to says farming won't support us like it used to do."

"Nee, I wouldn't give up farming, but there's been talk around here of switching from wheat to cattle." Thomas's tone said he didn't abide by the idea. "The start-up costs are high, but you're less vulnerable to the weather."

"You don't think it's a good idea?"

"Change is hard."

An undeniable fact, but one that Gabriel was surprised to hear from Thomas.

"Speaking of change, Thomas, don't you think the bakery would be a good place for Mary Elizabeth to work? She's a good cook and she likes to bake." Isaac leaned against the wagon, not looking at Gabriel. "Helen Crouch said your sister-in-law was looking for good help."

"If your father wishes Mary Elizabeth to work, the bakery is as good a place as any. Annie needs the help and she is devoted to the Ordnung." Thomas was always the diplomat. Gabriel liked that about his cousin. "What do you think, Gabriel?"

"I think Isaac wants an excuse to go into town and look at the building we bought for the repair shop. I think he's in a big hurry to get out of a hard day's work, chopping tree branches, mending fences, and shoveling mud. That's what I think."

"Is there harm in that?" Isaac's face turned red as the clouds at sunrise. He picked up a rock and chucked it into the field. "We came here to get a new start. What's the point if we do the same old thing?"

"We're enjoying Thomas's hospitality." Youth. Always in such a hurry for the next thing instead of taking care of the here and now. Isaac would get over that with time. Gabriel almost hated that thought. "You could go after—"

The sound of an approaching horse caused the Percheron to snort and do a half-step shuffle into Gabriel. Looking over the horse, he backed off to avoid getting stepped on.

Helen Crouch approached, her son seated next to her. The boy looked no worse for the wear despite his actions of the previous evening. She must've rousted him from his bed well before dawn to be out in the Brennaman homestead this early. Helen, on the other hand, had dark circles under her eyes that spoke of a sleepless night. The memory of how he'd scolded her the previous evening made heat coil around his neck and writhe along his jaw. She was only a woman, after all, and one without a husband to rein in their children.

"Good morning." Thomas spoke first. "You're out and about early."

"The big oak in front of our house toppled over last night. Peter says it was old and the root system weakened by the drought. By God's grace, no one was hurt, but we've much work to do to clean it up and rebuild the damaged wall and roof." Her tone stiff, she wrapped the reins around small, plump hands, her gaze flitting to Gabriel and then back to Thomas. "Peter, Tobias, and Thaddeus are there now, attempting to move the trunk and all the debris."

"We best get over there and help them." Thomas made a move toward the wagon. "We'll switch out the horses and be right there."

"You've done enough." Helen's face turned a dark red hue. "I brought Edmond over to help with your cleanup. Being he's not allowed to drive a buggy, I'll deliver and pick him up."

The boy's face turned as red as his mother's, and he hung his head. Gabriel almost felt pity for him—almost. Edmond had put people in danger, put himself in danger, and he'd embarrassed his family.

Gabriel moved around the horse. "Surely we can help your family out and then they can do the same for Thomas here. If it's a big tree, it'll take all of us to chop it up and prepare it for kindling. You'll be needing drywall, lumber, and glass for the windows from town."

"He's right, Helen." Thomas smoothed his beard. "Edmond should be helping his *onkels*."

Helen turned to her son. "Get down."

A reluctant look on his face, the boy slid from his seat and trudged around the horse. He stopped next to Gabriel. Despite his youth, he stood nearly as tall as Gabriel. His big hands hung limp at his side. "I'm sorry about what happened yesterday." He swallowed, let his gaze drop to the ground, then brought it back to Gabriel's. "I know your little girl could've been hurt and I'm sorry."

"I accept your apology." Gabriel began unhooking the horse from the wagon. "I reckon you learned a lesson."

"One he'll keep on learning for a long time." Helen's clipped tones brooked no argument on that. "Go on, Edmond, finish up."

The boy trudged over to Thomas. "I will pay back the money Mudder borrowed from you for the bond." His gaze swung toward his mother and back to Thomas. "I'm to do whatever you need me to do and then try to get a job in town. I'll turn the paychecks over to you."

"We have no wheat to harvest and our storm damage is little compared to what you have. I imagine your onkels need help on your farm—"

"Edmond owes you. We owe you." Helen interrupted Thomas in a manner that told Gabriel she wasn't used to interrupting a man—any man, least of all Thomas—but seemed very determined on this matter. "We appreciate your help. Now, I'll go home and start the noon meal. There will be many hungry mouths to feed after the hard work of removing the tree and rebuilding the wall."

"We'll take Edmond to your house with us." Thomas's tone was firm. "We're right behind you."

"As you like." She looked like a plump wren in her brown dress.

One who turned into a hawk the minute someone threatened her chicks. "Tobias will want to return the favor."

"If Isaac wants to start working on getting the repair shop ready, that is fine," Thomas added. "I see Luke and his cousins coming up over the hill there. My brothers will be along any minute. We'll take turns working each property until everyone's is cleaned up, starting with Helen's."

Thomas had missed the point, but Gabriel couldn't ignore the pleading look on his son's face. As a grown man with a mind of his own, Isaac had the right to make his own decisions. Hard as Gabriel found it to let go. "Fine."

Isaac grinned and gave a whoop that reminded Gabriel that he wasn't so grown up after all. "You'll see, Daed. I'll have that place whipped into shape and ready to open before you know it."

He didn't say it, but Gabriel knew he was thinking it. Thinking he could also look into the blacksmith job. Isaac had spent enough time working with his own daed. He wanted to spread his wings. So much for the family working together.

Chapter 7

Annie punched the dilly bread down harder than necessary, folded in the sides, and turned it over to reshape into a ball. If anyone saw her he'd wonder why a Plain girl had her hand fisted like that, pummeling the dough harder than necessary. It felt good. She had learned this technique from her Englisch friend Charisma Chiasson, who explained that kneading bread dough could be considered what she called therapy. That would be their little secret. The pleasing aroma of the fresh dill and chopped onions wafted through the bakery. It would welcome customers when she unlocked the doors in another hour. She inhaled and let it soothe her. Early mornings at the bakery were the best time of day. So peaceful.

Unlike her home. The memory of the previous evening's events invaded her peaceful refuge. Catherine had been gone this morning when Annie took her a plate of biscuits and sausage. Gone without even leaving a note. But then, that was Catherine's way. If she didn't come by the bakery today, Annie would seek her out. She would tell her she couldn't take photos, not of the family. It wasn't right for her to expect that—or anything—from the family and community she had abandoned. Annie punched down another batch of dough harder than necessary and began shaping it into a loaf. Catherine had no right. Annie would tell her that. Catherine had taken her by surprise on the previous evening, but now, in the light of day, she knew what she must do.

The look on Luke's face—that look of pain mixed with anger and hurt—haunted her. Luke was a stoic man most of the time, but Catherine's decision to leave on the heels of their parents' deaths had hurt him deeply. He'd been thrust into the role of head of the family at a time when he was starting his own family. Catherine had not made that transition any easier.

Catherine couldn't be blamed, either. She'd suffered a terrible trauma, witnessing the deaths of both their parents. Annie gently laid the bread dough in a greased loaf pan, spread a dish towel over it, and left it to rise a second time. No one was to blame. She hadn't told Luke about the camera or the pictures or the memoir. Or the doctor beau and the inability to have children. Better to let the shock of Catherine's visit ease before dumping the rest on Luke. He had his hands full with the storm damage and the harvest right now. Or the lack of harvest. One thing at a time.

Annie wiped at her damp forehead with the back of her greasy hand and sighed. The bumbleberry pies and the maple drop cookies were already baking, but she had so much more to do before the bakery opened. She needed to make two more rhubarb pies, an applesauce cake, and two batches of oatmeal raisin cookies. Exhaustion weighed her down. She needed help.

"I'm here! Sorry I'm late. The chores took longer this morning because of the mess left by the storm. Someone left the gate open and the pigs got out. It took me forever to get them rounded up. Then the fence had to be mended where the Morgan kicked it and then the dogs were chasing the rooster and…" As if in answer to a prayer, Mark trotted into the bakery, his freckled face alight with a smile and his mouth running fast as always. "Do you have deliveries? I left the horse hitched in case you needed something delivered this morning."

"Good morning to you too. Jah, I have deliveries. But first I need you to bring another bag of flour up here and a bag of sugar."

"Happy to oblige."

"Why are you so cheerful?"

"Catherine's back and have you seen the Gless girls?" He whistled. "Gabriel Gless is staying with Thomas and Emma and he has eight kinner just like us, four of them are girls, just like us, and one of them is close to my age—Mary Elizabeth—and…"

"I see, I see." Annie held up her hand. "I don't want you to get too carried away, because you know you're not supposed to talk to Catherine. She's not staying, anyway. The Glesses, on the other hand, are staying, according to Luke, but Gabriel Gless is very strict with his girls. Besides, you're not old enough to court yet. You can't even go to the singings for two more years."

"I know, I know. But once Catherine spends time with us she'll see. She'll want to stay." Mark popped his suspenders with an airy grin. "And once Gabriel Gless gets to know us, he'll see we're good company for his girls. We can be friends first. Singings later."

He looked so cheerful and sounded so optimistic, Annie didn't have the heart to argue about the Gless girls. "I don't know about Catherine."

"I do." He grabbed a snickerdoodle from the tray on the counter and munched as he headed to the storeroom. "Who could stay away forever? Not Catherine."

He disappeared from sight, still talking. Annie had to laugh. Her little brother always made her laugh. Asking him to work with her at the bakery after David's death and Sadie's retirement had been the right thing to do. Now she needed another person who could bake. She had more business than she knew how to handle, which was a blessing, no doubt about it. But she didn't want to lose customers because they had to wait too long for their baked goods. Maybe Miriam's little sister Delia could do it…

The door swung open and in walked a slim young girl in a dark blue dress that brought out the brilliant color of her eyes. Behind her strode a man who immediately sought Annie's gaze and held it.

"We're not open for another hour," she called. "Sorry. If you could come back—"

"Annie Plank? Emma's sister?" The man made her name a question and a statement at the same time, if that were possible. As if he were very sure of himself.

"Jah. I'm Annie."

"*Gut.*"

As if he'd known all along and she'd only needed to confirm. He towered over his companion and had a lean body. His whiskerless face told her he wasn't married, even though he looked to be close to her age.

"I think it's good most days," she responded, aware he'd caught her staring. "Today, I'm too far behind on my baking to be sure of it, however."

"Well, I think I have a solution to that problem." He introduced himself as Isaac Gless and the girl, who plucked at her apron and ducked her head, as his sister Mary Elizabeth. "Mary Elizabeth is a good baker and she needs a job."

"Does she, indeed? Then maybe we should get to know each other a bit."

"Good idea." He grinned, apparently unaware that Annie meant she and Mary Elizabeth should get to know each other. Funny job interview, when the interviewee couldn't get a word in edgewise. Isaac lifted his head and sniffed loudly. "You could start by letting us sample the wares. I smell bumbleberry pie and maple drop cookies."

"You have a good nose." Annie found herself smiling, although she wasn't sure why. "Right on both counts."

"With a honker like this, how could I miss?" He pointed at a nose that seemed suited for the size of his handsome face and grinned. "Got it from my daed. They say I look exactly like him, only better."

"Isaac!" Mary Elizabeth finally spoke. "Annie will think you're bragging on yourself. Remember what Daed says: No *hochmut*, only *demut*."

"I'm never prideful, always humble. I also try to always speak the truth." He laughed. His laugh was deep and natural and unfettered. It made Annie laugh too, something she hadn't done in a long time. He snatched a piece of cookie from the sample plate left from the previous day. "Let me have a taste—see how the goods are in this bakery."

"Nee, nee." Annie scurried forward and grabbed the plate. "Not day-old samples. I have cookies hot from the oven."

She whirled and scooped up the fresh, hot snickerdoodles and turned to give them each one. The look on Isaac's face made her stop. His sly grin said it all. She'd been tricked into giving him a fresh cookie free of charge. "You are quite the smooth talker, Isaac Gless. Now you best get along with your business while I talk to your sister about this job."

"I can't hang around while you talk?"

"Not unless you plan to be the one doing the baking."

"No, no, I'm either running my daed's implement repair shop or I'm working for your brother at the blacksmith shop—I'm not sure which it will be yet. I went by but his shop was closed. A sign on the door said he'd gone to make a house call."

He imparted all this information while leaning on her counter, grinning at her. He didn't sound unsure at all. Annie longed for that kind of self-assurance. Somehow hers had disappeared with David's death. She found his a little daunting. She turned to Mary Elizabeth. "Come behind the counter. I'll pour some fresh lemonade and we'll talk while I make the rhubarb pies. In fact, if you've a mind to, you could start the oatmeal raisin cookies for me. A bit of a trial run, how about that?"

"That would be nice." Mary Elizabeth put a hand on the swinging door that separated the bakery's public space from the work space. "I'm not so good at conversation, but my cookies are good."

"They're very good," Isaac interrupted. "I'll be a witness to that."

"Tell your brother he can go now." Annie cocked her head toward the door. "Job interviews are usually done by the person seeking the job, not a family member."

Mary Elizabeth's cheeks turned rosy. "Isaac means well."

The clink of the door closing told Annie that Mary Elizabeth's brother had taken the hint. *Gut.* "All the ingredients you'll need are on these shelves." She gestured to the oak planks that lined the wall. Shelves made with loving hands by Sadie's husband many years ago. Annie ignored the pang. She missed working with Sadie, but time marched along, taking prisoners, and leaving people behind. "Help yourself and I'll get started on the pies."

"My *bruder* doesn't mean any harm."

Surprised at her insistence, Annie glanced back at the girl. "I didn't think he did. I just have a lot of work to do. No time for silliness."

Mary Elizabeth selected cinnamon and nutmeg from the row of spices, then set them next to the enormous container of oatmeal. "He acts silly to hide his broken heart."

"It's hard to tell." Isaac had a broken heart? He didn't act like it. Anyway, it wasn't her place to know about Isaac Gless's heart. "We should talk about your cooking skills."

"My mudder died so Abigail and I do all the cooking and we take care of my sisters. They're special." Mary Elizabeth wiped her hands on her apron. Her eyes reddened, but her voice remained steady. "Both of them, even though Daed doesn't want to see it."

"I'm sure your daed believes he is blessed with each one of his children." Annie knew what it was like to lose a mother and try to help raise little brothers and sisters. "It's hard, isn't it? But you're blessed to have a big family to help care for the little ones."

"Jah." Mary Elizabeth looked doubtful, but she nodded. "I love Isabelle and Rachel. I...I hope to have many some day."

"Of course you do. It's what all Plain women want."

What Annie wanted more than anything she could imagine. Children with David. Many children. Gabriel Gless had eight. She couldn't imagine such bounty. Yet he suffered, just as she did. Perhaps more so with no fraa to care for those children. Maybe Isaac tried to help Mary Elizabeth get a job because of this. Otherwise she would be a substitute mother and miss her chance to be mudder of her own children. Annie put the thought away. She must not meddle in other people's problems. She had a penchant for doing that, and the results weren't always what she would have hoped.

"You're Mary Elizabeth Gless, aren't you." Mark's voice interrupted Annie's reverie. Her brother stood in the doorway, a twenty-five-pound bag of flour on his shoulder topped by another of sugar. He marched forward with a jaunty stride as if they weighed no more than a puppy. "I saw you at the parade."

The girl's face turned pink once again. She barely glanced at Mark, instead giving Annie an imploring look. Annie took pity on her. "Jah, this is Mary Elizabeth. She's come to work here. You'd best do the same. She's on a try-out and she wants to do well so she doesn't need you nattering on about parades and such."

"I only wanted to say hello and welcome." Mark wasn't one to be bullied—especially by a sister. "It's the neighborly thing to do."

Annie doubted Mark's intentions were that lofty. "Consider it said and take the pineapple sheet cake on the counter to Mrs. Fisher. While you're out, stop at the IGA and pick up a large can of shortening. I've run short and the restaurant supply truck won't be in town until tomorrow."

Mark dropped the bags at Annie's feet and made a show of dusting his hands. "I'm off then."

"Thank you for the welcome." Mary Elizabeth managed to summon the courage to take two steps in Mark's direction. Annie hid a smile. "We've only been here a few days, but everyone has been real nice. Makes it easier."

"We're pretty nice folks." Mark tucked his thumbs under his suspenders. "You'll see."

Annie suspected Mark would go to great lengths to make sure of that. She suppressed a sigh and turned back to cutting shortening into flour for the pie crusts. Those first baby steps in getting to know another person. The joy of the journey toward finding that individual who would be the one with whom a person could spend his life. Mark and Mary Elizabeth had that journey still in front of them. Perhaps with each other. Or with another. A journey full of delights and sorrows. Her own journey had ended abruptly in front of a white stone marker in a long row of identical headstones. She swallowed against the ache in her throat. She thought of Noah and began to count her blessings as she did each day. The ache didn't ease.

Helen added another dozen peanut butter chocolate chip cookies to a tray already laden with snickerdoodles, haystack cookies, and thimble cookies. She glanced around her kitchen. What else? Slices of banana bread. She wiped her hands on her apron and studied the tray. Enough? With Thomas and his crew, Gabriel and his boys, and Luke and his brothers, more than two dozen men and boys were working in front of the Crouch house. The tree had taken out two windows, knocked in part of the front living room wall, and damaged the wooden floor as well as any furniture in its wake. Rain soaked everything. The east side of the house stood in shambles.

Better add the blueberry muffins too.

Helen inhaled the scent of fresh wood planks and vinegar and water cleanser. Calm prevailed today. The storm, if nothing else, had put her problems in perspective. Everyone had survived safe and uninjured, just as they had been after Edmond's escapade. *Gott's* timing allowed for the children to be safe in their beds on the other side of the house when the tree fell. With the sun shining and the sky blue, the terrors of the storm dissipated, brushed away by the girls as they swept the areas the men cleared. Their excited, high-pitched chatter filled the air like birds singing in their nests.

"Helen, where are you?"

"Right at the counter, Mudder, getting ready to take snacks out to the men."

Mudder trundled into the kitchen, her cane making a clickety-clack sound on the vinyl linoleum. She didn't seem any worse for the wear after the night's adventure. No broken bones or even bruises, despite the force of Helen's desperate shove to the floor. "It seems drafty."

"That's because there's a big hole in the wall," Helen reminded her. "Remember, the tree fell into it."

"That's right. It did."

Sometimes, it seemed Mudder's mind might be going the way of her sight. The thought made Helen's stomach rock. Not Mudder's mind too. "Sit here at the table and I'll bring you a glass of iced tea and a cookie. Would you like haystacks or peanut butter?"

"Nee. You take the food to the men. I can take care of myself."

Between her failing sight, gnarled hands, and wandering mind, Mudder hadn't been able to take care of herself since before Daed's death, but Helen didn't argue. Her mother's continued presence brought her joy, and it lessened the blow a little of losing Daed too soon.

"Sit. Here are your cookies. I'll pour the iced tea when I come back." Helen picked up the tray. "I'll be right back."

She turned and smacked into Thomas's broad frame in the doorway. Cookies flew. The tray tumbled to the floor with a clatter. "*Ach!*"

"Sorry!" Thomas knelt at the same time as Helen. "I'll get it."

"Nee, let me." She narrowly avoided butting heads with him. "I'll have them cleaned up in no time."

"Here. I came to help fix a mess, not make a new one." Thomas's chagrined face surely matched her own. "Such a waste of good cookies too. They smell mighty good."

"There's plenty more where these came from." Helen scrambled to her feet, the tray in hand. "Did you come in for something in particular?"

"Gabriel sliced a finger. We'll need gauze and tape." Thomas lifted his hat and resettled it on his unruly hair. "Some antiseptic if you have it."

"Of course. The girls can sweep this up when they finish in the living room."

Glad to have a reason to turn away from the sight of a man who always brought her a mishmash of feelings that ran the gamut from friendship to aching disappointment that had to be buried—should've been buried deep, deep in the ground long ago, Helen dumped the ruined cookies and bustled about the kitchen, gathering supplies. *Keep busy. Work hard. God knows best. God has a plan.* "Bad cut?"

"Nee, just enough that he doesn't want to get blood on his shirt."

"This should do it, then."

She followed him through the living room, trying not to look at the gaping hole and the smashed hickory rocking chairs and the ruined sofa, its cushions ripped and squashed under the tree. What if her mudder had been sitting there? Better not to play the what-if game. God had brought them safely through the storm.

"You're making quick work of it." She cast about for a safe topic of conversation. "Are Thaddeus and Luke back with the supplies from the lumberyard yet?"

"Jah. They just arrived." He looked back at her. "Gabriel's a good man."

Startled at this direction in the conversation, Helen slowed her pace. "I'm sure he is. He's your cousin."

"Edmond's antics yesterday frightened him." Thomas scratched his forehead, a preoccupied look on his face. "He'll get over it."

"Or be upset for a long time."

"He's a forgiving man."

"Then I'll forgive him for being so stiff-necked."

"*Gut.* About Edmond."

Her own neck stiffened. "Is he not working hard out there?"

"Very hard." Thomas pulled the door open and paused so Helen could pass through with her medical supplies. "He seems bent on restoring my trust. And earning Gabriel's."

"That's *gut.*"

"I'm wondering if it might not serve him well to have Josiah talk with him."

"Josiah?" Annie's brother remained known for a reckless rum-springa despite the hard work and steadiness of the intervening years. "Having taken the path Edmond seems to be seeking now?"

"Jah. It might help to offer this as a solution when you speak with the bishop tonight."

"You think it'll help?"

"It won't hurt. Josiah has grown into a good husband and father. He's a hard worker. His mistakes are behind him."

"You're right."

Thomas smiled down at her. "Most of the time."

"Emma might differ with you on that." Helen grinned back. Thomas always made her feel at ease. Not awkward. Why had she not found that in anyone else since George? "But then, like any good wife, she allows you to think you're always right."

"She is indeed a good fraa. Just as you were to George." Thomas pointed to where Gabriel stood, a towel wrapped around his left hand. "Best take care of the wounded. Tobias and Thaddeus have this under control. I must go hunting for a good spot for a new well. If you need anything, let us know."

For a few seconds, Helen watched him stride across the front yard toward the corral and the buggies. "Thomas!"

He looked back, his face haloed by his straw hat and the sun behind him. "Did I forget something?"

"Danki."

He tipped his hat and walked on.

Letting Thomas's assessment of her wifely qualities settle upon her, Helen crossed the yard to where Gabriel attempted to wield a hammer despite the blood-soaked towel wrapped around his hand. He appeared to ignore her approach.

"You might want to stop a minute and get that fixed up." Any warmth she'd felt seeped away when she saw the polite but neutral look on his face. "Bleeding to death, are you?"

"Just a nick." He laid aside the hammer and faced her. "Thomas is making a big to-do about nothing."

Blood soaked the towel, which told Helen that Gabriel was downplaying the injury. Helen inspected it.

"Better sit down. How'd you manage that?" She waited for him to lower himself onto the porch steps. Then she laid the towel aside and began to blot the wound with a clean one. "Did the saw slip?"

"Got my hand too close to the area where Daniel was sawing." The set of his jaw and the white around his lips said her ministrations caused him pain, but he didn't jerk away or protest. "An accident."

"Jah, accidents happen, don't they?"

Their gazes met. His frown said he'd received her message. He opened his mouth, then shut it. Helen's upbringing kicked in after a second and she managed to drop her gaze to the bottle of peroxide in her hand. With a gentleness she didn't feel, she dabbed at the cut until it appeared clean, dried it, and began to cover it with gauze.

"You have a soft touch."

His tone made her glance up. The frown had been replaced with something that looked almost like longing. She could no longer force her gaze to the wound. He had a gingery scent that mingled with the soap used to wash his clothes. His breath came light and a little short. She hadn't been this close to a man in years and it had to be Gabriel Gless, who had studied her and found her wanting in her most important job—that of mother.

"There, all done." She slapped white surgical tape over the end of the gauze and backed away, hoping he couldn't see the trembling of her fingers. "You'll want to put some ointment on it tonight and a clean bandage."

He rose and turned back toward the workers as if dismissing her. He pulled on gloves that would further protect the cut and grabbed an ax from a nearby stack of tools. He lifted it as if it were no heavier than a toothpick. Gabriel might be forty or more, but he moved like a much younger man, all muscle and sinew.

"*Ach.*" She whirled and stomped up the steps. A woman her age thinking such thoughts. Ridiculous. Unseemly. Ungodly.

No. They were the thoughts of a lonely woman who longed for companionship and the love of a good man. Such things were gifts given by God, surely.

Chapter 8

Annie slipped the spatula under the last spicy molasses cookie and set it on the cooling rack. She swiped at a wisp of hair that had escaped her kapp. What a day. Noon had come and gone without time for a quick rest in the storeroom with the meal she'd brought from home. Thank goodness for Mary Elizabeth. She'd turned out to be a good worker who didn't flinch at a line of customers. She had the job if her father agreed. Annie hoped he would. It would be such a relief.

She'd barely had time to think about Noah and how he was doing under the watchful eye of Leah's sister Bethel, who came to the house each day to help out with the children and the laundry and the cleaning. The schoolteacher had yet to marry so she enjoyed spending her summers helping out with Leah's large brood. She had the added quality of being the opposite of her sister in every respect. Tall to her short, a smile to Leah's frown, a nonstop talker to her sister's silent introspection.

The bell over the bakery's door dinged, drawing Annie from her exhausted reverie. Her mind did seem to wander when she was tired. Pinging from one topic to the other without finishing one before another popped up. Despite her weariness, she smiled. Helen Crouch always served as a welcome respite on a busy day. The woman knew how to make Annie laugh. She gave Helen a closer look. Another weary woman, her hands full of a large box that held more jams and jellies. Annie rushed forward to relieve her of the box.

"You needn't have brought these today. I know you had a rough night with what happened to Edmond yesterday and then the storm during the night. Mark told me all about it."

"You said you were out of the peach and the strawberry jams. I can't afford to have the shelves empty." Helen shook her arms out as if her muscles were cramped. "I needed to pick up the proceeds from the last batch, anyway."

"Of course. I have the envelope ready." Annie set the box on the counter and began unloading the jars. Helen did a lovely job with the labels, each handwritten and illustrated with fruit. "Now come on, tell me, how are you doing?"

"The house is a mess, but what's worse is the garden. The hail destroyed the vegetables. We won't be doing much canning this summer." Helen blotted at her damp face with a handkerchief and shrugged. "We'll survive. We always do."

"Jah, we will. At least we'll still be able to get Colorado peaches." Annie grasped at straws. "I saw some at the farmers' market Saturday and I thought of you."

"I was going to buy three bushels today, but with the storm damage and Edmond's...mistake, I'll have to wait now." Helen set a jar of strawberry preserves next to a jar of blueberry jam. "I don't want to have them rot before we have a chance to have a canning frolic."

Silence held for a second. Annie contemplated her friend's face. She wished she dared to add some extra funds to the jam and jelly proceeds. The three bushels of peaches were an expense that Helen might not be able to afford right now, but they would mean more income in the long run. The tourists loved to buy homemade canned goods.

Helen would be anxious to pay back Thomas and her brother. Annie wanted to help, but she knew Helen would want to make her own way. "What's on your mind?"

"What makes you think something's on my mind?" Helen had a suspiciously bright smile on her face. "I have a whole crew of men at the house working like busy ants. I'm making a big roast and Emma's bringing over a casserole, but I've no time to make more bread so I thought I'd…"

"Of course. I'll donate to the meal."

"Nee, I'll pay for it. I can't have you—"

"No argument. If I can't be there to help with the cooking, the least I can do is offer what I've already baked." Annie shook her finger at her friend, whose mouth had opened again. "I mean it. No argument."

Helen crossed her arms. "Aren't you the bossy one?"

"I have two loaves of dill bread made this morning. Two of the whole wheat and a raisin loaf. Will that do it?"

"More than enough. You're too generous."

"You can't be too generous."

Helen nodded, but she studied the rows of jams and jellies with more attention than they warranted.

"Now, tell me what else is on your mind. Is it Edmond?" Annie moved behind the counter and selected the loaves of bread she would contribute to the supper. "The bishop will be fair. This is the first serious mistake Edmond has ever made. He's a good boy."

"I know. I know."

"Then why do you look so sad?"

"I'm not sad." Helen sat down on a bench across from the display cases. She smiled up at Annie. "Actually, I came by to see how you're doing. I missed you at the parade last night—before things got out of hand. You told me you would be there."

"I know I did." Annie examined her apron. It already had strawberry stains on it. She turned to the drawer where she kept clean ones. That way Helen couldn't see her face. "Noah was fussy, and I had a pile of sewing to do. I told Leah I would help her. I'm away all day long—"

"Excuses, excuses. Excuses are very close to being lies and lies are sins." Helen sounded so much like Annie's Aenti Louise she had to turn and stare at her. A deep frown had erased her friend's smile. "I've been where you are right now, missy, and the best medicine is to get out of the house. Learn to celebrate small things again. Life is in those moments, like sitting on a quilt, watching a parade, watching the children enjoy the fun."

"I meant to go." Annie sank into a straight-backed chair at the oak table where tourists often had a cup of *kaffi* or tea before leaving with their purchases. "I really did. I know it's been a year and that's what's expected. Leah and Luke let me know that. Even Emma. But when the time came…I don't know. I was too tired. I felt tired. Like I couldn't lift my feet."

"I remember that feeling. It's as if sadness makes you tired." Helen patted Annie's arm. "But once you get out there, you'll feel better. I promise. It takes your mind off it."

"I don't think anything can make me feel better, truth be told," Annie admitted. "It doesn't feel like a parade will make me feel better. It feels like I'm forgetting him. I'm already forgetting what he looked like. How can I celebrate without him?"

"Ask yourself if David would want you to be sad. Would he want you to mope around the house? Would he want Noah to miss out on the fun because you were too tired to go to a parade?"

"It's not as if you've moved on."

Silence reigned for several seconds. Looking at her friend's stricken face, Annie regretted her tart tone. Helen had been with her from the moment David passed. She'd been the one to hold her hand and walk her from the room when Annie had been unable to leave his side that last time. Helen helped arrange his clothes, oversaw the making of the food for the viewing, sat next to Annie at the funeral. She helped Annie walk away from the newly dug grave. She helped her give away David's clothes and boots and hats to families who needed them. She came by to make sure Annie arose, dressed, and cared for her new baby in the weeks after his father's death.

"You're right." Helen's voice cracked. "Who am I to give advice?"

"I'm sorry. I'm sorry, Helen."

"Don't be sorry. I've been alone for seven years and there are still days when I have to wrench myself from my bed."

"I see others—women and men in our community—who lose

a husband or wife and a year later they're remarried. Even Thomas remarried after three years." Annie thanked God for Thomas's ability to move on. He and Emma were meant for each other. "When do you and I stop being sad?"

"You have to insist on it. Our faith demands it." Helen sat up straighter as if the thought reinforced her spine. "The community expects it. To do otherwise is to show a lack of faith in God's plan for us."

"We're only human." Annie couldn't shake the anger mingled with grief that caught her in a stranglehold at the most inopportune moments. "We're only women who loved our husbands. Is that so bad? Isn't that what we're supposed to do?"

"We're women who've been blessed." Helen wiggled in her seat like a small child during prayer service. "I have no right to be sad about anything. I'm blessed with four healthy children, a family, and a farm that we work together. My mother is still with me."

The litany of blessings went on. Helen tried so hard to be a cheerful believer, but Annie saw something different in her eyes. "I can hear a big *but* in there that you're not saying."

"No big *but*. I try to do the right thing." Helen shook her head so hard her kapp strings flopped. "I try to raise the children according to the Ordnung."

"You have. I've watched you."

"Edmond is—"

"Edmond is running around. His escapade with the buggy might be the very thing that brings him back into the fold."

"A silver lining?"

"Jah."

Helen nodded, her expression hopeful. "Have you met Gabriel Gless?"

"Nee. But I met one of his sons, Isaac, and it looks like Mary Elizabeth will work here, if her daed allows it."

"Isaac looks like Gabriel."

"Naturally."

Helen tugged on her kapp strings until the kapp slid a little askew on her head. Annie wanted to tell her to stop, but realized it would sound like a mother admonishing a child. Given the difference in their ages, it wouldn't be right. "Why are you sad?"

"I went to the parade. I learned to go ahead. I accepted God's will for me." She raised her gaze to Annie's. "But still, things don't seem to work out."

"What does that have to do with Gabriel Gless?"

"I don't know. He got me all mixed up. I stumbled around."

"That's nothing new for you." Annie couldn't contain her grin. "You think you might…you think *he* might…"

"He thinks I'm a bad mudder." Helen glowered. "He already thinks badly of me and we just met. The first new man to come into our district in a long time and I already don't measure up."

"I'm sure he doesn't think badly of you. He only met you yesterday."

"You didn't see the look on his face when he realized Edmond was my son. Anyway, it's neither here nor there. If God's plan is for me to marry again, it will happen. How's Noah?"

"Don't change the subject."

"It's better if we do. No amount of nattering on about it will change what happens." Helen stood and scooped up the canvas bags that held the bread. "But you won't be able to discern God's plan for you if you don't step out in faith."

Annie held Helen's gaze. The purpose of the visit had not been to deliver jelly or pick up bread. "You're a good friend."

"David would want you to go on living. He would expect it."

"Everyone expects it."

"Because they know it's God's plan." Helen waved as she headed for the door. "Isaac looks like Gabriel. And he seems nice."

"Helen!"

The bell over the door dinged and her friend disappeared from sight.

"Nice," she said aloud. Helen gave good advice but she didn't seem to be able to take it herself. "Indeed."

Chapter 9

Gabriel leaned against the long-handled shovel with one hand and wiped at his face with the back of his shirt sleeve. The air steamed around him, his lungs ached, and his back muscles alternated between knotting and burning. They'd been digging steadily since before dawn. The hole Thomas hoped would be the home of his new water well now gaped over their heads. Gabriel eyed the walls. He saw no signs of crumbling or a potential cave-in yet. He grabbed the bucket hanging from the makeshift pulley, loaded it with dirt and rocks, gave a grunt, and tugged on the rope. Overhead, Eli, Seth, and Daniel took turns operating the crank they'd constructed between two enormous chunks of tree wood. They then emptied the bucket of its contents.

"We should be getting close," Thomas muttered, his back to Gabriel as he wielded his shovel. "We should hit the water table soon, if the chart the librarian gave Emma is right. If we don't, we'll have to start over in another place."

"This is the best location. Flat ground. Not too far from the house, but far enough not to be contaminated." Gabriel stopped to breathe. The still air hung around them, dank and close, making it hard to draw a breath. "Any time now."

The bucket descended in front of him and stopped with a clank on the bottom. Eli's giggle accompanied the sound. The boy enjoyed his work despite his disappointment in not being allowed to help with the digging. Thomas's concern over the potential for the walls to crumble had nixed that idea.

Thomas gave a whoop. Startled, Gabriel whirled to see his friend stomping his dusty boots in a small rivulet of water snaking across the bottom of the hole. Relief mixed with amusement. The ever silent Thomas had a grin stretched across his face. He held his shovel over his head and gave it a triumphant shake. "Water."

The boys heard the word and Thomas's whoop quickly became a chorus.

"Yup. Water, indeed." Gabriel grabbed a rung on the ladder they'd built from two-by-fours left over from the last room addition Thomas had constructed for his growing family. "I told you this spot was right."

"I picked the spot. You wanted to get closer to the creek." Thomas called after him. "Bring down the shorter shovels."

"That's what I'm doing."

In a matter of minutes, water began to fill the bottom of the hole. Digging under water proved to be a whole new proposition. Using a sawed-off shovel so the blade could lie flat, Gabriel continued to dig while Thomas employed a crowbar to loosen rocks, and Samuel handled a posthole digger to pick them up. It was hard to say whether they were covered with water or sweat. The liquid soaking Gabriel's clothes cooled him, but the lack of breeze deep in the pit made their enclosure suffocating. The minutes turned into hours. The muscles in his back protested and finally, blessedly, went numb.

"I think we've hit rock bottom." Thomas huffed. His ruddy complexion had turned a deep almost purple hue. "It's as deep as it's gonna get."

"We have almost four feet of water. We're good."

Thomas nodded, relief etched across his dirty face. Sweat dripped from his beard, and his shirt had gone from light blue to dark with perspiration. "Now for the casing."

Sharing in Thomas's relief, Gabriel shimmied up the ladder. He stood for a few seconds, letting the fresh air of an almost nonexistent breeze cool his face. He gulped water from a jug they'd brought from the house.

"You ready?" Thomas slapped his own jug on a tree stump. "We have to get the casing down there."

Gabriel nodded and shook out his arms, then cranked his head side to side, listening to the *pop-pop* sound. "Here we go."

It took all six of them to lower the fifteen-foot PVC culvert pipe into place, careful not to scrape the sides of the hole. Eli, Samuel, Daniel, and Seth had spent the morning using gas powered drills to punch evenly spaced holes throughout the pipe so water could pour in through the sides. Once the casing was in place, the boys moved on to their favorite part—filling in the space between the well's wall and the casing with rocks to hold it in place. They'd already made two trips to the creek for the rocks. They had way more fun slinging the rocks into the hole then Gabriel thought possible.

"Perfect." Thomas surveyed the work. He'd done his share of rock throwing, as gleeful as the boys. "We've got two feet left above ground."

"Right, the boys can work on capping it." Gabriel nodded, more than a little satisfied at their work. His back continued to ache, and the muscles in his shoulders and arms felt like jelly. On days like today, he felt downright old. "That'll keep the dirt and the animals out. Daniel can build the safety wall. We don't want the little ones falling in."

"Daed, how come the water looks so black?" Eli tugged at Thomas's sleeve with a muddy hand that left dirty prints. "Will we have to drink it that way?"

"The dirt will settle and the rocks will filter it." Thomas said. He squatted next to his son and stared down the well. "It's fine…"

Something in his tone caught Gabriel's attention. "What is it?" He squatted alongside the other two and peered at the swirling water below. Instead of being the clear, deep underground water he was used to seeing, the water was black. "What is that?"

Thomas's smile disappeared into a frown. His grip on the pipe tightened until his knuckles turned white. " I think we've found more than water, that's what I think."

Chapter 10

Helen took a deep breath and smoothed her apron. She glanced at Edmond. He looked clean and neat. Nodding, she knocked on Micah Kelp's door. Since her own living room still resembled a house under construction, the bishop had directed Edmond and Helen to come to his home. Micah Kelp opened the door on the first knock. He nodded and without a word, stepped back to allow them to enter.

"Sit." He gestured to two chairs on either side of a small pine table that held an overflowing sewing basket. For himself, he took a straight-back chair that looked as if it came from a dining room table set. "Susana has gone to visit her mother at the dawdi haus, so let us begin."

Helen glanced at Edmond. His thin face blanched white. Red blotches covered his neck. Her own undoubtedly looked the same. Edmond might have his father's blond hair and blue eyes, but he seemed to have inherited her social graces...or lack thereof. He squirmed in the chair, crossed his arms over his chest, and then uncrossed them. His Adam's apple bobbed.

"I'm very sorry for what I did. I overstepped the bounds of the rumspringa." His voice cracked—from nerves or from that awkward growing-up time of boys turning into men—Helen couldn't be sure. "I understand that. I take responsibility."

"Do you now?" Bishop Kelp leaned forward in his chair, rested his elbows on his knees, and interlaced his fingers in front of him. "What exactly are you taking responsibility for?"

"The drinking." Edmond squirmed some more. His face flushed a red darker than raspberries. "The buggy ride on the parade route."

"Those are only actions." Bishop Kelp shook his shaggy head. "Do you understand the results of those actions?"

"I went to jail. Bond had to be paid. We owe Thomas and Onkel Tobias money. I will pay them back."

"You're not seeing the bigger consequences." The bishop leaned back and tugged on his beard with thick, callused fingers. "Think harder. Much harder. Use the brain God gave you, son."

Edmond flinched. He glanced at Helen. She tried to give him an encouraging smile, but her face froze with embarrassment and mortification and shame. *Help him, please, help him to find the words. Help him to understand what he's done. Help him to show Micah he's learned his lesson.*

Part of her wanted to cry out that he was only a boy, but she knew better. Edmond had arrived at a crossroad. If he didn't pick the right path he could end up in a hospital like Josiah Shirack, or worse, choose to leave the faith as other members of their district had done. He had to choose. He alone could choose his path.

"I did not keep myself apart from the world." Edmond spoke haltingly, his voice just above a whisper. "I chose to be worldly."

"Speak up, boy. I can't hear you." Micah's tone was brusque, but Helen saw kindness in the faded blue eyes behind wire-rimmed glasses. "And what happened because of that choice?"

"I caused our community to be ridiculed."

"Worse. We don't care so much what the Englisch think of us, although we try to set a good example. You allowed worldliness to enter our community." Micah's voice deepened and rumbled like the thunder of a few nights before. "You allowed it to touch your sisters and cousins and friends. You set a bad example for each of them who will one day have their own time of rumspringa."

The bishop removed his glasses and began to polish them with a handkerchief. He seemed deeply engrossed in this task for a few seconds. "Try again."

"I'll have to deal with the Englischers' legal system." Edmond's voice sounded hoarse. "I'll have to go to court."

"Think about your mudder. Your actions affect her. Did you not think of how they affect her? Did you not think of how hard she works to raise you by the Ordnung without the help of your father?"

"Jah."

"I think not." He laid the glasses aside and fixed Edmond with an icy stare. "You thought of no one but yourself. You thought of your own enjoyment. You thought of your own appearance in the eyes of Englisch youth who no doubt took pleasure in your downfall."

Harsh words. Helen's hands were cold despite the July heat. She'd heard Micah reprimand more than one wayward member of the community over the years, but never with such ferocity as with this sixteen-year-old boy. Her son. She opened her mouth, saw the slight shake of his head, and closed it once again. She knotted her hands in her lap and stared at the white skin of her knuckles. *You reap what you sow.* Her mudder said that often enough when Helen and her brothers and sisters were growing up. *Be careful what you sow, or you might not like what you reap.*

"We are to keep ourselves separate from the world so that we don't become like the world." Micah rubbed bloodshot eyes, his expression making Helen wonder if he ever rued the day he'd drawn the lot to become the district's bishop. "On Friday, you became like the world. Take time and think about how that turned out for you. You're not the first to do this sort of thing, by any means, but each time it happens, I'm surprised and disappointed. Not nearly as surprised and disappointed as your mudder, I reckon. Now you must accept the consequences."

He paused and fixed Helen with an equally hard stare. "Do you have any words you would like to say before I pronounce Edmond's punishment?"

Helen breathed. In and out. She raised her head to meet his gaze.

"It was suggested to me that it might be good for Edmond to spend some time with Josiah Shirack."

Micah's white, bushy eyebrows rose and fell. "Not a bad idea." He glanced at Edmond. "Tomorrow you and I will go into town and speak to Josiah about the apprenticeship he's been talking about filling at his shop."

His eyes wide, breathing noisy, Edmond managed a nod. Most likely, his thoughts centered on days spent in the fields now exchanged for the heat of the anvil.

Micah turned back to Helen. "Anything more?"

"I take responsibility—"

"Nee. You do not."

Helen closed her mouth once again and waited.

"What we must do is minimize contact with this legal system. Edmond, I will go with you to the court. Only you and I will go. You will plead guilty and accept your punishment. No lawyer. No trial. As soon as possible. I imagine there will be a fine. It will be paid. There will be community service. We'll ask for a task that will not put you in further contact with these boys."

Edmond nodded. Helen nodded. Nothing more to be said.

"Then you will confess your sins in a kneeling confession before the community at our next Sunday service." Micah's gaze softened imperceptibly. "You'll confess and you'll be forgiven. We'll move on."

He stood. For a second, Helen remained seated, still contemplating his words. *We'll move on.* After the harsh words, forgiveness and grace. She tasted the sweetness of it, hoping Edmond saw it as well.

Micah lifted his eyebrows again as if inquiring. Helen hopped to her feet and jerked her head at Edmond. He rose. "I'm sorry," he said to the bishop. "It won't happen again."

"See to it that it doesn't." Micah opened the door. "Go on. Wait outside. I want a word with your mother."

Edmond stumbled over his own feet getting out the door. Helen longed to follow. She stood still, gaze averted.

"A word of advice." For the first time his voice held a note of uncertainty, something Helen had never heard in it in all the time since Micah had been bishop. "Look at me."

She forced her gaze to his.

"Word of advice. There's been talk about why you continue to remain single. I don't like gossip and chitter chatter among the women. Or the men, for that matter. Still, it would be best if you would try harder when the unattached men of this district show an interest. We are most at peace when our families are complete."

"None have shown an interest." To her horror, she blurted the words aloud. A wave of dizzying embarrassment washed over her. "That is to say, I'm so busy with caring for Mudder, Daed's death, the children—"

"It's long past time. You need a partner in raising your children. We've several men without fraas."

"I've not noticed them on my doorstep."

"They will be, sooner or later, of that I'm certain."

Did he mean to say he would tell them to make that journey to her door? Surely not. Courting was private. Not even the bishop interfered.

"Think on it. Pray on it."

"God's plan—"

"Keep your heart open to God's plan. Someone might walk through its door."

Helen closed her mouth and nodded. Silence served her best, even though everything in her cried out to ask him one simple question: *When?*

She slipped through the door, aware of his presence as he followed her into the yard and to the buggy where Edmond sat, head down, shoulders sagging.

With relief, no doubt. She climbed into the buggy, long past weary, to the point of exhaustion. She lifted the reins. A buggy came jolting up the road before she could pull forward. Eli Brennaman held the reins. Why had he come to the bishop's house? Had something happened? To Emma. The baby. Her heart slammed against her ribs with such force Helen feared bones would shatter. Thomas? Had something happened to Thomas?

"Bishop, bishop!" the boy hollered. He brought the buggy to an abrupt halt halfway between the house and barn. Panting, he jumped from the buggy. "Bishop, my daed sent me. He dug a well. He dug a well."

"Calm down, boy. Calm down." Micah slapped a hand on Eli's shoulder. "You're talking gibberish. What's happened?"

"Daed and Gabriel dug a well. We found water." Eli wiped sweat from his face with his sleeve. "It came up black. It's a gusher."

"A gusher?" Helen couldn't help herself. She climbed down from the buggy and went to Eli. "What do you mean?"

"Daed says we struck oil. We struck oil on our farm."

Chapter 11

Helen picked up her pace. Micah moved quickly for a big man, and Edmond had the long stride of a boy who'd shot up in height in the last few months. Everyone moved quickly to get this visit to Josiah's blacksmith shop over. The bishop had much more pressing issues to which he needed to attend. After Eli's arrival the previous evening, she and Edmond had been sent home while Micah rushed to the Brennaman farm. She knew from her brothers Thaddeus, Tobias, and Peter, who'd brought their families to supper, that a meeting had been set to discuss what happened next. Her brothers talked of nothing else during a meal of fried chicken, mashed potatoes and gravy, corn on the cob, and watermelon, none of which anyone seemed to taste.

Thaddeus's order that she and her mother not worry about it fell on deaf ears. How could one not worry? Telling her it was a sin didn't seem to help. She couldn't very well harness her thoughts. They rode willy-nilly through her brain like wild horses stampeding through an open pasture. She sighed. Her eyes burned with fatigue. Between the oil discovery and Edmond's transgressions, she'd slept little. Whenever she had managed to nod off, she'd had dreams the likes of which brought her upright in her bed, hair damp with sweat, her skin icy cold and hot at the same time. Dawn came as a relief.

Micah's order she come with them to talk to Josiah came as a surprise. "Come along," he'd said from her porch with a brusque wave toward his buggy. So come along she had, although she knew she would have no say in the conversation. Nor would Josiah. Micah had that plodding-oxen approach to discussion. Once set in a particular direction, nothing stopped him. Perhaps a good quality in a bishop. What would he have done with all that bossiness, had he not been the one to draw the lot?

Concealing a sudden, inadvertent smile at the thought, she slowed and waited for Micah to open the door to the shop. He entered first. Edmond followed, but he had the good grace to hold the door for her. She slipped in and gave him an encouraging smile. He didn't want to be here, that she could see, but he also knew he'd made his bed and he'd have to lie in it. He shrugged and let the door swing shut behind her.

The shop opened up into a huge room with rows and rows of horseshoes of all sizes on one side and a series of stalls on the other. In the middle stood a cart filled with tools next to the anvil. Josiah Shirack straddled the back leg of a mammoth black horse. He bent over, hammer in hand, and pounded the shoe onto the hoof with a quick, sure *pop, pop, pop*. Eight nails. He dropped the hammer and scooped up a large file, which he used with the deft movement of a man who had performed this task many times.

No one spoke. No one with any smarts at all interrupted a blacksmith in the middle of shoeing a thousand-pound animal. Although she'd never been in the shop before, even Helen knew that. Not that this horse seemed to mind. His head dipped now and again, but his body remained motionless as he gazed out an open window in front of him.

Josiah made quick work of it and let the leg drop. Muttering soft nothings to the animal, he moved away from the horse's hindquarters. "Good job, Smoky, good job."

He smoothed a hand across Smokey's back and then looked up. "Morning. What can I do for you folks?" He frowned as his gaze came to rest on Helen. "Helen, *gudemariye* to you."

"We were waiting until you finished the job." Micah shoved his hat back on his head. "No hurry."

"'Preciate that. I do." Josiah strode forward, wiping his hands on a rag that hung from his worn leather apron. "He's a good horse, but he doesn't like to be bothered when he's getting his new shoes."

"Getting to the point, then. I'm told you are looking for some help." Micah jerked his head from Edmond to Josiah as if to say *Here you go*. "This young man is in need of a job. And a stern taskmaster."

Josiah's hands stilled on the towel. He chewed on his lower lip, looking as if he were doing a hard addition problem in his head. "I've been thinking about taking on an apprentice, but I hadn't spoken to Caleb about it yet. He owns the shop, bought it from my brother Luke when my...a couple of years ago."

His voice trailed off. Helen could almost see when he put two and two together and got four. Edmond was being punished, and Josiah's shop would be the appointed place from which his punishment would be meted out.

"I'm aware of that." Micah crossed his massive forearms over a belly that must have been the recipient of one too many whoopie pies. "Edmond wants a job where he has to work hard. He wants to keep his mind on work and off the things that get a young man his age into trouble."

The shop door opened and in tromped Isaac Gless, looking so much like his father with his broad shoulders, big hands, and easy stride that Helen wanted to drop her gaze. It refused to go. *Stop it.* The room warmed, even though it wasn't even noon yet. Isaac brought with him a breath of the outside air. It might be eighty-five degrees outside, but the air was cooler than the ninety-five inside the building. He strode forward, and then halted, his mouth open in a half-spoken greeting.

"Well, gudemariye." He touched the brim of his hat. "Busy place, this."

"Becoming a bit of a meeting place, it is." A tiny undercurrent of sarcasm ran through Josiah's words. Helen hoped the bishop didn't hear it. Josiah didn't seem to care. "You don't, by any chance, have a horse you need shod, do you?"

"I came about a job." His face reddening, Isaac glanced at the bishop and then at Helen before planting his gaze on Josiah. "I don't mind hard work. I get up early. I go to bed early. I mind my manners."

Josiah wiped his face on the towel and grinned, a real smile for the first time. "I don't much care about the manners, unless you're helping a customer. As far as the rest, sounds like you have the basic requirements. Ever shod a horse?"

"A few times back home when…"

"Sorry to interrupt, but I haven't much time." Micah didn't seem sorry at all. "As I said, I'd like you take to Edmond on as an apprentice. You don't have to pay him much."

Josiah's dark eyebrows went up. He lifted his straw hat and his forehead wrinkled under rambunctious hair soaked in sweat before he settled the hat back on it. "I didn't know Edmond had a hankering to be a blacksmith."

"Nor did I." The bishop slapped the boy on the back. "All the same, I'd like you to show him the ropes. Never can tell. Might be exactly the right occupation for a boy who likes to use Main Street like a buggy racetrack."

Josiah had to be thinking punishment wasn't the best reason to take on an apprentice when a man wanted to make his business fruitful.

"I'm sorry, Josiah." Helen couldn't hold it in any longer. "I know it's a bit much to ask, but I thought since you had your own problems back in the day, you might have a few words of wisdom you could share."

"You think since I was a wild child, I'll know what to say?" His skin darkened to the color of ripe tomatoes. "Do as I say, not as I do?"

"You saw the pain that is caused by taking running around too far."

"I learned from my mistakes, as we all must do." His gaze whipped to the bishop, then to Isaac, and back to Helen. "This is a man's job. It can be dangerous. It requires a willingness to settle down and concentrate."

"Someone like me." The corners of Isaac's lips turned up. He thought he'd won. He didn't know Micah Kelp. "I only ask a fair wage."

"You'll have to look elsewhere," Micah intervened. "As Helen said, we want Edmond here to spend some time with Josiah. He can help him learn from his mistakes."

Josiah's face shuttered, became stony.

Silence beat down on them for a long second. Helen watched Isaac's expression as he tried to understand the undercurrents that swirled about the room. Surely, all he could see was a man about his age who ran his own shop, was married, had a child, and seemed content. What could the bishop find to criticize in that? Micah had a long memory. They had forgiven Josiah for his tempestuous rumspringa, but it remained the stuff of nightmares for many parents in their small district.

The door swung open once again. This time a young woman peeked her head in, glanced around, then stepped through the doorway. She had shiny blonde hair caught back in a tight French braid and hazel eyes. She looked so familiar, but her skirt and short-sleeved white blouse said she was Englisch. Helen looked toward Josiah, wondering if he knew this girl. Someone from his difficult past? Surely not. Then it hit her. Catherine.

Josiah dropped the towel in the middle of the floor. "Catherine?" He took a step forward and stopped. "Catherine!"

Bishop Kelp planted himself between Josiah and his sister. He stared at her long and hard, without speaking.

"Bishop, I only came to say hello to my brother." She smiled, not visibly intimidated by the bulk or stature—physical or otherwise—of the older man. "I've not seen him in four years, but I don't plan to stay. He knows I'm in town and I felt it would be rude not to at least stop by."

She smiled and her face lit up. She looked so much like Annie. They could be twins, if not for the clothes and her hair. Helen frowned. How could she wear her hair like that, for all the world, for men, to see? The look on Josiah's face said he felt some of that same disappointment. He probably saw Sarah whatever-her-name-was, the New Order Mennonite girl who had caused him such heartache only a few years ago.

Catherine glanced toward Helen and Edmond. "It's good to see you again, Helen."

Helen nodded but didn't speak. She knew better. She shouldn't even acknowledge Catherine's presence, but it went against the grain of every hospitable muscle in Helen's body. To not greet a member of Annie's family…Her neck stiffened, her hands felt clammy, and her stomach roiled. The bishop's gaze bore into her forehead.

"As it happens, I'd also like to speak with you, Bishop Kelp." Catherine hugged a leather-bound notebook to her chest with one arm and adjusted the long strap of the purse on her shoulder with the other. "I'm here in Bliss Creek because I'm working on a research project for my thesis at WSU. I'm also writing a memoir that will be published."

Bishop Kelp's features could've been sculpted from limestone. "That is well and good for an Englischer such as yourself."

"The topic of my thesis is the effects of living in a closed community." Her tone didn't waver. "The topic of the memoir is, of course, my life as an Amish girl who left her community."

"Why would you need to speak to me about it?"

"I would like to interview some members of my family and my community."

"Former family and community."

At that, she faltered a little. "In your way of thinking, which I respect deeply."

"Have you forgotten the fundamental tenet? Keep ourselves apart from the world."

"Maybe it would be easier to do that if people understood what we are about."

"We? Have you decided to return to the community?" Bishop Kelp looked hopeful. "We would welcome you back."

"I'm finishing my bachelor's degree in psychology. I'll begin my masters directly after that. My mentor thinks this is a good topic for me." She moved closer to the bishop. "I promise to be very discreet and quiet and respectful."

"I have to get back. We have important business to discuss tonight." The bishop turned as if her presence had already been dismissed. "Now then, Josiah, will you take Edmond as your apprentice? He's a hard worker, I'm told."

"If that is your wish."

"It is." Bishop Kelp pursued his lips. His beard bobbed. "Well then, I expect to see you at the meeting in my barn directly after supper. That gives everyone time to complete a full day's work."

"I'll go and let you finish your conversation," Catherine said. She lifted a thin hand, bare of rings or polish, and gave a tiny wave. "It's good to see you, Josiah. Say hello to Miriam for me. Kiss Hazel Grace for me."

Josiah cleared his throat. His gaze flipped to Bishop Kelp and back to Catherine. He settled for a barely discernible nod. She smiled and nodded back.

With an equally small wave and a polite smile for Isaac, who had not been introduced, Catherine turned and strolled from the shop, shoulders back and head held high. No hurry, no fuss.

Helen watched her, aware that the three men were doing the same. Catherine looked so much like Annie, only more worldly. She found herself grateful Annie hadn't gone the way of her sister. The thought surprised her. She should be thankful for every member of the community who chose to stay and commit to the Ordnung. Not just Annie Plank, with a spot of flour on her cheek and the scent of cinnamon wafting about her. Helen had needed a friend after Thomas's marriage, and Annie had chosen to be that friend. She sought Helen out. She asked her to the house for a visit. Invited her personally to her own wedding. Invited her to sell her wares in the bakery. Finally, she'd allowed Helen to be the one to guide her through those grief-stricken days and weeks after David's death. Helen had experience with this awful season in life, but she possessed little skill in choosing her words or offering comfort. Still, Annie chose her. Not her best friend Miriam, so happy in her new marriage, but Helen, a widow too.

Catherine surely missed the closeness of this community. How could she not? Helen turned and caught the expression on the bishop's face. Pure sadness.

"William and Ruth's beloved child," he murmured. His face shuttered and he lumbered toward the door. "Edmond, with me. We have another stop to make. Courthouse. Helen, I expect you'll want to have a visit at the bakery in the meantime."

Dismissed, she nodded at Josiah. "Danki," she whispered.

His rueful smile said it all. Did he have a choice? No.

"Sorry," she added, then to Isaac. "I'm sorry to you too."

"Don't worry." He smiled. Gabriel Gless's smile. She swallowed, feeling the color rising on her cheeks. He waved both hands airily. "I have other irons in the fire. So to speak. No pun intended."

He and Josiah burst into laughter, loud, guffawing laughs.

What was so funny about that? As always, Helen felt like the dense, not quite as smart woman in the room. Undoubtedly, Isaac would go home and share this little joke at her expense with his father.

No matter. Gabriel didn't think highly of her anyway.

Chapter 12

Gabriel made his way to the back row of the benches that lined Bishop Micah Kelp's immaculate barn. Farm equipment had been moved to a far wall and the doors flung open wide in hopeful anticipation of an evening breeze that might dissipate the humid July heat. A horse in a far stall nickered. The smell of hay and manure mingled with sweat. A sudden, unexpected wave of homesickness brought on by the familiar sights and scents nearly knocked him back a step. He never expected to miss Dahlburg. His parents had passed. His brothers and sisters had their own families. Laura was gone.

Gabriel buried the thought and took a seat. His recent arrival in Bliss Creek should make him more of a spectator than a participant in this discussion, but he would learn from watching and listening. Who led. Who followed. Who remained on the outside of the discussion. He had no doubt Thomas would be quiet until the moment when he had something important to say. And all would listen with respect to his cousin.

A steady stream of men, many of whom greeted each other in solemn tones, their faces somber, flowed around him. Thomas had insisted Gabriel would not only be welcome, but expected at this meeting. Still, it felt awkward. He'd come here to start a new life, but now he didn't know if he could stay. He squirmed on the bench. How could he uproot the kinner yet again? How could he tell them this community was too much like the one they'd left behind? And now the oil. Oil meant riches. He wanted no part of it.

"Gabriel, glad you came. Your help at the house was appreciated." Tobias Daugherty stopped in the next row up and nodded in a neighborly fashion. "It would've taken us days to remove that tree without the help of you and your boys. Even more to get the holes patched and the new wall built."

Unlike his sister Helen, Tobias stood nearly as tall as Thomas and had equally broad shoulders. Also unlike Helen, his hair flamed a deep auburn under his hat. His eyes were a startling blue against white skin touched by only a smattering of freckles. How could Helen, brown and plump like a sparrow, be from the same stock? Gabriel set aside the observation. Outward appearance meant little to him, but the contrast still intrigued him. The peacock and the sparrow growing up together.

Tobias's puzzled look said he expected a response. "It was no trouble," Gabriel hastened to say. "I'm sure we'll need the help returned at some point."

The man nodded, tugged at his hat, and moved on down the row. Gabriel sank onto the bench again. A second later, Thomas dropped onto it next to him. His legs were so long that his knees barely cleared the bench in front of them.

"Everything is well?" Gabriel sideswiped his cousin with a glance. He looked as he always did, unperturbed by the things of life. "You're late."

"Right on time." Thomas smiled. "I wanted to make sure the boys did the chores properly. We missed you at supper."

"I went in to look at the shop. Isaac has been going on and on about what he's done to get it ready." He hadn't told Isaac of his doubts. He couldn't. His son exuded youthful enthusiasm, buoyed up by youthful optimism. He showed signs of liking his new home. Gabriel couldn't bring himself to destroy it. Not yet. "The boy has no patience."

"And?"

"We need to build shelves and counters." He couldn't tell Thomas either. He had enough to think about right now. "Carry in my tools. Make the signs."

"You'll be open in no time." Nothing in his cousin's tone spoke of his own situation. Oil on his land. A possible move from a farm that had been in his family for three or four generations. "Emma and the other women made good work of the house today. You'll be able to move in soon. She's going on about making new curtains and painting the kitchen and who knows what all, but she'll oversee it, you can be sure of that."

"No doubt." No doubt God had blessed Thomas with this second fraa. Gabriel shied away from the import of those words. "I appreciate her efforts."

The bishop cleared his throat. Relief drenched Gabriel. He wanted no more of those thoughts. He directed his gaze to the front of the barn. Silence descended.

"Let us get right to it, then." Bishop Kelp's gaze floated across the rows of men. "I would like to hear from Thomas first."

Thomas nodded, rose, and walked without haste to the front. "I am sorry to place all of you in this position," he began, his deep voice steady. "We were looking for water, pure and simple."

"That's fine, Thomas." The bishop waved a hand as if to dispel Thomas's words. "What did the surveyor say?"

"He said it's a real find. A gusher. We've managed to cap it for now, but the problem remains that our old well is dry." Thomas wrapped his fingers around his suspenders. "We could plug this hole, but we would still need to find water."

Tobias Daugherty rose. "I know this is a surprise, but I've been thinking...maybe this is the answer to our prayers. It could be Gott's way of leading us through this time of hardship."

Bishop Kelp steepled thick, hairy fingers. "We must not presume to know what the Lord's plan for us is." His gaze traveled the room.

"None of us. Our focus must be on the Ordnung. On guiding our children on that path that keeps them far from worldly ways."

Bishop Kelp's gaze came to rest on Gabriel. He ignored the temptation to look away. After a second the bishop moved on. "What thoughts do the rest of you have?"

"Is it possible you could sell the property and find another in this area?" Solomon Yoder threw out the question. "Simply move down the road, so to speak?"

"Most of the property in this area is spoken for and prices are at a record high." Thomas smoothed his long beard, his face thoughtful. "I saw a piece of land up by Pretty Prairie where they wanted fifteen hundred an acre. Besides, that's a far reach from family and friends."

"What you would receive from the sale of your farm would be far more than you would need to buy another home," Timothy Plank pointed out. "The difference could be added to the emergency reserve to help with future barn raisings, medical expenses, and caring for our older folks and such."

"Still, I would no longer have a means of making a living here in Bliss Creek." Thomas's face had taken on a more stoic expression. He would accept whatever came. "I need to care for my family."

"We must all stick together." Luke Shirack, Emma's brother, spoke for the first time. "We'll not let one member of this community fall by the wayside, surely."

"It might be necessary for you to take a job in town." Deacon Pierce's gaze traveled to Gabriel. "Many others have done it. Our way of life is changing. We can no longer support our families with farming. Gabriel is opening a new shop. I reckon he needs a partner."

"He has grown sons in need of jobs." Thomas kept his voice even, but Gabriel could hear the slightest resistance in his tone. Thomas farmed because he had a connection to the land. Tearing him from it would kill him. Gabriel wanted no part in that, but sometimes circumstances forced difficult, painful change. Thomas's brown eyes darkened. "Gabriel's starting out. It's too soon to burden him with another person he must pay."

Not to mention another person who didn't want to be there. Gabriel already had sons who fell in that category.

"Gabriel, you've traveled a long way to become a part of this district." Deacon Altman nodded Gabriel's direction. "What are your thoughts?"

Surprised to be called upon, Gabriel drew a breath, then stood. All gazes were on him, expectant. If only he had greater wisdom for them. "I'll do whatever I can to help my cousin. To help this district. I would say, in the short time that I've been here, I've found this to be a strong community. Well centered on the Ordnung, for the most part." His gaze connected with Tobias Daugherty, who frowned and leaned forward a little. "For the most part. I left my district in Indiana because they had drifted far from our core beliefs. I would hate to see that happen here."

"So we should move?" Josiah Shirack asked. His hands were tight around his suspenders, knuckles white. "Just pick up and go?"

"Nee." Gabriel held up a hand to quiet the low murmurs of disagreement. "See the obstacles that lie ahead and overcome them. Don't give up. Commit to the Ordnung and make sure your families do the same. Oil means nothing to us. Let it remain so."

"But it's not only the oil." Luke Shirack spoke up. "We lost the wheat. Again. It's beginning to look like we might not be able to sustain our way of life here. Unless we do something different. Or move."

"Or sell the oil." Apparently Josiah liked to stir the pot. "Enough to sustain us this winter until we can get another crop in the ground and harvest it."

"That will not happen." Micah Kelp fairly thundered the statement. "It is likely, Thomas, that you will have to sell and seek a new home for your family. Let us think on this and pray about it. We'll meet back here two weeks from today. Begin to look at other properties for sale in the area. Take a look at what jobs are available in town. Talk with your cousin. Then we'll make a decision."

Thomas's stoic expression didn't change. He nodded, but when he returned to his seat, Gabriel caught a glimpse of his eyes. The deep pain that clouded them made his own heart clinch. Thomas must've seen his expression. Shutters descended. The pain became cloaked behind an opaque neutrality.

"It's likely there's oil on our farms as well," Luke said. "We need to deal with that possibility."

"No one does any searching for water without consulting with the community first." Bishop Kelp's shaggy eyebrows rose and fell. "Any more oil, and we will all relocate."

"There are more and more influences battering us now. As I've said before in these meetings, a move might be for the best." Paul Yoder stood, hands on his hips. He glanced sideways at Tobias. "There's land to be had in Montana and Colorado. Districts in Missouri and Arkansas are looking to increase their numbers. Our district has grown larger with each year. Some of us could start a new district. It might help us to move beyond some of the bad influences we're seeing here."

"If you're talking about Edmond, he's a boy. Pure and simple." Tobias didn't raise his voice, but steel resonated in the words. Gabriel respected the man for defending his nephew, but couldn't say he didn't agree with Paul. "It won't happen again. I'll see to it."

"I already have," Bishop Kelp said. "We'll hear no more about it until Edmond's confession at prayer service on Sunday. Then we'll forgive and move on."

With those words of grace promised, he stood, signaling the end of the meeting. The conversation immediately swelled as the men streamed toward the open doors. Like a massive ox, Bishop Kelp moved against the flow until he reached Thomas. He nodded at Gabriel, then turned to the other man. "The sacrifice you and your family may be asked to make does not go unnoticed."

Thomas nodded in return, but did not speak. The pulse in his jaw jumped.

Bishop Kelp touched the crown of his straw hat, then moved away.

Gabriel followed his cousin from the barn. Neither of them spoke until they reached the open field where the buggies were parked in neat rows. "I'm sorry," Gabriel began. "I recently left behind my farm. I understand how it feels."

"Don't apologize for something you didn't cause. It's only land. Only a house. Home is wherever your family is."

"You grew up in that house."

"Jah."

"Joanna lived in that house." Thomas's first wife had given birth to both their children in that house. "You have memories there."

Thomas hitched the horse to his buggy. "We will have new memories, many of them, with the new baby on the way."

It was the first reference Thomas had made to the impending birth of another child.

"How will Emma take it?"

"Fine."

"She's a good fraa."

At that, the gloom on his cousin's face lifted. He smiled for a brief second. "That she is."

Catherine's journal
July 5

What I did to Josiah wasn't fair. I hijacked him. Ambushed him. Whatever you want to call it. I drove out to the little plot of land he farms—if you can call it that—knowing he would make sure his rounds before going in for the night. Even after a full day at the shop and the big powwow with Micah Kelp, he'd still make sure the horses and pigs and goats and chickens were bedded down for the night, just like Daed used to do. I imagine Luke, with his much bigger farm and plethora of livestock, does the same. Not that I would try to ambush big brother. Instead I went forth, seeking the brother who'd once been a kindred soul. I parked the car on the road and walked up to the barn. Sure enough, he was in there, talking to one of the horses. That's his way. He's always had a way with animals.

He didn't even flinch when I called his name, quietly so as not to scare him. He looked up and grinned that Shirack grin. One rebel to another. Cat, he says, calling me a name only he ever used. A name from my running-around days. He looks so mischievous, like no time has passed, and we're two teenagers, our heads together, plotting our escape. For one night of fun, not for a lifetime. I take out my camera. He cocks his head, bushy eyebrows raised below his straw hat, and shrugs. I snap a few shots of the most handsome of the Shirack men, just a few as he clowns, then poses with the horses. After a few minutes he raises his hand, its fingers thick and wiry with hair above the knuckles. Enough, he's saying. He can go so far, but only so far. He has Miriam to think of, and the babies, he says. No one in Bliss Creek will see these images, I say. That's not the point, he says, knowing I know exactly what the point is.

How he manages to stay in line, I can only imagine. A combination of fervent faith and the even more fervent love of a good woman. By sheer will, Miriam Shirack holds on to him by her fingertips. My brother has been blessed. Knowing that, I don't bother to ask him the obvious. He doesn't disrespect me, either. Despite the choices we'd each made and the shunning I now endure, however earned, we met in that lantern-lit barn on equal footing. Josiah knows that but for the grace of God, there goes he. So I ask him to explain to me how he makes it work. His answer is simple. Each day, he looks at his wife and his child and begins a litany of blessings in his head. As he drives the buggy to the shop, as he shoes the horses, as he drives home, he recounts them, over and over in his head. Like a reformed alcoholic who prays, over and over, God, don't let me drink today, I will not drink today, and let tomorrow take care of itself.

I wonder if that would work for me. Could I give up my laptop and my social media and my smartphone and my ancient, on-its-last-leg mini-Cooper with its excellent gas mileage? Could I give up gourmet coffee, shorts, and tank tops? Could I give up classic movies and old TV shows—new to me, of course? Do I want to? The answer screams at me, just as it always has. I suppose I could. But I don't want to. I won't. The line in the sand has been drawn. I'm on one side and the Lukes of the Plain world are on the other.

Josiah tells me he sometimes still has dreams—nightmares—about the time he spent in Wichita. He dreams of car accidents in which his girl, Sarah, lies broken and bloody on the pavement. He dreams he's been drinking alcohol and smoking cigarettes. The whiny guitars of a country song blare on the car radio even as the tortured steel belches black smoke in the frigid winter night. What does that mean, he asks me. What does it mean after all this time that I still dream of her and our broken relationship? Am I being unfaithful to Miriam when I dream these dreams? Do I somehow summon them when I close my eyes? He looks at me with such guilt and concern in his eyes. I wish I could tell him. I wish I knew. Is it a subconscious desire for what he cannot have? On the surface, he's so happy. Father and husband. Husband and father. But he's not the farmer he *wants to be. He's sick of the heat and flame and smell of the blacksmith shop. Still, he refuses to admit it, even to himself.*

What does it mean? I'm the psychology major. Will an MS or a PhD tell me what common sense cannot? Josiah is a good man. Plain or otherwise, by all standards, he is good. He's where his faith would have him be. He loves and he is loved. By his wife, by his family, by his community, by God.

I tell him he should go with Thomas to find this new community they are talking of building in Missouri. His family could go where there might be enough land for him to farm. Maybe that's what those dreams are about. About being who he really is. A farmer.

He nods as if he's thinking about it, but I know he'll stay in Bliss Creek because the blacksmith shop is needed and Miriam's family is here and he will do what he thinks is right. What he knows is right. Because that is what makes him happy.

So why does it make me so sad?

Chapter 13

Helen forced herself to inhale. Her stuffy nose and congested throat didn't help, but the summer cold had nothing to do with the feeling that she might collapse from lack of air. She couldn't breathe. Not as long as Edmond was kneeling in front of the entire community, men on one side, women and children on the other. No murmur, no titter, no whisper. The only sounds came from a pair of blue jays chattering in the elm trees outside the barn doors and the occasional whinny of a horse or a dog barking in the distance. Her son had risen without hesitation when Bishop Kelp commanded that he come forward. Now he knelt, hands folded in front of him, his pale blue eyes bright with unshed tears. Red blotches smattered across the chalky white skin of his cheeks and neck. He worried his lower lip with his teeth.

Come on, come on. You can do it.

God, help him say what needs to be said.

The thoughts whirled in Helen's mind, the need for prayer tugging her one way, her desire to take matters into her own hands and help her son tugging her the other. The humid July heat lay like a stone on her shoulders and chest. Someone coughed. Someone cleared his throat. A baby whimpered and was quickly hushed by a young mother.

Helen forced her gaze to move back to the front of the barn. Her gaze collided with Bishop Kelp's. His expression seemed kind, but he shook his head as if in warning.

She swallowed and focused on her hands, clasped in her lap, her knuckles white with the force of her grip.

A hand touched her shoulder. She looked up. Annie smiled in encouragement. Helen tried to smile back, but her lips were frozen. She nodded. Annie knew how this felt. Her brother Josiah had done some pretty horrible things in his rumspringa. They'd survived. Barely. But now he was married, a hard worker, a good father. They all learned. The rumspringa insisted on it. She closed her eyes for a second and felt a smidgen of relief in not being able to see her boy, her only son, kneeling, shoulders slumped, head ducked, before his community.

No, looking away did him a disservice. If he could face this group, she could face him. She raised her head and sought his gaze. When it connected with hers, she nodded. His Adam's apple bobbed. He swiped at his face with his sleeve and then his shoulders went back and his head came up.

"What I did was wrong. I went to a party. I knew the boys. I knew what they were like." The red splotches spread until Edmond's face looked as if it were on fire, but neither his voice nor his gaze wavered. "I chose to drink the alcohol. I made it so the Englisch people saw me in a bad light and that makes us all look bad. I made a bad mistake. I'm sorry. It won't happen again. I know we…I know I…must keep myself apart from the world. I will do that. I will do it."

His voice trailed away. He looked at Bishop Kelp, who inclined his head. Moving as if chased by a rattler, the boy hopped up and dashed down the aisle that divided the men from the women. He didn't look at Helen as he passed her. She knew he would sit with Tobias, Peter, and Thaddeus. They would talk with him, give him guidance. All three had taken the time to tell her so during the days they'd spent repairing the house. She'd seen a bit of guilt written across each one's face. As surely they saw it in hers.

"See to it each of you searches your heart to make sure you harbor nothing there that would lead you in the way that Edmond went. Those of you who are of the age for rumspringa, you know that doesn't give you an excuse to embrace evil, to endanger others, to flaunt your running around in our faces. If that's what you want to do, make your choice. Leave your faith. Or embrace it. Learn of the outside world, if you must, but don't let it consume you to the point that there is no way to return. Mothers and fathers, counsel your children. Teach them to walk in our ways." The bishop wiped sweat from his face with a brilliant white handkerchief. He glanced toward the open doors as if hoping for a whisper of a breeze. None came. "We all falter. We all fail. We all make mistakes. That is why we are told to forgive. Not once. Not seven times. But seventy times seven. So that is what we will do. We will forgive Edmond. And move on. Showing him the grace that God shows us."

As the weight rolled from her shoulders, Helen closed her eyes again. All would be forgiven. Edmond remained on probation as part of his plea agreement hammered out by a city attorney and Micah Kelp. He still had to do many hours of community service. He still had to pay back the money for the bond. She still had to keep an eagle eye on her son so that he would not falter again. He could not be allowed to falter.

An elbow nudged her and she realized the final prayers were being spoken. She rolled off the bench and knelt, head down.

God. God. Words escaped her. The rest she left up to Deacon Altman, whose prayers enveloped her, his deep voice offering the comfort that surely he would be heard.

Then the service ended. She should go to Edmond. She murmured an excuse to Annie and slipped down the aisle. She should help with the food, but first she wanted to make sure her son was all right. Besides, the thought of facing all those women chattering like the blue jays made her shudder. She needed a few minutes to shore up her courage. She ducked through the tall men who seemed to fence her in, seeking Edmond. Eli and some of the other boys had him surrounded. He looked fine. He looked relieved. He even looked a little pleased with himself. Chagrined at the thought, Helen quickened her pace. She supposed the other boys would look up to him for his escapade. Exactly what none of the parents wanted.

Before she could reach him, Josiah Shirack stepped into the circle. The other boys parted and a second later, Josiah and Edmond disappeared through the doors on the other end. Helen breathed a sigh of relief and waded through the crowd toward the open doors. Sweat drenched her dress under her apron. Her hair felt wet to the touch around her ears. Light-headed, she pushed forward, wanting to get away from the crush of people. A tall glass of cool water. That would help.

Someone called her name. She didn't stop. If she did, she might crumple in a faint. She stumbled across the rock-strewn ground, rounded the corner, and started across the field behind the barn. A nice shade tree. That would do.

"The house is the other direction."

The voice stopped her in her tracks. Deep, rough-hewn, with a touch of honey. She lifted her head to see Gabriel Gless standing with one dusty boot on the fence, both elbows propped along the top railing. Sweat darkened the back of his shirt. His sleeves were rolled up to his elbows. His gaze seemed to see everything about her. Guilt, shame, insecurity, uncertainty, loneliness, helplessness. Nowhere in his stony façade could she see an inkling of how he reacted to all this. There was none of the soft sadness she'd seen that day as she labored over the cut on his hand.

"Getting some air." She lifted her chin, knowing the same red splotches that covered Edmond's face earlier now overtook her own. "It was stuffy in there."

"Can be uncomfortable." He shoved his hat back on his head and rolled down his shirtsleeves. "More for some than others."

"What is that supposed to mean?" She backed away. She shouldn't be out here, anyway. She belonged in the kitchen, preparing the trays of sandwiches, chips, pies, and cookies, gallons of tea and lemonade. Only the thought of facing all the women of her community—all better mothers than she—kept her from fleeing. "I felt fine in there."

His gaze studied her in a way that disconcerted her. "Lying is a sin."

"So is judging."

He moved in her direction. "It's probably cooler down by the creek."

"True. There's more of a breeze along the banks." What that had to do with her, Helen had no idea. "After the rain the mosquitoes will be bad, though."

"Mosquitoes don't like me." He gave her a lopsided grin. It was a poor excuse for a smile. Not like her joking George. But then, to be fair, George hadn't lost his wife. "My meat is tough and bitter."

"I expect mine is the same." That seemed to amuse him a little. Helen tried again. "Old too."

"I doubt that."

Their gazes met and for the first time, Helen realized there was something expectant, yet tentative, about his expression. She swayed a little. A night of restless wandering through the house combined with nightmares during the scant hours she managed to sleep had left her drained and exhausted.

"Are you all right?" He moved a little closer. "You look…kind of peaked."

"Fine."

"Jah, you said that before."

"You don't believe me?"

"If it were my son, I'd be in a sorry state."

"I'm not you."

"No doubt about that." He lifted his hat and settled it on his head. "I guess I'll take that walk down to the creek."

Again the expectant mixed with the tentative.

"Yell if the mosquitoes try to carry you away. I'll send my brothers to rescue you."

To her surprise, his expression darkened rather than reflecting the intended humor of her remark.

"You wouldn't come yourself?"

The question left her speechless for several seconds. Their gazes held. Finally, he touched the brim of his hat and nodded. "You'd best help with the food, I reckon."

He turned his back and began the trek across the field toward the tree line that signaled the spot where Bliss Creek meandered through the Shiracks' property. Helen couldn't for the life of her understand what had just happened. She dabbed at her sore nose with the handkerchief, coughed, and then sneezed.

He looked back. "On second thought, best leave the food to others or everyone will have that cold."

"You have knowledge of these things, illnesses, and such?"

"No, I have eight children."

"Jah."

He kept walking.

She had to say something. Why, she couldn't fathom. "Gabriel."

His name sounded funny on her lips. Such a beautiful name for such a prickly man.

"Jah." He kept walking.

"Sometime…if you…if you ever want company…on the walk, I mean…some other time, I mean, I have to help in the kitchen and like you said, I have a cold…."

He stopped walking, but didn't turn around. His hand went to his hat and lifted it from his head, then settled it back.

An answer of sorts, she supposed. An acknowledgment. But not a promise. Not even an assurance. She watched, despite her best intention to turn away, until he reached the trees. He had such a long stride. Measured. Unhurried. Lonely.

Voices tinged with laughter told her the moment had fled. Sure enough, a bunch of the boys rounded the corner, volleyballs flying, the net dragging behind.

"Mudder!" Edmond trotted toward her. "Mudder, I did all right, didn't I? Josiah said I did fine."

"That you did, son."

"You forgive me?" He ducked his head, his cheeks red once again. The other youngsters flooded past him, oblivious to his embarrassment. "I mean, I know I still have work to do. Josiah says he'll help me—"

"I forgive you."

"Okay."

"Go play volleyball. Have fun."

"Okay." He seemed to search her face for something. "You sure?"

"Go play, son."

He grabbed the end of the net that dragged behind one of the Glick boys and ran on.

Helen left them to their fun, still pondering her exchange with Gabriel. She couldn't be sure, but it very well could be that she would come to regret something about it. She couldn't be sure what.

Chapter 14

Annie dropped the cookie tray on the potholders she'd spread across the bakery counter and sucked at a fingertip that had strayed too close to the hot tray. She glanced across the room at the spot where her sister Emma sat near the front window, watching Helen arrange jam and jelly jars on a display shelf. Having both women arrive for a visit this morning seemed like a gift from God. Emma had been sick the previous day and unable to attend the prayer service. Helen had been enveloped in Edmond's situation, leaving Annie about to burst with her restrained fear and anxiety. "Thomas walked in and said you might have to sell the farm? No talking about it first."

"There's no talking about it. You know that. Micah will decide, and we'll do whatever he says." Emma sipped from her glass of tea and set it down with a clink. "Thomas feels as bad about it as I do. Maybe worse. He's farmed that land his whole life. He never says much, but when he suggested Rebecca and the twins watch Caleb while I come into town for a visit, I knew what he was thinking. It's his way of showing me he knows."

She lifted her glass of tea to her lips, then returned it to the table without sipping. "If we can find something else in this area, we're fine. If not, Thomas can take a job in town or we can move, maybe start a new district. They've been talking about doing that anyway, with ours having grown so much."

How her sister could be so matter-of-fact, Annie couldn't imagine. She wanted to howl at the news when Luke had returned to the house after the meeting. Stomp her feet and throw a fit like a child. Of course, she hadn't. The exhausted look on her brother's face kept her from saying much at all. Best to keep her thoughts to herself. In the days since he'd not mentioned the situation again. She'd thought baking would soothe her rebellious heart. Instead she only seethed more. The more she baked, the more she thought.

This morning, after snapping at Mary Elizabeth over something silly, she'd sent the girl on an early, extended lunch. Fortunately, Mark left to make deliveries so he didn't have to bear the brunt of his sister's bad mood. Emma's arrival, followed immediately by Helen's, couldn't have been better timed. A chance to speak her mind to two women who would undoubtedly do the same—since none of them would think of doing it at home. What if Emma and Thomas couldn't find anything nearby? Annie couldn't lose another sister. She needed them close. She wanted to be there to help with the new baby and to see Caleb grow up. And what about Mary and Lillie? They were her sisters too, after all, and there wasn't enough room at the Shirack house to move them home.

Unfortunately, Emma didn't seem to have any answers either.

"Tobias says there's a two-hundred acre spread for sale out near Wakefield." Helen grabbed two more jars of strawberry preserves from her box and added them to the display shelf. She smoothed the handwritten label on one. "He says we should consider starting a new settlement there."

"That's a two-hour drive by car." Annie caught the querulous tone in her voice and tried to calm herself. No need to make Emma feel worse. "The bishop didn't say anything about starting a new settlement. Luke would've mentioned that. He said they needed to sell the farm and find something new. Or start a new business. He mentioned working with Gabriel, didn't he?"

"Deacon Pierce did." Emma's expression grew more pained. "But you know Thomas. He's a farmer, through and through. He's not one to be in town much. Only for supplies and sales. It would be…"

She seemed at a loss for words to even describe the effect such a change would have on her husband. To leave behind working the earth with his hands. To know Thomas was to know this would be a travesty.

"Thomas will do what he has to do." She grimaced and rubbed her belly. "He understands what's at stake."

"Can't you leave the oil, pretend it's not there?" The words sounded silly to Annie the minute they came out of her mouth. She gathered the ingredients for a red velvet cake. Better she did something she knew how to do. "Not pretend, but leave it alone."

"Already John Slocum, the Englisch man who sells the houses here in town—the real estate agent—came out and talked to Thomas. He says he'll take the farm off our hands. That's what he called it, taking it off our hands." Emma's smile had a bitter tinge to it. "He says we'll receive lots of offers, and it'll be a nuisance so why don't we sell it to him and let him worry about it. Thomas said he would talk to the bishop about it. That's what he says about everything. We'll talk to the bishop. Mr. Slocum also said the other thing we could do is keep the farm and let one of the oil companies pay us for the oil rights."

"How would they do that?" Helen plopped down next to Emma and picked up her glass of tea. "Trucks and equipment and men streaming in and out of the farm, mingling with the buggies and the horses?"

"I guess others have done it. On Englisch farms. They have livestock and such too." The sadness in Emma's voice cut at Annie. Her sister had endured so much over the years. Now this. "But you're right. It wouldn't work, even if it were permitted. Even if Thomas were willing, which he isn't."

"Of course he's not." Helen's hands flew up in an emphatic gesture that bumped her glass and sent tea coursing down one side onto the table. *"Ach."*

She grabbed a napkin and dabbed at the spill, managing to knock the glass on its side. More tea soaked into the tablecloth. *"Ach,* I'm such a mess."

"Try not flailing about so much." Her voice gentle and soothing, Emma touched the other woman's hand. "Why are you in such a state today?"

"It's Edmond." Helen dabbed at the tea stains, making the wet spots grow. "He began his community service this morning. They have him picking up trash along the highway. Micah wasn't happy that they made him wear an orange vest, but they said he must, for safety's sake. Fifty hours, he has to do."

"He'll get this behind him. That's good."

"His confession on Sunday…that was hard."

"He did well." Annie meant that. Helen's son had been cleared-eyed and his voice had never faltered. Facing his neighbors, family, and friends, all gathered in one place must have been hard for a young man like Edmond. "Very well."

"He did, didn't he?" Helen's cheeks turned pink. "But it's the deed no one will forget."

"He's been forgiven."

"I know."

"That was the point."

"But he's so wound up now. He rushes around from one thing to the next, talking a mile a minute. It's like he's trying to make up for it all at once."

"He'll get over it." Annie understood Helen's discomfort. She too would face that challenge, someday. "Give him time. He'll calm down."

The door swung open and in marched Charisma Chiasson, little Luke David on her hip, Gracie skipping along behind her.

"Charisma! Gracie, you're getting so tall!" Annie smiled at the happy little parade. She didn't get to see the little ones often enough now that Charisma worked full-time at the Hometown Restaurant and spent her free time courting a certain chief of police. Annie bustled around the counter and rushed to give out hugs to all three. "I can't get over how big Luke David is getting."

"He weighs a ton." Charisma plopped the toddler on the floor and shook her arm for emphasis. "The pediatrician says he's in the top percentile for his age for height and weight."

Annie had no idea what that meant, but it must be good from the proud grin on Charisma's face. The woman passed out hugs to Emma and Helen and slid into a chair with a gusty sigh. "Got any more tea? I'm parched."

"Can I have a cookie?" Gracie followed Annie behind the counter, her little sneakers making a smack-smack sound on the wooden floor. "Peanut butter?"

Luke David toddled behind her, mimicking the words in a lisp that turned cookie into "ukie."

"Tell me how old you are now and I'll think about it."

"Five." Gracie held up the requisite number of fingers. "I'm five."

"My, my, then a cookie you shall have." Annie doled them out and then pulled a carton of milk from the gas-powered refrigerator to fill Luke David's sippy cup. "How about you, Gracie? Milk?"

"Soda pop."

"No soda pop. Milk."

"Okay, milk." Gracie's sunny smile never faltered. Like her mom, she tested the boundaries, then learned to live with them. "Chocolate milk."

"Milk."

"Milk." Gracie plopped on the floor next to her brother and took a big bite of her cookie. A muffled *yummy* followed.

"I'll get the tea. I want to refill my glass." Helen popped up and knocked over her chair. She dove for it and set it upright. "*Ach*, I don't know what's wrong with me today."

"You are a nervous Nelly. What gives?" Charisma patted the other woman's arm in a maternal air that seemed funny coming from the youngest woman in the room. "Are you in love?"

"In *lieb*?" Helen turned radish red. She held up both hands palms out. They shook. "Whatever would make you say that?"

Annie looked at Emma who shrugged and turned to Helen. "Has something happened?"

"No, nothing's happened. Nothing at all. I just…I don't know…it's the way…I'm sure it's my imagination…or something…I never thought I had much imagination."

"Well, something did happen to me, and I didn't imagine it." Charisma jumped in. She flashed her left hand around, first to Helen and then to Emma. "Dylan asked me to marry him. I said yes. I'm engaged. Isn't the ring beautiful?" She screamed a short, shrill scream after those words, jumped up, and then sat down. "Can you believe it?"

"*Wunderbaar!*" Annie rushed to join in the hugging and words of congratulation. "Wunderbaar. That is good news."

Charisma's face shone with a fierce, unrelenting happiness. She ran a finger down the condensation on Emma's tea glass. "I never thought, you know." She glanced at Annie, who knew all the details of her friend's life before coming to Bliss Creek, all about who had fathered her two children. "I never thought I would get to have this. I still can't believe it sometimes. I mean, why would Dylan want to marry a girl like me, someone with two children?"

"Because he loves you. Why else?" Annie patted her friend's shoulder. "Chief Parker is a good man and a good judge of character."

"I wanted you to be the first to know." Charisma disengaged Luke David's slobbery, cookie-covered hand from the pant leg of her faded jeans. "Since you were the one who pushed him my direction."

"I didn't do any pushing." Heat rose on Annie's cheeks. What had Chief Parker told Charisma? Surely not that he'd once admitted to having feelings for an Amish girl who had quite rightly sent him in another direction. "After what happened with Logan, he probably felt a responsibility for keeping an eye on you, what with having a new baby and being alone here with no family. When will the wedding be?"

"We haven't set a date. Gracie and I will be baptized first. That's real important. To get our new life started on the right foot. Plus, there's been another…development. That's the other part of what I wanted to tell you." The joy faded from Charisma's face. She dropped her gaze to the table where she wiped at the tea stains with an already sodden napkin. "Logan sent me a letter. He wants to see the children."

"He does?" Annie sank onto the last empty chair next to her sister. Luke David immediately climbed into her lap. She ran her hand over his soft dark curls, so like his father's. The memories flooded her. The gun, the shots, the glass breaking. Logan McKee had robbed the bakery. Then he'd broken out of the jail and tried to drag Charisma and the children away from the Shiracks' farm. Still, she couldn't bring herself to think badly of a man who only wanted to take care of his family. "Does he know…about Chief Parker?"

"You know you can call him Dylan, right? He's proud to have been promoted to chief, but he's also proud to call you a friend." Charisma dropped the wet napkin and leaned back in her chair. "I wrote to Logan and told him I'm dating Dylan, but Logan said it didn't matter. He's Luke David and Gracie's father, and he has a right to see them. He says he still wants to be their daddy."

"He does have a right," Helen pointed out. She seemed happy to have someone else's life to discuss. "He is their father."

"Like I don't know that?" Charisma sniffed. "They don't remember him. They only know Dylan. Luke David already calls him *daddy*. Well, he calls him *da-da*, but you know what I mean. Anyway, I stopped by to tell you the good news and the bad news."

"It can't be bad news that the children's father wants to be involved in their lives." Annie kept her tone gentle. "Logan isn't a bad person."

"If anyone knows that it's me." Charisma flipped her long, blonde hair over her shoulder. "I know what he did for me. He stole for me and Gracie. He went to prison for us. And I can't do the one thing he wants me to do for him."

"What's that?"

"I can't love him." Charisma swooped Luke David into her arms. "I can't go back to where I was two years ago when he went to jail for me. I can't go back to living the way we were living. I like my job. I like my little apartment. I like…I love Dylan."

"You've grown up, Charisma. Logan will see that. It seems to me…" Emma spoke slowly, her voice soft. "It seems to me he made his choices. Bad choices. You didn't make them for him. You needn't feel guilty about moving on with your life. He needs to do the same."

All of them looked at the baby boy on Annie's lap. Sometimes moving on meant figuring out a way to do what was best for someone else. Charisma had moved on. Annie wondered if she would ever do the same. How could she give Noah the father he would need to grow up a good Plain man? If Helen still lamented George's passing after seven years, how could Annie be expected to move on after one?

"I'd better go. I have to drop the kids off at Deborah's and hightail it to work." Charisma stood, snagged a chocolate chip cookie from the plate on the table, and lifted Luke David from Annie's lap. "Did I tell you Naomi made me a shift leader? I oversee the other two waitresses when she's out running errands, stuff like that."

Amid the congratulations offered by her sister and Helen, Annie took the opportunity to give Charisma another hug. "It'll be all right," she murmured. "You'll work through it. With Dylan. And with Logan."

Charisma nodded, but her lips tightened as if she held in a sob. "I know. That's what Dylan says," she whispered. "I feel terrible even laying this on you, knowing what you've been through, but I knew you'd understand."

"I do." Annie felt a stab of pain in her chest, thinking of what Logan must be feeling. "Congratulations again on the engagement."

She watched as Charisma shooed Gracie out the door and down the street.

"What are you thinking?" Emma asked.

"What do you mean?" She started to turn away from the window. "About what?"

"You're standing there, shaking your head. What are you thinking?"

"It's sad when families are broken apart. Dylan is a good man and he's good for Charisma, but Logan is the father of those children. I'm glad our ways are not their ways. It's too heartbreaking. I..." A woman getting out from a blue car across the street caught Annie's gaze. Catherine. She was crossing the road and making her way toward the bakery. "I love Charisma and her babies. But I still feel bad for..."

The door opened once again, this time bringing Catherine. She held the usual leather-bound notebook in one hand. A large handbag hung from a long strap over her shoulder. "Gudemariye. Perfect. Just the people I wanted to see," she said, a big smile on her face. She slid into the chair that had been occupied by Charisma and laid her notebook on the table. "I've been looking forward to a visit."

Chapter 15

Gabriel slapped another shingle down in front of him, pulled a nail from the pouch fastened around his waist, and hammered the shingle in place. Swinging the hammer occupied his mind and his body. No need to think about anything else. Shingle, nails, hammer. Shingle, nails, hammer. They had been fixing the Brennamans' roof, damaged by the July Fourth storm, all day. Muggy heat shimmered from the roof, and the sun beat down on the back of his sweat-drenched shirt. The billowing heat made it hard to breathe, the air hot in his nose and throat and lungs. Sweat ran down his forehead and dripped from his beard. He leaned back on his haunches and wiped at his eyes, but the salty drops only burned them more.

"Time for a break?" Thomas hollered from where he squatted over the row he had placed. He straightened, a dark, towering figure with the brilliant sun behind him. "I could use a long, tall glass of water myself."

"Jah. We may not have enough shingles after all." Gabriel stood and eased down the slant of the roof, careful to plant each step until he reached the eave. He squatted, swiveled, placed a boot on the second rung of the ladder, and clamored backward down to the ground. "We only have one pallet left."

Thomas followed him down the ladder and reached for the towel he'd left on the porch railing. His face ruddy with heat, he wiped down his face and neck in a vigorous motion like a man drying himself after a bath. "You're right. I'll head into town in a few minutes. I want to get more nails and some two-by-fours to patch that spot in the barn. The fence needs some work too. Might as well make a list and get everything at once."

"No rest for the weary." Gabriel grabbed one of the tumblers of water Emma had left on the porch before heading into town for a few supplies at the grocery store and—he suspected—a visit with her sister at the bakery. She'd left Abigail to watch the younger children and set off right after the noon meal. She and Annie would have much to discuss regarding the future of their family, perhaps divided by many miles. She hadn't said a word at the supper table when the sale of the property had been discussed. In fact, she hadn't said a word that entire evening. Biding her time until she had a moment in private with her husband? "Do we need to get the boys back in from the field to help?"

"Nee, I'd rather they get what's left of the alfalfa cut and spread so it can dry. We want to be able to turn it tomorrow and bale it later this week." Thomas drank deeply from his glass, then set it aside. He jerked his head toward the road. "Someone's coming. Looks like a car with all that dust it's kicking up."

Gabriel swiveled to follow his gaze. A huge silver pickup truck, not a car, roared along the dirt road that led from the highway to the Brennaman house. They stood in silence, watching it make a trip in a few minutes that took ten times as long in a buggy. Gabriel had ridden in vehicles enough to know the driver wouldn't be smelling the fresh cut alfalfa or seeing the birds flock in the tree along the road. The scenery would be a blur and the smells kept outside by the rolled-up windows. Inside, music would blare from the radio and fake pine scent would waft from a little tree hanging from the mirror.

Faster wasn't always better. Just different.

The truck with its shiny silver paint and brilliant chrome churned to a stop, fumes belching from double pipes in the back. Two men dressed in matching pale brown suits and skinny bolo ties emerged the second the engine ceased to roar. One was tall and bony, the other short and looking like he'd eaten more than his share of pie.

"Howdy, folks." The tall, bony passenger clomped toward them in slick, brown cowboy boots, his hand extended toward Gabriel. Gabriel took it, shook, and let go. The man, who had clammy, soft skin, grinned, his teeth brilliant in his tanned face. "You must be Thomas Brennaman. I'm Craig Shore. This is my partner, Bill Carpenter. We're interested in buying your property."

"I'm Thomas Brennaman." No note of welcome marked Thomas's words. Nor did fear, anger, or emotion of any kind. "This property is my family's farm."

Craig Shore's gaze darted to Thomas, his interest in Gabriel gone flat. "We represent a consortium out of Wichita interested in developing any potential oil reserves that may be available in this great state of Kansas. Oil is vitally important to the future of this country—"

"Mr. Shore," Thomas interrupted, his voice gruff, but respectful. "Mr. Shore, the decision to sell this property isn't mine."

"You said the property belongs to you." Bill Carpenter, who smelled of cigarette smoke and a heavy, sickening scent of cologne, looked confused. "Did you get another offer? Is it one of the big oil companies? We can match their offer…"

Shore held up a hand. "I know a little about these people, Bill. I'm sure what Mr. Brennaman means is he will have to check with the rest of the good people of his community before he considers an offer."

"It's a great offer, Mr. Brennaman." Bill Carpenter slid right back into his pitch, seeming to ignore the irritated look on his partner's face. "We're authorized to offer you a pretty penny for it. You got what— a hundred acres here? You won't do better. You'll be so rich you could buy a dozen farms with what you make. Just think, you could build a mansion for that bunch of kids I saw out there picking apples in those trees by the road. Those kids are gonna need an education. College costs money."

When Carpenter ran out of air and paused to take a breath, Thomas gave him a kindly nod. "The name's Thomas. I'm not interested in a dozen farms or a mansion. We educate our children ourselves."

The two men looked at each other, their expressions incredulous. The tall, bony man, Shore, recovered first. "We're talking three thousand an acre. I might be able to get more. The people I represent—"

"I don't mean to be rude, Mr. Shore, but what happens to this property is a matter that will be decided by our bishop who will consult with the other men of our community. We'll decide together."

"You people will want to make up your minds quick. The offer's only on the table for a short time." The short, pudgy man's voice increased in volume as if he thought Thomas might be hard of hearing. "We have other irons in the fire. Other properties we're looking at. It would be in your best interest to act now."

"When can we meet this Mr. Bishop?" Shore broke in. He appeared as calm as his friend was agitated. He tugged a package of cigarettes from the inner lining of his suit coat, extracted a cigarette, and offered the package to Gabriel. He shook his head, so did Thomas. The man proceeded to light his with a practiced motion. "As my colleague mentioned, we're on a timeline here. We need to get moving, get into production."

The reek of cigarette smoke in his nose, Gabriel quelled an urge to cough and to tell him he should move along on his timeline, but Thomas's simple approach was better. The man had the patience of Job. "We'll let Micah know that you have expressed an interest."

"In the meantime, can we see the spot where you sprung a leak?" Shore sounded as eager as a boy anxious to go on his first hunt. "We'd like to take a look at the existing infrastructure to determine what we'll need to bring in."

"Sprung a leak?" Gabriel spoke despite his intention to remain silent. The man rubbed him the wrong way, try as he might not to take offense at phrases like *you people*. "It's a farm, not a boat."

"Of course it is." Shore turned back to the truck. He tugged open the door and pulled a long roll of white paper from the cab, slid off a rubber band, and unrolled a map. "Is it here? Is it close to the road?

How much of a problem will getting our trucks in be? Do we need to clear an access point? Of course, we'll need to clear and level the land before we create the access road for our equipment. We'll need to bring in diesel engines—you folks don't have electricity, do you? So we'll need electrical generators. The diesel engines will power them, you see. We've got the hoisting system, the derrick…"

"You're getting the horse before the cart." Even Thomas's patience seemed to wane, even though his tone remained calm. "I'll let Micah and the others know of your interest. No decisions have been made. We'll talk and we'll think."

"Talk is good. Doing is better." Carpenter folded his arms over a gut that bulged through his fancy jacket. Sweat rings soaked his armpits. "We heard you folks can't make a living anymore. You lost your wheat crop. How are you gonna feed your family this winter? I'm hearing you don't have the money to pay your property taxes? Doing is better, Mr. Brennaman. We can write you a check today."

"Thomas told you what he'll do." Gabriel took a step closer to his friend. He tipped his hat to the two men. "Thank you for coming by. Careful pulling out up at the stop sign. The trucks on the highway speed by real fast up there."

Shore gave him the shrewd up-and-down look of a man assessing livestock at an auction. He scratched a spot on his neck, then turned to his partner. "We better get back to town. I got a meeting with a real estate agent about some office space. I also want to take the mayor's temperature, she might be able to…" He glanced from Gabriel to Thomas and then seemed to think better of the monologue. "Give me the keys. I'll drive. You drive like an old lady."

Carpenter mumbled something about wanting to live to see another day and tossed the keys to Shore. "Give us a call…Sorry… we'll come by in a day or two, give you a chance to talk and to think. We can get our lawyers to draw up the necessary paperwork. You won't have to do a thing, except cash our check."

Shore paused at the truck's door, then quickly retraced his steps. He pulled a small white card from a leather holder and handed it to

Thomas, who took it with obvious reluctance. "I know you people don't have phones, but I imagine that bishop fellow does. Or access to one. This is my card. Ask him to give me a call when you've had your pow-wow. Thanks, man. Thanks for taking the time to meet with us."

As if they'd been given a choice.

He slapped Thomas on the shoulder and once again held out a hand to Gabriel. Courtesy dictated that he take it. The moist, soft skin made him want to wipe his own hand on his dirty pants.

Shore got in the truck and pulled out, leaving behind a cloud of dust that billowed all the way to the porch. Gabriel held his breath until it settled down. Thomas threw out the water in his glass and poured a fresh one from the pitcher sitting on a table next to the hickory rocking chairs.

"Well." Looking sheepish, he smiled at Gabriel. "Don't that beat all?"

"Don't it, though?" Gabriel plopped down in a chair. "What's a consortium?"

"I don't know." Thomas sprawled out his long legs and took another swig of water. He removed his hat and poured the rest of the water over his head. It streamed down his face and darkened the collar and the front of his shirt "Whew, that feels good. It's mighty hot this afternoon."

"What happens now?"

"It's not up to me or you." He blotted the remaining water on his face with his bandana. "If it's best for the community, it will be best for me and Emma and the children."

"That's a lot of money."

"It is. The very reason Micah feels we must go."

"I understand."

"I'm not sure Emma will."

"She'll do what you want her to do."

"I know." Thomas's tone held a thinly veiled note of pain. "She's a good fraa."

A pain all his own jabbed Gabriel in the gut. Thomas and Emma had the bond of man and wife. Thomas didn't like the idea of hurting his fraa. Even if it were for the right reasons.

Gabriel longed for that bond. At moments like this he missed Laura with a longing so deep it drowned him. He tried to swim his way to the top so he could catch his breath. He swallowed and studied the horizon. The silence stretched.

"She'll want to do what is best for the community." Thomas broke it first. He seemed to be reassuring himself. "She always knows what's best."

Gabriel buried his own feelings under an avalanche of determined support for his friends.

"She does. You're blessed."

"I am." Thomas glanced his way, his expression one Gabriel rarely saw on his friend's face. Uncertainty. "So are you. You will be again."

Gabriel returned his gaze to the horizon. Not even with Thomas could he scale the heights of the fence he'd built. "When will you tell Micah?"

"Soon. I know there will be more who will come. I don't suppose there's any hurry. Might as well hear them all out first. Right now, I need to get into town and pick up those shingles. I want to finish this today." Thomas gave no indication he knew he'd wandered into dangerous territory where Plain men generally didn't go. He chuckled, a sound with no mirth in it. "All this work on a house that won't be mine much longer."

"The next family who lives here—if it comes to that—will appreciate your hard work and care when another big rain comes along."

"Indeed." Thomas clomped down the steps, stopped, and stared toward the corral and the barn. "I was selfishly thinking of myself. You're right. I'll get what we need to do a good job."

Gabriel watched him walk to the barn, his long legs eating up the distance. Thomas didn't have a selfish bone in his body, of that, Gabriel had no doubt.

Chapter 16

Annie laughed at the look on Emma's face. Her sister didn't like rhubarb much, but she didn't have to be such a baby about it. The strawberry-rhubarb pie had a sweet tartness Annie loved. She scooted the pie plate back across the table that separated her from Emma. All the awkwardness of the first few moments when Catherine had stalked into the bakery disappeared over pie and iced tea and catching up on who had babies and who was running around and who had moved away. Annie kept an eye on the door. Most of her customers were Englisch, but the first Plain woman who came in the door would recognize Catherine as someone who should not be here talking with her sisters. *God, I can't. I can't kick her out. She's my sister. My sister. You love sinners. We're all sinners. We've all made mistakes. Who are we to judge? Nothing Catherine says or does will draw me away from You.*

The mingled look of longing and sadness on Emma's face sealed it. Even Helen, despite the look of displeasure and distrust on her face, hadn't suggested Catherine should be made to leave. As a good friend who missed her own sisters, who'd married and moved to other communities, Helen understood. She disapproved, but she understood the choice belonged to Annie and Emma. Annie would willingly face censure from the rest of their family and from the community in order to spend a few moments with her sister. Then Catherine would go and they wouldn't see her again. For how long, none of them knew.

For now, they were friends and sisters catching up on a visit. Like all Plain folks, they loved a good visit.

Helen and Catherine both grinned as Annie defended her pie against Emma, who was arguing over the merits of ruining a good strawberry pie with sour rhubarb. They had devoured their pieces of the steaming hot pie with no complaint. Her sister needed to keep an open mind about such things.

"My customers love this pie. Come on, it's not that bad." To prove her point, Annie slid a second piece on her own plate, cut a bite with her fork, and held it up to her mouth. "Have another bite. I have to get back to work soon. The afternoon crowd will start flooding through the door any minute."

"It's delicious, Emma. No one makes pie like Annie," Catherine added. She chewed, her eyes closed, her expression blissful. "I've missed this. You can't get pie like this in Wichita."

"There's a lot you can't find in Wichita that you'll find here." Helen leaned back in her chair and clasped her hands primly in her ample lap. She'd eaten two pieces of pie and drank two glasses of sweet tea. No one ever accused her of having a puny appetite. "Like your family and your church."

Annie held up a hand. She wanted a little time with her sister, a little time to enjoy her company. To forget—or at least ignore—the chasm that separated them. "Helen, let's not get into that right now."

"Catherine, how does it feel to go around with your hair uncovered?" Helen had that stubborn look on her face Annie recognized, like Noah at bedtime. "Doesn't it bother you to know men are looking at you?"

"Nee." Catherine's voice dropped to a whisper. She leaned forward. "I'll let y'all in on a secret. It's only hair."

She giggled. Annie exchanged glances with Emma and Helen.

Helen looked shocked, Emma, sad. Annie turned back to her sister. "Mudder would be so ashamed."

"Don't tell me what Mudder would be." Catherine slapped a hand on her notebook. "If she were here, I would be a different person. If she hadn't died, we'd all be different."

"But she did die," Helen said, her tone troubled. "Don't disrespect her by disrespecting her beliefs, our beliefs."

"I don't mean to disrespect. I was…I wanted to give you some perspective. You're so isolated in your beliefs, you have no idea what a big, wide world it is out there." Catherine sighed. She ran her hand across the notebook. "Did you tell everyone why I'm here, Annie?"

"I didn't…not yet." She saw Emma's curious look and shook her head. "It's your project. You need to tell everyone and let them decide for themselves if they want to be a part of it. But you should know that I won't be."

"A part of what?" Emma glanced from Annie to Catherine and back. "Why are you here, Catherine?"

Catherine began to explain. Annie watched Emma's face. Her eyes widened. She toyed with the fork she'd used to play with the pie she hadn't eaten. Then she began to shake her head.

"Please, think about it." Catherine leaned forward. "It costs you nothing. You don't have to read the memoir or even see it in a bookstore. You're isolated here. No one will know it's you. How does that hurt you in any way?"

"How? Our job is to keep ourselves apart from the world. To not draw attention to ourselves." Annie jumped into the fray before Emma could respond. She couldn't help herself. How could Catherine have forgotten all this? "We don't hold ourselves up as examples of anything. We don't want graven images taken, let alone printed in a book for others to gawk at."

"It will help them to understand."

"No, it will help you to understand," Helen piped up.

Annie turned to stare at her, as did Emma and Catherine.

"I'm sorry. I know this is a family matter." Helen's plump cheeks reddened. "I can't help it. I feel like I should stand in, where your mother can't."

"Say what you think." Annie needed another perspective. Helen, despite her youthful awkwardness, was older and wiser. She had trouble expressing herself, but she had a grounding in the Ordnung that Annie respected. "We value your thoughts."

"Catherine wants to put on a piece of paper everything that has happened to her." Helen's face darkened to a brick red. She stumbled over the words, but to her credit, she kept going. "Those things involve the people who are important to her. Like her sisters and brothers. She thinks writing it down will make her feel better."

"So write it down. Feel better. But don't tell the world." Annie stood and began picking up the plates from the table. She didn't want Catherine to see how sick the idea made her. "Don't show them the inside of our family and our community. Don't use us as show and tell."

"I'm not using you."

"Jah, you are. To make yourself bigger in your career, whatever it is you plan to do with all this education, all this book learning you're getting."

"Nee, I'm only trying to understand what happened to me, why it happened." Catherine shook her head, her eyes suddenly wet with tears. "I only want to stop feeling like this. Can't you understand that? I don't want to feel like this anymore!"

"Then write it all down, but don't publish it." The look on Catherine's face made Annie feel like a mean, ugly person. If her sister needed to do this in order to heal after three years, shouldn't she be allowed to do that? Torn between her faith and her love for her sister, Annie felt ripped apart. She had to stand with her faith. She had to stand with her community. Didn't she? There had to be another way for Catherine to get better. "Don't take pictures of me and Noah and Caleb and Lillie and Mary. Write your story and let that be your therapy. Don't make us part of your therapy."

"What do you know about therapy?" Catherine dabbed at the corner of her eyes with a napkin. Her nose turned red, like Annie's did when she cried. "You didn't see what I saw. Besides, you're stronger. You have more faith. I can't help it I'm so messed up."

"I'm not stronger. I question. I question all the time. I question why I had to lose David." Her voice cracked and Annie forced herself to shut her mouth. She would not break down now. Not now. David asked so little of her. To take care of their son and to stay strong. That was it. She thought of Charisma and the dough punching. "I make bread. That's my therapy. I make bread every day. Day after day. I let it rise and I punch it down. I don't write books or take pictures and publish them for the whole world to see how I lost the person I love the most."

"You make bread?"

"Stop, please." Emma gasped and gripped the edge of the table with both hands. "Please stop arguing."

"I'm sorry, Emma. We're not arguing. We're talking." Annie laid the plate on the counter and rushed to her sister's side. "We didn't mean to upset you. It's okay. We'll work it out."

"It's not you." Emma's mouth widened, with it, her eyes. She gasped. Grimacing, she clutched both hands to her stomach. "The baby...oh, oh."

Annie's anger with Catherine dissipated in the rush of memories that deluged her. She remembered that enormous, grand feeling of having another human being growing inside her. That sensation of being exactly who God intended her to be. Wife and mother. She had relished those sharp kicks that said her baby thrived. An ache as sharp as any labor pain pierced her heart. Would she ever experience that feeling again? Hold her newborn child in her arms? She heaved those thoughts, those questions, into the box in the corner of her mind where she kept all things related to her murky, unfathomable future and padlocked it shut. "The baby's kicking. That's *gut*, right?"

Emma stood, knocking her chair back, and took two tottering steps away from the table. "No, not kicking." She grabbed the back of the chair and leaned forward, panting. "Pain."

"*Ach*, is it time?" A thrill ran through Annie. Her heart began to pound like a hammer against nails. Her legs shook. Thrill mixed with an aching, bittersweet remembrance. The excitement of it. The doubts that crept in and then dissipated when she heard Noah cry for the first time. Could she do it? Would the baby be fine, with all ten fingers and toes? "I know you intended to do this at home, but maybe we should go to the clinic since you're here in town."

"No, no, I need to go home. I need Thomas. He's working on the roof." Emma straightened, inhaled again, and staggered toward the door. "Tell Josiah to find Mariah Stockton. She's the midwife I'm using."

"Are you sure you have time to get all the way to the farm?" Annie grabbed Emma's canvas bag. "The clinic's two blocks away. We don't even have to hitch the buggy."

"It took Caleb ten hours to get here." Emma waved a hand, but her lips tightened and her face went white. She paused for a second and inhaled deeply. "I'll be fine. I don't want the expense of the clinic. We need to save our money…in case…well, you know."

She groaned and panted.

"Those pains are awfully close together." Catherine shot from her chair. She grabbed Emma's elbow. "Help her, Annie. Come on. Let's get to my car. It's parked across the street. We can be at the farm in twenty minutes, less if I speed."

"No, no car!" Emma protested. "We can't ride in a car, not with…"

"With me. The shunned sister." Catherine tugged at Emma's arm. "I don't care about the *meidung*. You're my sister and you're having a baby. Either you have it at the clinic or you let me drive you to the farm. Otherwise you'll have it in the back of a buggy. What'll it be?"

Emma bent over, hands on her knees. The gasp became a shuddering groan that reverberated off the walls of the bakery. Then she breathed in and out. "Car."

Annie grabbed her other elbow. "Helen, can you lock up and then go tell Josiah? He'll get the midwife." She plucked the keys from under her counter and tossed them to her friend. "Then come back here to wait for Mark and Mary Elizabeth to return. They can run the bakery for the afternoon."

Her face flushed, Helen nodded. "God bless you, Emma, and your new little one." Tears teetered in the corners of her brown eyes. "I'll pray for a safe delivery."

Emma managed a nod.

"Let's go, let's go."

Annie, conscious of the stares of passersby, helped Catherine lead Emma across the street. Catherine pushed a button on the little black thing in her hand, something beeped, and then she nodded. "The doors are open, hop in."

Annie helped Emma into the backseat and slid in next to her, enveloped in the smell of leather and something else. Something elusive that she hadn't smelled before. It was a far cry from the starless night when she'd helped Emma into the back of a wagon and ridden with her to the clinic in the cold and dark. That night Emma lost her first baby, and David had sat with Annie in the waiting room, offering her comfort, taking the first steps toward healing their relationship, toward a life together.

What she wouldn't give to have David's hand on hers right now, in this moment.

"I feel like I need to push." Emma grunted. "I need to push."

"No, no, don't do that!" Catherine started the engine. "No having a baby on the leather seats of my rental car."

Not words Annie ever expected to come out of her sister's mouth. Catherine driving a car was hard enough to fathom. Catherine worried about leather seats in a car she'd rented seemed even more unfathomable. She'd traveled a long road from cleaning Englischers' houses and walking barefoot to the produce stand to sell Annie's pies.

"Think about something else." Annie needed to think about

something else too. Catherine would leave soon, and they would go back to being strangers living in different worlds. She scrambled for another topic of conversation. "Have you picked out names? Do you want a girl this time?"

"I'll take whatever God gives us." Emma panted. "Thomas likes Adam if it's a boy, Lilah if it's a girl."

"Nice names."

"Jah. Nice names." Emma grabbed Annie's hand and squeezed hard. "I want this bobbeli to grow up here. In our home. On our farm. Is that selfish of me?"

"Maybe it is, but it's also human." Annie forced herself to sound cheerful—far more cheerful than she felt. "We can't rid ourselves of our hopes and wants. We have to set them aside for the greater good."

"You sound like Aenti Louise."

"I want to be like Aenti Louise, but I'm not."

"Me neither," Emma whispered, her grip tightening. "But she's had more years to hone her wisdom and her goodness."

"You are good, Emma."

"Nee. I want my way. I've always wanted my way. I'm selfish and unforgiving."

"You're the least selfish person I know."

Emma's hand tightened again. She cried out. "Lord, have mercy!"

Catherine glanced back, her face tight with tension and fear. "Is it…is she…we're almost there. You have to hang on, Emma!"

"Look at the road, Catherine!" Annie flashed to the day Emma and Thomas had come to tell her of the accident that had taken her parents' lives. "You must not look away from the road."

Catherine twisted back to face the front. The car shot forward as if Annie's admonition had caused Catherine's foot to slam against the gas pedal.

"Hang on," Annie whispered. "Hang on."

The drive passed in a blur that alternated between seconds that crawled along in an excruciatingly slow pace while Emma screamed in pain, then sped up as she sobbed, her head on Annie's lap. "It's happening so fast this time," she whispered between contractions. "I don't think we're going to make it."

"We will make it." The car shot forward again as if to punctuate Catherine's statement. "You concentrate on not having that baby until we get to your house."

Minutes later she made good on her words. Annie breathed a sigh of relief when the farmhouse came into view with its clean white paint and green trim. Gabriel Gless, wearing a tool belt and wielding a large hammer, stood at the top of a ladder leaning against one wall. Annie scanned the roof. No Thomas.

The second the car slammed to a halt, Annie burst from the car. She turned to help Emma slide out. "We're here, schweschder, we're here!"

Emma groaned in response. Her knees buckled and she sank to the ground. Annie pulled her to her feet. "Oh no, you don't. In the house you go. We're almost there. Your bed. The place where you want this bobbeli to enter the world. In your home."

"For now. Our home for now."

"Don't think about that. Think about the bobbeli." Annie helped her up the porch steps. "Nothing else matters right now."

Catherine slammed her door and ran around the car. "You must be Gabriel," she hollered. "Where's Thomas?"

Gabriel stomped down the ladder and strode toward them. "Thomas has gone into town for another pallet of shingles and more nails. Why? What's the matter?"

❧

Gabriel glanced from Emma to Annie to a third woman who looked to be Annie's twin, only dressed in Englisch clothes, car keys in her hand. They all wore the same horrified expressions.

"Thomas is in town?" Annie shook her head so hard her prayer kapp slid back a little. She slapped her hand on it. "This can't be happening."

"I have a cell phone. Fat lot of good it does me, since not one of the people I could call has a phone." The Englisch twin flashed the phone in one hand as if to show evidence of her preparation. "We need to get Emma into the house. She's in labor."

"So I gathered." Gabriel stomped up the porch steps in front of them and held open the screen door. "I'll ride into town and get Thomas."

"In a buggy?" The woman shook her head. "I'll go back in my car. It's much faster."

"Who are you, if I may ask?"

"She's our sister, Catherine." Annie spoke first.

Her tone was sharp, sharper than he liked to hear from a woman, but he would forgive that. She suffered from duress, with Emma about to give birth. Gabriel had been through this eight times. It never ceased to be a time fraught with a mixture of excitement, anxiety, and then blessed relief. The implications of what Annie had said hit him then. "Catherine."

"Yes, Catherine." Annie and Emma's sister lifted her chin, her voice steady. "The shunned sister."

"Then you best go on back into town."

"I want her here," Emma gasped. She grabbed the door frame and held on with one hand. "I need my sisters here."

"She'll be back with Thomas," Gabriel assured her. Now was not the time to argue with a woman about to give birth. Catherine could return, but she wouldn't be allowed into the house. "Go on. Take her in, Annie."

This house didn't belong to him, but Thomas had grown to be like a brother to him. Gabriel didn't want him to have trouble with the bishop, not on a day that should be filled only with blessing. Annie did as she was told, and Gabriel looked back at Catherine. "He'll be at the hardware store. He can leave the horse and buggy with Josiah. What about the midwife?"

"Helen was getting her, but it may be too late for that. She's far along."

"Then you best hurry. Get Thomas. He'll want to be here for his fraa."

"I will. And then I'll go. I know I can't stay."

Gabriel studied the dust on his scarred, scuffed boots, then raised his gaze to meet hers. "You can wait here, on the porch. Annie will want to share the news with you. She'll need you. As much as Emma."

Her green eyes looked wet in the bright sunlight, but she nodded. "It's hard to watch others go on with life when your own seems to be standing still."

He stiffened in spite of himself. What did she know? What had she heard? "You know that from experience?"

"Nee, but you do, Gabriel Gless."

"You don't know me." Heat burned its way across his neck and face. "We've never even met."

"I know of you."

Women and their nattering. It pained him beyond measure that they'd chosen him and his children as fodder for their incessant chatter. "Gossip is not a pastime one should admit to or participate in. Even though you've left this life for the Englisch ways, surely you remember that."

"No gossip." Catherine trotted around the car, her keys flashing in the sunlight. "Only a friend listening to another speak from the heart."

"What friend? What heart?"

She smiled for a brief second as she jerked open the car door. "Helen's heart, of course."

The door slammed before he could respond. The car spun around, spraying dirt and gravel, and sped out the driveway. Then he remembered to shut his mouth.

Chapter 17

Puffing, Helen raced up the porch steps behind Thomas. He pushed open the screen door and rushed in, letting it slap at her. She grabbed it just in time. He'd barely spoken since she'd stopped her buggy next to where he stood on the street outside Josiah's blacksmith shop. How could he be in Bliss Creek when his fraa had insisted on going home to have her baby because that's where her husband would be? He demanded she move over and let him drive. The bone-rattling journey had left her breathless and shaken. Inside he nearly collided with Gabriel, who stood at the bottom of the stairs.

"Is she all right?" Thomas demanded. "Is the bobbeli all right?"

Gabriel stumbled back and grabbed the staircase banister to steady himself. "The midwife arrived a few minutes ago. I don't know anything. What took you so long? I thought coming in Catherine's car would—"

"Catherine's car?" Thomas brushed past Gabriel and headed for the stairs. "Helen found me. I drove her buggy."

Gabriel's expression changed in an instant. Concern fled, replaced by something that looked like embarrassment. His ruddy cheeks darkened even more. Helen forced herself to nod at him, knowing her own face had turned the color of tomatoes. "It was happenstance. I had been watching the bakery for Annie, but then Mary Elizabeth and Mark both returned so I left them to take care of the customers. I wanted to—"

A half-muffled scream reverberated overhead.

Thomas bolted up the stairs and out of sight.

"Sounds as if things are progressing." Helen couldn't help herself. Tears welled and trickled down her cheeks. "The baby will be here soon."

Gabriel looked as if he wanted to be anywhere in the world except standing there with her. His gaze lingered on the staircase and then came to rest on Helen. The whites of his enormous brown eyes were red.

"Gabriel, are you—"

He brushed past her and headed for the door.

"Where are you going?"

"There's work to be done." His voice sounded gruff and strained. "You'd think no one around here had ever had a baby before. No sense standing around gawking."

"I'm not gawking. And things were a little tense because Emma was in town and then Thomas wasn't…" Stung by his tone, she pushed through the screen door and followed him on to the porch. "I'm here to help."

"Then you could go to the kitchen instead of standing there with your jaw flapping. Help Abigail get supper. Everyone will be hungry once things settle down."

"What is wrong with you?" She couldn't help herself. She folded her arms across her chest and glared at his back. "It's not necessary to be so rude."

He whirled and flashed her a glare. It almost sounded like he growled, but he didn't speak. After a moment, he swiveled and strode to the ladder, which he scrambled up in a manner that seemed less than safe in Helen's estimation. With any luck, he'd fall. Horrified at her own terrible thoughts, Helen sank into a hickory rocker and slapped both hands to her face. Gabriel Gless brought out the worst in her, the absolute worst. *God, forgive me. Please forgive me.*

The sound of an engine forced her to raise her head. Catherine returning. Poor Catherine. Hovering on the edge. Not belonging, but not able to tear herself away completely. Perhaps there was hope. Despite the trappings, the clothes, the car, the camera, the education, might there still be hope? Hope never ceased to exist.

"How is she?" Catherine hollered as she slammed the car door and trotted toward the house. "I couldn't find Thomas, but Josiah said he left with you, so I figured..."

"Still in labor." Helen nodded toward the other rocking chair. "Sit a spell with me. Annie will come down soon to tell us how things are going."

Catherine flopped into the chair and fanned her face with long, thin fingers. "I don't know about you, but I'm exhausted. I'd forgotten how hard it is to get anything done without telephones and electricity and you know, basic necessities."

"We have all we need." Helen didn't believe Catherine had forgotten anything. "You had a car, yet it was me who found Thomas in the buggy and brought him here."

"Luck."

"We don't believe in luck." Helen wanted to point out Catherine didn't either, but that was the old Catherine, the one who no longer existed, sucked up in the world. "God provides."

"For some."

"You don't believe anymore?" The thought made Helen sad. "You've lost your faith?"

"I can't have children." Catherine held both hands palms up as if to say that proved her point without any doubt. "God didn't provide for me."

"Is that why you were taking photographs of the girls?"

"What?" Catherine looked startled, then guilty. "I didn't...I mean..."

"I saw you. As we passed in the buggy, you were taking pictures of them when they were picking apples up by the road. Did you ask Gabriel and Thomas for permission? No, because they wouldn't have allowed it."

Catherine plucked at her skirt. She sighed and stared out at the road. "I took their pictures because they are beautiful and sweet and innocent and I love them. I don't even know them, but I love them."

"God gave you another role in life, Catherine." Helen felt herself relent, even though she knew what Catherine had done was wrong. The girl was mixed up, Helen had no doubt of that. She wandered around lost. That made Helen sad. "Take what He gives you and be happy. It's what He expects."

"As a student? I don't see why I couldn't have both."

"You had a dream of getting an education and having a profession. God gave you what you thought you wanted." Helen watched the emotions play on the other woman's face. "Yet you still long to be a wife and a mother to babies like the one being born upstairs right now."

"Jah." Catherine's lapse into *Deutsch* said it all. She longed for her old life—Helen was sure of it. Catherine patted Helen's hand. "And so do you."

⁂

Gabriel contemplated the two women sitting on the porch. Everything about their posture said they weren't enjoying a pleasant visit. He'd left the hammer in the house. He needed to retrieve it, but he didn't want to interrupt the conversation. No, he didn't want any part of it. The Shirack sisters, they talked too much, said too much, probed too much. Helen Crouch talked too much, period. It wasn't his way. It wasn't the Plain way. For the Shiracks, he blamed the loss of their parents at a time when they needed the discipline and direction provided by a father and a mother. Luke and Leah Shirack had done what they could, but there was no substitute, as he well knew. And likely Helen was born talking full tilt. Why did she make him feel so mean?

Blowing out a sigh, he tromped across the grass. Helen saw him coming and rose. "I'll bring out some lemonade. You must be thirsty."

How could she be so nice when he'd been so ugly with her?

"I left the hammer in the house."

"I'll bring it out when I fetch the lemonade."

"Danki," he managed, then ducked his head, feeling like a schoolboy. "It's heating up out here."

"Sit." She nodded toward the chair she'd left vacant. "Catherine won't bite."

"She shouldn't…"

"Be here. We know."

"As soon as there's word, I'll go." Catherine relaxed against her chair, belying her words. "I promise."

Gabriel eased into the rocking chair and gazed out at the open fields. Every muscle in his body tensed. He didn't want to sit next to this woman. Meidung happened for a reason, to keep the faithful away from those who couldn't shake the ways of the world. He had no desire to know the ways the world had touched this woman.

"Don't worry. I won't put you in my book." She smiled. Emma and Annie's smile. Helen had a rounder face with large, even teeth that made for a big smile. What possessed him to think about that woman's smile? He shook it off and tried to concentrate on Catherine's words. "Although, you do have a spot in my thesis. I hope you don't mind. I hope you'll even talk to me about it."

"Your book?"

"You haven't heard?" Her tone held bitterness, but she smiled. "Seems like everyone knows now."

She proceeded to explain her plan.

"What does that have to do with me? I wasn't here when you… were younger. I'm not part of your memories." Her words shook him.

He wanted no part in this. "I'm new to this what you called closed community."

Catherine nodded toward the flower garden that covered an enormous chunk of the Brennaman front yard. Rebecca, Lillie, and Mary were weeding while trying to keep Rachel and Isabelle out of trouble. Isabelle wanted to pull the flowers and stick them in her hair, while Rachel seemed more intent on eating them. Their giggles floated up to the porch, making Gabriel want to smile in spite of himself.

"Your paper is about happy Plain children who pull weeds and play in the flower garden? They like these stories in the Englisch world?"

"Not exactly. Like I said, my thesis is about the challenges of living in a closed community." Catherine said this as if it explained everything. "Those are your two little ones out there, right? Annie told me about them. Isabelle and Rachel, right?"

"Jah." He caught a glimpse of what she meant. "Nee, nee, leave them out of your writings, whatever they're called. They're kinner."

"Were you related to your wife?"

"What?"

"Were you blood relations?"

Perplexed Gabriel leaned forward and propped his elbows on his thighs. He studied his scarred, callused hands. He didn't want to think about Laura. Unbidden, her smiling face peeked at him from his mind's eye. The day of their wedding she'd never stopped smiling. She said her cheeks hurt from smiling so much. Their wedding night, she'd not only smiled, she'd giggled, and laughed aloud. He'd shushed her, sure his parents would hear. "We were third cousins. No shame there. It's allowed. It's common."

"Exactly. I'm not faulting you." She stared out at the children, her expression pensive. Isabelle plucked a flower from Rachel's plump fingers. The younger girl squawked and started to cry. Mary intervened, offering her a handful of dandelions. "Do you know what a recessive gene is?"

"We may not believe in a lot of book learning, but we're not stupid people." Gabriel knew where she was going. He and Laura had talked to doctors after Isabelle's condition became apparent. She'd been evaluated. They knew where they stood with her and they had been intent on helping her live a full life that blessed her and those around her. Catherine knew nothing of this. "My girls are fine."

"Isabelle and Rachel have Down's Syndrome." She softened her words with a gentle smile. "They're beautiful girls, Gabriel, don't get me wrong. They're precious."

A catch in her voice made him study her face. He saw longing there, not censure. "Rachel isn't…she's not…Isabelle yes, but not Rachel."

"You're in denial. Look at her face. They could be twins."

"It doesn't matter. It doesn't matter." Gabriel closed his eyes and pictured Rachel's almond shaped eyes and cherubic cheeks. He'd allowed himself to be blind to those features because he wanted a full life for his last born. Laura's last born. Isabelle and Rachel had their mother's eyes. They had her smile. But none of her unassuming intelligence. They would never follow recipes or measure a quarter teaspoon or understand how to operate the propane-powered wringer wash machine. They could never be trusted to give medicine to a small child or be left alone to care for a baby. "Both are gifts from God."

The words sounded weak in his ears. He cleared his throat. "They are blessings."

"I don't doubt that. You'll love them every bit as much as you love the rest of your children. You'll nurture them and watch over them. As you should. What I'm saying is the Amish only marry Amish. The districts are small, intentionally so."

Catherine sounded like a teacher now. Gabriel could barely remember his days in school. Only that they couldn't end quickly enough. He'd been ready for the fields. Ready to be a man. Ready to put schoolbooks and the things of children aside. He shook his head, trying to ward off the uneasy feeling he and Laura had done something wrong. That Catherine meant to say he was at fault for those little girls out there. For the way they were. Catherine's words droned on and he tried not to listen, but he had no choice.

"It becomes more and more difficult for a young man or woman to find an unrelated man or woman to marry. Did you know the Amish have one of the highest rates of mental retardation and dwarfism in any population in the United States? That comes from having such a small gene pool."

"So you want to put the girls in your paper as an example of why we shouldn't keep ourselves apart from the world?" Helen pushed through the screen door with her shoulder, a tray in her hands. "I'd say our treatment of these little ones shows the world how to be compassionate and loving."

"I don't want to show the world anything," Gabriel began, but Catherine cut him off.

"As an example of what happens when you don't open up to the world. But I'm not passing judgment."

"Jah, you are." Helen smacked the tray on the wicker table that separated the two rocking chairs. Lemonade sloshed over the edge of the pitcher and the glasses rattled. "You'd best move along, Catherine. You don't belong here."

"I'm letting people draw their own conclusions." Catherine looked distressed. She turned to Gabriel as if seeking his support. "I'm not saying you're doing anything wrong."

"The result is the same."

"You know, there are great programs in Wichita that could help children like Rachel and Isabelle reach their full potential." Catherine's voice took on a pleading tone. She cared. The thought hit Gabriel like a falling tree. Why did this Plain girl turned professor, turned Englischer, care? "Depending on the degree of disability, they can be educated, receive job training, work outside the home. They can even live independently in some cases. Some even marry."

"We educate our children." Helen intervened again. "We train them in our ways. Isabelle and Rachel will go to school with the other children. They'll learn to do chores, like the others do, to the best of their abilities. No one will ever tease them or make them feel stupid. They will be loved and never know anything but love."

Catherine kept her gaze on Gabriel. It drilled through to his core. "Don't you want your girls to have lives of their own someday?"

"I want them to have godly lives." He refused to let his gaze drop. How had he gotten into this conversation? He wanted out. "They will have godly lives surrounded by people who will take care of them."

"You think God wants them to live with you, be a burden to you until you die and someone else must step in to care for them?"

"They will never be burdens." He stopped. Why waste his breath arguing with a woman who had left their way of life? She'd lost any understanding of their world. He didn't need to defend himself or try to convince her. It wasn't his place. He stood. "Write whatever you want. I won't try to stop you. You know that."

He nodded at Helen, who nodded back and smiled at him as if showing her approval. He turned to walk down the steps.

"Because it's not your way," Catherine called out.

He looked back. "It's not our way."

Catherine's gaze drifted to the girls. Gabriel's followed. Both girls sat in the dirt, digging with spoons, and dumping soil in their laps.

"And they'll pay for that," Catherine said, her tone soft.

Isabelle's high-pitched giggle belied her words. Gabriel felt no need to respond. He kept walking.

The screen door slammed behind him. "Gabriel, wait," Annie's voice called after him. "Come meet the newest member of the Brennaman family. Lilah."

Gabriel turned to see Annie smiling. Helen crowded her, cooing over a newborn wrapped tightly in a small quilt. She had tears on her cheeks. Catherine stood. More tears. Babies were born in this community every day. Why were they so emotional? Women.

To his horror, his own throat tightened. He tried to swallow, but couldn't.

He breathed. *God, help me.* He turned and strode up the steps once again. The baby scrunched up her tiny, red, wrinkled face, and let out a wail far too loud for someone so small.

"She likes you." Annie laughed over the caterwauling. "You look like her daed."

"More likely my ugly mug scared her." He tugged his hat down so it would hide his face. "Tell Thomas...tell Thomas not to worry about the roof. I'll have the new shingles done before dark."

"Gabriel." Helen came to the edge of the porch. She hesitated. "Your lemonade."

"There's work to be done."

"Then I'll save you a glass for later."

Pondering the look on her face as she said those simple words, he walked faster, anxious to put yards between himself and all that womanly stuff on the porch.

Babies were born every day. Every day.

Chapter 18

Annie inhaled the scent of baby and leaned back in the rocking chair situated by the open windows in Emma and Thomas's living room. Lilah's head lolled against her shoulder. Her eyelids fluttered and she gave a sleepy, contented sigh. Annie knew how she felt. The quiet reigned, now that the children had been sent to do their chores. It had been a long day. Emma, tuckered out from labor, had finally agreed to sleep if Annie would care for Lilah for a few hours while Thomas oversaw the evening chores. It delighted Annie to be chosen for this task.

Her mind drifted back to Catherine's departure. They hadn't spoken of the argument at the bakery earlier in the day. Annie didn't know what to say to her sister. How to make her feel better. Catherine was wrong about so many things. So mired in her own loss, she couldn't see Annie too struggled to understand how God could take home the man she loved. She'd stepped out in faith with David, convinced their love would prevail. Only to have David get sick again, to have his cancer worsen, despite their prayers, and to have him slip away from her. She didn't allow herself to slide into the bitter morass that ate at Catherine because she'd promised David she wouldn't. And because she understood something Catherine did not. If she accepted the blessings in her life, did she not also have the responsibility to accept the hardships?

Her tiny brain didn't understand it all, but she would take it on faith that good things were yet to come.

She ran her hand over the baby's soft tufts of golden hair. It felt like baby duck down. Just like Noah's, her sweet boy. Her only boy. The thought made her want to weep. "Sweet girl, wait until you meet your cousin Noah. You'll be best of friends," she whispered. "Pretty, sweet girl. You look like your mama."

"A little early to tell, don't you think? Poor thing might have Thomas's chin."

She looked up at the sound of the husky voice with its playful tone.

"Isaac, I didn't see you there." She took a surreptitious swipe at her damp face. "I was talking to my new niece."

"They're nice at that age. They can't talk back." He strode across the room with an easy, long-legged stride, bringing with him the smell of sweat and earth. He leaned in for a better look. "I reckon pretty is in the eyes of the beholder. She looks like she hopped in a tub of water and stayed there too long."

"You'd look wrinkled and pruned too if you'd been through what she's been through today," Annie countered. He stood too close for comfort, towering over her. He would see her red eyes and wet cheeks. She shifted in the chair, looking for a way out. "Poor thing's tuckered out. I better put her in the cradle. She'll want her mudder soon. I expect my son is wondering where his mudder is too."

"Would it…I mean…could I…would it be all right if I held her, for a minute or two?"

In all the times Isaac had stopped into the bakery to pick up Mary Beth—why he felt it necessary to come in rather than waiting in the buggy, Annie didn't know—he'd never hesitated about anything. He seemed to think he knew everything there was to know about this world. He forecast rain. He suggested what kinds of cookies she should or shouldn't make. He recommended a new kind of soap for cleaning the floor. He had an opinion about everything under the sun. What was it about a tiny, sleepy baby that made him stutter and cast about for words?

"Of course."

"I'll try not to break her." A sudden grin stretching across his tanned face, he leaned down, then stopped. "What's the matter? Are you all right?"

"I'm fine. Why?"

"You look like you've been...well, crying."

"It's allergies. I've a bit of an allergy with dust and hay," she spoke hastily. She did have allergies. She'd never lie about such a thing. "It's worse in the summer."

Without acknowledging her explanation, Isaac took the baby from her arms and held her against his broad chest. He studied Lilah's face, then finally looked back at Annie. "They're so little, aren't they? You forget how small they start out."

"True, you do."

"I remember when Rachel was born." His gaze lurched away from hers. "She was a puny one, even smaller than this little sweet pea. Mudder called her the runt of the litter."

"Would you like to sit down?" Annie stood and moved away from the rocking chair. "You could rock her for a minute, if you like."

"You'd better take her." He shook his head and held out the bundle gingerly. "I'm such a big oaf, I might drop her or something."

"You're not going to break her." He handled the baby bundle as if he'd done it many times. That wasn't the problem. "Sit. I'll stay right here in case you lose your nerve."

The sadness in his face dissipated. "Gless men never lose their nerve." He smiled. Annie smiled back, at ease for the first time. Despite the rough edges, he had a soft center. "We muddle through, no matter what."

"I don't know what the problem is. You actually look like you know what you're doing."

"After Mudder died..." He stretched out his long legs and gazed out the living room windows, flooded with evening sun. "The girls had their aunts, it's true, but they needed their father. Daed was...he spent a lot of time in the fields. As a man should. He's not a talker, not much for touching, either. The younger ones were sort of lost."

"You stepped in."

"I helped some." His smooth cheeks ruddy, Isaac tucked Lilah's blanket around her with a practiced hand. "Some might not think it a man's place."

"Nee, you did what was needed." A knot formed in Annie's throat as she contemplated the role Isaac had been forced to take. He'd been willing to do it. A lesser man might have folded. Even his father bent, although none would fault him for it. He hadn't broken. "Some would think you were brave."

He made a sound somewhere between a snort and a growl, but didn't say anything for a few seconds. He rocked faster, the toes of his boots beating a rhythmic pattern against the braided throw rug under his feet. Unsure what to say or how to offer comfort if it was comfort that was needed, Annie waited in silence.

"I know we're supposed to accept death and move on," he said into the silence finally. The rocker creaked in protest under his solid frame. "Holding little Rachel made me feel…"

"Closer to your mudder."

"Jah."

"I know how that is. I lost my mudder and daed too."

"So you're muddling through like me."

"Like most people."

"Do you believe everything happens for a reason?" He set the rocker moving faster. "Even bad things?"

Annie thought of David and the pain that etched his thin, pale face at the end. She thought of his bald head, his cold fingers that gripped hers with surprising strength, even at the end. She thought of the way his hand fell away, finally, as he took his last breath. She thought of how alone she'd felt in that moment when his absence became a permanent void in her life. The same horrible, stubborn rebellion welled inside her that always came when she allowed herself to dwell on those memories for even a fleeting second. He had gone on ahead. He had left behind a broken world. They were only passing through. She knew all that. It didn't help. It took all her strength to beat back her rebellion, like an unbroken stallion that refused to be captured in a corral. She breathed. *God, forgive me.*

"Don't you believe it?" To her surprise, her voice didn't waver. Her tone didn't give her away. "Don't all Plain folks believe in God's plan?"

"What could God's plan be in taking the mother of a baby? The mother of eight kinner who weren't ready to be on their own without her?" An anger so like Annie's engulfed his words. He hadn't learned, even after three years, to corral the stallion. The thought gave Annie no comfort. How could she learn, if this man couldn't? "Nothing is the same anymore. Our family isn't the same."

His voice a hoarse whisper, he gazed at her, his pain swirling across his face. He looked so different from David. Tanned, healthy, his eyes a lighter, almost almond color, his shaggy brown hair hanging below his hat. He glowed with health and life, yet pain sought to douse that glow. "You lost your mudder and daed. How long did it take to bow down and accept it?"

"I didn't bow down. I kept putting one foot in front of the other." She'd moved forward, one step at a time, because life demanded it. She did the same with the loss of David. It took time. Time would heal the wound. Only time. "Every day, it got a little easier to bear. Our family changed too. But we're still a family. Families can change shape."

Suddenly light-headed, she eased into the chair across from him. The distance between them was far enough for propriety, but not so far that comfort couldn't be had. Something about his face and his voice, something about the way he held that newborn baby in his arms told her she could talk to him. "I lost my husband last year."

"I know."

He didn't offer empty words or condolences. She appreciated that. "David was a wise man, considering how young he was. He said we needed to take the time God gave us and use it to the best of our abilities. To step out in faith that He knows what He's doing. David said he wanted to spend whatever time we had together." She brushed at a stain on her apron, then forced herself to look at Isaac. He needed to know things would get better. It would get better, for both of them. "It turned out to be much shorter than either of us wanted. But it's all the more precious because it was so short."

"You wouldn't have chosen not to marry him if you knew how it would turn out?"

"Never. Never. That's the whole point of faith. You don't know how it's going to turn out." She tried to swallow the familiar, aching lump in her throat. It refused to go. "We had something. We had each other. And now there's Noah, my son. David's son."

"Jah, there's that." Isaac looked down at the sleeping baby, then back at her. "Who could regret this?"

"Just like your father doesn't regret marrying your mother." Annie didn't know that for a fact, but she saw the way Gabriel looked at his children. The same way Annie looked at Noah. With heartfelt gratitude and a sense of awe at the blessings they'd been given. "We have to be thankful for what we have and who we have in our lives and not demand to know why we can't have more."

His full lips turned up in a faint smile. "I'm trying."

"Your sister says you have a broken heart." Any other time Annie wouldn't have dared to raise the subject—or any other of such a personal nature—but something about this quiet moment shared only by the two of them made it possible for her to say the words. "Is that true?"

"Mary Elizabeth is a blabbermouth."

"No. She loves you. I knew that from the first day she worked with me."

"She's my sister." Lilah hiccupped a small cry. Isaac had forgotten to rock. He began again. The baby quieted. "It's not much of a stretch to say she loves me."

"She defended you. Not all sisters would." Annie saw that he hadn't answered her question. She let it go, as she would've wanted him to do for her. She wore her broken heart on her sleeve, but not everyone—especially men—chose to do so. "She said you were pushy because you wanted to help her have her dreams. I thought that was nice of her and of you."

"Did I need defending?"

"You were a little pushy."

"Me? Pushy?" He smiled, a sad, forlorn smile, but still, a smile. "Annie Plank, if I shine a flashlight in your window some night, will you do me the honor of taking a buggy ride with me?"

Annie froze. Had he heard nothing of what she'd said? She had loved David with every muscle and every bone in her body. "I…" She closed her mouth. Swallowed. "I don't…"

"Didn't you say you had to step out in faith?"

"I didn't mean…"

"You didn't mean with me."

"We've only met."

"Yet I've talked more to you in the last few minutes than I have to anyone the entire time I've been in Bliss Creek." Something in his voice forced her to meet his gaze. The smile was gone, replaced by an expression so mesmerizing she couldn't look away. "Come out with me, Annie Plank. Have a little faith…in me."

Much to Annie's relief, Lilah picked that moment to open her eyes and wail. At least, Annie thought it was relief.

Catherine's journal
July 6

    I don't know where to start. With the chasms. Or with the things that connect us. So much happened today. Emma gave birth to a healthy baby girl. I wasn't allowed in the house so I sat on the front porch like a pariah with leprosy, banished outside the walls of the village. I know why. I accept it. I don't want to cause them trouble. I only want to understand. How they can move on, move ahead, move beyond?

    I have the car and the fancy education and the cell phone and the laptop, but I'm the one who's stuck in the past. How did that happen? They move forward by the sheer force of habit. By sheer faith. I can't.

    If I had more faith, I would've insisted I be allowed to hold my niece. Surely the bishop wouldn't begrudge that. The Ordnung wouldn't speak to such a specific act, surely. I'm Emma's sister. That baby is my niece. My unwillingness to be yoked to their ways doesn't change that. Even Annie knows that. I can see it in her face. Helen's too. Even Gabriel Gless felt hardhearted in not allowing me to stay and hold the baby.

    Truth be told, I'm not sure I wanted to hold the baby. To hold Emma's baby would be so close to holding my own, it's more than I can bear to think about. Throughout the entire conversation with Gabriel, all I wanted to do was scream at him. Doesn't he know how blessed he is? Eight children? Two with Down's Syndrome, it's true, but they are beautiful and I would've loved them with every ounce of my being. How could God deny me that? Am I being punished?

    I look at these photos on my laptop. Little Isabelle and Rachel. Lillie and Mary—my sweet sisters. They didn't know their photos were being taken or they would've hidden their little faces. They look so much like Annie. Like me. I don't see Gabriel in Isabelle and Rachel so they must look like their mother. Except the almond shaped eyes and cherubic cheeks and stubby arms and legs give them away. These photos will be perfect for the thesis.

The thesis. Is it worth it? To take these pictures for a dry academic paper that only a handful of people will read? Is it worth it to further alienate a family already shunning me?

I can't say. I just know that this is the path I've taken. The life I've chosen.

It doesn't matter. This will be another chapter in my memoir. New memories to supplement the ones of my childhood. Nothing changes here. It's not allowed. I did the right thing, leaving here. Otherwise I'd be stuck in the nineteenth century too, with my buggy and my washboard and my woodstove. Scrubbing floors and hanging laundry on the line. People want to idolize this way of life. If they had to make every meal from scratch, make all their own clothes, grow vegetables in the garden, and can them in a kitchen with no air conditioning, they'd stop.

Or would they? No inane TV chatter. No celebrity gossip. No cell phones ringing in church. No email. No texts morning, noon, and night. Working close to the earth with people you care about. Knowing when you get up each day exactly what that day will hold. Reaping what you sow. The bounty of your labor. They are happy. I can see it in their faces. Whatever life brings them, they're happy. I forfeited that brand of happiness when I chose to leave here.

Maybe what I need is balance. Perspective. What I need is Dean. I'll call Dean and tell him I need him. He'll understand. He's the only one who understands.

Chapter 19

Raised voices greeted Annie when she finally pushed through the screen door and trotted into the house. Luke and Leah's voices. Annie slowed, torn between wanting to know what Leah would dare to argue with Luke about and knowing she shouldn't be listening. After the events of the day, starting with Catherine's visit to the bakery and then Emma's labor and delivery, and ending with Isaac's proposal that they take a buggy ride together, Annie felt numb with exhaustion. She could barely lift her feet, let alone face an argument between her brother and his wife.

Even after all these years of marriage, Leah hadn't learned her place. Or how to state her thoughts and opinions while still giving Luke the support he needed. As a woman, Annie could understand Leah's frustration, but she hated to see her brother constantly trying to placate a woman who didn't know when to stop arguing and let her man be the man. Annie liked to think of it as Plain diplomacy. That would've made David laugh. He laughed at all her daffy ideas. And then he told her he loved her. That was David.

Managing a smile at the thought, Annie trudged toward the stairs. The aroma of pot roast still lingered in the air, tempting her to head to the kitchen for a late supper. She hadn't been able to eat after her conversation with Isaac. She'd felt his gaze following her as she helped the girls put supper on the table. He hadn't pursued an answer to his question, but she could see it still lingering in his face every time he looked at her.

She was too tired to try to contemplate what her answer would've been had the baby not chosen that moment to wake up crying. Her stomach rumbled now, making her wish she'd tried harder to eat the ham, navy beans, and hot cornbread Abigail had served at the supper table, but the loud voices deterred her. She could wait until breakfast. Better to get up the stairs before they found her and decided she'd been eavesdropping on a private conversation.

Luke, an angry grimace plastered across his face, strode into the room before she could make it up two steps. He halted at the sight of her standing on the staircase, shoes in her hand. "How's Emma? The baby?" He slapped his hat on his head so hard it must've hurt. "I expected you home earlier—to let us know how things went."

"They're both doing fine. Didn't Mark tell you?"

"Just that the baby came. I sent him out to mend a fence. The hogs got out again today. We lost two of them. Looks like wolves."

No wonder he seemed so out of sorts.

"They named her Lilah. When Emma went into labor at the bakery, I thought we might have to help her deliver right there. It was a good thing Helen and Catherine were there."

"Catherine? What was Catherine doing there?"

"Just visiting. She drove us to the farm."

"Drove you to the farm. In a car?"

"Yes, Emma was in hard labor. We were afraid…"

"Did you ask Josiah? He could've taken her in a buggy."

Annie found it interesting that Mark hadn't filled Luke in on the details. Smart boy. "There wasn't time."

"*Ach.*" Luke slapped his hat against his dusty work pants. "We'll hear it now. I'm sure Micah already knows."

"We did what we thought was best. Catherine didn't go into the house. She didn't hold the baby, even. I felt mean, not letting her hold the baby."

"Nee. She shouldn't even have been there."

"Soon it won't matter. She'll go back to college, and we won't be here the next time she shows up." Leah marched into the room. She stuck her hand through the crook of Luke's arm. "I'm sorry, Luke. I didn't mean to argue..."

"We won't be here?" A chill raced up Annie's spine. The shoes dropped from her hands. "What do you mean, we won't..."

"Leave it be." He tromped past Annie and shoved open the screen door. "I'm checking on Mark. He needs to finish up. The sun is almost down and he'll be out of light soon. Don't wait up for me."

The screen door slammed.

"What was that all about?" Annie came back down the stairs. Leah's scowl melted away, replaced by trembling lips and scarlet cheeks. Annie had never seen her sister-in-law look so forlorn. "What is it?"

Leah plopped into the rocking chair and put her head in her hands. Her shoulders heaved.

"Leah? Leah!" Annie scurried across the room and laid a hand on Leah's shoulder. "Please, what is it?"

"Micah spoke to him today. He says we're to be one of the families that will move." Her words were muffled, but Annie got the gist of it. "The bishop wants him to lead a group to start a new district. It'll be us and Thomas and Emma. And four other families."

"Nee."

Leah raised a tear-stained face. "Jah."

"Is it because of the oil?"

"Jah. Thomas and his family are to go because of the oil. Micah fears there may be more. Besides, the rest of us can't make a living anymore here with our wheat, milo, and alfalfa. They think it'll be better in Missouri. Or maybe Oklahoma. There's been some talk of Arkansas, even. We don't know yet."

"Thomas didn't say a word."

"He may not know yet, with the baby coming today."

This news on the heels of the baby's birth. Joy married to pain. "Why only six families?"

"The ones who have businesses here can keep this district going. He says it's gotten too big, anyway. He says too many families make it harder. I always thought it made it easier. Easier to keep to ourselves and to help ourselves, to help each other."

What Leah said made sense. Her sister-in-law had given much thought to these things. Annie sank into the other rocking chair. "So that's why you were arguing with Luke? You know he will do what Micah asks. You don't think it's a good idea?"

"I don't know if it's a good idea. I'm only a wife and a mother, but I know how I feel. I know I don't want to go. I don't want to leave my family and friends." She lifted her apron and smothered a sob in it. "I don't want to leave my home. This is my home."

"If Luke must go, so must you." The words sounded harsh in Annie's ears, but the truth often was. "You won't be alone. You'll have Emma and Thomas and the others."

Cold comfort, Annie knew. Leah and Emma had never been close. Emma had struggled to come to terms with Luke and Leah moving into the Shirack home after their parents' deaths. The strife had been alleviated when Emma married Thomas and moved away.

Leah sniffed hard and wiped her nose with a hankie. "I know. I know." Her thin lips formed a stern line. "It's not right. Why us? Why can't it be the Yonkers or the Glicks?"

Annie had no answer to those questions. The bishop decided. That was that. She rocked for a few seconds, trying to absorb this news. "When?"

"Luke and Thomas are to make a trip up there next week, Monday or Tuesday, depending on when Michael Baldwin can drive them. They'll scout out the farm land that's for sale. Micah's been corresponding with another new community in that area. They say there's land to be had, the weather is decent, and they've been well received by the Englisch folks out there."

"I can't imagine living anywhere but here."

"You don't have to."

"What do you mean?"

"Micah says those with businesses that are supporting their families can stay. They want the community to continue with the families that can make it here."

Most months, the bakery paid for itself. Annie could stay.

Did she want to stay? Alone in this house with little Noah. She tried to imagine the rooms empty, without Mark, William, Joseph, little Esther and Martha, Jebediah. How strange it would be. Since Mark worked in the bakery, perhaps he could stay with her. Would that be fair to him? Would he want to stay? How would she keep up the garden? Who would farm the land without his help?

Josiah. Josiah would want that. He was a farmer at heart, as much as he'd embraced the blacksmith shop as a way of supporting his growing family.

Her mind raced ahead to all the changes they faced. Emma and Thomas would take Lillie and Mary, their little sisters. She wouldn't see them grow up. Trips during the holidays…that would be it. It wouldn't be the same. She relied on Emma. She needed Emma. Miriam was wrapped up in her husband and her kinner. She couldn't always make time. "What about Helen Crouch and her family?"

"Her brothers Tobias and Thaddeus are offering to go with Luke and Thomas on the scouting trip. They are chomping at the bit for a new start." Leah sounded tired and bitter. "Helen will have to decide whether to go or try to make it on her own with her jams and jellies and her produce."

Helen would be at home having the same thoughts and fears swirling around in her head as Annie. Maybe Helen would want to work in the bakery. Annie tried to imagine that. Helen, with her clumsy falls and her awkward way of talking to Englischers. Annie's head felt heavy. She could barely hold it up. Her arms and legs were drained of all energy. She closed her eyes.

"I'd better get myself up to bed." She stood. "I'm sorry I wasn't here to put Noah to bed."

"Noah went to bed without a peep tonight."

She sank back into the chair at the implied criticism in Leah's words. "No fussing?"

"None."

"How did you do it?" A spurt of something ugly and mean ran through her like a snake slithering after its prey. Jealousy. Leah could make Noah do something his own mother couldn't get him to do. Sleep. "I've been trying for months. What did you do?"

"I didn't do anything."

"You must've done something. Did you rock him first?" Annie wanted to grab the words back and soften them. Too much excitement and too little sleep made her cranky. "Did you give him a cup of milk? A snack?"

"Nothing." Leah's thin lips curled up in a half-formed smile. "I relaxed."

"I don't know what you mean."

"You're so tied up in knots when it's time to put him to bed, and he feels it. He gets all tied up in those same knots."

"So it's my fault he won't go to sleep." Of course it was her fault. She didn't have much experience and no mother to show her how to do it right. *Stop it. Stop wallowing. God, help me look forward instead of backward.* "I make it so he can't fall asleep?"

"Not intentionally." Leah stretched and cranked her neck from side to side. Her bones made little popping sounds. "He feels your sadness and your grief and all those bottled-up feelings you have inside you. Let them go and he'll sleep fine. You'll sleep fine. You know, you need to find yourself a husband. That will solve your problems at home and at the bakery. Why, you won't even miss us at all."

"I…I…" Annie sputtered. "I don't think…"

"Goodnight." Leah stood and trudged to the staircase. "I'll check on the babies on my way to bed. You go to sleep. You look all done in."

Leah might be older. She might be married to Luke and the mother of five children, but she didn't know everything. She didn't know when or if it was time for Annie to marry again.

Sleep. Annie could sleep now. David had left her. Now the rest of her family would do the same. She stood, feeling like an old woman, and went to the kitchen. Noah might be able to sleep now, but she might never sleep again.

Chapter 20

Gabriel ladled another scoop of potato salad onto his plate, his mouth watering. Despite having eaten a helping of everything on the picnic table in Thomas's yard already, Gabriel had to have one more serving of the potato salad. A few more bites wouldn't hurt, especially since all his pants had grown too big around his waist since the move from Indiana. For the first time in a long while, he had an appetite. Watching the kinner play volleyball, eating good food, and not thinking about the future for a few hours proved to be a balm to his cranky heart.

Still, the celebration of the arrival of Lilah Brennaman was muted by the silent acknowledgment that these gatherings would soon be a thing of the past. The knowledge that Thomas and Luke would set out for Missouri the next day hung over the farm like a thick, scratchy wool blanket donned in the scorching heat of midsummer. Gabriel wanted to go with them, but he wouldn't. Let them determine a course of action and then, if he still felt it necessary, he would tell his children of the change in plans. Only then. Let them enjoy this new place for now.

"You like the potato salad?"

He glanced up at the now-familiar voice. Helen Crouch. He'd figured she'd be here. Still, he looked around, uncomfortable. Everyone else already had seats near the volleyball net so they could watch the children play. No way for him to avoid a conversation with this woman.

"It's real *gut*." He stuck the serving spoon back into the greatly reduced mound. "It has something different in it. Did you make it?"

"I did. It's a recipe I copied from a magazine from the library." She looked pleased with herself. "It has dijon mustard and dill weed in it. I'm glad you like it."

"Jah." He couldn't for the life of him think of anything else to say.

"Your boys are good volleyball players." She nodded toward the good-natured game punctuated by gales of laughter and teasing shouts. "The girls too."

"We used to play all the time back home—back in Indiana." He grabbed his glass of cold tea and backed away from the table. "With so many kids, we can almost make our own two teams."

"George—my husband—was a big believer in playing games. He liked baseball the best, but he was pretty good at volleyball. We played a lot before we were married and even after."

"Not anymore?" He didn't mean for it to sound like a challenge, but it came out that way. "I mean, *you* don't play anymore. George—your husband—"

"I will if you will." Her impish grin made her look ten years younger. Gabriel could almost imagine what she must've looked like as a schoolgirl. "I used to be pretty good."

A challenge that couldn't be ignored, it seemed. Why not? Everything was about to change for these people. They could take a moment to have fun together, as a community. Why not, indeed?

Still grinning, Helen rushed onto the field and yelled to her daughter Naomi that she would take her place. Gabriel had no choice but to put his plate on the table and follow. He squeezed in between Isaac and Seth in the back row and prepared to make a fool of himself. He hadn't played in years. Many years.

"Here goes." Helen hoisted the ball in the air and smacked it over the net with an overhand serve that sent Gabriel reeling back trying to keep the ball in front of him. Helen clapped and crowed. "I still have it!"

"Whoa!" Gabriel raised both hands to knock it back and missed entirely. He stumbled, nearly lost his balance, and grabbed Isaac's shoulder to steady himself. "And I don't."

The kids roared with laughter. He joined them. "Ball's all yours." He trotted to the sidelines, scooped it up, and tossed it back to her. "I didn't know the girls' team had a secret weapon."

"We can still come back," Seth cried. "Come on, Daed, get ready!"

It didn't take long to see that Seth's optimism had no grounds in reality. If Helen was clumsy in social situations, she proved to be completely the opposite behind a volleyball net. She smacked the ball with great enthusiasm, dove for it, and rushed about congratulating her teammates when they made good hits. Out of practice, Gabriel could only laugh at his own awkward attempts to keep up with his boys, who humored him by letting him get an occasional hit.

"You need to practice, Gabriel Gless," Helen called to him, her face red with exertion, her kapp askew, and her apron spotted with grass stains. "Your boys are making you look bad."

Gabriel popped the ball into the air and smacked it over the net. Mary Elizabeth met the volley with a neat pop that set the ball up for Helen to return it. Despite her short stature, she managed to spike the ball right back.

"Nice!" Isaac did his best to keep the ball from hitting the ground, but to no avail. "Game!"

"Okay, that's it. I've had enough," Gabriel admitted breathlessly. "I'm old and out of shape."

"Giving up already?" Helen clapped her hands, then put them on her knees and heaved a big breath. "Good. I'm done in too, if I were to admit it."

"You were good, Mudder." Naomi patted her mother on the back. "For a mudder."

Everyone laughed, Helen the loudest.

"I need my glass of tea." Gabriel returned her smile without thinking. She smiled back, the picture of health and contentment. She looked happy. She looked...pretty. Gabriel took another quick breath. "And that potato salad you made."

"Worked up a powerful hunger, did you?" She fell into step next to him. "That was fun. I haven't had that much fun since...since I don't remember when."

"Me neither," he conceded. "It's a good way to spend a Sunday afternoon. Playing with the kinner."

"Makes for good memories."

She didn't say it, but he knew what the rest of the thought was. They both knew how important it was to make good memories. Because tomorrow things would change and the loved ones who'd played in that volleyball game might not be there for another game. Whether they were forced to move by circumstances beyond their control or because they were called home by God. When had he become aware of his own beating heart? So aware of the sound of his own breath? When had he stopped taking for granted the hugs and kisses of his little ones? *Laura.*

"It does." He cleared his throat. "Can't have too many of those."

"No, you sure can't." She straightened her kapp, dabbed at her sweaty face with a crumpled handkerchief, and then brushed ineffectually at the stains on her apron. She seemed a jumble of motion. "If my daed were here, he'd say I should act my age, but I'd tell him I am. Acting my age, I mean."

"He wouldn't approve of you playing?"

"He worried about what others might think."

"You don't?"

"I'm trying to do better."

"It shows. You seem a little less..."

"Doplich?" She smiled as if to show no offense had been taken.

"Less nervous."

She cocked her head and picked up her glass from the picnic table. "I'm trying," she said again. "I feel..."

"Mudder, Mudder, I fell out of the tree. I hurt my finger." Her daughter Ginny darted toward them, holding her hand against her chest. "I think I broke it."

"Out of the tree? What were you doing in the tree, child? You're a girl, not a squirrel." Helen examined the girl's hand. "You probably need to put some ice on it."

She looked up at Gabriel, a curious expression on her damp face. "It's nice to have ice around the house, even if it is a break from the old ways. I'd best tend to her."

"Take care of her." He nodded back, not sure why she felt she owed him an explanation. Was that a jab at him, who'd moved his family here because the district had a stricter Ordnung? Clinging to a traditional way of life kept them from the way of the world. He didn't have to apologize for that. "Good game, all things considered."

"Good game." The uncertain Helen disappeared again. She grinned like a teenager. "For an older man."

Older. Whom was she calling older? She took her daughter's hand and trotted toward the house.

Still feeling out of breath—and not from playing the game—he took his time with his plate and his glass. Helen Crouch reminded him of the salamanders he used to see at home. Changing colors with the landscape, camouflaging themselves. They wanted to protect themselves so they changed in order to blend in. He never knew which Helen would appear. There was challenge in that. And mystery. *Ridiculous.* He looked around to make sure he hadn't said the word aloud. Loneliness had given him mush for brains.

Still giving himself a silent tongue lashing, he joined the other adults in a row of lawn chairs under a row of massive oaks. No one commented on the game or his participation, for which he felt grateful. Someone brought up the unseasonably nice weather. Luke mentioned a wolf sighting. The women chattered about a quilting frolic they would have next week. Everyone avoided giving voice to what occupied their minds. Would this be the last time they all sat together under these trees?

A nice breeze ruffled his beard. The smell of fresh cut hay mingled with barbecued brisket. They accepted their lot. That was what it came down to. No sense in talking about what they couldn't change. He needed to accept his lot, and in doing so, he felt almost at peace. Almost. If Laura were sitting in the chair next to him, chattering on about something the boys had said or done, that would have made the picture complete. He had to stop doing that. Imagining her in every scene in his life. Now, he had to stop.

He let his gaze roam. Thomas had both elbows on his knees, deep in conversation with Luke. Planning their trip? He couldn't tell from his seat.

Babies on each of their hips, Miriam and Annie replenished the dishes at the picnic table and giggled about something while Emma sat in a chair, little Lilah in her arms. Leah sat on the porch rocking Jebediah, who had been fussing since company arrived. Gabriel looked down at the neatly bandaged cut on his hand. Since the day Helen had wrapped it for him, he'd been confused whenever he thought about her. Why, he didn't know. Something about her soft touch had unnerved him and he didn't like it. At least that was what he kept telling himself.

Better to think on other things. The house was ready. They would move in within the week, most likely. Then he could focus on the shop and getting his business up and running. If it was successful and things improved in this community, maybe he wouldn't have to think about moving his family yet again. He didn't want to face that possibility. *Please, God, if it is Your will, let this be home.*

"Is this seat taken?"

Gabriel looked up from his reverie to find Bethel Graber, Leah's sister, standing over him, a plate of peach pie in one hand and a glass of iced tea in the other. She wore a wide, dimpled smile, something he'd yet to see on Leah's face.

"Nee."

She sank into the chair next to him with a contented sigh. "Some mighty deep thoughts you were having, I reckon."

"Hmm?"

"I asked you twice before you even looked up." Bethel gave him a quizzical look. "I thought maybe you were sleeping with your eyes open."

"Now that would be a trick." He shifted in the chair, sat his glass on the ground next to it, and settled back. "No deep thoughts. I don't sleep very well, eyes open or closed."

"New place, new surroundings."

He would let her believe that was the problem. "You're Leah's sister?"

"Jah, and I'll be Seth's teacher come the end of August." She took a big bite of pie and chewed, a blissful look on her face. "Annie's outdone herself, as usual."

"You help with the kinner in the summer too, Leah and Annie's little ones?"

"I do. I enjoy all of them very much. It's hard for Annie, but she makes the best of it, all things considered."

"I reckon that's what we're all called to do." Bethel looked to be in her early twenties. He wondered why she hadn't married. Working as a schoolteacher was an honorable calling, but the look on her face when she talked of caring for Noah and the other bobbeli told Gabriel she wanted more. "I figure it's pointless to try to figure it all out. My gnat-sized brain can't do it."

"Still, it's hard to understand." She set aside her plate. "David was a good man and a good husband. He'd have been a good father."

"Hard to understand." He stopped. He didn't know her. Didn't know Annie's husband. How had they moved to this topic so quickly? He gave her a sideways glance, realized she was doing the same, and returned his gaze to the volleyball game where his three oldest sons, along with Mark and Mary Beth, proceeded to make mincemeat out of the rest of the Shirack and Brennaman children.

"I didn't mean to be forward."

"It's all right." He stood and looked at her full face for the first time.

She had blue eyes, wheat-colored hair, smooth skin, and an easy smile. Nothing like Leah in looks or attitude. And she looked at him with a direct gaze that seem to hide nothing. "I best make sure my little ones aren't getting into trouble."

She nodded and smiled. "It was nice talking to you."

Something about her tone seemed to hold an invitation. He whirled and nearly stumbled in his haste to get away. After three years he should be ready for this, but he couldn't quite get a handle on how to start. He was too old for flashlights and buggy rides. True, the older boys and girls were old enough to watch over the little ones if he left the house after dark. But it had never occurred to him to do so. He strode toward the house, pausing only long enough to ask if Emma or Annie had seen Abigail and the little girls.

"I saw them headed toward the barn earlier. I think she was going to show them the new batch of kittens." Annie brushed Caleb's hand from the plate of brownies. "Nee, little one, you've had enough sweets for one day. You'll give yourself a tummy-ache."

Gabriel headed for the barn. He trusted Abigail to watch the girls, but she should have some fun too. She was sixteen and her rum-springa should've started a few months earlier, but in the move and the upheaval she'd said very little about it. She took far more responsibility for the household than did Mary Beth, who was only two years younger. Time for them to switch places for a few hours. And it gave him an excuse to get away from the social tomfoolery he couldn't make heads or tails out of.

He pushed open the barn door and peered inside. Light streamed through the loft overhead. "Abigail?"

She sat on a bale of hay. Edmond Crouch sat next to her.

"Abigail!"

"Daed." She rose hastily. Edmond did the same. "I was just...we were just..."

"Where are the girls?"

"Right there, right there in the last stall, playing with the new kittens."

Anger burned through him, a hot, writhing curtain of fire that took his breath away. "You best get back there and make sure they're all right. Now." He let his gaze bore into Edmond. "I don't want to see you anywhere near my daughter."

"Daed, we were just talking…"

"Hush. Get the girls."

Her face flushed, she gave him an imploring look but brushed past Edmond without another word.

Edmond stared at the ground, his neck and face a mottled red. "I didn't mean any disrespect."

"Stay away from Abigail."

"But I…"

"I won't have her passing time with a boy who drinks and goes to jail."

"I've been forgiven."

"Not by me, you haven't."

"Who does that make worse?" A high, tight, angry voice made him turn around. Helen Crouch stood behind him, her face as red as her son's. "Edmond, go hitch the horse to the buggy. It's time to go."

"Mudder…"

"Go."

His expression mutinous, Edmond stomped past Gabriel, squeezed around his mother, and left the barn. Gabriel stared at Helen, waiting to see what she would do next. Would she contradict his words? Dare she?

"Begging your pardon for my son. I reckon he knows better than to pass the time alone—well, almost alone—with a young girl in the barn." Her chin lifted. "The others things…well, I hope you'll find it in your heart to forgive him for them as well."

Nonplussed by her soft tone and conciliatory words, Gabriel's anger fizzled. "It's hard to find a happy medium, isn't it? Abigail is in her rumspringa as well, but she's been so busy helping with the little ones, she hasn't had time to do the things a girl her age…wants to be doing."

"A happy medium would be good." Helen's gaze dropped and her hand came up to her throat. Her cheeks were pink. "If you ever need help with the little girls, I'd be happy to watch them. They're so sweet at that age and mine are quite a bit older now."

"It's kind of you to offer, but there's no need." His words sounded stiff in his own ears. Her hand fluttered and her gaze hardened. Gabriel hastened to clarify. "Between Abigail and Mary Elizabeth, they're fine."

"I heard Mary Elizabeth is working at the bakery."

"That's true. Still, we're fine."

"You don't want them influenced by the loose morals of the Crouch family." Helen offered the words as a whispered statement, not a question. "You're letting first impressions…"

"We don't need the help."

"You don't need *my* help." She whirled around to leave. Her skirt caught on a nail head sticking out along the edge of the barn door. Material ripped. "*Ach*, no!"

She grabbed the skirt tight and rushed away, still murmuring to herself.

Gabriel could only watch as she went. Why did he insist on ruffling her feathers? Why couldn't he accept that her son's drunken buggy ride had been a simple mistake that wouldn't be repeated?

Because his children's lives and their futures in this district were in his hands and he couldn't afford to take any chances. He didn't want to have to move them again. Edmond couldn't be allowed to spend time with Abigail, and Gabriel couldn't afford to soften his heart toward Helen. It simply couldn't be done.

❦

Annie stretched her aching shoulders and back, then eased into the lawn chair. Noah had finally succumbed to a much-needed nap. It wouldn't last more than an hour at the most, but she intended to enjoy every minute of it. At fourteen months he was toddling about now, getting into anything and everything. His last exploration had involved dumping a sack of flour on the floor and then rolling around in it. She craned her neck side to side. He was getting heavy too. Especially when he threw himself backward in her arms, bawling and trying his mightiest to escape being taken to his crib.

She reached for the glass of tea she'd deposited on the ground next to her chair. At least she could watch a little of the volleyball game before it was time to return to her motherly duties. The dishes were washed and the leftovers packed up to be shared among the guests when they were ready to leave. The Gless boys had the upper hand in the game. At least she thought they did. No one kept score, which made it difficult to tell. But the chortles and high-pitched whoops told her where the game stood. She closed her eyes for a second, enjoying a slight breeze that picked up the leaves on the boughs overhead and dropped them back into place.

"Whoa, whoops!"

Something—or someone—kicked Annie in the leg. She opened her eyes in time to see Isaac do a wild two-step trying to avoid her chair. His arms flailed. He managed to deflect to one side, but his hip crashed into her, knocking her sideways. She dropped the glass and tried to catch herself, but over she went. She landed in the grass with an ungraceful plop. The ball bounced next to her head and rolled away.

Isaac zigzagged and managed not to sprawl on top of her. Annie covered her face with both hands for a second. Her skin felt hot to the touch. Embarrassment raced through her like a raging flame feeding on a stack of old *Budget* newspapers.

"Sorry! I'm sorry!" Isaac popped back to his feet. Panting, he leaned over her, his tall frame blocking the sun. "Are you all right?"

"Annie, are you okay?" Miriam knelt, squeezing between her and Isaac. She glanced up at the man "I'll take care of her."

"It's okay. I'm fine." Annie sat up, ignoring the hand Miriam held out. She tried to stifle the urge to giggle, but it burbled out anyway. Miriam started to grin, then she giggled. In a second they were both laughing. Miriam laughed so hard she snorted, a sound that made them both laugh more.

Isaac stood there, a look of confusion mixed with concern on his handsome face.

"Nice play!" Annie smiled up at him. She sucked in air, trying to catch a breath, winded more from laughing than from the unexpected fall. Isaac's face turned an even darker shade of red, if that were possible. "I thought you were playing volleyball, not football. And I wasn't even playing. I'm just a poor bystander."

"Or bysitter, as the case may be," Miriam chimed in. They both began laughing all over again. "I think that's what they call out-of-bounds."

Isaac opened his mouth, then closed it.

"What's the matter, cat got your tongue?" Miriam asked. She picked up the ball and tossed it back on the field where Mark chortled and grabbed it. Miriam glanced at Annie, then back at Isaac. Her grin grew. "Isaac? Isaac, can you hear me?"

"Jah, jah, I hear you." He still didn't take his gaze from Annie.

Feeling too exposed, Annie decided the teasing had gone far enough. She was a grown woman, after all. A woman with a child. Luke and Leah wouldn't be happy if they noticed her sprawled on the ground in front of Isaac Gless.

She sat up and dusted her hands off, then smoothed her skirt around her ankles. She tried to look as if she were settling in, there on the ground, as if she was perfectly accustomed to people nearly running her over. "You missed." She spoke evenly, without all the unnecessary mirth. "Our team wins."

"Your team? And who's keeping score?" He picked up his hat from the ground and settled it on his head. His hand shook. Why was it shaking? From fear he'd hurt her? Surely not. His smile had returned, but something about it seemed more tentative. "We didn't lose. Nobody loses in these games."

"Unless you're the team with fewer points. The game's over."

She pointed toward the field. The clapping had stopped. The other folks had viewed Isaac's sprint to the sidelines, saw that he missed, and gone back to their visiting. His brothers and sisters were already angling to start a new game.

"Annie's right. You lose," Miriam added. "Are you a sore loser?"

"Forget it. They can win if it makes you happy." He held out a hand to Annie. She looked up at him, all the frivolity gone. The question he'd asked her the day of Lilah's birth floated to the surface, as it had done every hour since despite her best efforts to quash it. The question she'd failed to answer. So far he hadn't shone that flashlight in her window. Maybe he'd changed his mind. Maybe her failure to answer his question had served as all the answer he needed. He offered her a hand up, nothing more. She took it. His big hand swallowed hers. It felt callused, like the hand of a man who worked hard. Those calluses told her so much about him. He would be a good provider. A good husband and father.

"I'm sorry I knocked you over." He sounded breathless even though he'd been standing there long enough for his breathing to return to normal after his mad dash. "I got carried away with the game. I like to play hard, in case you haven't noticed."

"I noticed. You play hard like you work hard. No harm done."

She allowed him to pull her to her feet. He lifted her up as if she were light as a feather. True, she'd lost some weight in the last year. Her dresses hung on her, but she lacked the incentive to take in the seams. Did Isaac like the way her dresses looked on her thin body? Probably not. The thought made her cheeks burn. She shouldn't be thinking of these things. Better she wear a flour sack. She tugged her hand from his and tried to steady her breath. One would think she had been playing volleyball and running about like a wild man.

"At least let me get you a fresh glass of tea." He seemed to be studying her face. For some reason, he grinned. He had a sweet smile, white, even teeth, full lips. "You've spilled yours."

"You mean you've spilled it." Glad to think about something so simple as spilled tea, Annie shook her finger at him. "All your fault. Your team lost, you knocked me over, and you spilled the tea. You're a regular bull in the kitchen."

"I'll refill the tea." With an expression that could only be described as pleased, Miriam looked from Annie to Isaac. She took the glasses from Isaac's hands. "For both of you."

Isaac waited until she walked away, then he turned back to Annie.

"You have dirt on your dress. I guess I made more laundry for you too." He picked up her chair and sat it upright. "Do you want to try to clean up?"

"Danki." Grateful to get off legs that were shaking for no apparent reason, she sank into the chair. Another simple topic she could handle—laundry. "Nee. No point. Grass stains don't come out. I can try to bleach the tea stains, but they probably won't come out either."

He squatted on his heels next to her. "So I owe you a new dress."

"Nee." She ran her finger over the wet, brown spots. "The apron will cover it. They're good for that."

"I thought they were for the little kinner to wipe their noses on."

"Isaac!"

He could make her laugh. David had not been one for silliness or games. Maybe it was the Hodgkins. She tried to remember if he had told jokes before he got sick. Sadness curled its tendrils around her heart. She couldn't remember. She couldn't remember what his laugh sounded like. Did that mean his memories would one day stop intruding in moments such as this when she tried to move forward with life? Or when life attempted to pull her kicking and screaming into her new future? Did she have to forget him in order to go on with her life? She didn't want to do that. She couldn't do that. For Noah's sake, she had to remember.

Isaac let one knee come forward and kneeled so close to her chair, she could smell his woodsy, salty scent and see the droplets of perspiration on the back of his neck. "You never answered my question." He leaned toward her, his expression holding a tenderness that surprised her. She'd forgotten what that looked like too. A man's tenderness directed at her. He had a longing there that she recognized. The longing she felt to be close to someone, to be special to someone.

She tried to breathe through the pain the thought brought her. "I don't..."

"Here's the tea." Miriam rushed at them, a glass in each hand. "How about cookies. Anyone want cookies?"

She glanced from Isaac to Annie and back again, her expression almost gleeful. Annie shook her head. If a conversation were to be had, it had to be between Isaac and her only. Miriam backed away. "Then I'll just get some for me. I think I saw brownies. I love brownies."

Annie heard her voice trailing away, but she couldn't help herself. Her gaze had already returned to Isaac's. The ferocity of his tenderness held her, alarmed her, yet told her something she wasn't sure she was ready to hear.

"If I show up at your doorstep, will you come out?" He kept his voice low, gruff, barely above a whisper. "Or will you leave me sitting out there all by myself? All alone?"

Her hand fluttered to her neck. She tilted her head, contemplating, imagining that scene in her head. She saw his buggy parked in front of her home. She saw the glow of the flashlight dancing on the wall in the living room. She saw herself moving toward the door. Surely, she would open the door. She heard the sound of a baby crying. She stopped.

"I don't know," she whispered.

"If you don't know, who does?"

Her heart pounding so hard in her chest, she was sure he could hear it, Annie jerked from the chair. It tumbled back. Isaac scrambled to his feet. He picked up the chair without taking his gaze from hers. "What are you so afraid of?" He leaned forward, his voice barely above a whisper. The others were so engrossed in their conversations, they didn't seem to notice.

"I need to check on Noah. He's been napping too long," she stammered. Since when did he make her stammer? No man had ever made her stutter. Not even David. "If I don't get him up now, he won't sleep tonight."

Determined to escape his riveting gaze, she tried to bolt around him. He stepped in her path.

She took two steps back, aware that Emma and Leah, engaged in conversation in the chair swing hanging from the tree a few yards away, had both stopped talking. She shook her head slightly at Emma's questioning look. Emma nodded, but her gaze remained on Isaac.

Annie had to end this before Leah caught on. She looked up at him. "Don't ask me that now, please."

"Annie." Pain, surely it was pain, imbued the two syllables that formed her name. "Annie."

"I don't know."

He deserved an answer, she knew that, but she couldn't find it in her heart to give him one. Not at this moment, not on this day. She picked up her skirt with both hands, whipped around him, and fled into the house.

Chapter 21

Annie folded the pants on which she had finished letting down the hem and stuck them in the mending basket that sat at her feet. Exhausted, she let her hands drop into her lap. Her eyes burned and her fingers ached from holding the needle too long. The silence of the evening told her everyone in the house had turned in for the night. One pole lantern illuminated the small area in the living room allowing her to see to sew. Everything else had been turned off to conserve fuel. The breeze that came through the open windows did nothing to cool her face. She should go to bed. Instead, she sat, not moving, contemplating the day. Despite Luke's pending absence hanging over them and the reason for it—moving to another state—it had been a good Sunday.

The family gathering with the volleyball and the visiting had been fun. She enjoyed holding the new baby and chatting with Miriam and Helen. She enjoyed watching the kinner play volleyball. Truth be told, she especially enjoyed watching the Gless men play. They looked so much alike, all tall, sturdy, and strong. They smacked the ball around like they knew what they were doing. Especially Isaac, who kept looking over at her as if to see if she were taking note of his ability to send the ball soaring over the net.

The girls didn't stand a chance. Until Helen played. She showed them not all girls were puny players. Isaac took it in stride, laughing as hard as the rest. Each time the ball rolled her way he loped over to pick it up, gave her a wink and a grin, and strode back to the field where he and his brother Seth had set up a lovely spike that sent the girls dashing out of its way. It'd been fun, even when he'd nearly run over her on the sidelines. Miriam insisted it had been intentional. But Miriam saw what she wanted to see. Annie shoved aside the question he'd asked her. She had no answer. Better to savor the good time they'd had up until he'd asked that question. The question she didn't want to think about.

After all, when would they have that much fun again? She wished David had been there to see it. David. *Ach*, David. When would she stop seeking to fill her new memories with past ones? She sighed, knowing it was time to plod up the stairs and face her empty bed. In the last year, she'd taken to staying up later and later out of sheer cowardice. *Go on, get up.* Get going up those stairs. Monday would come early, with Luke's departure and the bakery to open. Mondays always required so much more baking to get ready for the coming week. She'd darn one more sock and turn in. One more pair of socks. The boys were so hard on their socks…

A glowing circle of light danced on the wall in front of her. "What?" she spoke aloud despite being alone in the living room. She turned and craned her head over the back of the sofa. The light traveled across the room, striking all the familiar objects, the rocking chair, the table. A dawning realization brought with it a feeling of dread mixed with something else, something like…anticipation. Anticipation and pleasure danced with dread and a certainty that she couldn't, she *shouldn't,* think of anyone but David. She dropped the sock back in the basket, rose on trembling legs, and went to the window.

A buggy was parked by the porch. Isaac Gless stood on the steps, flashlight in hand. The light floated, then hit her square in the eyes. "*Ach.*" She shielded them with her hand, then pulled open the door. "What are you doing?"

Silly question. She knew what he was doing.

"You didn't know the answer to the question, so I decided to help you figure it out. I've come calling."

It couldn't be any clearer than that. Annie hesitated, hand on the door. She tried to sort through her feelings. They were all topsy-turvy. A sense of delight mixed with a deep, dark hands-around-her-throat feeling that she couldn't betray David. Not like this. She had married David. In her heart, she still felt married. *God, God, how can I do this? How can I let him go?*

"Come out with me. We'll take a ride down by the creek. Now that the sun is going down it's not so hot."

"It's late," she stammered. "Luke's leaving in the morning, and I have the bakery to open. Mondays are very busy. I was just going to…"

"A short buggy ride." He held out his hand as if to take hers. "I promise."

I promise. Like David had promised to love her and honor her for the rest of their lives. Such a short life. Annie slid through the door and closed it behind her. Despite the muggy July heat, a chill ran through her. She hugged her arms to her middle. Isaac's hand dropped. She couldn't see his expression in the dark behind the flashlight's glow.

"Turn off the flashlight, please."

He complied. In the gathering dusk, his white teeth glinted in a smile. "Hop in, we'll take a spin." He offered his hand again. "Then we'll both have our answer."

"I can't. I have to get up early in the morning."

"You mentioned that. Is that really the reason you won't go, or is it because you don't find me…suitable?"

Suitable. She couldn't help herself. She giggled. "Suitable? I don't think suitable is what a girl wants when a beau comes calling." She stopped. Heat burned her cheeks and neck. "Not that I think of you as a beau, I mean, I…"

"You find this funny? Women are lucky." His hand dropped and he shook his head, a painful expression on his rugged face. "They don't have to take the first step. They don't have to be the ones who get rejected."

"I'm not rejecting you." She couldn't find it in her heart to send him away, knowing as she did how hard it truly was for a man to get up the nerve to come calling on a woman who might turn up her nose or not even come to the door at all. She trotted down the steps and stopped in front of him. "I hardly know you."

"Then get to know me. They say there's no time like the present."

"I don't know…"

"What don't you know? If you could like me? Give me a chance."

"I do like you." Annie stopped, startled by her own admission. The heat on her cheeks and neck deepened to a searing broil. The truth often sallies forth without a person knowing it. The feelings gave credence to the words. "I mean, I think I could…you know…like you."

She did like him. *Lord, how did that happen?*

"Then come for a ride with me." The note of pleading in his low voice reduced Annie's reservations to ashes. She felt soft, through and through. Something about his cadence had that effect on her. She'd felt it in the bakery, the first day when he'd teased her into giving him a fresh, hot cookie. She'd felt it when she watched him hold baby Lilah. As much as she didn't want to admit it, she felt it now.

David's face flashed in her mind. His dark eyes, filled with emotion as he said his vows. His delighted smile when he held Noah in his arms the day their son was born.

No.

No, no.

She simply didn't want to be mean. How could she be so mean as to turn away a man who, as he said, had put everything on the line, to come here and ask a girl for a simple thing? A buggy ride.

She swallowed the knot in her throat. "But Noah."

"Noah sleeps through the night, doesn't he?"

"Not often."

"Your brother's fraa is here."

"Leah's here."

He held his hand out yet again. "Let me help you up."

With his help, she climbed in. His hand, hard and callused, gripped hers with almost painful strength. His touch set her hands to shaking. No matter, they matched the trembling of her legs. She sank onto the buggy seat. He let go. With relief—it had to be relief—she clasped her fingers together in a white-knuckled grip and thanked God Isaac hadn't asked her to take a walk. She'd have fallen flat on her face in a knock-kneed tribute to her own fear.

"That wasn't so bad." Isaac picked up the reins, made a clucking sound, and guided the buggy away from the house. "Not so bad at all."

For whom, Annie wanted to ask.

She stayed quiet, fearful her voice would give her away. After a second, she recognized the hitch in his low voice for what it was. Nerves. He took a deep breath and exhaled.

"Not so bad? Then why are you sweating?" She couldn't let him get away with sounding so smug. To her relief, she sounded just like she did when she asked him if he wanted a cookie on his almost-daily visits to the bakery. No nerves in her voice. "Don't tell me it's the heat of summer in Kansas that's turning you into one big puddle."

"Nice. Good of you to point that out." He didn't sound the least put-out. "Moving right along. Let's talk about something besides my ability to sweat at the drop of a hat."

"What do you want to talk about?" She gazed out at the passing fields, reminding herself periodically to breathe. This was a bad idea. A very bad idea. "Maybe you should start."

"Should I tell you a joke? Would that make you feel better?"

"What makes you think I don't feel well?"

"You look like you could heave any second."

"Wouldn't that be lovely?" It might be true but he didn't have to point it out. "Maybe supper disagreed with me."

"You didn't eat supper."

He'd been watching her. The thought unnerved her more.

He tugged the reins until the buggy slowed to a snail's pace and turned his head toward her. "I know this is hard for you. I watch my daed struggle every day to move on. I know it's time for him to do it. All of us know it. I think he even knows it. But his heart has to get to where his head is. So does yours. Is it there yet?"

"I don't know." Stupid answer. Isaac's assessment of his daed's state of mind was very knowing. His question merited a thoughtful response. "Sometimes I think so, and then I think it's just that I'm so lonely and I'm tired and I'm not sure I can raise Noah to be the man he deserves to be without a husband at my side."

"A time will come when you can think of your husband without being sad."

"I can't imagine that time."

"But it will come." Isaac clucked and set the buggy in motion again. "I'm counting on it. And I will be there when that time does come."

His declaration sent her mind reeling again. Her hands clenched tighter. She tried to breathe, but her throat felt so constricted. "I think I should go home now," she whispered, unable to get enough air to speak more loudly. "Please take me home."

Isaac didn't answer, but he guided the buggy in a slow, careful turn.

"Danki."

"I didn't mean to upset you. I like you, Annie."

"You didn't upset me." She managed to raise her head and meet his sideways gaze. "I think I like you too."

The surprise—and the fear—in that realization would keep her up for nights to come.

"And that scares you."

"Jah."

"It scares me too."

"Really?"

"Why do you think I'm sweating so much?"

He grinned then, a smile that took her breath away once again, this time in that kind of fell swoop that makes a woman's stomach drop right down to her knees, knocks her feet out from under her, and sends her flying through the starry night.

She'd been sure she'd never feel that way again. She didn't want to feel like that again. Look how it had ended the first time.

They didn't talk anymore on the road back to the house, but the silence teemed with unspoken words.

Isaac halted the buggy in front of the steps. Annie hopped down before he had a chance to come around and help her. "Annie…"

She turned and faced him. "Give me some time. Don't come back for a while."

"I won't come back until you give me leave." He doffed his hat in a jerky motion. "Just don't make me wait too long."

He drove away. Annie stood on the porch, watching him go, and wondering what would happen if she did, indeed, make him wait too long.

To her surprise, she didn't want to find out.

Catherine's journal
July 30

It's almost daybreak and here I sit on my bed, laptop in front
of me, sleepless, exhausted, but so keyed up it's impossible to lay
my head on my pillow. Another odd night in a row of many
odd nights. My mind keeps going round and round, thinking
about Emma's new baby and Helen's assessment of my life and
Gabriel Gless's sad face when he looked at those little girls. So
many images I can't get out of my head. I can't even decide what
approach to take to my thesis. I haven't written a word of the
memoir. A rough draft of the manuscript is due in three months
and I haven't written anything new since I arrived here. Just
these journal entries, fragmented notes, fragmented feelings,
fragmented sentences. Too many new memories crowd the old
ones or awaken things I didn't remember before, memories I'd
hidden under rocks and behind stone walls.

I couldn't sleep so I drove out in the country with the windows down and the breeze cooling my face. I could smell the
alfalfa in the fields and hear the bullfrogs singing. Memories
flooded through the windows, nearly taking my breath away.
I drove up the road that leads to a pond on the Glicks' farm. I
wanted to take a walk, wear myself out, and I remembered that
place as being so quiet and peaceful.

Not anymore.

I parked along the road and decided to walk to where
it dead ends into the pond. The stars were out and a nearly
full moon lit up the sky. I had a flashlight in the glove com-
partment, so I grabbed it and decided to throw caution to the
winds. How often did I get to take a stroll on a moonlit night
in Wichita? Never.

As I got closer to the pond, I could hear unexpected sounds.
I slowed, surprised, a little scared. Then I realized it was kids
talking and laughing. The high-pitched chatter of girls mixed
with the lower voices of boys trying to sound older than they

were. They weren't trying to be quiet. I guess they figured no one would be around at that time of night. In their world, everyone goes to bed when it gets dark. No electricity. No TV. No reason to stay up. I knew then this was one of those running-around parties I'd missed in my youth. Back when I thought I would never leave my faith or my community. There were cars mixed with buggies. The burning ends of cigarettes bobbed in the night air like fireflies. The music swelled and died away, an old George Strait song about Amarillo.

Let them have their fun, I thought. It would end soon enough. Most of them would choose to be baptized. They'd pick their life's mate at the age of nineteen or twenty and spend the rest of their lives in hard labor and parenting. And what's more, they would like it. They deserved this little bit of what others would call a normal life. I started to turn back, but the engine of a car rumbled behind me and headlights flashed in my eyes. After a minute I could see it was an old beat-up car with rust on the sides and gray paint in swatches along the doors. Edmond Crouch peered out the window at me. Edmond Crouch driving a car. I nearly fell over.

He looked up at me. We stared at each other. He seemed as speechless as I felt. One of Gabriel Gless's daughters was in the seat next to him. It took me a minute to pull her name from the recesses of the things I'd learned since arriving in Bliss Creek for this visit. A visit that's seeming less and less like a good idea.

Abigail. Her name was Abigail.

Helen Crouch's son had already had so much trouble with the buggy ride and the DUI. What was he doing out here in the middle of the night? Not my problem. Without speaking, I turned and started walking toward my car.

He called my name.

I wavered. Mosquitoes buzzed my head. Even at eleven o'clock at night, the heat sweltered around me and sweat ran down between my shoulder blades. The muggy air coated my face in droplets of perspiration that trickled down my temples.

Let it go, Edmond, I won't tell anyone, I wanted to say. But I didn't. I turned back. He said something to the girl. She argued softly with him, but after a second, she slid from the car and trotted up the lane toward the others.

He asked me to get in. Of course I didn't. No one in her right mind would get in a car driven by a sixteen-year-old Amish boy. Still, it was almost comical how proud he was of the car. I asked how he could drive a car after what had happened with the buggy. He said he wasn't allowed to drive a buggy during his probation, but they never said anything about a car.

They didn't think they'd have to tell an Amish boy not to drive a car. Naïve of them.

Edmond called the car a classic. He and some of the other boys had pooled their money to buy it off an Englisch farmer who no longer had need of it. They keep it hidden behind an abandoned barn on the Stoltz property. He told me all about it as if recognizing that confession is good for the soul. Or because he thinks that since I left the community, I'm a kindred spirit. I thought of Mudder and Daed and how they died. He assured me they never take the car on the highway. They don't have licenses and the car isn't registered. So they haven't completely gone around the bend.

If things were different, he'd be just another kid learning to drive, a rite of passage for most sixteen-year-olds. But things aren't different. He has no one to show him. No one willing to show him. He learns by doing.

His hands smoothing the wheel underneath them in a movement almost like a caress, he asks me the question. He looks up at me the picture of innocence on his whiskerless face. His skin shines white in the light of the moon. He looks so earnest and so young. He and his friends think driving a car without a license and smoking make them English. I don't have the heart to tell him those things only make them young and stupid, a universal, but not irreversible, condition.

I take out my camera and ask him if I may take his picture. He considers. It will be evidence of the depth of his running-around. By the same token, it is his running-around. He grins and nods. I snap the shots of his face shining through the open car window. He gets out and leans against it. Snap. Snap. *We walk down the road to the others. They consider my question, talk among themselves, then nod at me. I take pictures of them laughing and talking. They seem like average teenagers. And they are, for the most part. Less worldly, no doubt. They want to think they're doing something rebellious and out of line, but most of them will go no further. They won't cross lines Englisch teenagers cross every day. Most of them will turn their backs on this phase of their lives, choose their faith, be baptized, and go on to be good Plain folks. Like my parents and my sisters and brothers. They're good kids.*

Edmond wants me to take him back to Wichita with me when I go.

The exception to the rule. Like me.

How can I help him into a life like mine?

Of course I tell him no. Under no circumstances. He's only sixteen. I urge him to talk to Josiah about what it was like to be apart from family, living in a big city at such a young age. He claims he has. I doubt Josiah intended for Edmond to find his stories to be like notes from the Pied Piper's flute, luring him to a fate he can't begin to imagine.

How could I tell him? When the excitement dies away, what's left is an excruciating loneliness. A sense of desolation. A longing for something familiar. An aching loss. He'll long for the smell of fry pies cooking and the clatter of the dishes in the tub and the familiar sound of the hymns from the Ausbund. *He'll want the taste of fresh milk on his tongue and the feel of crackling hay between his fingers. It'll all be gone, lost in the cacophony of the traffic and the spewing fumes of the buses and the taste of metallic, bitter convenience store coffee.*

The look on his face. It seemed so familiar. Like a memory etched on my brain. It was the look I had on my face when I gazed into the tiny, cracked mirror Emma held in her hand on my wedding day. That horrified realization that I had allowed myself to become trapped. I'd awakened in someone else's skin and somehow had to find my way out.

Edmond's only sixteen. He's not of age.

Taking him away would only compound my sins in the eyes of my family and this community.

He's not old enough to make this decision.

He's only sixteen.

Yet, I see his face in my mind's eye and I wonder: How can I leave him here?

No wonder I can't sleep.

Chapter 22

A steaming cup of kaffi in one hand, Helen opened the front door. The night sky had just begun to lighten with the impending dawn. Another day. The beginning of another week. Tobias, his face lined and tired, stood on the porch. It could've been Daed standing there were there a little more gray in the beard. Despite the early hour, her oldest brother had a sheen of sweat on his face. His shirt looked damp around the collar. "We're on our way, then."

She studied his weary face and then looked beyond him. A dusty brown minivan stood in the driveway. Thaddeus and Thomas waved at her from the backseats. She returned the gesture. "You're off. To Missouri."

He nodded.

"Safe trip, then."

"If you need anything, Peter will come by. His fraa can help you with Mudder when you go into town. My fraa can help you with the canning and the jelly making."

That Tobias even knew how she spent her days surprised her. His awkward attempt to offer her encouragement surprised her more. He'd never been much for talk about feelings—of affection or otherwise. "We'll be fine."

"We'll find a new home for our community in Missouri, schwe-schder. It will be better for all of us there. You'll see. You'd best start thinking about moving too."

Helen eased the full cup onto a table next to the door. She carefully considered her brother's words and his tone. Did he mean to say she had a choice? She was thirty-six years old, a widow with four children. But her brother, six years her senior, was the head of the family. In her lifetime, she'd rarely had the opportunity to make her own choices. Only George. George had been her choice.

"Helen, do you hear me?"

"I've been thinking about it."

She had. About how she didn't want to leave this house with its smooth wood floors and the spot where wax from a candle had burned the linoleum in the kitchen. And the place on the porch where Ginny had dumped a bottle of bleach, leaving a huge white spot. The place behind the corral where they'd buried Chipmunk, a silly dog who'd made their front yard his home without so much as a by-your-leave. She stared at the spot where the oak tree had stood, now a mere stump. Like her life. Stunted.

"Good."

"I want to stay here." She blurted it out. She'd meant to wait until he returned, until she heard all about what it was like in Missouri. Instead, the words tumbled out. "This is our home."

Tobias swiveled and glanced back at the van. "We don't have time to talk about it now. Just know that you can't make it here on your own. Eggs and jams and canned vegetables and pickles aren't enough. That's the whole point of this move. A fresh start. Better opportuni-ties for our families."

"Is this about Edmond? Because if it is, he's doing better."

"It's not about Edmond." Tobias scuffed a boot against the porch as if to remove mud from the sole. "It's about making sure we stay together. As a family."

"We can't move Mudder. This is her home even more than ours."

Helen had a flash, an image, of her mother stumbling about in the dark, even in the brightest sunlight, lost in a strange new house. "She knows her way around here. She'd be lost."

"We'll talk about it when we get back." Tobias's voice grew gruffer with each word. He cleared his throat. "Our brothers and me, we'll talk and we'll figure it out."

"Jah. We will." He wouldn't catch her meaning, but Helen didn't care. She'd been on her own a long time. She'd earned a voice in this decision. "When you get back."

"Tell Edmond I said there's a huge chunk of fence down on the back side of the pasture." Tobias's expression lightened. He was back on solid ground. "He'd best get over there and mend it. When he puts the horses out to graze they'll wander off."

"I'll tell him."

Tobias glanced at the sky. "It'll be light soon. He should get up and get moving before he has to go to the blacksmith shop."

"I'll tell him."

"Tell him I said he'd best stay out of trouble."

"I'll tell him, Tobias."

He shifted from one foot to the other. "Well, then."

It was the best he could do. From years of experience, Helen knew how to read into his words, to unearth the unspoken ones between the lines. "Take care. Come home soon."

"That's the plan."

He turned away, a big hulk of a man made in the image of her father, who'd taken his leave only a few months earlier. Only Daed would not be returning. The thought made tears well in her eyes as she watched Tobias lumber down the steps, his boots making a *clump, clump* sound on the wood.

Thomas and Thaddeus were waiting for Tobias to join them. Helen waved at them both. She'd have to stop by Emma's and make sure she was doing all right with the new baby. It must be salt in an open wound for Thomas to have to go with a new baby at home. But women took care of the babies. He knew Emma would be fine without him. That's what women did.

Inside, she trotted up the stairs, Tobias's words still ringing in her ears. Edmond would have to step up and do more work, both here and at the farm Tobias and Peter shared with their brother Thaddeus. Emma would need help too, although Helen had no doubt that Josiah and Gabriel would make sure she lacked nothing. All those Gless boys seemed to be good workers and good-natured. Unlike their prickly, dark-eyed father with his long legs and know-it-all opinions.

Stop it.

At Edmond's door, she paused and lifted her hand to knock. No sound filtered through the door. "Edmond, Edmond, time to get up." She opened the door and peered through the dusky dawn. "Edmond, Tobias says the fence is down again…"

She blinked, sure the darkness played tricks on her eyes.

No Edmond.

His bed stood empty, the covers as neatly arranged as they had been the previous day.

Edmond wasn't asleep in his bed. So where was he?

⌐⌐

Annie stood on the porch, watching Luke shove a scruffy duffel bag into the back of the minivan parked in front of their house. Dawn hadn't quite arrived yet and the air felt damp on her cheeks. She inhaled the smell of exhaust mixed with the scent of the roses on the porch trellis. Nausea roiled in her stomach. This scouting trip would lead to other trips until one day they'd be loading furniture into a moving van and leaving for good. *Don't think about it. Don't think about it.* She didn't dare think about it. She had to be strong for Leah. Her sister-in-law bustled in and out of the house, bringing this and that, little things she was sure Luke would need on this trip, all the while murmuring to herself.

"We're not going for a month," Luke finally said, exasperation written across his weather-beaten face. He grabbed his fraa's arm. "Stop."

Annie had to turn away at the emotion in Leah's face. She slipped down the steps and walked around the van. It was big, big enough to carry five men and their baggage all the way to Missouri and back.

"We'll be fine." Thomas popped out of the open door. "Don't worry."

"I'm not worried. Worrying is a sin."

"It is." He fixed her with that levelheaded stare that always reminded her of her daed. "Still, it's human."

"I think Leah has enough worry for both of us." She peeked around the van. Luke had his arm around his wife. They huddled together on the porch, Luke talking to her in a low voice. Annie averted her eyes. "I need to be strong for her."

"Could I ask you to do something for me too?"

"Of course."

"Help Emma." His voice sounded hoarse. He wasn't so steady after all. "She has the new baby and Caleb. Gabriel and his kinner are moving into their house tomorrow so she won't have them to feed, but she won't have them around to help, either."

"I'll help her. Don't you worry."

"You have so much on your plate with the bakery and Noah. Leah will need you. I hate to ask."

"Leah has her sister. Rebecca, Eli, and the twins will help Emma. We'll all be fine." She forced a smile. "Like Luke says, you won't be gone that long. You know Gabriel will help too. He doesn't strike me as someone who'll abandon his friends."

"Nee. He's a good man." Thomas lifted his hat, resettled it. The whites of his eyes were crisscrossed with red lines. The pouches under them were dark. Another person who hadn't slept. "So is Isaac."

"Thomas!"

He smiled. "I'm only saying."

"Don't."

"I won't, then." He turned and smacked a hand on the roof of the van. "We need to be off, Luke. We still have to stop for Silas. At this rate, we won't get to Missouri until next week."

Luke clattered down the steps. Leah remained where she was on the porch, her hands gripping the edges of her apron as if she were afraid it would blow away.

"Have a good trip." Annie gave her brother a quick hug. "Come home as soon as you can."

"Help out my fraa, will you?"

"I will."

To her surprise, Luke held onto her for another moment in a bear hug that took the air from her lungs. "It'll be fine. You'll see."

He let go and gave her a grin. He was actually looking forward to this new venture. She could see it in his face. Startled, she nodded. "It'll be fine."

"We'll be back in five or six days, tops."

"Safe travels."

He waved, folded himself into the middle seat of the van, and pulled the sliding door shut. The van took off, spitting gravel and dust at them. Neither Thomas nor Luke looked back or waved.

Annie stood next to Leah on the porch, watching until the van's tail-lights disappeared into the darkness. Even when Leah went inside, letting the screen door slam behind her, Annie found she couldn't move.

It'll be fine.

Chapter 23

Despite the early hour, the hot sun beat down on Helen's prayer kapp. Sweat formed on her neck and rolled under her collar as she slowed the buggy and brought it to a stop in front of Josiah's blacksmith shop. She hopped down and tied the reins to the hitching post. All the way into town she'd contemplated what she would say. She'd come here first in hopes of finding Edmond working and not where she was afraid he'd been during the night. Rumspringa or not, she'd have a word with him. Her mind made up, she marched across the sidewalk, flung open the door, and entered. "Edmond!"

Josiah looked up from the shoe he was hammering onto the hoof of a very large chestnut horse. "Easy, girl, easy," he said. To the horse, Helen assumed. He glared at her. "Do you mind? Easy, now. My fraa prefers I come home in one piece, what with the crops in the field and the colicky baby."

"Sorry." She eased the door shut with a gentle tug. "I'm looking for Edmond."

"Give me a minute to finish up."

She glanced around the long, narrow room with its collection of tools and horseshoes and the row of stalls, currently empty. No Edmond. Her stomach roiled. "But…"

"Just a minute. I'd rather not get fed my teeth for breakfast."

She gripped her hands so tightly in front of her she could feel her fingernails digging into her skin, but she nodded and waited while he popped in the last two nails, examined his work, and then let the horse's leg drop. He smoothed the animal's rump, making murmuring noises as he moved to the front and then patted its long, graceful neck. "That's a good girl. All done."

Turning to Helen, he pulled off a leather apron and hung it on a hook next to the rows of all sizes of horseshoes and leather tack. "I'm done here. Walk with me to the bakery so I can get me a couple of fry pies, will you?"

"Didn't you have breakfast?"

"My fraa does the best she can." He wiped his hands on a towel and gestured for her to go first through the door. "I've never seen so much sickness."

"The baby or her?"

"Her. Much more than the first time."

It was the most he would say about Miriam's condition, but Helen gathered what he was getting at. Morning sickness that lasted morning, noon, and night. She'd experienced it with Betsy. Or was it Ginny?

"Tell me where Edmond is. Do you know? Why isn't he working?"

"Whoa." He held up a mammoth, callused hand. "I sent him home. You just missed him. I'm surprised you didn't pass him on the road."

"Why? Why did you send him home?"

"He hadn't slept. I could tell it from the wrinkled clothes and the bloodshot eyes." Josiah looked both ways, paused for a car to pass, and then started across the street. "I don't need him burning himself or nailing a shoe to his hand—or worse yet, getting trampled—because he's too tired to think straight."

"I thought you were going to talk to him." Helen scrambled to keep up with Josiah's long stride. She didn't really mean to blame the man for her son's misbehavior. "I mean, Micah thought you might…"

"That Edmond might learn from my mistakes?" Josiah snorted. "You're his mudder. Do you really think children learn from the mistakes of others? I know I didn't. Did you?"

Helen's rumspringa had been singularly boring. She hadn't done one thing, not one thing that would've bothered her parents—not even embarrassed them a little. She'd always been proud of that. Now she wondered if she'd missed the whole point.

"Where was he?"

"What do you mean?"

"You know what I mean. Last night."

Josiah glanced at her sidelong. He clomped along the sidewalk to the bakery, walking as if he needed that fry pie right now or he might die of hunger.

"Josiah."

"I didn't agree to be a tattletale. Edmond trusts me to keep quiet about the things he tells me. Otherwise he'll stop talking to me."

Helen gritted her teeth and fought for control. Josiah opened the bakery door for her. She exhaled and went through it.

"Helen! I'm so glad to see you. I imagine you're as worried as I am." Annie came around the counter, wiping her hands on a towel. "Oh, Josiah, I didn't see you there. Is everything all right? How's Miriam? What can I get you?"

Josiah held up his hand to stem the flow of his sister's chatter. "Miriam's fine. I'm fine. A dozen fry pies. Surprise me with the flavors, why don't you?"

Her face wrinkled in puzzlement, Annie glanced at Helen. "What are you two doing together at the crack of dawn?"

"Dawn has long passed." Josiah poured himself a cup of kaffi from the thermos Annie kept on top of the long glass counter. "I've already shod a horse this morning."

"And I've made six dozen haystacks for Mrs. Carmichael," Annie countered. "What is going on?"

"It's Edmond. He didn't come home last night." Helen blurted it out. She felt the heat that billowed from her skin. Now her neck would be all blotchy. "I came to see if he was at work. Which he's not because your brother sent him home and he won't tell me where he was all night."

"He took Abigail for a buggy ride." Annie smiled as if her words would placate. "They stayed out longer than they should, but then that happens when two young people are running around at the same time."

"Longer than they should…how do you know this?"

Annie cocked her head toward the back of the bakery. "Mary Elizabeth. She's in the storeroom unpacking the spices that came on Friday. She seemed a little frazzled this morning so I asked her if something was wrong. She said she heard Abigail come in right before it was time to get up. Abigail barely had time to change and wash up before she had to help Emma get breakfast."

"This is awful. This is *awful*." Helen sank onto the bench next to the front door below a sign that read *Sweets Waiting Room. The wait will be worth it.* "She's sure she was with Edmond?"

"She said Abigail told her so. She said they took a picnic down to the pond on our property and went fishing." Annie's expression grew far away, as if remembering something. Something sweet. Or bittersweet. "Stayed up all night talking. Just talking."

"Gabriel forbade Abigail to see him."

"She's running around."

"With someone her father doesn't wish her to see."

"A sticky situation."

"I've got to go home and talk to him. I've got to set him straight."

"Nee." Annie and Josiah spoke at the same time.

"What do you mean, no?"

"What Edmond does during his running-around is his business. That's the way it works."

"Emma and Luke came for you when you were in Wichita," Helen pointed out to Josiah. "They brought you back."

"Because my parents died." Josiah said the words without emotion, but Helen saw the pain flicker in his eyes. She regretted bringing it up, but he forged on without pause. "I chose to come back. Then I left again. Idiot that I was. But I had to find out for myself. I had to make my mistakes before I could come back and know this was where I wanted to be. Just be glad Edmond has taken up with a Plain girl and not an Englischer."

"Sarah was Mennonite," Annie said, as if to absolve Joshua of a little of the guilt written across his face. "And she did pursue you."

"I let her. Like I said, I was an idiot. I lost so much time with Miriam…" Joshua set his empty cup on the counter. "I have to get back to work."

"Gabriel Gless doesn't want his daughter seeing my son."

"Like you, Gabriel needs to let go. Let them be. Let them find their way. That's what we do. That's why we have this running-around period." Josiah tipped his hat at his sister. "Thanks for the kaffi and the fry pies. How much do I owe you?"

"Get out of here!" Annie gave him a look of mock horror. "Like I'd charge my own brother."

"You're a good schweschder."

Annie's expression faltered. "You said goodbye to Luke?"

"I'll stop at the house tonight, make sure Mark gets the chores done." Josiah picked up the bag of pastries. "You've given him the week off here?"

"Jah. He'll be busy at the farm."

"You need help here…"

"I'll be fine."

"If you need deliveries made, send Mary Elizabeth to tell me."

Helen watched the exchange, ashamed of the tendrils of envy that tried to wrap themselves around her throat, like weeds threatening to snuff out roses. The Shirack brothers and sisters had a bond like few other families. Still, she'd been blessed to have her parents so much longer than they had. She had no right to feel anything but blessed.

"You want to make a point with Edmond?"

It took Helen a second to realize Josiah was now talking to her. "Jah. I do."

"Go roust him from bed and make him work. He'll be dragging, but he'll get the message that he can't stay out all night and if does, he's still expected to carry his weight."

"All right."

"And stop looking so worried." Josiah pulled the door open and paused halfway through it. "We all survived our rumspringas. So will he."

Not if Gabriel Gless found out.

Chapter 24

Gabriel hopped onto the back of the wagon and wedged himself between the sofa and the table that lay on its side. Sweat rolled down his face and trickled onto his shirt collar. He swiped at his cheek with his sleeve. Whose crazy idea had it been to move in late July? Oh, yes. His. He needed the fresh start now. Not later. To top it off, he'd waited until Thomas and Luke were gone to Missouri. Two sets of hands he could've used this morning. No matter. He didn't want to impose on Emma any longer. She had her own hands full, what with her husband out of town. She didn't need to cook and clean for his brood.

"Give me a hand with the sofa," he called to Isaac, who loped down the steps of their new home with the energy of a much younger man. Gabriel longed for that energy. One good night's sleep might produce it. At this rate he would never know, such were the tossings and turnings of his nights. "Once we get it out, it'll be easier to move the table and chairs."

"Everything is covered with dust and straw from having been in Thomas's barn." Streaks of sweat had made tracks in the dust on Isaac's face, attesting to the truth of his statement. "The girls can get busy wiping everything down."

The girls were in a tizzy over the new kitchen, a bit larger than the one they'd had back home—back in Indiana, Gabriel mentally corrected himself. Bliss Creek was their home now. He liked seeing them excited about a kitchen. It meant they had their priorities straight in a world where it could be easy to lose sight of them. They'd cleaned and mopped and dusted and waxed until the inside of the house shone. The boys had freshened the paint on the outside, straightened shutters, repaired the steps, and generally polished the outside. The place looked neat and clean, as it should. Now to make it their home.

"I'd be happy to help."

At the sound of Helen's voice, Gabriel let his end of the sofa drop back onto the wagon. Helen trotted up the road from the cluster of buggies parked by the corral fence. She carried a large pie—pecan from the looks of it—and her children were following her. Including Edmond.

She apparently hadn't understood their conversation Sunday afternoon. He didn't want her son anywhere near his daughter.

"What are you…"

"Hey!" Isaac objected from his position on the ground with half the sofa hanging on his shoulder. "This is heavy!"

"Right." Gabriel stooped to pick up his share of the weight. He focused on the job at hand, hefting the sofa to the ground, and then scrambling down himself. "You want to go backward or forward?"

"Backward," Isaac said, the picture of youthful assurance. "Tilt it so it'll fit through the door frame."

"I'll just take this to the kitchen," Helen called after him. "Edmond can help with moving the furniture and the girls will help unpack the dishes."

"*Gut*," he managed.

Helen nodded but didn't move. She stood there, watching them manhandle the sofa. It was heavier than he remembered. At this point he saw no alternative but to be thankful for the help she offered. He would keep an eye on Edmond himself. And with so many people showing up to help, there would be no possibility of the young ones trying to sneak off on their own. Besides, Abigail knew better, especially after the talking-to he'd given her Sunday night.

Not to mention it wouldn't be neighborly of him to reject her help. And they were going to be neighbors now. The Murphy place bordered the Daugherty homestead. Close quarters in the country. He and Isaac shoved the sofa against the far wall in the living room, both of them grunting at the same time. "That should do it," Isaac said, and sat down on it. "I don't remember it weighing so much."

"Me neither."

He should, though. The sofa was the only piece of furniture he and Laura bought after their marriage. Everything else had been made by his daed and her Onkel Obediah, who ran a carpentry shop in Dahlburg. They'd picked out the sofa at a discount furniture warehouse not long before Isaac was born. Really, Laura had picked it out. She liked the sturdy wood frame children could climb on and not hurt. She liked the dark blue fabric that wouldn't show stains from little hands and feet. He liked it too, but for different reasons. It brought out the blue in her eyes when she sat on it, sewing in the evenings or reading letters from her family back east in Pennsylvania.

"That's where you want it?" Helen stopped in the doorway, the pie still in her hands, her nose wrinkled. "In that spot?"

"What?"

His response sounded gruffer than he'd intended, but he didn't see any way to soften it now.

"It's just…are you sure that's where you want it?" She took a tentative step forward. "It's so far from the fireplace."

"And?"

Another step.

"I'm just imagining…when it gets cold. Aren't you going to want it situated in front of the fireplace?" She craned her head to one side as if picturing Gabriel and Isaac sitting before a blazing fire on a cold winter night. Instead of gasping and sweating as they moved furniture on a blazing July day. "Otherwise your feet and hands are going to be mighty cold."

"Well."

Gabriel thought it over. He looked at Isaac, who shrugged and stood. Together, they hoisted the sofa again and moved it several feet so that it faced the fireplace mantel.

"Back a little farther so you have room for the table. You'll want room to put a rug under it. Rugs will make the room seem cozy and are warmer than the wood floor." She sat the pie on the mantel and pointed to a spot. "You have long legs; you'll want to give yourself plenty of room."

"You are a bit bossy, aren't you?" The words were out of his mouth before Gabriel could stop them. Isaac guffawed. Gabriel gave his son a stern look. Isaac stifled the sound and shoved the sofa back a few more inches. Gabriel managed to make eye contact with Helen. "Good advice, though."

"A woman's touch is what makes a house a home." She smiled, giving her round face the same softness he'd noticed at the Brennaman house. "Everyone knows that."

"I reckon you're right." Bethel Graber popped into the room. She carried a pie. A pecan pie just like the one Helen held. "I brought pie and my brothers. We'll have you settled in no time."

The two women looked at each other. Then at Gabriel.

"Emma says pecan is your favorite, Gabriel," Bethel said, a big smile on her face. Her blue eyes sparkled with something—he couldn't be sure what. "I made two. Leah has the other one."

"I like pecan all right." Gabriel managed to get the sentence out. Once again, he felt like a schoolboy. Only thing was he didn't know why. It was just pie, wasn't it? He looked from Bethel to Helen and back. "I like pie in general."

Isaac guffawed. This time he didn't try to stifle it, even when Gabriel gave him a blistering look.

Helen's cheeks burned. With the pie in her hands, she couldn't cover them. She marched into the kitchen and set it on the counter next to a platter of brownies, a chocolate-frosted cake, and half a dozen loaves of bread. The prep table held casseroles and sandwiches and other goodies. The Gless girls wouldn't have to do any cooking for several days while they got settled in their new home. They didn't need her help. Why she'd felt compelled to come here, she couldn't imagine. Yes, she could. It was the neighborly thing to do. She had to forgive Gabriel for his attitude toward Edmond. He was only trying to be a good father by protecting his daughter from untoward influences. Even if he thought her son represented the untoward influences.

Her talk with Edmond on the previous day had yielded little. His expression morose, he'd done her bidding, rising from his bed and stalking from the house to tend to the fields. She'd also done her best to convince him he couldn't continue to pass the time with Abigail, but his expression said he had no intention of changing his behavior. None.

This morning she'd drilled him before leaving home about his conduct during this move. Their purpose consisted solely in helping their new neighbors move in, to be neighborly. That's what she wanted Gabriel Gless to see. That she knew their responsibility to help make the Gless family feel welcome in this community. Edmond would work and nothing more. Gabriel would see that her son could behave himself. No little chats in the corner. No running into the kitchen to seek a glass of iced tea. Just work. His sullen face did nothing to convince her he planned to do as she told him.

Helen sighed and looked down at the pie in her hands. It had been a peace offering, but now she saw that it could be construed as something else. What with Bethel Graber prancing around with her pecan pie.

"Do you want to work on the kitchen or help the girls set up the bedrooms?" Bethel, the picture of friendliness as always, bustled into the room. "Gabriel says they want to get the beds made up so the little girls can take naps after dinner."

"I'll unpack in here so they'll be able to make sandwiches and such." Helen did her best to sound equally friendly. She'd always liked Bethel. She taught her scholars well, and the children flocked to her whenever they saw her. "You go ahead upstairs."

After the other woman disappeared through the doorway, Helen surveyed the room. Like most Plain folks, the Glesses owned a great number of kitchen utensils, necessary for baking and cooking for their large broods, and for the moment they were all in boxes. Best get started.

"Helen, can I ask you a question?"

She nearly jumped out of her skin, only realizing Isaac Gless stood behind her at the sound of his voice. She turned around. "I thought I'd help your sisters unpack the dishes and the pots and pans."

"They can use your help. We have more stuff than I remember." He moved through the doorway. "I wanted to ask you something. It's… of a private nature."

Surprised, she felt her skin go hot again. It would get all red and blotchy, and he'd know she was embarrassed. Her skin betrayed her every time. "Are you sure you don't want to ask your daed or Thomas when he comes back?"

"It's not that kind of question." Now his face had turned red. "This is…something they can't answer. Luke, maybe…but he's gone for who knows how long."

"What is it?"

"I…I wondered…Annie…well…" He took off his hat and bent the brim in his big hands. "Has anyone been courting her?"

Helen surveyed the man. Tall, with his father's features. Dark hair, nice eyes. He was different from David, who'd been sick most of his adult life. Isaac had the build of a man who worked hard and the demeanor of a man who enjoyed it. "Her husband died a year ago. She's taken her time in grieving, as she should."

"I know that. It's just that I took her for a buggy ride…"

"You took her for a ride." Good news, indeed. So why didn't he look happy? She picked up a box filled with dishes wrapped in newspapers and placed it on the counter. "That's wunderbaar."

"She didn't seem to think so." He looked as if he might pass out from the embarrassment. "I thought maybe…She's not courting anyone else, is she?"

"Nee, nee." Helen hid her smile and began to unwrap the plates. Heavy, white, unadorned china just like the ones she and George received as gifts after their wedding. She remembered that feeling of knowing a new beginning hovered on the horizon. "No one. She's been waiting until she's ready."

"Ah, *gut*. She said that, but I…" His face flushed beet red. *"Gut."*

"That's all I'll say."

"Jah!" He grinned, looking like a little boy for a brief second. "That's enough."

"Don't you have more furniture to move?"

"Danki…for the advice on where to put the sofa. We're no good at that stuff."

"You should ask Abigail to oversee the placement of the furniture. She'll know."

His forehead wrinkled. "We didn't think of that."

"You should." Helen placed a plate on the shelf and reached for another one. "It's her place in this house."

Isaac seemed to think it over. Then he grinned. "For now."

Then he slapped his hat back on his head, whirled, and disappeared through the doorway.

Helen stared at the spot where he'd stood. To be that young and hopeful. Gabriel strode into her line of sight, so like his son that for a second she thought Isaac had returned. His lined face and the dark circles under his eyes registered. Gabriel. His sleep didn't come easy, either. His gaze glanced off her. "I thought I'd get a glass of water." He squeezed past a stack of boxes by the prep table. "If we still have glasses. The boys don't seem to know how to handle with care."

"I saw a box that had *glasses* written on the side." Flustered for no reason at all, Helen rooted among the boxes. She stubbed her toe on one and nearly toppled another. "I think this is it."

"I can find it."

"No, no, this is it." She ripped off the packing tape and tugged the box open. "See, they're fine. They're nicely wrapped in newspaper. I'm sure they're fine."

They reached for a wrapped glass at the same time. His hand brushed hers. "I can get it." He ducked his head, and his hat hid his expression. Helen wanted to see it. She wanted to know if he had any inkling of what that touch did to her. *Stop it.*

He tugged the glass from the box and removed the newspaper with long, steady fingers. "Laura bought these glasses at a yard sale back in Dahlburg." He didn't sound sad. He sounded as if it were a nice memory that somehow cheered him. "They've held up well."

"She made a wise and frugal purchase, then."

"She was both." His hand gripped the glass, still suspended in the air between them. His gaze met hers. "I'm surprised you're here. After Sunday."

"I wanted the opportunity to make amends for my son."

"He needs to make his own amends." Gabriel set the glass on the counter as if he'd forgotten why he came into the kitchen. "He needs to learn to speak and act properly for himself."

"True and he will. In the meantime, neighbors help neighbors." Helen took another glass from the box and moved to the sink. She needed to put space between them. She didn't like him towering over her. At least that's what she told herself. "In Bliss Creek we help each other. I expect my children to learn that lesson too."

"Then you're also wise." He smiled at her. Helen had to remind herself to close her mouth. He had a nice smile. He should use it more. "Danki."

This surprised her more than the smile. She groped for a response. "I'm sorry about Edmond."

"So am I. It must be hard for you."

That he acknowledged this provided yet another surprise. "I want him to be a good, Plain man."

"What we all want for our children."

"I talked to him. I told him he's too young to court. That Abigail is too young."

"Danki for trying to talk some sense into him."

She busied herself by pulling a pitcher of water from the refrigerator. "Here, let me get you some water. You still have much work to do."

"Jah."

He took the water from her, nodded, and left without another word. Helen sagged against the counter, arms and legs weak as the tension drained from her. She didn't recall George ever having such an effect on her. With each encounter she became more and more certain of her feelings for Gabriel and less and less certain of what to expect from him. But as long as he didn't trust Edmond, it didn't matter. He would never trust her either.

Chapter 25

D ay eight.
  Annie thought of each day this way since Luke and the others had left. She slid the hot bread from its pan and laid it on a rack to cool. Perhaps today would be the day they returned. Luke had said five or six days. Day five had come and gone, as had days six and seven. At the Sunday prayer service, the bishop told them he'd received two phone calls from the men. One on day three, when they'd arrived in western Missouri and another on day five, when they had stopped for the night in the southeastern part of the state. They had decided to visit Arkansas as well. Beyond that, he shared little of the conversation. Annie knew he'd call a meeting of the men later. Discussions of land purchases and new districts weren't for the prayer service. Instead, they prayed for the well-being of the men and for a fruitful trip.

Unable to see her way through the morass of this problem, she set it aside. Immediately her argument with Catherine rose in its place. Catherine sauntered about town talking to Miriam, to Miriam's daed, to Josiah, to Mark, to Mary Beth, and even to Rebecca. She didn't write anything in her notebook while she talked to them, but she scribbled away while she sat at the table and drank cup after cup of kaffi and ate Annie's cookies by the handful. She always left money on the table, like a tip. Like Annie had served as her waitress. She didn't know whether it was meant to be a contribution to the bakery as a business or if her sister didn't want to assume any privilege that might belong to a sister. She didn't take any photos—at least not in Annie's presence.

When Annie had voiced her misgivings and asked Catherine to leave them out of her thesis and forego the memoir, Catherine had called her selfish. Called Annie selfish. She snorted aloud, then looked around. No customers to hear. Catherine's willfulness reflected a deep selfishness, and her expression said she knew it. The argument didn't last long. Catherine simply swept up her things and departed without another word.

Annie rubbed the spot on her forehead just above the bridge on her nose. It continued to throb in a steady *thump, thump* like a drum beating. With Luke gone, she couldn't very well talk to him about Catherine. He'd left without saying another word about their wayward sister. It didn't matter. She knew what he would say. Catherine should go home. Write her book or not write her book, it was of no concern to them.

The door opened and in tromped Mayor Gwendolyn Haag. Despite the heat, she wore a long-sleeved black blouse and black slacks. Her silver slip-on sandals were her only accommodation to the heat. Behind her, a half-dozen women who frequented the bakery at least once a week marched in. They milled around behind the mayor, their arms folded over their chests, their stares indignant. Before Annie could speak, the mayor held up a hand and glared.

"Is it true?"

"Is what true?" Annie looked at the other women. They clustered together by the waiting benches. They didn't seem intent on buying anything. "What can I do for you? The cinnamon rolls are fresh, and I just put a pan of apple cookies in the oven. They'll be out in a jiffy."

"Your community is leaving? You're leaving Bliss Creek? All of you? Because of oil on one farm? That's ridiculous. Let Thomas Brennaman sell his farm and move on. You don't all have to go." The shrill accusation in her tone made Annie's ears ring. "How could you make such a decision? Without telling anyone? Without giving us a chance to win you back?"

"Win us back? I'm…I…" Annie stuttered. How had the mayor found out about the scouting party? This had nothing to do with wanting to leave Bliss Creek. Far from it. "We're talking about…"

"Talking? Talking!" The mayor ran her long, painted fingernails through short, silver hair. "Your men are in Missouri right now, looking for a new place to settle. I saw your sister at the restaurant. She told me, so don't try to prevaricate!"

"Prevari-what?"

"Don't lie to me."

"I don't lie." Stung, Annie folded her towel and laid it on the counter. Then she walked with deliberate care around it so she could face the mayor. "When did you talk to Emma?"

"Not Emma. Your sister Catherine. Life in the real world agrees with her, by the way. We had a lovely chat about her book and then she started asking me how the community's move would affect Bliss Creek economically." The mayor's voice started to rise again. "I nearly fell out of my chair. It would be a disaster, an absolute disaster. I can't believe you people didn't…"

Catherine had no business telling the mayor anything about the district's intentions. She'd truly forgotten her place. *You people.* A defensive response rose in Annie, but she managed to squelch it. *Her* people kept themselves apart from this town as much as possible but changing times had led them to start businesses and work in town. The exchange benefitted both. "The bishop hasn't decided." Annie kept her tone low. "None of us know what will happen. We're all waiting to see."

"I want to meet with Bishop Kelp. With all of you. Today."

The other women crowded around the mayor, nodding their heads, murmuring in agreement. The murmur rose and swelled. "Yes, we want to meet with the bishop," said Leila Cockrell, a tall, skinny lady who looked like she'd never eaten a cookie in her life. "We need this bakery. We need the tourists to come here. Our bed and breakfast depends on it. So does the motel out on the highway. And Mr. Brewer's tour bus. And the restaurants—Hometown and the German place. We need to meet with the bishop. Immediately."

"The bishop. That Micah Kelp. We want to talk to him," added another woman who bought a pecan pie every Friday for her husband who worked out of town and only came home on the weekends. "Immediately, if not sooner."

Immediately, if not sooner? How was that possible?

"Mayor, it's not up to me." Annie brushed past her and threaded her way through the crowd to the table where she picked up a napkin a customer had dropped there. She had work to do. If they didn't plan to buy anything, they should leave. How did she get them to leave? "Really, I don't have any say in this, ladies. Please, just wait until we know…"

"Then run and tell your brother—the older one, not the blacksmith." The crowd parted for Gwendolyn, who stalked behind Annie to the table. "Right now. Please."

She'd clearly added the please as an afterthought.

"You mean Luke? He's out of town." Annie dropped the napkin in a wastebasket and began restocking the napkin holder. "But he'll be back any day now."

"Ah, so he *is* out looking for a new place to live." The mayor sounded triumphant. She poked one long finger in the air to punctuate her sentence. "A new place where tourists will go and buy your cakes and pies and your quilts and your jams and jellies and your cute little faceless dolls. Instead of coming to this beautiful town. Bliss Creek has been good to you, all of you…"

The door swung open again. This time Charisma Chiasson stormed in. Her face red and her full lips turned down in a pout, she shouldered her way through the cluster of women. They parted like tree boughs whipped back in a strong wind. She planted her feet, ripped off her HomeTown Restaurant apron, and crumpled it into a ball. "You're leaving! You're leaving and you didn't even tell me. I thought we were friends. I thought we were more than friends." Her voice broke. "You're not even going to be here for the wedding. You won't be here to help me with Logan…"

"Charisma. Charisma!" Annie tried to stem the flow. Charisma talked like a roaring river when she got started. Stopping her took a dam of major proportion. "I'm not leaving," she shouted. "I'm not going anywhere!"

All the talking ceased.

"Those of us who have businesses will be given a choice." Annie rolled her shaking hands into her own apron to hide them. She breathed and got her voice under control. "Luke says we'll be given a choice. It's the families who depend on farming who might go. We don't know anything for sure. Nobody knows yet."

"What's going on here?" Chief Parker loomed in the doorway, his towering body nearly reaching the top of the wooded frame. His knowing gaze lingered on Mayor Haag. "Do I need to do crowd control?"

Annie let go of her apron. Chief Parker's calm expression and take-charge tone caused the band around her chest to loosen. Pretty soon the entire population of Bliss Creek would be squeezed into Plank's Pastry and Pie Shop. Too bad not one of them had given any indication they planned to buy anything.

"We're fine, Chief Parker." Annie made her tone brisk. She crooked her arm through Charisma's. "Except for this girl, everyone else was leaving."

"But I want…"

"You heard the lady," Chief Parker interrupted the mayor as he held the door open. "Either buy a cake or move along."

"You can't tell me what to do. I'm your boss," Mayor Haag huffed. "I'll take this up with the City Council."

"You might want to think about your approach," Chief Parker held the door wider. "You want these folks to stay, try showing your appreciation instead of bulldozing them."

"Nobody is bulldozing anyone."

Chief Parker made a shooing motion with a mammoth hand. "Out. Out."

"But…"

"Out. Don't make me arrest you for trespassing."

"You wouldn't dare!"

"Try me." Chief Parker's hand rested on the butt of the big, black, ugly gun he wore on a belt around his hips. "It's been a long time coming, Gwendolyn."

"Mayor to you." Her angular face crimson with fury, the mayor took her sweet time strolling past the chief of police. She glanced back at Annie. "We're not done. You tell Micah Kelp I'll be out to see him."

"Yes, ma'am." Annie tightened her grip on Charisma's arm. Charisma patted her hand. "I'll pass that message on."

She would. To Josiah. He would talk to Micah. She had no business bothering the bishop with anything—even this. It wasn't her place. Josiah would know what to do.

The women flounced through, chattering to each other like a bunch of chickens clucking in the barnyard. Chief Parker doffed his police hat to them, revealing tousled blond curls that made him look like a child who rolled out of bed late to school and forgot to comb his hair.

"Well?" Charisma tugged lose from Annie's grip and turned to face her. She didn't look much friendlier than the mayor had. "Seriously? When were you going to tell me? I heard your sister talking to the mayor over meatloaf and mashed potatoes. Your sister says y'all have decided to move, lock, stock, and barrel."

"Catherine had no right…"

"No right? No right! What about your friends? You do have non-Plain friends in this town, you know!"

"Whoa, whoa!" Chief Parker grabbed Charisma from behind and wrapped his long arms around her at the waist. "Slow down there, firecracker. Give Annie a chance to talk."

"Thank you, Chief." Annie took a breath. "I appreciate someone giving me a chance."

"That's Dylan to you, as you well know." He kissed the top of Charisma's head and let her go. "I'm sorry Mayor Haag ambushed you like that. If I'd known, I would've tried to head her off at the pass."

"Thank you... Dylan." Annie gestured to the table. "Sit down and I'll bring you some lemonade and cookies. I'll tell you everything."

After Charisma had heard the whole story, she seemed lost in thought. She broke the oatmeal-raisin-pecan cookie—her favorite—into little pieces, then shoved them around on her napkin with a fingernail painted the color of bubblegum.

"Well?" Annie couldn't keep quiet any longer. "You see my problem, don't you?"

"I do." Charisma sat back in her chair. "I know what it's like to be away from family. Not that I have much of a family. Not like you. Your family is great. Emma is great. And Luke. And y'all did so much for me. I can see why you don't want to get left behind."

Her voice quavered.

"*Ach*, don't cry." Annie handed her a fresh napkin. She heard a catch in her own voice and swallowed against it. "I meant it when I said I wasn't going. I have a good business here."

"And good friends. Friends who are like family," Charisma raised her gaze to Annie. "I know you have plenty of sisters already. But you're like a sister to me. You're the only one I have."

"I know." Annie blotted at her own cheeks with a napkin. She thought of Catherine's blabbering mouth telling Mayor Haag about the district's plans. "And some of the sisters I do have need a talking to."

She had work to do now, but later she would straighten Catherine out.

"I've seen that look before." Dylan settled his coffee mug on the table and leaned forward. "Easy, Annie, your sister has her own problems."

"What do you know about Catherine's problems?"

"I know she's been without family for three years." He cocked his head. "You surely must have thought about what that's like for her."

"But now she's back and she's causing rifts."

"She's back and she's trying to find something she lost."

"By talking out of turn and causing upheaval."

"Yeah, yeah, that's not important right now. What's important is you staying and being here for my wedding." Charisma sounded like a small, cranky child. "Let's stay focused here."

Annie laughed despite herself. "I've never been to an Englisch wedding."

"Will they let you come? Will Luke let you come?"

"I think so." Annie contemplated. She was a grown woman, a widow with a child, but still, she would ask. In the interest of doing the right thing. In the interest of not bringing more problems on her poor brother's head. Catherine and even Josiah had done enough of that. "If I can't, we'll have our own celebration."

"I want you to be there. There's nothing about it that's wrong or bad. I bet it's nothing different than what y'all do."

"Except for the flowers and the music and the rings and the rice and the honeymoon trip," Dylan pointed out. "And the fancy dress and the toasts. Maybe you could come to the reception, if coming to the church is a problem."

"Rice and toast?" Annie asked, perplexed. An interesting menu. She preferred to bake a cake herself. "That's all you eat at the reception? I could make something nice for you."

They both laughed. "You'll be a guest, not the caterer," Dylan said. "You'll have to come and see."

Annie wasn't sure what Luke would say about that, but she was willing to find out.

If he ever returned home. She had a lot to tell him.

Chapter 26

Gabriel strode into the house, intent on gathering up the ledger and the other office supplies he'd set aside in a box to take to the repair shop. Opening day. Finally. The house was livable. The barn was in good shape. A small, late garden had been planted. Seth had mowed the yard, and Abigail had planted flowers in the beds along the front porch. The first steps toward making a house a home. Now Gabriel could concentrate on making a living and supporting his family. Maybe then he would feel as if he'd made the right choice in coming here.

He sniffed. An unpleasant odor wafted through the air. Not the smell of clean laundry he usually enjoyed on Tuesdays. It smelled… like a dirty diaper. But they didn't have any more children in diapers. Abigail had worked hard to potty train little Rachel. She'd been almost as difficult as Isabelle, if not more.

"Abigail? Abigail!" Where had that girl gone? A wail poured from the upstairs. One of the girls was crying. "Abigail!"

He stormed up the stairs two at time. He didn't have time for this. Isaac had gone ahead to be at the hardware store when it opened so he could buy a few more tools they would need. Gabriel's job was to open the store. Abigail had a job to do just as Mary Beth did at the bakery, or Daniel and Samuel working at the Glick farm and the Yoder farm.

The crying intensified at the top of the stairs. He rushed into the girls' bedroom, nearly tripping over a box of clothes sitting by the door. Abigail knelt next to the bed where Isabelle and Rachel cuddled side-by-side, still dressed in their nightgowns. All three were crying. The little girls appeared to have dirtied their undergarments and Rachel had vomited.

Abigail looked up at Gabriel, then leaned over and vomited all over his boots.

"I don't feel good," Isabelle announced. Then she rolled over and did the same.

Gabriel stifled a groan. *God, please.* He needed Laura. He needed her more today than he'd ever needed her.

You need a fraa. You need a woman. You need a companion.

The voice sounded loud in his head. His ears rang with it.

Laura is gone. Gone forever.

Yes, she is. You need a fraa. You need a woman. You need a companion.

"Abigail, I'll get towels and water." He backed away. The stench in his nostrils made his stomach roil. "I'll be back. We'll clean this up, and then y'all can rest while I go into town."

Abigail nodded and wiped at her mouth, but her blue eyes were stained red and her cheeks went white with bright red spots in the middle.

Holding his breath, Gabriel backed away from the mess. He pounded down the stairs and stalked into the kitchen, where he managed to unearth towels and a bucket. Water. He pumped water with the long handle and managed to carry everything upstairs without spilling it.

Back aching, jaw clenched, he started with Abigail, then directed her to help with the two smaller ones.

It took a good twenty minutes, but finally they were clean and the dirty towels and nightclothes had been deposited in the second bucket he'd brought for that purpose.

"Now, I need to go into the shop for a few hours." He adjusted a sheet over the two younger girls, then touched his oldest daughter's cheek with one hand. "Can you handle it for that long? They should sleep now."

Abigail nodded. Then a look of dread mixed with misery slid across her face. "Daed, I…" She flung herself from the bed and scurried toward the door. She didn't make it.

Gabriel sighed and remembered just in time not to inhale through his nose. Time to ask for help. Much as he hated the thought, he couldn't be both daed and mudder to these girls. He had to earn a living. That was his job. If he didn't find a way to do both, they were all lost.

⁂

Helen dried her hands on the dish towel before opening the front door. She froze. The last person she'd expected to see on her porch was Gabriel Gless. He stared down at her with a wary look on his face. The woodsy scent she normally associated with him had disappeared, replaced by something…awful.

"I need your help." He spoke before she could say anything.

Gabriel Gless needed her help. Helen clamped down on the uncharitable thoughts that ran through her head. She moved aside and opened the door wider. He seemed to hesitate, then stepped across the threshold.

"Who is it, Helen?" Her mother called from the kitchen where they were feverishly trying to finish canning a bushel of tomatoes before they went bad. Helen had gotten behind, what with the damage to the house, Edmond's problems, Emma's baby, and helping the Glesses move. "Invite them in for lemonade and cookies, why don't you?"

That was Mudder. It didn't matter who it might be. Company was company.

"Would you like something cool to drink? We have ice."

Gabriel shook his head. She could see the vein pulsing in his jaw. Whatever he needed from her, he didn't want to ask.

"What is it? Is something wrong?"

"The girls are sick."

He stopped, as if that explained everything.

"Do they need a doctor?" She glanced around for her bag. "Doctor Chapin sees my kinner when they're ailing."

"It's some kind of stomach flu. It'll pass." He grimaced. "All over my boots, mostly."

She buried a smile. Men weren't built to deal with bodily fluids. Women were used to cleaning up floors and washing clothes when children were sick. She didn't even flinch anymore.

"The thing is, Abigail's sick too." He stopped. Again as if that explained it all.

"Poor thing," Helen murmured. "They need lukewarm tea and toast. Keep the liquids in them so they don't get dehydrated. Ginger ale and saltine crackers will help settle their stomachs."

"*Gut, gut.*" He nodded. "That's *gut.*"

"Are you coming, Helen?" Her mother stomped into the living room, leaning heavily on her cane. "The tomatoes are boiling. The jars are in the bath. I can't see well enough to…"

Her voice trailed off and she stomped closer to Gabriel. "Is that you, Thomas? I didn't recognize your voice or I would've come out to say howdy sooner."

"No, it's not Thomas," Helen intervened. "This is Gabriel Gless. Remember how he helped repair the house when the tree fell on it?"

"Jah, jah, I remember." She moved still closer, peering up at Gabriel. "You do look like Thomas, don't you? Come on out, have some lemonade. Helen made apple-rhubarb coffee cake. Helen makes good pastries. Mighty fine pastries."

"Mudder, Gabriel's children are sick. He doesn't have time for coffee cake right now." She glanced at his splattered boots. Or the stomach for food. "He stopped by to…"

"I stopped by because Abigail is sick too. She can't take care of Isabelle and Rachel when she's sick. Mary Beth already went to the bakery. Isaac's at the shop. The other boys are all working too."

"An industrious bunch, you've raised. That's *gut*." Mudder eased into the rocking chair, looking ready for a chat. "You moved here from where?"

"From Indiana. The reason I stopped by is because I can't leave the girls alone with Abigail. She needs help herself. But I can't stay with her. I've got to get into town. We don't have any family here and Emma just had a new baby. She can't be watching over mine." He pulled at his suspenders. "I wondered if you could…if you would mind…if you would stay with them, just for today."

That had been like pulling teeth.

"You have the makings for soup?" Helen bustled toward the kitchen. Gabriel followed and watched, his dark eyes filled with what looked like relief, as she grabbed items from the kitchen shelves—crackers, medicines, tea bags, a big bottle of ginger ale. "Chicken, noodles, and such?"

He nodded.

"*Gut*. Mudder, Naomi and Betsy will help with the canning. Gabriel, go to town. Get your shop open. I'll stay with the girls."

He nodded again and disappeared through the door.

He didn't say thank you, but Helen didn't mind. One didn't have to thank a person for doing the neighborly thing. She thanked God Gabriel thought enough of her to allow her to take care of his girls. Maybe he'd finally forgiven her for not being the kind of parent who could prevent her son from doing something foolish and dangerous, like driving a buggy while drunk.

It took another thirty minutes to hitch up the horse to the buggy and drive to the Gless farm. The minute she walked into the house she put her hand to her nose. The stench made her stomach rock. One look at the pile of dirty laundry on the bedroom floor and the mess on the sheets, and Helen swung into action.

This she knew how to do. She sent Abigail back to bed in her own room after helping her strip off her sweaty, soiled nightgown and replace it with a clean one. Then she cleaned up Rachel and Isabelle, stripped their sheets, and replaced them. Admonishing the girls to stay in bed and rest, she carried the dirty linens and nightclothes downstairs. Before starting the laundry she washed her hands and put a big pot on the stove. She jostled the wood to bring up the flame before pouring in the chicken stock she found in the propane-operated refrigerator. Leftover baked chicken, a few peeled potatoes, and egg noodles followed.

Feeling as calm and collected as she had in weeks, Helen moved outside. She turned the knob until water flowed through a garden hose that ran in through the back porch window. She filled the tub with water and began adding buckets of hot water heated on the stove. While the dirty clothes soaked, she took a glass of ginger ale and a plate of crackers to Abigail's room. The girl's eyes opened as soon as Helen entered.

"How are Isabelle and Rachel?" the girl asked through cracked lips. "I'm sorry you had to clean them up. I wanted to do it, but I felt so weak."

"They're fine. They're sound asleep. No need to apologize." Helen took the damp cloth she'd slung over her shoulder and used it to dab at the girl's feverish forehead. "Try to eat a cracker and drink a little ginger ale and then you need to do the same."

"I don't think I can swallow." Abigail eyed the plate of crackers. "I'm sorry you went to all that trouble to bring me…"

"You need to stop apologizing." Helen paused for a second. She always apologized for everything too. "Don't worry about it. I'll leave the plate. Take a nap and when you're feeling better, you can have a snack."

Abigail squirmed under the blanket and then sat up. "Wait, don't go."

"Did you need something?" Helen paused at the door. "If you feel sick, just use that bucket I set on the floor there. Don't try to get out of bed."

"It's not that. It's just that…I mean." Her cheeks, already rosy from fever, darkened. "Edmond says you don't want him to see me anymore."

"Your daed doesn't want it."

"But it's my rumspringa…"

"You should talk to your father about it."

"Don't you like me?" Her chin trembled and her voice quavered. "I try to be nice. I know I'm new here and you don't really know me. There's probably other girls who would be better for Edmond, but I promise I'll try…"

The girl slapped both hands to her face and burst into tears.

"Abigail, Abigail!" Helen rushed to the bed. She sat down so she could put an arm around her. "Honey, I like you fine. You seem like a nice girl. I haven't given any thought to Edmond courting. I hadn't even thought of him as being old enough. Silly me, he seems like a little boy to me."

"I miss my old house," Abigail sobbed, her shoulders heaving. "I miss my mudder."

"I know you do." Helen patted her thin shoulders. "You'll get used to it, and in the meantime, Edmond gives you company."

"Jah. He talks to me. And he listens to me. He asks me what it was like in Indiana. And he knows what it's like to lose a parent. He knows how I feel."

So Edmond had given this girl the company she needed. Remorse at how she'd treated her son roared through Helen like a stampede of horses. He was nice. Her son was a nice person who felt bad for a young girl far from home.

"I'm glad you two can talk."

"Are you?"

"Jah, I am."

"Why can't my daed see that?"

"He's scared."

"Scared? Daed isn't scared of anything."

"He's scared of not being a good parent. I know. So am I."

"You're *gut*. He's *gut*. He takes care of all of us every day."

"That's right. That's why you need to give him some time to get used to you and Edmond. Just give him some time. Now go to sleep. You need to rest so you can get better."

The girl's eyes closed before Helen finished the sentence. Feeling ashamed of herself, Helen tiptoed away from the bed and slipped down the hallway and checked on the little ones again. She'd let Gabriel's view of the situation between Abigail and Edmond color her own opinions. She'd been wrong to do that. Edmond was a good boy. Abigail was a good girl. Edmond had shown kindness toward her. Welcomed a stranger into their midst. He should be commended, not condemned.

Determined to do better by him, Helen turned her attention to the little girls. Rachel had worked her way to the side of the bed—precariously close to falling off. Helen tugged her small body back toward the center. The little one felt hot to the touch. Helen smoothed her blond curls from her face. Such a cute face, with the same almond-shaped eyes and round face as her older sister. Two special children. A handful.

She sighed. Special children were gifts from God. But for a widower with eight children, these two presented an even bigger challenge. They had no mudder to help them learn what they could and take care of what they couldn't. She pressed a kiss on her fingertips and touched the girl's cheek with them. *God, help Gabriel with these blessings. You have not given him more than he can handle. Help him to rise willingly and lovingly to the yoke.*

She tucked a sheet over Isabelle and moved back into the hallway. Something banged in the next bedroom. Helen plowed to a stop. She and the girls were alone in the house. Or so she had thought. Shuffling noises followed. Perhaps Gabriel had returned? No, he asked her to come to the house because he had the shop to open. It couldn't be him. Unless he'd forgotten something. Or one of the boys? They were supposed to be working. Her palms sweaty, hands shaking, Helen tiptoed toward the open door. She peeked in. "Gabriel?"

A young man spun around—Gabriel's son Daniel, she thought—with a folded shirt in his hand. "What? Oh, it's you. Helen."

"That's me. You're Daniel, right?"

"Jah." His gaze traveled beyond her. "What are you doing here? Where's Abigail?"

"Abigail's sick." Helen glanced at the bed. Daniel had thrown open a battered suitcase over the quilt. The suitcase held a small pile of pants. "So are the little ones. Your daed asked me to take care of them until he could return."

"Well, okay." He dropped the shirt on top of the other clothes, then stood there, hands dangling, his expression uncertain. "I…I just…I'm…"

"Looks like you're packing."

"Jah." He turned his back on her and went to a row of hooks on the far wall. There he removed another pair of pants and a nightshirt. "I am."

"Can I ask why? Where are you going?" It was none of her business, but something in the young man's rigid posture and flushed face told Helen the question needed to be asked. "Does your daed know you're taking a trip?"

"It's not a trip."

"What then? You're too old to run away from home."

"I'm not running away from home." He turned and faced her then. His expression said she had no right to probe into his life. "I'm going back to my home."

"*Ach.*" Helen's heart contracted. Surprised, she tried to grasp the reasons why. Gabriel might evoke all sorts of mixed emotions in her, but she recognized the symptoms of a lingering broken heart in another. He didn't deserve this new pain. A child leaving. Without saying goodbye. Without offering an explanation.

"I've made soup. It's good. Have some before you go." Maybe she could stall him until Gabriel returned. "Fortify yourself for the long trip. Indiana is a mighty long way from here."

Daniel glanced out the open window where a white curtain

fluttered in the soft midday breeze. "I can't stop for food. Like you said, Indiana is a mighty long way."

"Then let me pack you a sandwich. No sense wasting your nest egg on food along the way."

"Nest egg?"

"Surely you've saved money for the journey. How are you getting there?"

"Bus. Mr. Carver from the Stop-N-Go is giving me a ride to the bus stop."

"And you have enough money to get to Indiana."

"Enough." He shrugged. "Phoebe...my...my girl...she helped. She sent me half. I had half."

"Well, then." Helen tried to think. He couldn't leave without saying goodbye to his daed. Without Gabriel having a chance to dissuade him. "I'll pack you a lunch."

Daniel snapped the suitcase shut and glanced around the room. Helen saw nothing in his face to suggest he had any connection to it. He'd barely lived there a week. Just passing through. He followed her down the stairs and into the kitchen without speaking.

There she made him a sandwich with thick slices of ham, cheese, and mustard on slabs of homemade bread. Finally, when he'd demolished the first half of the sandwich and gulped noisily through most of the milk she'd poured, Helen dared to try again. "How old are you?"

"Nineteen."

Old enough.

"You've been baptized?"

"Jah. Same as Phoebe. We were going to announce our marriage next winter when I'd saved enough to build us a house on a few acres her daed was willing to give us. She's only seventeen. Her daed wanted her to wait another year."

"What did your daed say?"

"He said we had to move." Daniel's voice didn't betray his emotions, but his hands shook as he lifted the glass to his mouth and drained the last of the milk. He sat the glass down harder than necessary. "He said if we were meant to be, then Phoebe could come out here when she was old enough."

Helen wrapped another sandwich in plastic wrap and slid it into a baggie. She dropped it in a brown paper bag along with two apples and a dozen cookies. As long as she didn't look directly at him, he seemed willing to talk to her. "Have a piece of pie before you go." She slid a wedge of pecan pie onto a saucer and laid it on the table in front of him. "You can't wait another year?"

"I can't." He looked up at her, his blue eyes fierce with emotion. He looked nothing like Gabriel so he must be like his mother. His determination to have his own way—now that surely came from his father. "I'm a man now. I'm ready to start a family with the woman I've…" He swallowed. He pushed the plate away. "I'd best get going. Mr. Carver said he'd take me to the station when he goes home for lunch. I don't want to miss the noon bus to Topeka."

"You'll go without saying goodbye?"

He wiped at his mouth and laid the napkin by the plate. "It's better."

"For whom?"

"You don't know my daed."

"I know what's right." And, truth be told, she didn't want Gabriel to suffer this pain. He'd suffered enough loss. She knew about the ache caused by these gaping voids. "I know sons should honor their fathers."

"I left him a note."

"Not very brave."

He stood, towering over her just as his father did. "He'll be glad I did it this way."

"Nee."

"He doesn't like goodbyes."

"Who does?"

"He didn't say goodbye to any of our friends and family in Dahlburg. He got in the van and told the driver to leave. He never even looked out the window until we crossed the line into Kansas."

"You're his son."

"Jah. All the more reason."

Helen shook her head as she watched him disappear through the kitchen doorway. Daniel missed the woman he loved. Surely he missed his mother. Yet, in his youth, he couldn't see how his father must feel the same pain. Instead of drawing closer, he stepped away because his father had been the one to stand between him and his girl. Phoebe. Helen contemplated the empty doorway. As much as it would hurt Gabriel, Daniel needed to go home. The woman he loved wasn't dead, wasn't beyond reach. She was alive and waiting for him. Gabriel should be glad for that. He should be glad his son could still have that happiness. Once he waded through the pain of the separation, surely he would see that.

She padded through the house and slipped through the front door to the porch. "Take care," she called to him.

"Tell Daed Mr. Carver's son will bring the horse back tonight." Daniel snapped the reins and the horse began a slow canter. "He'll need a ride back to town."

"I'll tell him." If he gave her a chance. "Any other messages?"

"Tell him I'm sorry. Tell him I'll write. Tell him…tell him I'll be fine."

The other words remained unspoken, but Helen filled them in for the boy determined to be a man. *Tell him I love him.*

The afternoon passed in cleaning up Rachel and Isabelle, who still couldn't keep ginger ale and crackers in their stomachs. Helen considered putting them in the buggy and taking them into the clinic, but it didn't seem right without asking Gabriel first. Instead, she busied herself by rummaging through the pantry for the ingredients and making a chicken pot pie. The men would be hungry after a long day's work and they would still have chores to do when they returned to the farm.

Abigail and Mary Elizabeth had done a good job in the kitchen. Plenty of bread, cookies, and pie to go with the main dish. Corn on the cob. Pickled beets. She considering running out to the garden to pick some fresh tomatoes—if any of the plants had survived the storm earlier in the month—but she decided against leaving the house. She didn't want the girls to wake up and find themselves alone, even for a minute.

After a few hours, Abigail appeared in the kitchen. Her gait was unsteady, but her face seem less flushed. Helen fixed her some toast and tea. After a few bites, the color returned to her face and her body seemed to droop less. "I should get supper started."

"I have a pot pie in the oven." Helen took the plate from Abigail's weak grip. "Back to bed with you now."

"I want to help with the babies." She stood, swayed a little, sat back down. "I'm just a little dizzy. It'll pass."

"Up to bed now." Helen followed her up the stairs to make sure she didn't come tumbling down. "I'll check on the girls. You rest."

Rachel rolled over when Helen entered the room and immediately began to whimper. "Want Mary Liz. Want Abby."

"Mary Elizabeth is at the bakery. Abigail is sick, just like you are."

The girl began to wail.

"Now, now, now." Helen scooped her up and whisked her down the stairs. She didn't want Isabelle joining in the fray. She would just rock the girl a bit. "You'll wake up your sister and she needs her sleep."

She settled into a rocking chair in the front room and tucked the sobbing girl's head against her chest. Her arms felt heavy and her legs weak. It had been a long day. She sighed and leaned her head against the back of the chair and began to rock. They could both use a good cry, but only the little one would get one.

Chapter 27

Wiping at his face with a semi-clean handkerchief, Gabriel pounded across the yard and up the steps to the back porch. He paused to wipe his work boots on the rug. The first day at the shop had been successful—if success could be measured by the number of farmers who'd passed through the door with repair jobs. Mostly small ones that would earn him little fees, but it was a start. It felt good to be working at something he knew how to do. Since leaving his own farm behind in Indiana, he'd felt a strange void. Like he didn't know what to do with his hands. Or his feet. Where to put them. They seemed unusually large and all thumbs and big toes. In the way. Work relieved that feeling.

The girls being sick had marred an otherwise good day. He pushed through the door and into the kitchen, anxious to make sure they were better. Helen seemed capable of caring for them. She had three girls of her own, after all, and she'd done a good job, fixing up his cut after the storm. Still, she was such a clumsy one, sometimes. It might have been better to take them to the doctor and let Isaac handle the shop. In the past, he'd never had these moments of uncertainty. Laura had known what to do with the children. He'd relied on her for that. As a husband should do.

The soft sound of a woman's voice—Helen's voice—penetrated his reverie. She sang an old hymn he recognized in a sort of sing-song, almost talking, almost praying sort of voice. Inhaling the mouthwatering scent of something—chicken pot pie?—he crept closer to the door, curious.

She sat in the rocking chair of his front room, little Rachel wrapped in her arms. The girl seemed to be asleep, but still Helen rocked and sang in English and then in Deitsch. With no one around and the late afternoon sun filtering through the green blinds on the windows, her face seemed to relax from her customary anxious, eager to please but not quite sure how expression. She looked as if she belonged exactly where she sat. In a rocking chair, holding a baby, singing what might pass as a lullaby. He stood transfixed by the sheer goodness of her presence. How could one miss it? Because she managed to bury it the second his path crossed hers?

Her hand lifted and she smoothed Rachel's hair from her cheek with a gentle touch. "Poor baby, you're just tuckered out, aren't you?" she whispered. "Being sick takes all the spunk right out of a person. You must look like your mudder. I don't see your daed in those cheeks and that blond hair. She must have been lovely. You are so sweet. Pretty is as pretty does, of course. Not that the boys will be running after you, poor sweet thing."

So she knew what he had only begun to accept. Rachel, like Isabelle, would never be a wife and mother. Gabriel hadn't taken her to the doctor yet, but he knew. He'd known before the conversation with Catherine. Before her insistence that he face facts. Rachel would always have the mind of a child. Isabelle had an innocence and a sweet disposition. She loved to pick flowers and chase hummingbirds and pet kittens. She loved to sing and play hopscotch and jump rope. She would always love those things. Gabriel had no doubt Rachel would be exactly the same.

A sob caught in his throat and he stuffed it back to the heart of its origin. God had blessed this family with two special little girls. Gabriel didn't know how he would bring them up, but he would. Without Laura, the task seemed endless and insurmountable, but it wasn't. It wouldn't be.

Helen sighed and rocked some more. The wooden floor creaked under the chair. Her head drooped and he thought maybe she'd gone to sleep as well, but the soft singing resumed for a few seconds.

The scent he'd enjoyed a few seconds ago seemed different now. He sniffed. A little burnt? Grimacing, he started forward. "I…"

Helen jumped up from the chair, her eyes wide, her mouth open. To her credit, she didn't drop Rachel in her fright. "Gabriel! You scared me! Why didn't you say something? How long have you been standing there?"

"Hush, you'll wake the baby."

"The poor thing is exhausted from vomiting and taking repeated baths…"

"I think whatever you're baking is burning." He put up both of his hands, palms out, to try to stem the flow. "I just came in. I saw you there…"

"Jah, well." She trotted across the room and held the sleeping child out to him. "Could you take her while I check on your supper?"

"You didn't need to start supper. Mary Elizabeth will be here any minute. Isaac intended to stop at the bakery to pick her up on his way out of town."

"We're here. Hi, Helen." Mary Elizabeth slipped through the front door at that very moment. "How is she? Isaac told me the girls were sick. Let me take her."

"Better not. Not if you want to go back to work at the bakery tomorrow," Helen objected before Mary Elizabeth could reach them. "Wash up and I'll check on the chicken pot pie. Your daed seems to think it's burning."

"I know when I smell burned pie crust." For some reason, he felt a need to defend himself. He cradled his youngest daughter against his chest, pleased that she didn't feel as hot as she had that morning. Her cheeks were rosy, but not burning. She stuck a thumb in her mouth and snuggled closer. His throat tightened. He cleared it and followed Helen into the kitchen. "I'll run her upstairs. Then I best take care of chores."

"You best eat first. While it's hot." Helen pulled a steaming pot pie from the oven and sat it carefully on a thick pile of potholders made by Laura many years earlier. "I set the table. There's bread, applesauce, pickled beets, corn on the cob, and some pecan pie. That should fill you up."

"You're not staying for supper?" Isaac tromped through the back-door and eased a bushel of peaches onto the floor next to the sink. "Did you invite her to stay, Daed? After all, she took care of the girls all day and that couldn't have been much fun."

No one generally gave much thought to whether childcare or other women's work was fun, but Gabriel knew what Isaac was getting at. He should've asked her. It would've been the neighborly thing to do. "Jah, of course, you must stay."

"I have to get home. My mudder doesn't see well and she lets the girls get away with a little too much for my liking…" Her voice trailed off. "Anyway."

Thinking, no doubt, that he would be judging her parenting skills once again.

"You made the pot pie, you should have some."

"I don't know."

"You didn't set enough plates. We need two more." Mary Elizabeth padded on bare feet into the kitchen. "Daed, me, Isaac, Seth, Samuel, Daniel, and you, of course. You didn't know you would be eating with us, but even without that, we're one short."

"Nee, that's not it. I…you see…" Her expression had become strained again. Gone was that soft, motherly gaze that seemed so sure of what to do and how to do it. "I…well."

Seth burst into the kitchen with Samuel right behind him. The room was too crowded now. "Where's Daniel? Isn't he having supper? Did he say he was staying at Thomas's tonight?"

The boys jostled each other, jockeying for position to wash their hands.

"He didn't say anything to me." Gabriel looked at Helen, aware that she no longer met his gaze. Her neck and cheeks were mottled red. "Has he come home?"

"He's come and gone."

"Gone? Gone where?"

"Home."

"I don't understand. This is home."

"Home. Home." Isaac broke in. "He's gone home. To Indiana?"

Helen nodded, her gazed fixed on Gabriel's dirty boots as if she were offended that he'd tracked dirt into his own home.

"When?"

"Before lunch."

"And you didn't tell anyone." Anger simmered and boiled up in the words. He knew she had no fault in this, but he couldn't help himself. "You didn't try to stop him?"

"I couldn't leave the girls." Her gaze came up. Her chin lifted. "I did try to talk him out of it."

"But you couldn't, so you gave up."

She had the good grace not to remind him that Daniel wasn't her son, but rather his. "I couldn't talk him out of it, so I made him a sandwich and I sent supper with him for the trip."

She'd taken care of him the only way she knew how. By feeding him. Gabriel's throat closed up. Tears welled close to the surface. He fought them back. They'd made the long trek to Kansas together as a family. Now, Daniel had chosen to break away and return home. Make that trek alone.

"He had no message?"

"Only that he loves all of you and Phoebe is waiting for him, so not to worry."

Something in her tone caught at Gabriel. She'd made up the message. He was sure of it. The fact that she sought to comfort him—even if lying were a sin—only made his heart hurt more.

Unable to utter another word, he strode past her and out the door. He needed to put as much space between Helen Crouch and himself as possible before he did something untenable, like cry. Or worse, seek the comfort of her arms.

Chapter 28

Helen chuckled as she smoothed her hand over the material. The success of a quilting frolic depended not only on the sewing ability of the quilters, but also on the quality of the visiting. Emma's stories about Eli, Rebecca, Mary, and Lillie always made her laugh. The four of them were having fun showing the Gless children all the best places to fish, climb trees, and collect rocks on the Brennaman farm. Emma and Thomas's children were as generous with their time and friendship as the adults in their home. She wished Annie could've come, but having the frolic on Saturday, the busiest day at the bakery, precluded her attending. They'd settled on Saturday so the girls could contribute to Aenti Louise's birthday present. Annie had already done her share of the sewing.

"What about you? How's Edmond doing?" Emma asked as her needle flew across the alternating rows of light and dark triangles in maroon and mauve. If she were frazzled by the extended absence of her husband, she gave no sign of it. "Has he settled down?"

"I don't know if I would consider it settling down." Helen let her needle stand still for a second, suspended in air. "It almost feels more like he's waiting for something. Just waiting."

"Boys his age *are* waiting. They're waiting to grow up." Emma studied her stitches, then adjusted the material in front of her. "Eli's only thirteen and he's itching for the day he can stay home from school and work next to his daed in the field all day every day."

The chattering of the other women subsided and the room grew quiet, something that never happened at these gatherings. Emma looked around, her expression placid. "No sense in inviting worry, is there? We will find our place in the world, and Eli will work next to his father, whether it's on a farm in another place or in a homegrown business. Thomas will be home soon, and we'll go on from there, according to God's plan."

"You're right." Helen began stitching another triangle. "God will provide."

"He always does," a voice boomed from the doorway.

Thomas's voice. Thomas had returned. He was here, in the house.

Helen's needle stabbed her thumb. "Ouch!" She stuck it in her mouth and stood, as did Emma and the other women. They all spoke at the same time.

"Whoa, whoa, one at a time." Thomas held up a hand as if in self-defense, but he had eyes only for his fraa. Helen forced herself to look beyond him, over his shoulder, toward the door. To her surprise, Gabriel stood behind his cousin, a grin stretched across his rugged face. Their gazes met. His head dipped in a fractional nod that a second later she wasn't sure if she hadn't imagined.

He made his way through the throng that surrounded Thomas and approached her with a certain trepidation apparent in his expression. "Helen."

"They've returned," she said unnecessarily. "What are you doing here?"

Helen wanted the question back the instant it left her mouth. Not only did it sound rude, but it was none of her business. This house didn't belong to her. Gabriel could visit his good friends anytime he liked.

Still, he took pity on her, it seemed. "I happened upon the van on the road as I drove to make a delivery. A plow we'd repaired."

"It's so good to see them back. Did you speak to my brothers?"

"Jah." Gabriel studied the group crowded around Thomas. "They went on home, as did the others. They all seem very glad to be back."

"Did they say anything? Anything about what they saw? What they'll tell the bishop?"

Gabriel's gaze hadn't left her face, but he didn't seem to hear her questions. His eyes were dark, almost opaque, and she couldn't read his expression. He glanced toward the others, then back at her. "Come outside."

"What?"

He jerked his head toward the door. "Come outside. Please."

He strode away. Nonplussed, but curious, Helen considered the tilting in her stomach that threatened to bring up her breakfast. *He's just a man. Just a man.*

A man who made her want to pull her hair—or his—out by the roots and hold tight to his hand all at the same time.

She squeezed past Emma, who was grilling Thomas on whether he'd gotten enough to eat on the trip, insisting he looked thinner than he had ten days ago. Thomas denied it, but then allowed that he'd missed her mashed potatoes and chicken fried steak something fierce.

Helen followed Gabriel out the back door. A picnic table stood empty near several long rows of clothesline. They were also empty except for dozens of clothes pins awaiting their weekly burdens. A brilliantly colored robin sat on the line, chirping until he was joined by his more subdued mate, a mousy brownish-red bird. Helen knew how she felt.

She pressed her damp hands together and waited.

"Could you sit?" Gabriel pointed toward the bench. "I'm tired."

She sat, giving him leave to do the same. "What is this about? Did Thomas say something? Are they leaving for sure? Did they find property in Missouri?"

He lifted his straw hat and resettled it. "I'm sorry."

"You're sorry. For what? What's going to happen?"

"This is not about the trip. Thomas and Tobias and the others will bring that information to the bishop first. He will decide when to tell the rest of us." He spread his huge hands, palm down on the picnic table and began to rub them against the rough, sun-weathered wood. "I'm sorry for being so…my oldest daughter calls it being so daed."

Helen felt a laugh burble up in her. "So you?"

"Jah." He didn't smile. "They don't say anything, but I can tell my children think I wasn't very kind to you after you took care of the girls. You cleaned up after them and cooked for us and then I was ungracious."

"You were upset."

"And I took it out on you."

On impulse, Helen placed her hands on the table, palms down. Her fingers didn't touch his, but they were close. She watched him as he stared at the four hands. He looked tired and not a little discouraged. Why? A new business took time to get off the ground. It took time to become part of a new community. "What's wrong, Gabriel?"

His jaw worked. His right hand inched forward until the tip of his index finger touched her. She felt that touch down to her toes. "Gabriel?"

He cocked his head and lifted his gaze. "I wanted to say I'm sorry."

"You're sure that's all you wanted to say?" *Say it, please say it. Say something. Please.* "There wasn't something more?"

"The girls thought it would be nice if we tried again. You could come to supper tonight."

"The girls thought?"

"Abigail especially. She took it hard, the way I treated you. She scolded me right good. Reminded me of…" He stopped. "Anyway, I'd be grateful if you could see your way to forgive me and come to dinner. You could bring your children."

That was indeed a peace offering. Helen could imagine what it cost him to set aside the notion that her son was not a good influence for his children. She wanted to say yes, but she was still stuck on the sentence he hadn't finished. *Reminded me of…* of his late wife.

"Are you sure you're wanting to do this?"

"Wanting to do what?" The gravel in his voice deepened. "Invite you to supper? It's only right, considering how you helped me."

"And that's all it is? A thank-you?"

This time all five fingers on his right hand inched forward. They slid over hers and wrapped themselves around her wrist. He met her gaze head-on. "It's what I'm able to do right now."

Mesmerized by his gaze, she didn't try to escape his grip. "I can't live in someone else's shadow."

"I don't expect you to do that." His grip slackened and his hand withdrew. "I'm just trying to find my way."

"Me too."

"I know."

The second his hand left her wrist she felt doubly alone. She wanted his hand back. In order to get it she would have to take it on faith that he would find his way into the sunshine where the only shadows that fell were his and hers. She would go and he would catch up.

"I'd be happy to accept your invitation to supper."

Chapter 29

Gabriel inhaled the aroma of frying pork chops. His mouth watered, but his stomach did a strange see-saw like the lapping of the water in the pond when a strong wind hurled itself against it. He gritted his teeth. *Stop being an idiot. She's a woman. Just a woman.* He glanced around the kitchen. Abigail and Mary Beth had everything under control, it seemed. Mounds of mashed potatoes, gravy, pork chops, creamed corn, beets, hot rolls, watermelon, a lemon pie. A decent meal for family and friends. Too bad Isaac had gone out after finishing his chores. Gabriel would've liked to have his oldest son as an ally in making conversation, never his own strong point. With Daniel back in Indiana, that left Samuel, Seth, and the girls. They'd be more interested in talking to the Crouch children, leaving him to fend for himself with Helen.

Just friends.

"Shoo, shoo!" Abigail made a flapping motion with her apron. "Go on."

"Are you talking to me?" Gabriel frowned, not bothering to keep the irritated surprise from his voice. "Do you think you should speak to your daed that way?"

"You've been mooning around the kitchen and the front room for at least half an hour now." Her tone sounded equally tart. Her cheeks were rosy and she kept looking toward the battery-operated clock on the wall. "We know how to cook. We won't embarrass you. You should wash up. They'll be here any minute."

"I never thought you would embarrass me, and I know what time it is." Gabriel studied his oldest daughter. She looked flustered. "It's just the Crouches. Friends. Why are you in such a state? Is this about Edmond? You know how I feel…"

"I'm not in a state and it's not about Edmond." Without looking at him, she began lifting the pork chops from the skillet and laying them on a platter. "You're in a state."

"Nee."

She turned and they glared at each other. Gabriel won the match. "I expect you to keep your distance from Edmond. You may be on your rumspringa, but I still know what's best for you. And he is not it."

"How can you know that? He only…he only listens to me."

"Listens to you?"

"Jah. He listens. He knows how I feel. He lost his daed."

"Like you lost your mudder."

"Jah."

Gabriel lowered his head, not wanting to absorb the pain in his daughter's eyes. He should be the one she shared those thoughts with, but she couldn't because he worked and he did chores and he left her to raise his little girls. "I'm sorry."

"Sorry?" She looked shocked by his admission. "You didn't do anything."

"I should've been more…here."

"You do what daeds do."

"No matter." He drew a breath. "Edmond is not for you."

"He's a friend. We're too young for courting."

The words sank in. Could he trust that it wouldn't become more? He knew too much about the ways of the heart. He'd fallen in love with Abigail's mother long before the age of courting. "If you don't honor my wishes, we'll have to move again."

Her mouth dropped open and she began to shake her head. "Nee. Please. Don't make us move. Not again. We're just getting settled. And Edmond is…well…he's…"

"More than a friend. Just as I thought." Gabriel hated to be so hard on her, but her future, their future, depended on her obeying him. "I'm your father and I'm asking you to honor my wishes."

Abigail didn't reply, but her gaze darkened. She bit a lip and he knew she was doing exactly what Laura did in those moments they disagreed. Harnessing the words and thinking ahead to how she could get what she wanted without thwarting his authority. Laura had been good at it. Good at making him see her way—eventually.

He opened his mouth but before he could remonstrate further, Seth hurled himself through the doorway. "They're here, they're here!"

Suddenly feeling as bashful as a five-year-old, Gabriel followed the children to the front room. He opened the door. Helen smiled up at him, her face flushed, a pie—lemon meringue from the looks of it—in her hands. Caught by her pink cheeks, clean-scrubbed face, and bright brown eyes, he forgot to say anything.

"May we come in?" Helen asked, her smile fading. "Are we early?"

"Right on time." He meant to sound friendlier, but the words came out flat in his ears. His conversation with Abigail hung over them. Did Helen know how close her son and his daughter were becoming? "I mean, come on in, supper is ready."

Helen slipped by him, so close he could smell the fresh scent of her soap, followed by the children. Edmond managed to make eye contact before he ducked his head and rushed past. He didn't stray too far, but veered toward Seth, who immediately engaged the older boy in a discussion of what he thought of going fishing after they ate.

Heaving a breath, Gabriel showed Helen to the table while her girls trailed after Abigail into the kitchen. "Have a seat."

"How was your day?"

"I can't do that."

"What?" Her quizzical expression made her look half her age. "Answer a simple question?"

"Make small talk." He waited until she sank into a chair and took the one opposite her on the other side of the table. Having the expanse of wood and tablecloth between them helped for some reason. "Laura used to say...Sorry. See what I mean?"

"We can't not talk about our spouses. We were both married before." She smiled. Her dimples popped out. "Obviously. You have eight children. I have four. They got here somehow."

The tension that held hostage the muscles in his shoulders and neck eased its grip.

"You're right. Laura used to say I missed the class at school where they taught us how to visit."

Helen grinned. "I'm just the opposite. I go on and on until people get annoyed with me."

"I won't be annoyed. If you talk, I won't have to."

"That wouldn't be fair. Isn't the idea for us to get to know each other?"

"Is it?" He found himself very much wanting an answer to that question. Did she want to get to know him? "Is it possible for us to set aside..."

"You mean for you to set aside," she cut in.

"For you to set aside how I've acted since I've been here in Bliss Creek. I haven't been very nice to you."

"We got off on the wrong foot, that's all." She offered her hand. Uncertain, he took it. "Gabriel Gless, I'm pleased to meet you."

"Same here, Helen Crouch."

At that moment the girls began streaming into the room, carrying the bounty of food Abigail and Mary Beth had prepared. The boys quickly followed, their hands clean and their hair slicked back with the water they'd used to wash their faces. The room filled up then and there was no time for personal conversation. The children laughed and chatted as if they'd known each other all their lives. Helen looked so pleased, she looked almost at ease. Gabriel found himself imagining what it would be like for this to be an everyday scene. Their combined families sharing meals. *Whoa, slow down the horses.* What about Edmond and Abigail? What if he decided to move his family with Thomas's to Missouri? Did Helen plan to move? How could she stay here if her brothers went? All these questions swirled around him like a swarm of gnats.

Helen's gaze sought out his. "This is nice."

"Jah."

After the meal had been cleared and the girls began the dishes while the boys went to do the evening chores, Gabriel got to his feet. What now? The heat in the house pressed against him. He hadn't thought this through. Inviting her into his home. What did he do with her now? She looked at him, her expression so expectant, so unsure. Did his expression look the same?

"It's so warm." She waved at her face with plump fingers. "A walk might be nice. There might be a breeze down by the creek."

"There might be."

"Besides the food was so good, I ate too much. I expect a walk would help me work it off."

"Would you like to take a walk?" Feeling like an idiot, Gabriel moved toward the door. His boot caught on a chair leg. He stumbled. Now who was the clumsy one? "I mean, I don't know how much cooler..."

"I'd love to take a walk."

They took a meandering path down by the creek and into the stand of woods that separated his property from the Brennamans. Neither spoke until they could see the trickle of water that had once been a flowing stream reduced by the drought.

"This is nice too." Helen swiped at a fly buzzing her face. Perspiration dampened her forehead. "It's a beautiful evening."

"You're not too warm?" He'd been wrong to follow her lead. Better to save walks for another time, later in the evening when the heat was less oppressive. "Walks in August aren't really that pleasant, I reckon."

"I'm walking with you." She said the words so simply, so without artifice, that Gabriel knew he'd been given a great gift. Helen's gaze traveled over his face to his mouth. "I'm content."

"All the same, we'd best not stay out long." This thing between them—whatever it was—only served to make his life more complicated. "Who knows what trouble the little ones are getting into."

"You're a good daed."

"Danki." Her compliment burned like salt in a wound. If she only knew how he chafed at his inability to make decisions, his uncertainty about the family's future. Daniel had left him. The little girls were growing up without a mother to guide them. "It doesn't always seem so."

"I know. I suffer the same anxieties."

"And I've made them worse with my censure."

"I've made mistakes." Her face colored. "But I've learned from them. You know, Edmond isn't a bad boy. In fact, he has a good heart and he's trying to be a good friend to Abigail. That's all."

"They're too young."

"The more you try to keep them apart, the more they're drawn together."

"Not if I take the family to Missouri."

She stopped in the middle of the road. Gabriel kicked himself mentally. He hadn't meant to blurt it out like that.

"You'd do that because of my son?"

"Nee. Not because of Edmond. Not only that. I'm trying to figure out what's best for them. If Thomas goes…"

"Then why are we here? Why are we taking this walk in this horrible heat?"

She sounded so disappointed. This meant something to her. As it had him. He couldn't be sure what. Had he started something he couldn't finish? His heart did a strange hiccup. Something he wanted to finish?

"I haven't decided anything."

"But you're thinking about it."

"Aren't *you* thinking about it? Won't you go if your brothers go?"

"I can't. My mudder's sight is leaving her and I won't uproot her. I have my home business. I can sell at the bakery."

"What do your brothers say?"

"Nothing has been decided. They think it will be up to them." She kicked at a rock. "I'm not sure they've thought it through. They haven't thought of Mudder. They haven't thought of me as a woman who can take care of herself. Who has taken care of herself for a long time."

"You don't need anyone's help." He had no doubt she could take care of herself. She didn't need a man. She didn't need him. "So you'll stay."

"Jah, I'll stay." She started walking again. Her gaze stayed on the ground. "I hope you'll do the same."

The last words were spoken so softly Gabriel could barely hear them. He lengthened his stride to catch up, but she kept her face averted.

He grabbed her elbow but she jerked away. "Helen, nothing's been decided."

"You still think of me as the bad mudder and Edmond as a bad boy. We have nothing more to talk about."

"I don't. I'm trying."

"You have one foot out the door already."

"Nee. The kinner won't want to move again. I don't want to move again. I want to do what is right for them."

She said nothing more, instead trudging toward the house, head down, face somber. Gabriel stayed by her side and searched for something to say. Nothing came. Everything had been said.

Mary Elizabeth waved to them from the front yard. She and Naomi sat on the front step, each with a glass of sweet tea. Betsy and Ginny had engaged the younger girls in a rousing game of tag.

Gabriel managed a smile at the enthusiasm with which they dashed around the yard, squealing and laughing. "To have that much energy."

Helen didn't answer him. She went to Naomi. "Where's Edmond?"

Gabriel followed her gaze. No Edmond. No Abigail. "Mary Elizabeth, where's Abigail?"

Mary Elizabeth sighed. Her gaze didn't meet his. "Edmond took her for a buggy ride. They took our buggy. She said not to wait up. She said she would give Edmond a ride home later. Edmond said you shouldn't wait up either."

"They said not to wait up?" The slow burn worked its way up his neck and across his face. "Not to wait up?"

"Gabriel, I'm sorry." Helen held up both hands. "I gave him a severe scolding before we came here. I thought he would contain himself. I thought they both would."

"It's late. I'd best get these girls to bed." It wasn't her fault. Her son had a wayward heart and no father to set him straight. Still, Gabriel couldn't imagine how they could come together, two families as one, with this lack of respect for his wishes. Better he take the family and go. "Tomorrow will be another long day."

"I'm sorry." Helen's voice caught in her throat. Her face reddened. "It's their rumspringa. You know that."

Her crestfallen face hurt his heart. He tried to see his way through it. How could they ever work this out?

"Gabriel?"

"I know that and I'm sorry too." He called to Seth who trotted from the barn. "Hitch up Helen's buggy for her. It's time for them to head home."

⁂

Annie took a sip of lemonade from the thermos Isaac offered her, aware that he watched her every move from his spot on the blanket he'd spread under an enormous oak tree. The branches provided ample shade. If only there were a cooling breeze to go with it. "It's good. Very good."

"I'll tell Mary Beth you liked it." He opened the picnic basket and brought out cold chicken, bread, and a slab of cheese. "It's not much, but Abigail and Mary Beth had their hands full cooking for company."

"Company?"

Isaac grinned. "Helen and her children came for supper."

"Indeed. Wunderbaar." Finally, Helen might have a chance to find new happiness. "I mean, if you're happy about it."

"Who wouldn't be?" Isaac shrugged, his expression light. "My daed needs companionship as much as the next person. Someone to talk to about his kids, to help him raise them."

"Is that all you see marriage as?" She arranged the food on his plate and handed it to him. "Two people taking care of their children?"

"Nee." He let the plate hover in the air between them for a few seconds, his dark brown eyes piercing her. "Do you?"

"I've been married before." She said the words gently, knowing he didn't need the reminder, but she did have some experience in this arena. "It's a balancing act. Time for your children, time for the house, time for the man you love."

"Same for the man, I suppose."

"It is. Both take their responsibilities to heart. One of those responsibilities is seeing to it that you spend time with your husband. Give him your attention."

He took a bite of his sandwich and chewed, his face thoughtful. She did the same, wondering where this conversation would take them. He continued to eat without speaking until she wondered if she'd said too much. She laid her plate on the blanket, her appetite gone.

"Don't you like it? Mary Beth's bread is good. Not as good as yours, but good."

"It's good." She picked up the plate to show her approval, but she couldn't have swallowed another bite. "I've eaten Mary Beth's cooking before, remember?"

"What's wrong?"

"Does it bother you that I've been married before?" The words tumbled out on top of each other. Relief at getting them out made her legs feel weak. "None of this is new to me."

"If it did, do you think I'd be here?"

"It's one thing to have something in your mind. It's another to start to see it take form in front of you, to begin to see how it would be to live it."

"True. I like what I'm seeing in front of me." He set his plate next to hers, then he leaned forward and traced her check with one finger. "I like it very much."

The rush of heat that roared through Annie made her jerk back. "That's not what I meant. I don't fish for compliments. I'm not a vain girl who needs admirers."

"I'm sorry." His smile fled. "I didn't mean to take liberties. I thought…"

"It's fine. I'm just a little jumpy." Forcing herself to breathe, she picked up her sandwich, then laid it back down. He seemed so sincere. He meant what he said. He shouldn't have to apologize for saying something nice about her. "Thank you."

"Thank you?"

"For the compliment."

"Do you like what you see?" He leaned in close again, his voice low, husky, his expression eager yet uncertain. "Annie, do you think you could like me?"

Annie breathed. "I do. I do like you."

He leaned closer. His warm breath grazed her cheek. His lips touched hers. Only for a second. Then they brushed against her cheek and he drew away.

"Oh, my." She dropped her plate, and the sandwich and the chips slid from it and landed on the blanket. "Oh, sorry." She scrambled to her knees and began tossing them back on the plate.

Isaac grabbed her arm. "Stop. Stop. It's okay. I didn't mean to fluster you."

"Yes, you did." She couldn't help it. She glared up at him. "You did, Isaac. You know you did."

"Is that a bad thing?" He chuckled and pushed back a lock of her hair that had escaped her kapp with a touch so gentle she barely felt it. "Come on, Annie, was it so bad?"

"Don't laugh at my expense."

"I'm not. I'm laughing because the thought of doing that every day for the rest of my life makes me very happy." His grin reinforced the words, as did the way his hand gripped hers. "Do you think you could be kissed by me every day for the rest of your life? Would you get tired of it?"

"Isaac!"

"I'm sorry. Am I going too fast again?"

"Most definitely, and I think you know it."

"I can't help it. That's how you make me feel."

Annie forced herself to breathe. She settled back on the blanket. "Don't do that again."

"I won't."

"You promise?" She didn't want him kissing her again. Did she? "Tell me you promise."

"I promise I won't until you give me leave."

"Good." That was what she wanted, exactly what she wanted. "That's what I want."

"I don't believe you."

"What?" He was infuriating. "What are you talking about?"

"You want me to kiss you again. Now."

He looked down at her with that smile. She liked his smile. He had nice lips and nice teeth. *Stop it.* "Have a cookie." She thrust the cookie at him with a shaking hand. He opened his mouth and let her stick it between his teeth. "There. Now be quiet and enjoy the scenery."

He took the cookie and began to chew as he leaned back on one arm, his legs crossed in front of him. He looked perfectly at ease. Annie, on the other hand, knew she did not. She dropped her hands into her lap and willed them to stop shaking. *Breathe. In and out.*

Isaac knew too much. He saw too much. And he was right too often for her liking. She did want him to kiss her again. The idea scared her more than anything she could imagine. She couldn't do this again. She couldn't love a man who might on any given day be taken from her. She didn't want to love him.

It scared her too much. The thought that it might be too late scared her even more.

Chapter 30

Helen settled onto the bench next to Annie and Emma. The smaller children had been left in the charge of the older children. Only adults could attend this community meeting. Nothing in Emma's expression told Helen anything. If Thomas had shared his impressions of Missouri or his recommendations with her, it didn't show in his fraa's face. She looked calm, peaceful, and content. Helen tried for the same, but expectations that hung in the air made it hard. She squirmed on the hard bench, trying to get comfortable.

"For goodness sake, Helen, stop fussing and sit still." So Emma did feel the tension. Helen heard it in her tone and saw it in her expression. "It will be a long evening."

"What does Thomas say?" Helen leaned closer. "Is he recommending we all go?"

Emma shook her head, but before she could say anything Micah Kelp and the deacons filed down the aisle between the two sets of benches neatly arranged in Micah's barn. He cleared his throat. The soft murmur of conversations died away. "Thomas."

Thomas stood and went forward. When he turned to face the members of his district, exhaustion and tension lined his face. He bowed his head for a few seconds, eyes closed, then raised it. His expression eased.

"Tobias, Luke, Thaddeus, Silas, and I spent ten days in Missouri and Arkansas. We passed some of those days with our brethren in Seymour and Jamesport as well as some of the smaller communities. We had a good visit. I've been asked to report what we found."

He went on to say the districts had been friendly and welcoming. Seymour and Jamesport were the biggest and most well-established of the districts. The communities in Seymour appeared more conservative, less touched by tourism. "Jamesport is like Bliss Creek," he explained. "They have a lot of tourist trade."

"What about the farming?" Paul Yonkers asked, his face anxious. He shouldn't have interrupted, but Helen understood the desire to do so. "What about the land?"

"The communities have been blessed. The weather has been kind to them. The farms do well." Thomas's gaze didn't waver. "Land is available and reasonably priced."

"So what you're saying is it would be a good move for us." Levi Grable rubbed his neck with a huge hand. "Do you recommend we go?"

Thomas's gaze strayed to Emma and then to Helen. She held her breath. *Don't be silly.* She let it out.

"Tobias, Thaddeus, Luke, Silas, and I agree we should consider starting a district in one of the smaller towns. Not Jamesport, for sure. Or even Seymour. They're too big for us. Some place smaller where we can get our own fresh start." Thomas spread his hands, his fingers long, tanned, and callused. "But the decision belongs to all of us. For me, I would not have us abandon Bliss Creek. It has been a good place to raise our families and a good place to worship. Not always easy, but then we don't require that it be easy, only godly."

"Well said." Micah Kelp returned to the front of the room. Thomas took his seat. "I've spoken with these men at length. We agree another trip must be made, this one to look for tracts of land suitable for our purposes. Farms such as Thomas's will have to be sold. I doubt this will be difficult given the discovery of the oil. That will give us the seed money for the new district."

"Then we'll move to Missouri," Thaddeus said. "All of us?"

"Nee. I have also met with Mayor Haag and the Englisch City Council members at their request. They wanted us to know their banks are willing to give loans to any members of our communities in need." Micah removed his glasses and polished them on his sleeve. "I told them that would not be necessary. Mayor Haag also said they could help with the purchase of Thomas's farm and finding another property for him."

"That is kind of them." Thomas said, his voice gruff, but his expression placid. Helen longed for that kind of serenity. Thomas never wavered. "What did you tell them?"

"To be honest, I suspect their offer stems more from the benefit they receive from our presence than from a desire to help us. But no matter. I told them we will consider their offer and we will." Micah's gaze floated over the room. "Their offer only serves to highlight our problem. We do not want to rely on the Englischers in order to stay here. Mayor Haag has plans. Plans for bus tours and advertising in Englisch magazines. More Englischers will come to gawk at us. Those with farms that are failing must move quickly to get this fresh start. I am meeting with those families separately. We will have the names at our next meeting."

"What about those of us who are just getting started here?" Isaac stood, his hat in his hand. Helen couldn't keep from looking beyond him to Gabriel. Would they go too? They'd only just arrived, but Gabriel seemed set on fleeing from her and her children. Her throat ached with the effort to swallow back her emotion. She focused on Isaac, who gripped his hat so hard his knuckles turned white. "We don't know yet how our business will do, and we don't have crops in the ground yet."

"You might do well to think of moving before you sink a lot of effort into land that may not produce and a store that may not do well." Micah shrugged. "It might be wiser to move now, but it's your daed's choice."

Helen saw the look on Gabriel's face. He'd wanted to run since the day they met. He needed no excuse. His gaze caught hers. He didn't look away, but his face revealed nothing. Whatever he'd decided to do, it didn't involve her.

Annie settled into the rocking chair on the porch. After the stuffy air of Micah's barn and the long ride home in the stifling humidity of early August, it surprised her to find a slight breeze wafting across her face. She leaned into it. The sun had begun to sink behind the horizon. Noah slept. Everyone slept. Except her. The excited buzzing of the crowd after the meeting still filled her ears. The somber, yet expectant looks on the faces of her neighbors danced in her mind's eye. Their community would soon fracture and no one seemed worried.

"You're up late." Luke shoved open the screen door and trudged barefoot onto the porch. "You'll be sorry in the morning when it's time to make the bread."

"I know." She sighed and rocked, letting the familiar motion calm her swirling emotions. "I'll go in soon."

"Don't rush off on my account." He eased into the other chair. "Nice breeze."

"Nice." She rocked some more, wondering what went on in the head of her oldest brother. One could never tell from his face. "All things considered."

"Nice."

They fell silent.

"What's it like?" She swiped a sideways glance at his plain face. "This town where you've decided to settle?"

"Like this, only greener." His expression grew more animated than she'd seen it in many years. "More trees. I imagine in the fall they'll be red and orange and yellow. And the town is a lot like Bliss Creek, only even smaller."

"Even smaller." She mulled his words. "The winters will be the same since it's almost due east."

"Should be."

"And the town?"

"Filled with people minding their own business."

Annie watched dots of lights flit and dive in the front yard. Fireflies. Like miniature flashlights. "Are you happy to go, Luke?"

"Strange question."

It would seem so to Luke, who never questioned his lot in life. Who clung to the rules. She hadn't expected him to answer the question. Being happy wasn't the point. "I know. I only wondered."

"I'm...excited isn't the word. I don't reckon I know what it is exactly." His rough cadence gave away the emotion in him. In the light from the gas lamp that shone in the open window, his face was half-hidden in shadows and light. Annie never saw much emotion on his face, and it gave her a strange sense of contentment to know her big brother hadn't lost the ability to feel happiness. His lot in life hadn't robbed him of those wonderful feelings of possibility. "I'm waiting to see what comes next. It's good to know something will come next. I haven't seen it all or heard it all. There's more. God will show us more."

He looked at her as if to see if she understood. She did. "A little bit like an adventure?"

"I'm a grown man. No need for adventure." His tone belied the words.

Annie smiled at her stoic, grown-up brother who'd been forced to take the reins and lead them on a rough, pit-filled road. "An adventure," she said again.

"Jah." A grin split his face for a second. "Don't you go repeating that."

"Never." She rocked some more. "What's the town's name?"

"We haven't decided which town for sure yet. It depends on whether we can afford the land. Which farms are for sale."

"Which one are you hoping for?"

"The ones God chooses for us."

"Luke."

"New Hope. The town's name is New Hope."

"New Hope." She whispered the name to herself. "New Hope. You and Leah will be happy there, then."

"I expect. As well you could be." His tone roughened. "You could use a new beginning too."

She thought of Isaac. "I have the bakery."

"You would let Emma go without you?"

"She has Thomas and the babies. And Mary and Lillie."

"Who will you have?"

"Josiah and Miriam are here. I have Noah to think of."

"Josiah and Miriam are busy with the shop and the farm and the babies."

Annie listened to the words her brother couldn't say. "I'll miss you too."

"Come with us."

The fact that Luke asked rather than ordered her to join him on this adventure touched her. "I can't."

"You can."

"I have the bakery. This is my home."

"Your home is where your family is."

"I can't leave here." She couldn't tell him about the anguish caused by the thought of leaving the last place where David had been part of her life. She couldn't tell him of the need to face the future squarely in this place. She wouldn't tell him about Isaac. Not yet. "My life is here."

Luke stopped rocking. He smoothed his beard and exhaled. "Jah."

"Jah."

"Best get in to bed." He stood and stretched. "Morning will be here soon enough."

He was right. A new day awaited them both.

Chapter 31

Annie slathered more cream cheese frosting on the German chocolate cake. She picked up the pastry bag of pink frosting, turned it upside down, and squeezed, carefully guiding it as she formed the letters *Happy Birthday* across the broad expanse of the two-layer cake. Aenti Louise's favorite. Annie inhaled the scent of baking lasagna and her mouth watered. She hadn't been able to eat breakfast or dinner. Her stomach twisted in a knot. One year since David's death. Why must the anniversary occur on the same day as her favorite aunt's birthday?

If she were any other person, she'd have called it unfair. But Annie knew better. Being fair didn't enter into it. Luke and Thomas sat in the front room making plans for moving their families to another state. Tomorrow they would leave for another trip, this time to scout properties. The *For Sale* signs had been installed on their gates. The real estate agents in town had been informed. Mayor Haag, who sputtered and spit fire, had been informed.

She willed her shaking fingers to steady. What would she do without Emma to rely on? And Mary and Lillie? She longed to ask Emma to let the twins stay with her, but it wouldn't be fair to them. She would be at the bakery all day long. Six days a week. Not the family life they needed. Resolute, she focused on the meal she'd made. Aenti Louise

loved lasagna. Leah argued that they should have had a pot roast or a
ham, but Aenti Louise had trouble chewing meat these days. Noodles.
Ground beef. Cheese. Those she could handle.

What else needed to be done? Lillie, Mary, and Rebecca had set
the tables. With the Gless family arriving along with the Brennamans,
the house burst at the seams. They'd pulled out two folding tables and
stuck them together for the younger children while the adults would
sit around the two pine tables. Annie's fingers trembled again as she
thought of Isaac's dark gaze on her when he strode into their house, little Rachel on one hip, Isabelle on the other. He looked the picture of a
family man. They could've been his girls. But they weren't. She forced
her gaze from his face. She wouldn't think of those soft lips grazing
hers. She wouldn't think of the way he'd bent close and cupped her
face with one hand as he kissed her. No, she'd spent enough time daydreaming about that. To her utter despair, she couldn't drive the memory from her mind.

"Annie?"

Had her thoughts brought him into the kitchen? She jumped, and
the *y* in birthday streaked and ended in a long, scraggly tail.

"Isaac." She turned. The icing dripped on her apron. *"Ach."*

"I didn't mean to startle you. I was only going to ask for a glass of
lemonade. Emma said you…"

"Jah, jah. Right here." She turned too quickly and bumped her hip
on the counter. "Ouch."

"I thought we were doing better after our picnic the other night."
He took two steps in her direction. "Now we're back to you acting
more nervous than a mother cat with her litter being attacked by a
wolf."

"Nee." She laid the pastry bag on the counter and picked up the
pitcher of lemonade. "I didn't hear you come in the room."

"Does that mean you'll come out with me again? I wasn't sure, the
way we left it."

"I think so."

"You think so?" Incredulity made his voice rough as sandpaper. "Annie, it's one step forward and two steps back with you."

"I'm sorry. This is hard for me." She handed him the glass. His fingers brushed against hers. A warmth like cocoa on a winter night coursed through her. "I'm trying."

"I know." The hoarseness of his voice made her throat tighten. He sipped from the glass and then set it on the prep table. His gaze never left her face. "I'm trying not to go too fast for you, but it's not my nature."

Annie couldn't help but smile at this.

"What are you smiling about?" He looked confused. "It's not funny."

"I'm smiling at you. No truer words were spoken. You want to run before we walk. You want to gallop."

"Fine. No galloping." He dabbed at the frosting with his long, tan finger and popped it in his mouth. "But could you not walk like an old lady? We'll never get there."

Annie smacked at his hand and missed. "Don't eat that!"

"It's sweet like you—when you're not being crabby!"

"Crabby!"

Isaac took another swipe at the frosting and Annie pushed his hand away. He snagged her arm at the wrist and held on. His touch sent heat crackling up her arm and through her chest. To her heart. They stared at each other. She should move. She should step back. He should release her. Or he should kiss her. No, not here. Not now. Annie willed herself to relax. Small steps. Seemly steps. The steps of two Plain people who knew how to go slowly and carefully into a union that would last them a lifetime. Neither of them moved. It seemed they'd ceased to breathe. Or they breathed at the same time in a barely noticeable rhythm all their own.

"What are you two doing?" A frown plastered across her face, Leah stood in the doorway. "Annie, haven't you finished that cake? John has gone to fetch Louise. They'll be here any minute."

Annie's face burned. Her whole body burned. She jerked back and Isaac's hand dropped. He picked up the glass of lemonade and turned to Leah. "This lemonade is *gut*. Did you make it?"

"Jah, well, it's only lemonade." Leah bustled past him and planted herself next to Annie. "Luke and Thomas are talking about the trip—what they saw and about the land. They're trying to decide where the best place is to settle. I expect you'll want to hear about it," she said to Isaac.

"I have no plans to leave Bliss Creek." Isaac's gaze landed squarely on Annie when he said these words. His tone made them a promise. His gaze made them a promise to her. "But I'll leave y'all to finish up here. I don't want to be in your way."

Without haste, he strode from the room.

Annie grabbed the pastry bag and touched up the spot where Isaac had swiped the frosting.

"It's about time."

"What?" She concentrated on the frosting, knowing her sister-in-law stood close by, judging.

"Noah needs a father. Even more when we leave and there is no man in the house to teach him." The emotion in her sister-in-law's voice made Annie look up. Sadness etched lines in Leah's face. "This is a big place for one woman and a child."

"This moving must be hard for you." Annie wanted to go to Leah, but her sister-in-law abhorred shows of emotion or physical affection. "I'm sorry."

"Don't wait too long." Leah would never acknowledge what she perceived to be weakness. "A hard-working man like Isaac Gless can have the fraa of his choice."

"Is that the baby crying?" This was private business between Isaac and her. Determined not to think about it, Annie cocked her head. "Yours or mine?"

Leah shook her head, but she left the room all the same, as Annie knew she would.

Wiping her hands on the towel, she glanced around the kitchen. Green beans, rolls, creamed corn, baked potatoes—all Aenti Louise's favorites had been prepared with love. Time to visit with family. Even if that meant living with Isaac's knowing stare all evening.

In the family room, Annie found Emma putting the finishing touches on the wrapping of the gift she, Annie, and the other quilters had made for Aenti Louise—a lovely Sunshine and Shadow quilt in bright maroons, blues, and a lighter mauve, along with a crocheted blanket in a matching pale pink yarn. Glad the prohibition against wearing bright colors didn't extend to their quilt making, Annie touched the white tissue paper. It crinkled under her fingers. Aenti Louise would love the pattern. It needed bright colors to make the contrast work. And colors didn't make the quilt any less useful.

Her aunt never complained, but more often than not her frail body shivered with cold because of poor circulation. Come winter, she would delight in the warmth provided by the quilt and the blanket. At eighty-two, she seemed to be disappearing. There was a little less of her to hug each time Annie saw her. Annie brushed away the thought, along with the dark clouds that surrounded this anniversary. Today, they celebrated the birthday of the oldest member of their family.

"Very nice!" she told her sister when she held up the wrapped box. "She'll have no idea what it is."

"They're here, they're here!" William bolted into the room, reversed directions, and headed for the door. "Onkel John is pulling the buggy up to the house. Daed says we should all greet her on the porch."

Smoothing her apron, Annie paused to lift Noah from his play pen. He gurgled and smacked his hands together as if clapping. On the front porch, William popped up and down like a jack-in-the-box next to his brother Joseph, who was chanting "happy birthday" in a sing-song tone. These boys had none of their father's calm, slow-as-molasses approach to life. Nor Leah's morose outlook. Maybe they were a throwback to Luke and Annie's daed and mudder, who so loved to celebrate these special occasions.

"Stop it, William. Joseph, settle down." Leah shifted Jebediah from one hip to the other. "No need to get so excited. It's just a birthday."

An eighty-second birthday. What exactly would excite Leah? *Forgive me, God, for such an unkind thought.* Annie bounced Noah on her own hip and plastered a smile on her face. "Aenti, happy birthday, happy birthday," she called as Onkel John helped her aunt climb down from the buggy. "We're so glad you're here."

"I'm happy to be here. Happy to be anywhere at my age." Aenti Louise chuckled, then coughed, a deep, hacking cough. Annie started forward, but Aenti Louise clutched Onkel John's arm with clawed fingers. Her wrinkled face gray, she grimaced and straightened once her feet were on solid ground. "Where is that new baby? Where's Emma?"

"Here, Aenti!" Emma waved from the front door with her free hand. She cradled Lilah in the other.

With Onkel John on one side and Luke on the other, Aenti Louise made it up the steps and into the crowd clustered on the porch to celebrate her arrival. She didn't get out anymore, except on special occasions. This qualified, of that Annie was certain. They were only passing through this world, but the time spent here could be made special and spent well with loved ones. She focused on the smile on Aenti's face as she touched Lilah's face with a gnarled finger.

"What a fine baby. You do good work, Emma." Aenti patted Emma's arm. "Come, come, let's go inside. What are we standing out here for? I hear there's cake. Chocolate cake. Can we start with the cake? Is there vanilla ice cream?"

"We made the ice cream!" Rebecca squeezed past Josiah and Miriam and tugged on Aenti Louise's arm. "Me and Eli and Mary and Lillie, we all made it together. We took turns with the crank."

"I thought my arm would fall off," Eli added. "The twins complained, but I didn't. I didn't mind at all."

"As it should be. A big boy like you. Besides, making ice cream should be a family affair. Now let's eat."

Everyone laughed and waited for Aenti Louise to pass through the door before jostling for position to follow. She looked back. "Annie, come give your old aunt a hand, why don't you?"

Surprised, Annie took her arm at the elbow and guided her through the door. Her aunt's arm felt like thin bone through her sleeve. When had she become so skinny?

"You do fine work too." Aenti's whisper, gravelly with age, sounded like a mix between honey and vinegar. "Noah is a strong, healthy boy who will grow into a man every bit as hard working, strong, and faithful as your David."

Annie could only nod.

Inside, Aenti refused to stay in the living room, tottering instead to the kitchen. "What can I do to help?"

"Nothing, Louise." Leah intervened. "You're the guest of honor tonight. It's your birthday. Sit. Sit!"

"I'm not a dog." Aenti Louise shook her finger at Luke's wife. "And I'm not on my deathbed yet. I can serve the rolls or toss the greens. Make myself useful."

"The lasagna still has about twenty minutes," Annie said as she handed Noah to Lillie. "The rolls are done. If you want to toss the greens, that's fine, just please sit to do it."

"Presents!" little Esther cried. "Presents!"

"The presents are for Aenti Louise." Leah frowned at her daughter. "Greed is unbecoming."

Aenti Louise took Esther's plump hand in her own clawed fingers. "Why don't I tell you a story, little one, to pass the time until we eat? That will be my contribution to the meal."

The nearly dozen children in the room chorused a collective *jah*. Annie smiled. She'd loved storytime with Aenti Louise too. To be taken on the wings of her words to another place and time had been a treat that had made holidays even more special. In those days, Mudder had been there to bustle about in the kitchen and to tell Aenti Louise her job was to keep the children out from underfoot. Time ran on. Nothing could stop it. Trying to escape her thoughts, Annie rushed into the kitchen to check on the lasagna.

"She's right, you know."

Annie paused from peeking under the tin foil to check the lasagna at the sound of Miriam's voice. Her friend moved from the doorway to stand near the prep table. Her apron barely covered her enormous belly.

"What do you mean? Right about what?"

"You're doing fine. Noah is growing and he's healthy. It won't be long before you'll find yourself ready to share your life with someone else."

"Would you?" To her horror, Annie heard bitterness in her voice. Miriam had no fault in her present situation. She only wanted to help. As did everyone. She tried to soften her tone. "Would you be ready to move on to someone new if something happened to Josiah?"

Miriam's face crumpled. Tears wet her cheeks and her nose turned red. "I can't imagine if it were my Josiah. I surely can't." Her voice quivered. "I know we're taught to be happy for those who go on ahead. They go with Gott. But I can't imagine my life without Josiah. I'm sorry, Annie."

"I'm the one who's sorry." Annie rushed across the room to her friend. "I shouldn't have said that. You're only trying to help."

"It's this bobbeli. He keeps me awake at night." Miriam laid her head on Annie's shoulder for a second. "Between little Hazel Grace's colic and my heartburn, I'm worn out. But I'm not complaining. I know I'm blessed. Every day I remind myself of how blessed I am."

"I try to do the same."

"Try harder." Her face gaunt, Aenti Louise put her hand on the door frame as if to hold herself up. Her clothes hung on her spindly body as if they'd been meant for a much larger person. "It's time."

"Time?" How could she say that? Annie thought Aenti, of all people, would understand. After Onkel Samuel died, she'd never married again. Her children, Annie's cousins, had many children, but none lived nearby. She didn't see her own grandchildren. "It was never time for you."

"Not true. I had my chance and I missed it."

Annie contemplated her aunt's pensive face. Aenti Louise looked as if she no longer saw the oak prep table or the propane oven or the wood-burning stove or the enormous tub where they washed the dishes. She didn't see the cake on the table. Her gaze went far beyond the walls of the house. Annie wanted her back from the place that caused her pain. "I didn't know. We never knew."

"I let my grief rule the day for too long." Aenti sank into a chair at the table. She grasped its edge as if for support. "I never told anyone, because I was ashamed to admit I turned him away. Besides, it was between him and me. He moved on. He married again. His life is complete."

"Who? Him who?" Annie dropped in the chair across from her. "Tell us."

Aenti coughed, a raspy, ugly sound. Annie scurried to the counter to pour her a glass of water. Aenti drank greedily, coughed again, then sighed. "Can't shake this cold." She sniffed and wiped at her nose with a hankie. "Even now, to tell you would be wrong. It was between him and me. No one else."

"But you regret it."

"That's the only reason I bring it up now. I could've been married all these years instead of alone. When your onkel went, I was too old for more children, but not too old to want companionship, to want to have my own home and family around me. But I couldn't bring myself to let go of the past and have faith in the future God had planned for me."

They were silent for several seconds.

"It smells like the lasagna is done. From the aroma, it'll be mighty fine eating." Aenti rose and shuffled toward the door. In the doorway she stopped and turned back. "It's not enough to know God has a plan for you. Have faith in His plan. You can't just sit around waiting for it to happen. Step out in faith. For Noah's sake." She smiled. "Now, I'd best tell those children their story."

She disappeared into the dining room.

Annie looked at Miriam. Her friend shrugged and smiled. "Has your aunt ever been wrong?"

"Never."

"Then take her advice."

"It's not that easy."

"So what do you think of Isaac?"

Annie dropped the bread basket. Fortunately, she hadn't put the rolls in it. She glanced at the doorway, sure saying his name would make him reappear again. "What about him?"

"I saw the way he looks at you. Just hearing his name makes you drop things." Miriam grinned. "Josiah's right. He makes your heart quiver, doesn't he?"

"No one makes my heart quiver." Annie scooped up the basket. "No one."

"We'll see about that. Let's eat. I'm starving."

Grateful to let the conversation go, Annie turned her back on Miriam and grabbed the potholders. She wished Helen were here. Helen would understand. Miriam was her best friend, but she had her first love. She had her husband. She couldn't understand.

Annie squared her shoulders, pasted a smile on her face, and went to serve the lasagna.

The next two hours passed in a blur of serving food, eating, laughing, and recalling other birthdays, some of their loved ones long gone, some more recent, all happy moments. They were stuffed and barely able to move when Mark dropped his napkin on his plate and let out a contented burp. "Remember when me and Luke and Josiah got David that new hat for his birthday, and it was too big and he insisted on wearing it anyway, even though it covered his eyes?" Mark grinned at the memory. "He walked around bumping into chairs and tables on purpose just to make us laugh. We offered to get him a smaller one, and he asked if we could get him a wig instead. We laughed so hard. I miss him."

The chuckles scattered and faded away. Annie knew they all looked at her. She pushed her half-eaten lasagna around on her plate with her fork. Aenti Louise stilled Annie's fingers with her own hand. Annie forced herself to look up. "I miss David too."

"Me too." Josiah plucked another roll from the basket and broke it in half. He didn't eat it. "We all do."

"But that doesn't mean we have to be sad. David would be the first to tell you that. He lived his time. He went on ahead of us." Aenti Louise picked up her glass of lemonade and slurped noisily. She'd hardly touched her food. No one spoke, waiting for her to continue. "Life goes on. If you learn anything from what's happened, learn that. God gives and He takes away. He is the Almighty, the Everlasting, the Great I Am. That means He knows what's He's doing. Praise Him for that. And let David go in peace. Just as I let my Samuel go in peace. Just as we let your mudder and daed go in peace."

She set the glass down with a thud. "Now, let's open those presents and then we'll have cake."

Annie stumbled to her feet and began to clear the plates.

"Leave them." Emma touched her arm. "We'll get them later. Let's enjoy this, for now."

She was right. Annie helped Mark and Lillie carry in the pile of presents. Aenti Louise took her time, fingering the wrapping paper, praising each gift, offering hugs of thanks.

At last she picked up the final gift. Her face lit up when the wrapping dropped away and she removed the box's lid. She held the material, then touched it to her wrinkled cheek. "It's beautiful. Danki, all of you. Sunshine and Shadow." She rubbed her hands across the squares of fabric arranged by color and turned on point to form alternating rows of light and dark triangles. The colors were bright against her pallid skin. "What made you choose this pattern?"

As if she didn't know. This was Aenti Louise, after all.

"You know, Aenti."

"I do know. I know it's been hard for you." She stood and accepted Annie's hug. "Danki."

She clung to Annie, not letting go of the hug, her head close. "You've been touched by death," she whispered in her ear. "You will be touched by birth again. You'll see. Sunshine and shadow. We will always have both in our lives."

"I know, Aenti." Annie turned her head away from the table and wiped at her face with the back of her sleeve. "Who wants cake and ice cream?"

"Me, I do, I do." Aenti's voice carried over the cries of the children. "Lots of ice cream."

Annie rushed to the kitchen to retrieve it. A series of raps on the front door made her stop midstride, whirl, and head to the living room. Everyone who had said they were coming to the birthday supper already sat around the tables.

She opened the door. Catherine stood on the porch, a package wrapped in brown and green paper clutched in her hands. Next to her stood a dark-haired man dressed in navy pants and a short-sleeved shirt, open at the collar, keys jangling in one hand.

"*Ach*, Catherine, what are you doing here?"

Chapter 32

Annie stared at Catherine and the stranger standing on the front porch in their Englisch clothes, their shiny blue car out of place next to the line of buggies. Indecision rendered Annie immobile. She couldn't invite Catherine and her Englisch friend into the Shirack home, even though it had once been her sister's home too. Luke and Leah would be furious. "What are you doing here?"

"I invited her," Aenti Louise called from the supper table. She couldn't possibly see Catherine at the door. She surely had keen hearing for a woman of her age. "Let her in. I want all my nieces here for this birthday."

Annie stared at the couple on the doorstep. "But…"

"This is my house." Luke appeared next to her. He clomped past Catherine as if he didn't see her there and tromped down the steps headed for the barn. "Last time I checked."

"She's not going to be around forever. I want to see her." Catherine stopped. Her gaze dropped. "You understand, don't you?"

Annie did understand. Aenti Louise's failing health had never been more apparent than it had been this evening. But she couldn't go against Luke's wishes. His house. Their Ordnung. "I'm sorry. Not here. Not tonight."

"Could you at least give her this?" Catherine proffered the package to Annie. "I don't want to cause any trouble. I stopped by to see her when I arrived in town. She mentioned the birthday supper."

Annie glanced back and saw Leah hovering near the door to the kitchen, her face tight with a thin-lipped frown. No help from that quarter. Annie squeezed past Catherine and her friend, whom she still hadn't introduced. With care not to slam it, Annie shut the door behind her. "Let's talk on the porch."

"Annie, this is Dean Barlow." Catherine took the man's hand. "My friend."

"Her fiancé, if she'd just admit it." Dean had a nice smile, even teeth, white against his tan. "Catherine talks about you all the time. You look just like her."

"Yes." Annie put one hand on the wooden railing to steady herself. For some reason, her legs felt weak. "You're the doctor. The student doctor."

"I am." He joined her at the railing while Catherine remained where she stood, looking down at the package in her hand, looking like she wondered how it got there and what she was expected to do with it. "I'm also in love with your sister."

"You are?" Annie looked up at him. His eyes were a clear blue, his tone untroubled, his posture relaxed and easy. So unlike the Plain men she knew. They didn't go about discussing their feelings with someone they'd just met. But then, maybe it took courage to do that. "Does she love you?"

"I expect she does." He grinned then, his gaze sliding toward Catherine. "She says she does and she says she never lies. She says the Amish don't lie."

"I'm sorry I can't invite you in."

"We'll live. Won't we, Cat?"

Cat?

"I'll live." Catherine sank into the hickory rocking chair. "We've no choice."

"You did have a choice and you made it," Annie pointed out. Catherine couldn't make this out to be anyone's fault but her own. They'd gone far beyond what was permitted in the time they'd spent together at the bakery. "Are you regretting it now?"

"Only our—your ways."

"Then you made the right choice."

"I made the choice I could live with."

Dean put both hands on the railing and leaned forward. He took a deep breath and let it out. "I don't know. I could get used to living in a place like Bliss Creek. It's so peaceful, so quiet. The air's fresh and the people pleasant. Not like the big city. Wichita is so loud and obnoxious sometimes. I wonder if Bliss Creek could use another doctor."

Annie turned in time to see the startled look on Catherine's face. She saw there, in that expression, the truth. Catherine would never return to Bliss Creek for good.

"Catherine." She went to her sister, knelt at her feet, and took the package from her hand. "Catherine, you know why you came here. It wasn't to see Aenti or me or to work on your thesis. It's another year away, that paper. You came to make your peace."

"There's no peace for me." Catherine shook her head, her eyes shimmering like the water in the pond in the afternoon sun. "You're supposed to forgive. Plain folks forgive. Why can't Luke forgive me?"

"He does forgive you, but he also believes in following the rules. That's what holds his world together. You know that. It's how he manages. He keeps going, taking care of this farm and all of us by following the rules."

"What about the rule that says you forgive?"

"Meidung isn't meant as a punishment. You know that. It's meant to force you to see what you're giving up. What your life will be like if you don't return to the fold. It also helps us to make sure we don't stumble and fall into your worldly ways. You know that as well as I do."

"It feels like punishment. Like I'm being punished for having seen that awful accident. For having watched them die and not being able to help them. I didn't even try to help them."

"You couldn't help them. No one could. You weren't a doctor, you were a young girl. No one blames you."

"Then why do I feel so guilty?"

"Because you loved them and they're gone and you're still here."

Catherine put her head in her hands and began to rock.

Dean squatted next to Annie. "Let me have her," he whispered. "I'll take care of her. I promise."

Annie rose. She went to the door, but she looked back, not able to stop herself. Dean drew Catherine from the rocking chair and folded his arms around her. Catherine's head fit in the crook of his arm, and he had to bend down to hold on to her. Her tears were muffled by his shirt, but his soft mutterings carried. He told her he loved her, God loved her, and her family loved her.

Catherine had indeed found the right man for her. Relief flooded Annie. Dean would do. She might never see him again, but she would know Catherine had found someone who understood her and would take care of her. Dean knew her sister needed reassurance. She would always need reassurance. Something about the accident she witnessed had ripped away everything solid and stable in her life, leaving her on shifting sands where her sense of security waned instead of grew.

Dean looked up and caught Annie's gaze. He nodded as if to say *I've got her*. Annie nodded and mouthed *Thank you*. She turned and went in. No need to look back. That chapter was closed.

Chapter 33

Annie slid from the buggy, lifted her skirt, and ran toward the dawdi haus. Onkel John stood at the doorway, his massive arms crossed over his chest. His hat hid his face, but she could see the emotion in the slump of his shoulders.

"She's been asking for you." His gruff voice scraped like sandpaper against her ears. "Best hurry."

Straightening her shoulders, she squeezed past him. The air in the house hung still and dank as if empty already. *She's not gone yet.* The birthday celebration the previous week seemed to have taken the last of her aenti's strength. She was failing quickly. Too quickly. Every day a little weaker. Annie picked up her pace. The door to the bedroom hung open. She inhaled a quick breath and entered. Aenti Bertha sat by the bed, knitting needles clacking, moving quickly, row after row. Annie tore her gaze from the frowning concentration of her face to the bed.

Aenti Louise lay on her side, her eyes closed, both hands clasped under cheek, the Sunshine and Shadow quilt pulled up over her shoulders despite the sweltering August heat.

"Aenti Louise," she whispered. "It's me, Annie."

"It's about time." Louise opened her eyes. She sniffed and squinted. "Speak up, girl, this isn't a funeral. Not yet, anyway."

"Aenti Louise!" Annie giggled. Aenti Bertha looked up from her knitting and frowned. Annie frowned back. The other woman dropped her gaze. "Onkel John said you wanted to see me."

"Bertha, could you get us some lemonade? I'm so thirsty." Louise rolled over and faced her sister-in-law. Bertha stood and tossed her knitting in a basket at her feet. She didn't look happy, but Louise didn't seem to notice. "And some cookies."

For someone on her deathbed, she seemed awfully chipper. And bossy.

"What is it, Aenti?"

Louise pulled herself up so she half sat, half lay against the pile of pillows behind her. She patted the bed. "Sit, sit, girl, you're giving me a crick in my neck towering over me like that."

Annie sat.

"They act like I'm dying or something." Louise's querulous tone made her sound like a child. "They won't let me out of this bed. Your Onkel John treats me like a little girl. I'm older than he is by twenty years."

"He's just worried about you. That's all." Annie smoothed the quilt. She was worried too. Her aunt's cheeks were sunken, her lips tinged with blue, and her scalp showed through the wisps of white hair that clumped over her forehead. She looked older, if it were possible, than she had at her birthday only a week earlier, and far more frail. "What did Doctor Corbin say?"

"He said I'm old." Louise thumped both hands on the quilt in frustration. "He'd better not send me a bill for that diagnosis."

"Onkel John said you fell. He found you out in the yard, sprawled on your back. He said you hit your head."

"So I took a tumble." Louise touched her hand to the back of her head, behind her ear, in an unconscious gesture. "It's not the first time an old woman's fallen. Won't be the last."

Bertha entered the room carrying the lemonade.

"Where are the cookies?" Louise fussed. "I know there are cookies in that kitchen. I made them myself last week."

"The doctor says the sugar is bad…"

"I don't care what the doctor says. If I'm dying, what difference does it make?"

Bertha's face crumpled. "Don't talk like that, Louise."

"*Ach*, come here."

Louise flapped her knobby hands. Bertha set the glasses on the small side table and rushed to embrace her sister-in-law. The two women made murmuring sounds. Annie had to look away. She wiped at tears that surprised her. Nothing to cry about. Louise was fine. Same crabby old woman she'd been since Annie sat at her feet listening to stories as a little girl.

"Now, you go do your laundry." Louise pushed Bertha away. "I want to have a visit with my niece."

"I can't leave you."

"Bertha, your husband will need clean pants tomorrow, and I won't be the reason he's hollering at you when he can't find none. Go."

Bertha threw up her hands, slid from the bed, and marched toward the door. "I'll be back," she tossed over her shoulder. "Don't you tire her out, Annie. She needs her rest. The doctor says rest is the best thing for her."

She left the door open but disappeared from sight. Louise stared at the door as if waiting to make sure she didn't pop back in. After a few seconds, she threw back the quilt with such force Annie jumped.

"Come on, don't just stand there."

"What? Where are we going?"

"Anywhere. I want to take a walk. I want to be outside." Louise held out a hand. "Help me out of this bed. I don't want to die without having one more look."

"One more look?"

"At God's beautiful earth."

Annie helped her from the bed. Louise swayed. Her hand went to her mouth. She swallowed, her face ashen. Annie tightened her grip. "Are you sure?"

"Where are my shoes? Get my shoes, girl. I can't be wandering around outside without my shoes."

Afraid to let go, Annie guided her to the chair where Bertha had been sitting. She found the shoes and gently slid them on Louise's tiny feet. "Ready?"

"Ready." Louise stood again, this time steadier. "Back door. Hopefully John went along with his fraa, but let's take no chances."

Feeling like she'd undertaken a secret mission, whisking her aunt away from kidnappers, Annie found herself holding her breath. Through the living room of the small, sturdy house, through the kitchen, neat as a pin and smelling of freshly baked sweet bread, and toward the back door. "Where to, Aenti?"

Louise plowed to a stop. "First you get me some cookies from the counter, there, and then it's on to the big wide world."

Annie did as she was told, wrapping four cookies in a napkin as she erased the picture of Bertha's disapproving glare from her mind. Then she helped her aunt through the back door and down the steps.

"Let's go toward the stand of pecan trees out there." Louise waved a hand toward the east. "Where we always walk."

Where they'd walked when Louise had been a little younger and a little stronger and a little steadier on her feet. Annie shortened her stride to match the older woman's and kept her fingers tight on Louise's arm. Sweat dampened her face and neck and made her dress hang damp and heavy on her legs. She should've brought the lemonade.

"You don't have to worry." Aenti Louise wheezed in a breath. "I'm not afraid."

"I'm not worried." Her aunt had always known what Annie was thinking. She knew what every one of her children, grandchildren, great-grandchildren, and nieces and nephews thought. "You'll live to be a hundred. You're too cranky to die."

"I'm ready to go. I just wanted one last look."

"You're not ready to go. I can tell." Annie fought to get the words out over the lump in her throat. "You're still giving orders."

"That's because they're afraid. John and Bertha and the rest. You'd think they'd have learned by now. You go when it's your time. No worrying. No fretting. We've always known we're just passing through. I'm relieved. I'm ready to taste the dirt on the tip of my tongue and feel the warm earth all around me."

"Aenti."

"You of all people should understand." Louise nudged Annie with a bony shoulder. "Your parents left you. David left you. And look at you, you're still putting one foot in front of the other."

"Jah." If only Aenti Louise knew how many days Annie contemplated whether she would be able to get out of bed. How many days she smothered sobs with her pillow so Leah and Luke and Mark wouldn't hear. "I have no choice."

"But you do." Breathlessly, Louise pointed at two stumps on the edge of a line of trees that stretched beyond their sight. "Let's sit a minute."

Relieved, Annie moved in that direction, careful to keep a hand on Louise's arm. "I don't have a choice. I have a bakery to run. I have a son to raise. People depend on me."

"You have a life to live. Best get started. And the only way to do that is stop being so mad about it."

"Mad? I'm not mad."

Aenti Louise cackled, then coughed. Alarmed, Annie patted her back. "Maybe we should turn around."

"Stop fussing and listen to what I say. You're mad? Admit it. You're mad at David."

"I'm not mad!" Annie stopped, trying to corral the emotions that built like an angry river straining against its banks, threatening to spill over and flood everything in its path. "David's dead. How could I be mad at him?"

"He left you. He made you love him and then he left you."

"Jah. He did. He did!"

Tears soaked Annie's face. She couldn't breathe with the pain of it.

How could he? He'd never promised to stay, but he'd told her to take it on faith. She had. And now she couldn't rely on her faith. It had let her down.

"David had the right idea, Annie."

"Nee. How could this be right? How could feeling like this be right?"

"Love is right. The love you and David had was right. For that moment and for that season of your life. But your life isn't over. David has gone on ahead. Your turn will come, but it's not now."

"I'm doing the best I can."

"It's not good enough." Louise plopped down on the stump. She sucked in air and wiped her face with her sleeve. "God expects more. He expects us to step out in faith. To believe He has a plan."

"God expects more? God's plan was for me to raise my son without his father?"

"Don't dare to believe you know God's plan, child." Her tone cut Annie like a butcher knife. "Don't presume. None of us is that smart."

"I'm only going by what I see and what I feel."

"Do you not see Isaac Gless standing in front of you? Do you not feel what he feels for you?"

"Aenti! How did you…"

"It's written all over his face. Who could miss it? I didn't come out here for my health, child. I came out here to talk some sense into you." She stopped, panting a little. The ashen cast of her skin scared Annie. She shouldn't have let her aunt talk her into this walk. "Others would say it's private business between you and him. I say I've earned a say. I've watched you grow up your whole life. I know what's best and your mudder's not here to tell you what's what, so I'm standing in for her. I won't be here much longer. This is my last chance so I'm talking plain as I can. I don't have the breath left to dress the words up nice. You're a smart girl, but sometimes you're dense as a stone."

The river of words rolled over Annie and finally, blessedly, stopped. Annie tried to marshal her thoughts. As if Louise had ever bothered to dress up her words. "I'm not dense. I'm…I'm…I don't know what I am. I'm married, that's what I am. I put all my faith into that marriage and now I feel…I feel so…"

"Like God let you down? That's mighty prideful, isn't it? God gave you a good man. He gave you a good marriage. He gave you a fine, healthy son. He's asking you to have faith that there's more. More blessings. More than you will ever deserve. David is dead. You are alive. The vows say until death do us part. You parted. It hurts, but there it is. Don't make the mistake I made."

She paused again, leaned forward, her hands on her hips. Her breaths were raspy now. Annie wanted to make her stop, but the torrent of words kept coming. "I could've loved again and I was too bullheaded and too stubborn and too blind. I didn't have faith. You remind me too much of myself. I won't have it. I won't have you throwing away a perfectly good love. You have a life in front of you. Your son can have a father. Have a little faith, child. Have a little faith!"

She stopped. Smiling, she began to rock. Her breathing seemed to ease. She stared at something Annie couldn't see. "That's it. That's all. I can go now."

Annie wished she'd brought her bag. She needed a hankie. She sniffed and wiped at her cheeks with her fingers. She had no response so she remained silent. Blessedly, so did Aenti Louise. Annie unwrapped the cookies and handed two to her aunt. They ate without speaking.

The cookies were the best Annie had ever eaten, better than any she'd ever made. The sweet crumbs melted in her mouth, butter and brown sugar and peanut butter baked together in a mixture that had never tasted better. It was as if the emotion of the moment sharpened her taste buds and made her want to hang on to the last crumb, not let it go, because when it was gone there would be no more. There would never be a better cookie or better company. The finality of that made Annie's heart turn over and twist in tight knots that hurt her chest.

Even after the cookies were long gone they sat in silence, letting a tepid breeze blow across their warm faces. The leaves rustled. A cow mooed in the distance. Another answered. The scent of fresh cut hay and manure wafted through the air like the perfume of summer. Annie didn't want to move. She didn't want to think. She didn't want to know what came next. Her muscles relaxed and her eyes closed.

"Sweet girl, you're so tired."

She jumped at the sound of Aenti's low, soft voice. She didn't sound mad now. She sounded content.

"It's all right, Aenti. I'm fine."

"We're both fine. Isn't it a lovely day God has made?"

Annie opened her eyes and gazed at the cloudless, blue sky, so blue and bright it hurt her eyes. "Jah, a lovely day."

"One more thing."

One more thing. Annie straightened and took a breath, not certain she could handle one more thing.

"The move. Stop railing about it. Whatever happens, happens. God has a plan. I don't know how to say it more plain. His plan. Not yours."

"To uproot some of us. To take our families and break them apart?" Annie tried to control her trembling voice. She wanted to be as strong and sure as her Aenti Louise. The woman who had been almost a mother to her when Mudder had gone on ahead. "I don't understand how that can be His plan."

"You don't have to understand. I can tell you this. A family is a family. It doesn't have anything to do with place. A home is where family is. It's not a building. A family isn't always about blood, neither. Figure it out."

Figure it out.

Louise rose. "Take me back now before Bertha comes looking for me and throws a big fit."

Annie stood. Her legs shook more than her aunt's. Someone watching them would've wondered which of them was sick. She sucked in air and straightened her spine. If Aenti Louise could be so sure and strong, so could she.

The walk back to the house took a long time. Louise shuffled along, barely raising her feet. Annie wrapped an arm around her shoulders to keep her upright. Louise hummed a song, a hymn. Annie couldn't remember the words, but the familiar tune calmed her aching heart. Onkel John met them at the door, his gaze lingering disapprovingly on Annie. He jerked his head toward the porch. Catherine sat in the rocking chair, her hands folded in her lap.

"She says she isn't leaving until she talks to her aenti."

Annie didn't respond. She nodded at Catherine as they passed by. Her sister started to rise, then sank back into the chair. "I'll be out in a minute," Annie told her. "Wait here."

Together she and Onkel helped Louise back into her bedroom. Annie once again knelt, this time to remove the shoes.

Louise slipped under the quilt and pulled it up to her chin. She closed her eyes and began to snore, a light, rhythmic sound that comforted Annie. Her aunt still breathed in and out.

"I'm staying. You can go on to work," she whispered to John. "Leah has Noah. Helen is covering the bakery. I can spend the day."

"No more gallivanting around the countryside," he growled. "Doctor says she needs rest."

"She needs what she needs."

He tugged his hat down on his forehead. Annie followed him out to the porch.

"She doesn't have much time, does she?" Catherine began to rock. "I want to see her."

"Where's Dean?"

"He went back to Wichita."

"You should've gone with him." Annie sank onto the porch step.

"I'm stuck. I can't seem to go forward."

"You have Dean. He seems like a good man."

"He is, but I can't have a life with him until I figure out what to do with all this." She waved her hand about as if to encompass everything around her. "The nice thing about it is he'll wait for me. He promised me he would wait. He said he would live here if I wanted. Or anywhere in the world—it's up to me."

"He is a good man." Annie struggled to make sense of her sister's problem. "Would you...would you want to live in Bliss Creek? Not as a member of the community."

"You mean like an Englischer?" Catherine's laugh held no mirth. "So everyone could continue to rub my nose in my meidung? I don't think so. That part of my life—the Bliss Creek part—is over. It's finding my way to the next thing that seems to be the problem."

Annie didn't answer. She didn't have the words. Her sister, with all the education and experience in the real world, didn't have any more answers than Annie the baker did.

"I spoke to Luke."

"You did?" Now that surprised her. "Did he speak back?"

"No."

They both chuckled a little, the sound strange and out of place in the darkness brought on not by the lack of sun, but by the cloud of impending grief that hung over them.

"No, he didn't talk back, but he listened. I could tell by the way he kept clearing his throat like the words were trying to fight their way out. He kept right on working, feeding the horses, checking on the pigs, doing this and that so he didn't have to face me."

"So you made your peace with him. That's good. Aenti would tell you to make peace with the past. It's the only way."

"Is that what you've done?" The barely controlled sarcasm stung. "Sorry, that was mean of me. It's not my intent to be mean. Sometimes it just seeps out of me. Luke's stubborn, hardheaded, Plain man's way of doing things just makes me mean."

"You're not mean. You're right—about me making peace, I mean, not about Luke's head. He's trying to do what he believes he's called to do. And I'm trying to make peace." Annie bit her lower lip until it hurt. Not hard enough. She saw that now. She'd paid lip service to the promises she'd made to David. She'd pretended to accept her lot, but inside her anger raged. Anger that had to be allowed to burn itself out before she could go on and live the life God called her to live without her David, without her rock.

"Aenti is right. I've been trying so hard to fulfill my promise to David I haven't allowed myself to have my own feelings. I have a right to be angry and mad and upset and to grieve. My David died. He died. He wasn't supposed to die. He told me to have faith. To take it on faith. I did. And look what happened. He died!"

The tears burst forth in a torrent that surprised her. "God, forgive me," she cried. "I find it so hard to accept. But I will. I promise I will."

Catherine darted from the chair and scurried to Annie's side. She slung an arm around her. "That's the first step."

"The first step?"

"Letting it all out."

Annie blew her nose on her handkerchief, then wadded it into a ball. "Do you want to talk to her?"

"I don't need anything from her, Annie. You're wrong about that." Catherine sounded so sad that Annie fought another wave of tears. "I only want to say goodbye."

Together they rose and Annie led the way. Louise hadn't moved. Her breathing seemed even more labored. She didn't stir when Catherine kissed her cheek and smoothed a hand across her forehead.

Annie pulled up another chair. They sat, side by side, sharing the glass of lemonade Bertha had left on the bedside table. Together they waited, without speaking. One or the other shed tears, but quietly so as not to disturb Aenti's rest. Sometime later, the snoring ceased and the room filled with quiet. Annie couldn't find it in herself to weep anymore, as much as she wanted to dissolve the lump where her heart had been.

She sat still and imagined Aenti Louise savoring the dirt on the tip of her tongue and embracing the warm earth in her arms.

Chapter 34

Annie straightened her apron and smoothed her skirt. For the fourth time, she ran her fingers over her kapp to make sure it properly covered her hair. She glanced at the battery-operated clock that hung over the double sink. Any minute Isaac should come through the bakery door to fetch Mary Elizabeth home. Annie glanced around. Everything was spotless as usual. She'd finished cleaning up and all the ingredients sat in a row, waiting for her to return in the morning for another round of baking. She felt silly. What did she think she was doing, acting like a schoolgirl?

She grabbed the broom and began to sweep with more energy than necessary. It felt good to be back in her regular routine. Aenti Louise's funeral had been bittersweet. She'd lived her life as God intended and she'd been ready to leave this world. That didn't mean Annie wouldn't miss her with every bone in her body. She sighed and swept harder. Aenti Louise expected her to get on with her life. She would try her hardest to do as her aunt had asked—no, demanded.

"I think I'll wait for Isaac outside." Mary Elizabeth came through the storage room door, her small lunchbox on one arm. "Surely it's cooler out there than it is in here. I feel like I'm melting. Did you turn off the ovens? It feels like it's four hundred…"

"Nee!" Annie broke in without thinking. If Mary Elizabeth went out, Isaac had no reason to come in. She couldn't tell his little sister that. "I mean...did you finish unpacking the spices and make a list of the things we need to have Mark pick up at the bulk food store tomorrow?"

"I did. And a list for the dent-a-can store too. All finished." Mary Elizabeth flapped her hands in front of her face. "If it gets any hotter, I'm going to run home and jump in the creek, clothes and all. Won't that make Daed laugh?"

Annie tried to laugh with the girl, but her mind whirled. *I'm trying to move on, God, really I am, but this isn't helping.* If Isaac didn't come into the bakery, she wouldn't see him. She certainly had no reason to go into the implement repair store. She glanced around the bakery, not a tool in sight that needed work.

"See you tomorrow, bright and early." Mary Elizabeth jerked open the door. Isaac strode in. The two nearly collided. "Bruder! You nearly knocked me down!"

"Sorry, schweschder." Isaac laughed, that deep, hoarse laugh that sent a chill up Annie's arms. "You're so short I didn't see you down there!"

"I'm not short." Mary Elizabeth's indignant retort lost its effect when she stumbled and Isaac had to grab her arm to keep her upright. "It's hot in here and I'm hungry. Let's go."

"Whoa, hold your horses!" Isaac let go of her arm. His momentum kept him moving in Annie's direction. She hung on to the broom, letting it hold her up in case her legs suddenly gave way. "How was your day, Annie?"

"*Gut.* It was *gut.*" She heard the stutter in her voice and felt her cheeks heat up. Pure silliness. That's what Leah would call it. Tomfoolery. She was a grown woman with a child. Not a schoolgirl with a crush. Next she'd be headed to the singings on Sunday night and hanging around waiting for him to offer her a ride home. "Busy. We were blessed."

"Same here. Lots of farmers with things that need fixing. Daed's happy. And that's *gut*. Maybe he'll stop talking about uprooting the family again." His father's happiness seemed to make Isaac happy. Annie found that endearing. He stopped within arm's reach. "I'm starving. Abigail didn't pack enough sandwiches in my bag today. Got anything left?"

"Anything left? Oh, you mean, any cakes, pies, cookies…" She pointed toward the display cabinets. While they were a little sparser than earlier in the day, they were by no means empty, a fact obvious to anyone with seeing eyes.

"Come on, Isaac, I want to get home and help Abigail with supper." Mary Elizabeth tapped her foot and yanked open the door. "You know she's been with the girls alone all day. She gets pretty worn out, running after them and trying to take care of the laundry and the cleaning and the garden and the cooking."

"I know, just give me a minute." Isaac's meaningful glance at his sister was not lost on Annie. She relaxed a little. He looked as nervous as she felt. "Wait in the buggy, why don't you? It'll be cooler out there. I think I felt the tiniest little breeze when I pulled up in front of the bakery. Or maybe that was you talking!"

"Funny, funny." Mary Elizabeth frowned. She didn't move to go through the door. "And leave you alone with Annie? I don't think so. Daed wouldn't…"

"Daed would say courting is private. Daed would tell you to mind your own business."

"Ah, this is courting business then." A grin spread over the girl's face. "I'm so…"

"Mary Elizabeth!"

Still grinning, she waved at Annie and went. The door closed with a ding. Isaac took a breath. Annie took a breath. She squared her shoulders.

"So."

"So."

"We still have lots of apple cookies and the walnut-raisin-oatmeal cookies turned out really well this time—"

"Annie."

"I don't know what to say," she admitted, turning to face him. "Baking is what I know."

"I made my pitch. Time for you to step up to the plate."

Baseball had always been Annie's favorite sport. David had once tossed her a soft pitch that she had hit all the way to the creek. Everything rode on her response. The look on Isaac's face said he had no idea which way she would hit the ball.

"I'm ready."

"Ready for what?"

"For the next step." She gripped her hands together to keep them still. "The next little step."

"Ah, little step." He seemed to study the racks of cookies. "Would another attempt at a buggy ride fall within the boundaries of a little step?"

"It would." She forced herself to loosen her hands before the flow of blood stopped circulating. "I'm sure of that."

"You're sure?" He looked at her directly then, his brown eyes tender and tentative at the same time. His voice had dropped until it had that same gruff quality Annie had heard in Gabriel's when he talked to his youngest kinner. "You know, yours isn't the only heart at risk here."

"I know."

"I'll take two dozen of each."

"What?"

"Two dozen of the apple and two dozen of the oatmeal." He lifted his hat and extracted the money from the band inside it.

Not sure whether they'd made it to the next step or not, Annie took the money he offered, slipped around the counter, and began loading sacks with the cookies. She peeked at him from the corner of her eye. He seemed absorbed in studying the cookies.

"Not that one."

"What?"

"Not the broken one and that one looks a little burnt."

"I don't burn my cookies!"

He grinned. "Never?"

"Never."

"Fine."

"Fine. I'll get your change."

She went to the old cash register David had found at a secondhand store, pulled the lever, and settled the bills into their slot.

"Keep the change."

"What?"

"Keep the change."

"No, I..."

"I'll see you tonight."

"Tonight?"

He picked up the bags, tossed her a smile that curled her toes, and left.

She sagged against the counter. Why did a small step feel so big?

✳

Gabriel trudged into the kitchen in search of a glass of sweet tea. It had been a long, hot day. Despite having every window in the shop open, the temperature had risen higher and higher during the afternoon until the air seemed to sizzle and pop around him. He felt like a piece of meat roasting in an oven. Cooked too long, he was now well-done, like a long strap of leather. He strode past Abigail, who was standing at the stove stirring a pot of navy beans and ham. She looked up and smiled, the picture of her mother, with damp tendrils of blonde hair escaping her kapp and drops of perspiration shining on her face. She looked as warm as he felt.

"What I wouldn't give for a breeze," she said, jerking her head toward the three open windows. "All we're getting are flies and mosquitoes. I can't keep them off the pies!"

"There are some thunderheads on the horizon, but the Farmer's Almanac says no rain for another two weeks. I don't reckon we'll get any relief until then." He pumped water into the tub and washed his face, cupping his hands and pouring the water over his head and neck, washing away the sweat and grit of the day. Abigail stood by and handed him a towel.

"Danki," he said, with one eye open and water dripping down his face. "I needed that."

"I've been doing that all afternoon." She turned and poured him a glass of tea from a pitcher sitting on the counter. "Having the oven on in this heat seems like a silly thing to do, but the bread has to be baked and I needed cookies for the sack lunches. I made pies for supper too."

"Everyone will appreciate that." He took the glass from her, glad to find pieces of ice floating in it. After all these years, ice was still a treat. They hadn't had ice in their home when he was a child growing up. "Especially the girls."

The girls in question didn't look up from the big pan of green beans Abigail had apparently given them to snap for supper. They were doing more playing than snapping, but it was a good chore. They couldn't hurt the beans or themselves. Before Gabriel could greet them, Isaac burst through the back door, his hands laden with white sacks. He plopped them on the prep table. Her eyebrows arched, Abigail walked over to peer into one of the bags. She looked up at her brother, surprise on her freckled face. "That's a lot of cookies. Why would you buy cookies? I just made a whole batch of peanut butter chocolate chip— your favorite."

"Cookies, cookies," Isabelle piped up.

Rachel immediately joined in the chorus. "Want cookies!"

"Not until after supper." Abigail sounded so like Laura, Gabriel winced. She crossed her arms. "Don't you like my cookies, Isaac?"

"I like your cookies a lot."

"He's sweet on Annie Plank," Mary Elizabeth interrupted with a chortle as she trotted in behind him. "Our bruder is in lieb."

"That would not be any of your business."

With that curt statement, Isaac stalked from the kitchen. Gabriel looked at Abigail. She shrugged and went back to chopping up bacon and throwing it into a frying pan. Acting as if she hadn't heard Isaac, Mary Elizabeth chattered on about someone who'd come into the bakery that day to order two enormous cakes for a wedding.

Perplexed, Gabriel inhaled the mouthwatering aroma of frying bacon, left them to their chatter, and went in search of Isaac. All he wanted to do was eat his supper in peace and do his chores. He was exhausted and his day was far from over. Like it or not, he also had the chore of being a daed to all these kinner. Straightening his spine, he glanced into the room that served as both dining room and living room, with a long table situated by the windows and five chairs on each side. Isaac sat at the table reading last week's copy of *The Budget*, an intent look on his face as if the information contained in the newspaper were being committed to memory.

"What was that all about?"

Isaac looked up, a picture of innocence. "What was what all about?"

"Snapping at your sister. She was just being silly." He didn't say it aloud, but it was good to see the girls act silly. Act normal. Like the dark cloud of their mother's death had finally lifted. "They're just being girls."

"I know." Isaac dropped the newspaper onto the table. "Can I ask you something?"

"Jah." Gabriel eased onto the chair across from Isaac. His son's expression put him on guard immediately. It had been a long day, and he wasn't sure if he was up to a heart-to-heart. He hated heart-to-heart discussions. But to whom else could Isaac talk, now that Daniel had fled? "You can always talk to me."

"I know." Isaac picked at the folded napkin on the table. He began to refold it. "Do you think you will remarry?"

The air whooshed from Gabriel's lungs. The question he'd been asking himself for years now. More and more lately. The image of Helen

Crouch smacking the volleyball over the net, her dimples deep around a wide smile, filled his vision. He batted it away. He cleared his throat and drank from a glass of sweet tea, set it down, and then coughed.

"Daed, it's not a commitment. I mean, do you think about it at all?"

"Why do you ask? Did someone say something? I haven't done anything yet."

"Yet? Then there's someone."

He hadn't meant to say that or imply that. He had no idea if there were someone. If that someone was even the right someone. Plump. Awkward. A mother hen. So different from Laura. Wasn't that the point? There would never be another Laura. But there was hope of something more, something different. Someone different. "Why do you want to know? It's a private matter."

"I don't want to know about your business." Isaac squirmed in his chair like a little boy being asked to recite his times tables in front of the whole class. "I'm asking because I'm trying to figure out something."

"What is that something?"

"What do you think it would be like to be married to someone who has been married before?"

Gabriel had given this topic a great deal of thought. He and Laura had been so young. They'd never shared their thoughts and dreams with anyone other than each other. From the early grades of school they'd been drawn together. First, as teammates who scrapped and pushed each other on the walk home, later on buggy rides after singings, and during visits late at night to her home, long after her parents had gone to bed. Those nights on the front porch, seated side by side in the rocking chairs, had been filled with conversations about the lives they would build together, the children they would have, the memories they would share. Surely a woman like Helen had done the same with her husband. They had had four children together, shared a home, made a life. How did two people who had lost something they thought would last a lifetime make new memories, a new life, together?

"Daed?"

Gabriel started, realizing Isaac was still waiting for a response. "I think it would take time."

"Time?"

"Time to get used to each other. To figure out how it will be. Because it would be different. For the person who's been married before."

"How?"

Gabriel groped for the words. "Your mudder had known me since the schoolhouse, before even. She knew what I liked for breakfast. She knew how I liked my pants to fit a little loose and the way I liked time at night to myself to think. She knew all about me. I knew all about her. What flowers she wanted to plant in the garden. How she didn't like beets. The way she liked the sheets tucked in. Her favorite blackberry jam. Her favorite kind of cookies—oatmeal-walnut-raisin. The way she cut the sandwiches corner to corner instead of across."

He stopped. Heat burned his face.

"I know." Isaac's voice softened. "She knew everything about you."

"Everything. Just as I knew everything about her."

"But you think it can happen more than once?"

"Jah."

"I don't see how I can take the place of another man when a woman has loved only him."

That was it. The crux of Isaac's worry. He feared he would be found lacking.

"You won't take his place." Gabriel picked his words with care, realizing as he said them that he meant them as much for himself as Isaac. "That can't be done. No one can take the place of your mudder. But I reckon there might be room in a man's heart for more than one such love in a lifetime. Look at Thomas."

"Jah, look at Thomas." Isaac nodded, his face hopeful. "He seems mighty happy."

"He is happy."

They were both silent then. Gabriel contemplated how these things happened. He and his son were at similar crossroads, despite the years of difference in their ages. Isaac had set his sights on a widow with a child. A widower himself, with eight children, Gabriel suspected his row was a much harder one to hoe. Eight children plus four. Helen's Edmond, so willful and rebellious. Gabriel's Abigail, seeking to fill a void in her heart left by a mother gone too soon. How could these people live together in the same house as a family?

Hold your horses. Don't get ahead of yourself. He'd been nothing but harsh when it came to Helen. Why would she give him the time of day? Yet her expression when she'd given him the lemonade at Thomas's house had said she would. He was no expert at these things, but she seemed willing that day when they played volleyball. Then he'd gone and spoiled it by overreacting about Edmond and Abigail.

"You don't have any more idea than I do about all this woman stuff, do you?" Isaac cocked his head and smiled for the first time. "But you're thinking about taking a gander at it, aren't you?"

"Never you mind." Gabriel stood. "I'm getting some more tea. You'd think those girls would have supper on the table by now."

"You'd think. It seems ham and beans take a long time to prepare."

"Or Abigail was daydreaming and got a late start on it."

"Most likely."

Gabriel paused in the doorway. He studied his son's bent head. He looked so much like Gabriel, but he had his mother's heart. "Tread softly."

"What?" Isaac looked up from the newspaper he didn't seem to be reading, but rather folding and refolding. "What do you mean?"

"A woman's heart is a strange thing." Gabriel looked at the empty glass in his hand, wishing it were full. His throat still felt dry. "I surely can't figure it out."

Isaac shrugged and smiled again. "You will. We both will."

The optimism of youth.

Catherine's journal
August 20

Dean left this morning to get back to the hospital and to his residency. I've gassed up the rental car and packed my bags. All that remains is to check out and leave Bliss Creek once again. This visit didn't turn out the way I expected, but I do believe in the adage that everything happens for a reason. That we don't know what the reason is still serves to baffle and irritate me. I had to come here to see Aenti Louise before she passed. To talk to her before the possibility no longer existed. In coming here, I finally faced my fears and put to rest my anger and resentment. Strangely enough, it wasn't the time spent with Annie or Emma or Aenti Louise or even Josiah that allowed me to do that. It was talking to Luke. Or talking at him. He wouldn't look at me, but the pain of his rejection radiated from him. It hurt him as much as it hurt me. Yet he did it out of an abundance of faith that shunning is what's best for both of us. He loves me that much. I look at my family and I see how much they love each other and me. I can't go on hanging around here, causing a fissure in their lives. I chose my life and I'd choose it again, so I can't expect to have it both ways.

So I'll go and I won't look back. No published memoir. Yes, I will write all those memories and bind them together and send them as a gift to my brothers and sisters. My memories are their memories and so many of them are good, wonderful, beautiful memories. I want them to know how much those early memories mean to me. They are our memories, for us only. Not to be bought and shared by others. I see that now. Their faith requires that they keep themselves apart from the world. I have no right to take that from them. I cannot benefit at their expense.

My life in Bliss Creek is over, but my childhood memories will always be of a warm and loving family.

I will write my thesis next year but without the photos. Those I'll keep in a scrapbook for my eyes only.

Only one question remains. What to do about Edmond. The day of Aenti's funeral I stood on the far edge of the cemetery and watched as they laid her in the ground. He came to me, asking me for a way out. His mother saw him talking to me and nearly fainted. She rushed him away as if he might contract a deadly disease. I saw the fear on her face. She looks at me and sees what her future may hold. I'm caught between knowing the drowning sensation Edmond experiences at the thought of remaining here and the hurt I would cause his family by helping him. The psychologist in me says he will run whether I help him or not. He will run just as Josiah did. Whether he comes back to his community depends on who reaches out to help him during his time away. That could be me. Maybe God put me here to be a witness to Edmond, someone who can make sure he stays safe in a city where he will know no one.

Maybe everything does happen for a reason. Maybe God does have a plan. Maybe I'm part of His plan for Edmond.

I wonder what Aenti Louise would say.

I know what she would say. Catherine, stop messing around and follow your heart.

Chapter 35

Gabriel tugged on the reins and brought the buggy to a halt several yards from the front door of the school. It might be the first day of the new school year, but the sun beating down on him and Seth announced that the brutally hot Kansas summer refused to make an exit. Murky clouds hung low in the sky. The humidity weighted down his damp shirt, making it cling to his back and shoulders. And this at seven o'clock in the morning. What would midafternoon be like? He longed for a breath of cool air. He longed to throw himself in the creek, clothes and all. Even the movement of the buggy brought no relief in a soggy, hot rush of air that didn't serve to dry the sweat on his face.

Seth had insisted the ride wasn't necessary, but Gabriel had no intention of ending the time-honored Gless family tradition of taking the children to school on the first day. In Dahlburg they'd lived close enough to the school that Laura and the children could walk the short path to the one-room building. They'd done so each year. Now only Seth attended and he only had Gabriel to accompany him. The little girls would go eventually, but there was no hurry, given the little they could be expected to learn of reading, writing, and arithmetic. Gabriel didn't want them to be a distraction that kept the teacher from applying herself to the other students' learning. She would have to have an assistant to work with his girls. Time enough for that when they turned five or six.

Seth made no move to hop from the buggy.

"What's the matter, son?" Gabriel studied his youngest son's somber face. "Got the first-day-of-school jitters?"

"Nee." Seth's expression belied his answer. Balancing his lunchbox in one hand, he climbed down from the buggy with the movements of an old person. "I'm sorry summer's over."

"Fewer chores," Gabriel offered. "Less time keeping an eye on your little sisters."

"I don't mind the chores or the girls." Seth sniffed and blew out a sigh. He sounded much older than his eight years. "I like fishing when I get done with the chores. And swimming in the creek. And playing baseball."

"And you aren't looking forward to being the new scholar, I reckon."

Seth shrugged, but the misery in his eyes told the real story.

Gabriel hopped down. No reason he couldn't provide a little backup for his youngest son. Being the new boy at school wasn't much fun, as he recalled. But the Plain children would make him feel welcome. That was what they were expected to do.

"Look, they've got a game of volleyball going." He put a hand on Seth's skinny shoulder. "Look, there's Eli and Rebecca. And Lillie and Mary. You know a bunch of these kinner. And you like volleyball."

"I like baseball better." Still, Seth's face brightened. "I don't like math. Or spelling. Or English."

"Learn to like them."

"Hey, Seth!" Ginny Crouch skipped toward them, her smile stretching across her chubby cheeks. She had Helen's dimples. Gabriel shut the door on that unwanted thought. "Wanna play? School doesn't start for a few minutes."

Enthusiasm poured from the young girl. Seth trotted after her. Gabriel settled his hat back on his head and watched as the group of children flocked around Seth, carrying him into their game. The teacher would have a fine time getting them settled down on the first day of school.

He turned back toward the buggy. Beyond it he saw Helen standing next to her buggy. He could tell from the guilty look on her face she'd been watching him. She looked as if she might climb into her buggy and run away. In fact, she immediately grasped the handle and started to haul herself up.

"Helen. Wait."

She stopped, one hand still on the buggy, but she didn't speak. He wished she would. If she'd start the conversation, he could find a way to keep it up. The starting part—that was the part that gave him trouble.

He strode toward her, wanting to say something. He only had a few yards to figure out what that something would be. She stood motionless, looking like a roly-poly robin in her brown dress that had just a hint of red in it, nothing garish or bright. "How are you?"

That wasn't it.

"Fine."

Not helpful. "I mean, I haven't had a chance to talk to you since supper the other night."

"Three weeks ago, you mean?"

"With the store and the house and the children, time has gotten away from me." That didn't mean he hadn't thought of her. "I thought I might have time in the evenings, but the girls…"

"No excuses necessary."

"Or no excuses accepted?"

He wanted his angry retort back immediately. What was it about this woman who got his back up every time they ran into each other?

"Gabriel! Gabriel!" Bethel came flying across the front yard of the school. "How are you? Good of you to stop by. We plan to have a parent meeting to talk some about the curriculum next week. You'll be there?"

"I will."

Gabriel glanced at Helen, waiting for her to join in. Surely, she would come to the curriculum meeting as well. All the parents did. To his surprise, sharp emotions were tumbling across her face. She harbored jealousy toward the teacher. Why on earth? Bethel was tall for a woman and thin and she had a nice face, but she had none of that earthiness that made it hard for Gabriel to dismiss Helen from his mind. She had a roundness that made him want to touch her, much as he tried not to think about it. Beauty in the eyes of the beholder? Not beauty. An inner strength that fought with insecurity and a kind nature that made her a caring mother. These qualities would make her a good fraa. If he could stop putting his foot in his mouth about her son. Instead, help her to guide Edmond and let her help him guide Abigail. Together they could be a team.

If he ever learned to control his tongue.

"Helen, what about you?" Bethel turned to Helen. "Your girls are getting so big. I might ask Naomi to be my helper this year."

"She'd be honored." Helen's frown stretched into a smile. Proud, no, grateful, mother appeared. "Thank you, Bethel. Naomi tries hard, and she'll be so pleased to help you. I'd best be going. I need to take some jams and jellies into the bakery this morning."

Gabriel opened his mouth to say something, anything, but the two women were already turning away, each going on with their day's tasks.

"Time to go in, children. The first day of school has begun," Bethel called. She clapped her hands. "Let's begin on the right foot, shall we? Everyone in."

Gabriel took a step toward Helen, willing her to wait until the children filed into the school. She looked up at him, then looked away. When she started to climb into the buggy, he put his hand on hers. He heard the audible breath she took. Startled at his own forwardness, he withdrew it. To his relief she stayed put, her cheeks scarlet, but her gaze steady on him.

Seth waved as he went by and then disappeared through the school door. When the door closed, Gabriel breathed. "I'm sorry."

"Sorry for what?" Helen raised her eyebrows and climbed into the buggy. This time she didn't stop. "You've done nothing wrong."

"I've done nothing but criticize and judge."

"Jah."

"Why is this so hard?" Gabriel flung his hands up in self-defense.

"I want to do this, but I don't know how to find a balance. They're my children."

"And Edmond is mine. He's not perfect. Not one of us is. Only Jesus." She looked down at him. "You have to decide if you'll trust me to be a good mother to my son and daughters. If you'll trust me to be that for your children someday. If you do, then all I know is that it's the man's job to court. It's a woman's job to wait for him to do so."

"The man's job is harder."

"You're wrong about that." She looked down at him, then shook the reins and clucked. The buggy jolted forward, leaving Gabriel standing there in the dust kicked up by the wheels.

"Nee. Don't go," he said, but he knew she couldn't hear him. She couldn't hear the jumble of thoughts. His own dilemma. Should he uproot his family again? Or should he try to make Bliss Creek work? With Helen at his side, he could make it work. "Don't go. Stay here with me."

Chapter 36

Annie shifted the basket of baked goodies into the crook of her arm and smoothed her apron with the other. She'd never been to an Englisch wedding. She'd feared Luke would say no, but he'd surprised her by simply nodding and telling her to carry his good wishes to Charisma and her policeman. Even Leah looked a little wistful at the idea. She hoped Charisma would like the Broken Star patchwork quilt they'd recently finished at a quilting frolic. Its burgundies and blues looked so pretty together.

Annie glanced at Helen. She carried the quilt, carefully wrapped in soft white tissue paper. She looked as nervous as Annie felt. Together, they slipped through the door of the small white building with its steeple and its colorful stained glass windows. Annie had heard the church's bell ring many times during her growing-up years, but she'd never been inside. Curious, she glanced around. One big room was filled with wooden pews. Not that much different from a barn filled with wooden benches. Except for the piano. The pews were full at least three-quarters of way back. Garlands of sunflowers and daisies had been intertwined and strewn from pew to pew, giving the sanctuary a festive air.

"Bride or groom?" asked a young man dressed in a blue suit with a bow tie askew. He held a stack of folded papers in his hands, which he bent back and forth in a nervous gesture.

"I'm sorry?"

"Bride or groom. Which side do you want to sit on?"

Perplexed, Annie looked at Helen. She shrugged. Annie turned back to the young man who was running a bony hand through his hair, making it stand up in dark spikes. "We would like to sit with the other women."

He frowned. "Are you friends of the bride or the groom?"

"Both."

Annie had never heard of the idea of dividing people up this way. Weren't they all there to support the taking of the vows by two people who professed to love each other?

"Annie. Mrs. Crouch." Officer Bingham lumbered toward them. Annie had never seen him out of uniform before. He wore the same blue suit as the young man, but the buttons on the white shirt underneath it looked in danger of being flung to the far reaches by the pressure of his protruding belly. "I got this, Frankie. Charisma asked me to save a spot for you right up front next to Mrs. Bolton from the restaurant. She's keeping an eye on the kiddoes."

Annie would have preferred a spot at the back, but she obediently followed Officer Bingham. He took the wedding present from Helen and laid it on the table in the corner with stacks of wrapped gifts with silver bows and sparkly paper. Muttering appreciative sounds under his breath, he set Annie's basket on the table with an almost reverent touch. "Snickerdoodles and monster cookies," he whispered as if to himself.

"I didn't know if we should have brought food for the wedding dinner." Annie looked at the piles of presents. She didn't see any food. "I thought of a cake, but I imagine they have one."

"Oh, you can take this over to the restaurant after." Officer Bingham looked like he might take it for her, given the chance. She doubted a single cookie would make its destination.

"The restaurant?"

"Yeah, Mrs. Bolton closed for the rest of the day so the boss and his bride can have the reception and dance there. She's making all the barbecue, and she isn't charging them a dime."

Annie studied her hands. They could come to an Englisch wedding, but she knew better than to think that extended to a dance. "It's very nice of her. She's making this an even more special day for Charisma."

"And for the boss. I never seen a man so in love."

"Are you married, Officer Bingham?"

"It's Joe, and no ma'am, no way."

Annie laughed at his emphatic tone. "But you think it's great for the boss?"

"He's a lot more relaxed—at least he will be when all this wedding stuff is over. It's been making him crazy. He says he wants to settle down with his wife and kids. Those kids are awful lucky. He's already a daddy to them."

"I'm happy for all of them."

"Me too." Officer Bingham snatched a cookie from the basket, a grin on his face. "Me too. I get cookies and wedding cake. He gets all the headaches."

With that definitive statement, he turned and led them along the side aisle to the first row of pews. At the front of the chapel stood Chief Parker—Dylan—dressed in yet another blue suit with a bow tie. Did all English weddings require such a suit? Next to him stood a man Annie didn't know but he looked an exact replica of Dylan, maybe a tad bit younger. He also wore the blue suit. Dylan grinned and nodded when he saw Annie and Helen. He lifted his hand and gave them a wave, followed by a thumbs-up sign. Annie glanced around, then returned the thumbs up, feeling like a kitten in a barn full of puppies.

Once seated, Helen turned to Annie and whispered, "Have you ever seen the citizens of Bliss Creek so dressed up? I never thought they'd make such a fuss over Charisma."

Music began to play. It emanated from the front of the chapel where an older lady with hair piled up several inches over her head in a thick plait played the piano. Chattering ceased and all heads turned toward the back of the church.

Little Gracie traipsed down the middle of the aisle in a white frilly dress and white shiny shoes, a basket of flower petals hanging from one arm. Smiling from ear to ear, she flung the rose petals about in front of her with such enthusiasm they floated into the laps of those closest to the aisle. A murmur of soft laughter floated through the chapel. Annie couldn't begin to imagine what the purpose of the petals could be.

Then everyone stood as Charisma started down the aisle toward her husband-to-be.

Annie couldn't help but think of Isaac when seeing the look on Dylan Parker's face as he stood at the front of the chapel, waiting for his beloved. Charisma had two children from another man. She was sassy, stubborn, and an incurable cynic. But Dylan loved her and he was willing to take her, warts and all.

Isaac claimed to have those feelings for her. Despite her stubbornness, her cheekiness, her reluctance. Like Dylan, he would take the woman he loved and her child, knowing the two were inseparable. Annie had never been a cynic. She'd always believed in love. Isaac believed in her.

That Annie should be so blessed for a second time.

And then she turned her thoughts from Isaac and focused on the couple at the front of the church. She didn't want to miss the happy moment when Dylan Parker and Charisma vowed to love, honor, and cherish each other from this day forward—the moment they became husband and wife.

She wanted a moment like that of her own.

Chapter 37

Gabriel mopped his face and glanced at the sky as he climbed into his buggy. Black, menacing clouds scudded overhead. A moist wind slapped him in the face like a damp washcloth that clung to his skin. Thunder rumbled. Lightning answered, quick and razor-sharp. What a day for Seth to leave his lunchbox on the kitchen counter. With the second week of school underway, he should have his routine down by now. The boy showed signs of being a scatterbrain sometimes. Gabriel had work to do, and his mood hadn't improved as he spent his days repairing equipment and his nights wondering what to do about Helen. Her words still rang in his ears. *A man's job to do the courting.* He wanted to do it, but something kept him from showing up at her house, flashlight in hand. Pride? Surely not. Fear? He was a man, not a boy. Then what?

All the grumpier at the thoughts he couldn't corral, Gabriel slapped the reins and the buggy took off with a jolt. Better he focus on what he knew how to do. Isaac had left early to deliver a repaired hay mower to the Yoders. Samuel had followed shortly after that to work for Thaddeus. That left Gabriel to run this errand. A trip to the schoolhouse would delay his arrival at the shop. That would mean he wouldn't finish converting the wringer wash machine to propane until after lunch. Michael Glick would be waiting at the door for him.

A gust of wind brought with it the first enormous drops of rain. They were warm and held none of the refreshing coolness he associated with rain showers in the fall. Never mind. It hadn't rained since the Fourth of July holiday. Its arrival should be counted as one of this day's blessings. From a bountiful God. This errand wouldn't take long. "Come on, Bess, let's get this over with and get to work."

The horse picked up her pace. The rain came down harder. Irritation crawled up Gabriel's neck, already damp with sweat. Seth needed to be more responsible. Gabriel should probably leave his lunch and let Seth learn from his carelessness. No. He couldn't bear the thought of the boy, who'd grown three inches over the summer, going hungry. Of course the other children would share with him, but Gabriel didn't want them giving up their food either.

Why was he obsessing over this? Because it kept him from thinking about other things. Like the decision to stay in Bliss Creek. He had decided. In the middle of the night, when sleep wouldn't come and he'd grown tired of staring into the darkness and seeing nothing but question marks hanging over him, he'd finally admitted it to himself. He wanted to stay. He argued with himself that he wanted to stay because he didn't want to uproot the family again. But the truth was that he wanted to stay and he wanted Helen Crouch to stay.

"Giddy up, girl!" Lightning crackled overhead, now too close for comfort. Gabriel ducked, a reflex that made him chuckle aloud even though nothing about this situation truly amused him. Thunder boomed and Bess nickered, a high, nervous sound whipped and carried away by a wind now so strong that it knocked Gabriel's hat from his head and launched it into the back of the buggy.

Rain pounded his face. Turn back or carry on? Gabriel searched the sky. No roiling clouds that signaled the formation of a funnel. Only blackness, thick and heavy as molasses. Day had turned to night. His clothes were already soaked. No point in turning back. He carried on, the strength of the wind taking his breath away. He wanted his hat back. The rain slid from vertical to horizontal, smacking his face like a swarm of stinging bees. Gabriel wiped at his eyes, trying to clear his vision. "Come on, Bess, come on," he shouted over the roar of the wind in his ears. "We're almost there."

The schoolhouse came into sight. It seemed to take hours to race across the last five hundred yards. He needed cover for the horse and buggy. Having no barn meant leaving them exposed to the fierce rain and wind. He settled for securing both on the east side of the school where the building blocked a little of the westerly gale. "Sorry, girl!" He patted the horse's flank. "I hate to leave you out here, but I have no choice."

Bent almost double, he fought his way around the corner. The wind knocked him back. He wrapped his arms around the lunchbox and clutched it to his middle. Rain and hail pelted him in a blistering fury. *Lord, have mercy.*

Hunched over, Gabriel climbed the steps and pushed the door open. It flew back and smacked against the wall. One of the little girls in the front row screamed.

"Hush, Ruth Ann." Bethel scurried across the room. "Gabriel! Let me help you with the door."

Together, they managed to propel it away from the wall. It took their combined weight, but it finally clanged shut. Bethel leaned against it. "Whatever brings you out here in this weather?" She gasped as she readjusted her kapp. "Surely, whatever it is could've waited."

"This." Gabriel held up Seth's lunchbox. "Seth left home without it."

"*Ach*, no!" Bethel shook her head and laughed. "I suspect you aren't real happy about his timing on that."

Grinning despite himself, Gabriel wiped at his face with a sodden sleeve. The children, arranged like stepping stones from smallest to largest, front to back, sat quietly, watching, their faces shining in the light of lanterns and candles that had been lighted when day turned to night, he imagined. Gabriel sought out Seth, seated toward the middle of the dozen rows of desks. His son wore a sheepish look on his face. "Sorry, Daed."

"Sorry isn't enough, son. You must be more responsible. I should be at the shop now, working."

"I'll do better."

"Should we go to the basement?" Bethel interrupted. "It was a heavy rain so I figured it wasn't a tornado."

"It's raining too hard for a tornado and there's no bank of clouds that I could see." Gabriel walked to the window and looked out. It was so dark he couldn't see anything, but rain and hail pounded in a staccato on the roof. "I'm no expert. You probably know more about the weather here than I do."

"Just an end-of-summer storm, I reckon."

All of a sudden the windows shattered. Wind ripped through the room, bringing with it a blinding rain. Boards creaked, groaned, and ripped apart. Lunchboxes, lanterns, books, and papers whipped through the air. Children shrieked, the sound like sirens mingling with the wind. Gabriel felt himself lifted and propelled forward. He tried to stagger toward the little girls. He wanted to give them cover, but he couldn't seem to control his arms and legs. The force of the wind captured him and held him captive.

The seconds seemed to stretch and stretch. Rain beat down on them and the wind whirled and snatched at things and hurled them about with all the fury of an unseen foe. Desks flew. Chairs knocked into children. Seth. Where was Seth? Gabriel had to get to him. "Seth!" He hollered, but the wind swept up the word and sent it dashing against the black sky overhead. The whirling wind sucked all the air from the one-room schoolhouse as the small building came apart at the seams.

Screaming filled the air around him. The wind picked Gabriel up like a rag doll and smashed him against a wall. Seth flew past him and hit a desk, his body limp. Gabriel landed on his back. He tried to roll to his side, determined to crawl to his son. Hail and rain pelted him.

Tree branches smacked him in the face. He pulled himself forward on his hands and knees, broken glass and wood grinding into his palms. "Seth? Seth!"

Something hard and heavy slammed into him.

Seth. Son.

Chapter 38

Helen hurled herself from the buggy and tore across the uneven ground. She stumbled and fell to her knees. Thaddeus grabbed her arm and dragged her up again. She scrambled to keep up with her brother. His long legs ate up the distance that separated them from knowing the fate of their children. His four. Her three. And all the others who belonged to their friends and neighbors. Her brother had arrived at her doorstep with a message spreading across the community. Powerful winds had ripped through the schoolhouse. Wind shears, he called it. Took the roof right off. He didn't know any more than that. But it was enough. They had to go. Peter and Tobias had gone ahead.

Rain puddles soaked her shoes and the hem of her skirt. She lifted it and climbed over a mammoth tree branch that lay across the road. Ahead, she saw the schoolhouse. What once had been the schoolhouse. The building no longer existed. The force of the winds had sheared off the roof and shattered the walls. *Lord, have mercy. God spare them.* She prayed the same words she'd prayed over and over again during a buggy ride that had lasted a lifetime.

Ambulances and a fire truck parked at odd angles served as more obstacles. Buggies filled the spaces in between. More parents poured in with the same terrible fear driving them along the road. Helen dodged an EMT and ignored the warning of another to keep back. She couldn't take it in fast enough.

"Naomi? Betsy! Ginny!" The names stuck in her throat. Little Mary. Lillie. Gabriel's Seth. Thomas's Rebecca and Eli. Luke and Leah's William and Joseph. And on and on. Each child a precious son or daughter of a friend. *Ach, Gott. Please.*

"Stop, ma'am. Stop! You can't go in there." An Englisch firefighter put a hand out. "The building isn't safe. What's left of it may collapse."

"My girls. My girls were in there!"

"We're tending to all the children. Please stay back, ma'am."

She tried to circumvent the barrier he created with his body and he stepped in front of her once again. "Who did you have at school today?" He looked down at a clipboard in his hand. "We're making a list so we can account for all the children."

She drew a shaky breath and gave him the names.

"Mudder, Mudder!"

She turned and Naomi scampered toward her. A long, red welt snaked across her forehead. Mud stained her torn apron, but she looked whole. "Naomi, my girl." Helen enveloped her daughter in a hug that held them both up. "Betsy? Ginny?"

"Betsy's fine. She doesn't even have a scratch on her. She's with Onkel Peter and his boys. They're fine too. Just banged up. With bruises and bumps." The girl began to cry, quiet sobs she tried to hold back with a hand over her mouth. "They have Ginny over there in that first ambulance."

Helen's heart ceased to beat. Light-headed, she tried to move toward the ambulance, but her legs wouldn't cooperate. They'd gone soft. They collapsed underneath her. The firefighter grabbed one arm, Naomi the other.

"She's not dead, Mudder. The EMT says she's unconscious." Naomi's grip tightened. "She has some broken bones."

Together they managed to make their way through the crowd. Helen saw Thomas and Emma huddled over Eli and Rebecca. Both seemed to be in one piece. *Thank you, Gott.*

Beyond them stood Peter and his wife, Cynthia, who gathered around their flock like protective mama and papa birds. Betsy looked up from her seat on a tree trunk, saw Helen, and ran to her. Helen hugged her tight. "Stay here with Onkel and Aenti," Helen whispered in her daughter's ear. "You're safe here. I have to see to Ginny."

The words caught in her throat.

"Teacher helped us stay down on the ground. I wanted to run, but she kept us under the desks." Betsy hopped up and down as she spoke. "The ambulance took her away. I want to go with you to make sure she's all right."

"You have to stay here with your onkel. I'll let you know how teacher is. I have to go to Ginny."

Frowning, Betsy sank down on the trunk. Cynthia patted her back. "We'll take care of her."

Helen nodded her thanks and moved on.

Thaddeus waved at her. "Mine are fine. Yours?"

She nodded and waved back. They'd be fine. *Gott, let Ginny be fine.*

In the ambulance, the EMT bent over Ginny. She had a brace around her neck that dwarfed her face. Either the wind had taken her kapp or the EMT had removed it. Her blond hair feathered around a face so white and still. Helen tried to breathe. It would do her child no good if she fainted. She inhaled and climbed into the ambulance. "Ma'am, you can't be in here."

"This is my girl." She knelt next to the stretcher. "Ginny. Ginny, girl. Can you hear me?"

Ginny's eyelids fluttered. She moaned. "Mudder?"

"You're fine." Helen glanced at the EMT. He nodded in confirmation. Helen stroked Ginny's arm with a gentle hand. "They'll take you to the medical center and get you fixed up in no time."

The EMT motioned toward the open doors. Helen squeezed Ginny's hand and forced herself to let go. Outside the ambulance, a second EMT took a look at the welt on Naomi's face. "This is superficial. It'll heal in no time," he said. He pulled a tiny flashlight from his pocket and flashed it in Naomi's eyes. "Any pain? Did you hit your head? Anything fall on you?"

"Another doctor already looked at me." Naomi leaned on the ambulance bumper and wiped at her face with a shaking hand. "She said I was fine. How's Ginny? How's my sister?"

The first EMT turned to Helen. "It looks like your daughter may have a broken clavicle and fractured left arm. They'll have to do X-rays at the clinic to confirm. She took a blow to the head. I'm not sure if she fell on something or it fell on her, but she's got a lump on her noggin and she'll have quite a headache for a few days."

"But she'll be okay?"

"They'll want to determine if she has a head injury, a concussion." He smiled at her. "The docs at the medical center are good people. They'll get her fixed up in no time. You can ride in with her."

"Naomi, you stay here with your onkels and Betsy." Helen forced her voice to be steady and strong. She needed Naomi to be steady and strong. "Go home with them. I'll come for you when I can."

"I want to go with you." She clung to Helen's arm. "Can't we all stay together?"

"I need you to be strong for Betsy." Helen held the girl at arm's length. "You're her big sister. She'll be scared."

"I'm scared."

"The storm is over."

"The wind screamed. It knocked us around." Naomi shivered and wrapped her arms around her middle. "It even knocked over Gabriel."

"Gabriel?" Gabriel couldn't have been at the school. Shouldn't have been there. He would be at his shop working. Surely, he was at the shop. "Why would he be at the school?"

"Seth forgot his lunch."

"We're leaving, ma'am." The EMT slapped one ambulance door shut. "If you're going with us, you need to get in."

"Go to your onkel." She patted Naomi's cheek. "You'll be fine. Tell him where I am. Tell him I'll come when I can."

Over Naomi's shoulder she saw another stretcher being loaded into an ambulance. Gabriel's long, gangly body lay supine, his hair dark against the snowy white sheets. "Gabriel?" she whispered. "*Ach*, Gabriel!"

Chapter 39

Mark and Josiah on her heels, Annie threaded her way through the crowd in the medical center emergency room. Her entire community seemed to be crammed into the waiting room. She searched the faces. Waiting. Stoic. Troubled. Praying. There they were—Emma, Luke, Thomas, Leah. Her family. She squeezed past the Glicks and the Hostetlers. One of the older women patted her shoulder as she passed.

"Are they all right? Is everyone all right?" Annie pulled Emma into a hug, including baby Lilah in the embrace. Her sister's body trembled, but she managed a smile. A smile. *Gut.* Very *gut.* "Where are they?"

Her brothers and sisters parted. All six of the family's children sat side-by-side in the padded waiting room chairs. Lillie leaned against William, her eyes closed, face peaceful in sleep. Rebecca, who held baby Caleb on her lap, had bandages wrapped around both wrists while Eli sported a Band-Aid over his nose and a second one on his cheek. Bruises darkened the skin around both eyes. He seemed quite pleased with his appearance. "The wind knocked the school down, Annie! It knocked it down and it knocked us down!"

"*Ach.* Thank Gott you're all right." Annie hugged each child, careful not to wake the smaller ones who had succumbed to the exhaustion of such an exciting day. "My sweet babies, I'm so glad you're okay."

"Jah, thank Gott." Luke's arm went around Leah's shoulders. His fraa's lips quivered, but she shed no tears. She hugged little Jebediah closer to her, her gaze steady. Luke's hand rubbed against her sleeve. "Thank Gott we didn't lose anyone. Every child survived. Only Gott's grace…"

He stopped, his voice choked.

"Any bad injuries?" Annie tried to collect her thoughts. She prepared to pray. To seek God's mercy for the children of her neighbors and friends. "Who?"

"Bethel." Leah's face worked, but she managed to contain her sobs. "She covered the smallest children with her own body. Her back may be broken."

"*Ach.*" Annie whispered. A good teacher. A good person. "I'll pray."

"Pray," Leah repeated. She sank onto the chair next to Esther and Ruth, who slept side-by-side.

"Jonah and Ruth's boy Solomon has two broken legs," Thomas added. "Letty Brier is unconscious with a head injury."

"Has anyone seen my daed? Gabriel. Gabriel Gless." Isaac's deep voice carried over the crowd. Annie turned to see him weaving his way among the clusters of families, stopping to ask his question here and there, his face dark and miserable. "I can't find him. What about Seth Gless? He's eight. Has anyone seen him?"

Annie slipped past the Grables and called Isaac's name. He swung around. His face lightened for a second, then darkened again. "I'm looking for Daed and Seth. Have you seen them? Abigail said he went to the school to take Seth his lunchbox. He forgot it…"

"Did you ask at the desk?"

"I just got here. I need to find them. My daed." He stopped, his lips pressed together so tightly they turned white. He pulled his hat from his head and turned it in his hands. "He's my daed."

"I'll ask." Annie moved through the crowd. Her friends and neighbors parted for them. Isaac didn't touch her, but somehow it felt as if he held her hand. "This way."

The nurse at the counter studied the computer screen. "Mr. Gless is in examining room three. So is Seth Gless. He'll be admitted shortly. The boy, I mean."

"Admitted?" Isaac gripped the counter with both hands, but his voice remained calm. "Seth's to be admitted? Are his injuries…are they bad?"

"You'll have to ask the doctor. He'll be out shortly."

Isaac turned, leaned over, and slapped his hands on his knees.

"Let's walk down the hallway," Annie whispered close to his ear. "The examining rooms are that way."

He nodded and straightened. They slipped along the corridor until they reached the double doors. "They survived and they're back there somewhere." Annie peered up at him, trying to imbue her voice with all the encouragement and peace and certainty he needed to hear. "Good doctors are taking care of them. They are in good hands. Gott's hands. No matter what happens, they're in Gott's hands."

Isaac nodded. His Adam's apple bobbed. He chewed on his lower lip.

"What is it?" She stepped closer, longing for the freedom to give him a hug the way she had the children. Why was it different between a man and a woman? He needed comfort. She wanted desperately to offer it. "You can tell me anything, Isaac."

"Anything?" Emotion roughened his voice. "You might think less of me. A man who lets his emotions ride roughshod."

"You care and you show it. I don't consider that a character flaw."

"Not very manly."

"It is to me."

This time his hand really did grip hers, his skin rough and callused. "How about this emotion? I'm afraid I'm growing to love you."

After a second, Annie managed to close her mouth. "You thought you might lose your father and your brother. This isn't the time for declaring love or any other big declarations. When you mind is clear…"

"Were you the one asking for Gabriel Gless?"

They jumped apart at the man's inquiring voice.

"Jah, I mean yes, that's me." His neck and face red, Isaac stepped back but he didn't let go of Annie's hand. "Gabriel and Seth Gless."

"Who are you?"

"His son."

"Mr. Gless is trying to leave. Maybe you can convince him to stay overnight. He has some fractured ribs, a broken finger, lacerations, and he received a blow to the head. We'd like to keep him for observation."

"If my father has made up his mind about something, there's no changing it."

Like father, like son, Annie thought, but she didn't give voice to those thoughts. What a time for an interruption. She couldn't be selfish and wish the doctor had waited to step into the hallway. Isaac's father and brother were hurt. Still, her mind reeled from his declaration. Did she love him? The truth made her heart do a strange, small, painful dance. She might. She found herself on a cliff, looking down at a raging river. She could stay where it was safe or dive in.

Swallowing against the tide of conflicting emotion, she followed Isaac into the small exam room. There would be time to discuss this later. Right now, they needed to see to his family. She tugged her hand from Isaac's and stopped in the doorway. Gabriel stood, shoulders bent as if it hurt to straighten. His fingers fumbled with his shirt, trying to tuck it in. His skin had a gray cast and white lines tightened around his lips. Seth stirred and moaned on the bed next to his father's. His eyelids fluttered but didn't open. Gabriel froze, his gaze on his son.

"Daed, what are you doing?" Isaac strode toward his father. He put his hand out as if to help him. "You should be lying down. The doctor said…"

"Quiet. They gave Seth something for the pain. He's resting. I have to go. Stay here with him. The doctor says he'll be fine, but they're keeping him." The rough staccato of the whisper told Annie the older man labored under great emotion. "I'll return as soon as I can."

"Where are you going?" Isaac lowered his voice to a whisper, but the urgency remained. "You're hurt."

"I came here for a new start and I didn't have the strength to take the chance when it was handed to me." Gabriel's gaze came to rest on Annie and seemed to register her presence for the first time. "I see you found the chance as well," he said to his son.

"I…I…jah, I think I did."

"He did," Annie whispered, seeing the need for assurance in Isaac's eyes and hearing the uncertainty in his voice. He needed to know she would join him in this new territory. "He did."

"*Gut*. I have to go." With a tenderness on his face that made Annie want to look away, Gabriel leaned over the bed and laid one hand on Seth's cheek. The boy didn't stir. "I'll be back, son. Soon."

Then he limped past Isaac. When he reached Annie, he smiled down at her, a fleeting smile she almost missed. "Danki."

"Danki? For what?"

He didn't answer. He pushed through the doorway and disappeared down the hall.

Isaac moved to his brother's bedside. He pulled up the sheets and tucked them around the boy's thin shoulders. Annie watched the emotions play across his rugged face. Then he turned so she couldn't see his face anymore.

"Isaac?"

"He's so little." He cleared his throat, then cleared it again. "He looks beat up."

"Flying furniture can cause a lot of damage, but the doctor says he'll heal." Annie went to his side and slid her hand in his. "Gott is merciful."

"Jah," Isaac whispered. He turned to face her. "You know yourself how short life is. We have no guarantees. I lost my mother. You lost your husband. You didn't have the time you wanted with him. We could've lost brothers and sisters today. You and I, we know that you can't wait when it comes to feelings of the heart."

"What are you saying?" Annie tried to calm her breathing, but it seemed to get away from her, racing faster and faster. "What do you want?"

"Marry me." His hands tightened around hers. "I want you to

marry me. If you're not ready in November, we'll wait until next year. I'll wait for you, Annie. I'll wait for you to be ready."

"Isaac."

"Do you think you can learn to love me?"

"Jah." The word escaped of its own volition, but the second she uttered it, Annie knew she spoke the truth. "I do love you."

"I love you. So marry me."

"We're in the middle of a medical clinic."

"Marry me."

"Give me time to know you, truly know you."

"I know. I'm racing ahead again."

"You are, but I want to catch up. I will catch up. I promise." As she said the words, Annie felt the fluttering of hope, optimism, and tenderness as they bloomed inside her. "We'll have our new start, here in Bliss Creek."

"Jah. A new start." He leaned closer. "Do I have your leave to kiss you now?"

"You do."

So he did. Everything stopped. The fearful voices died, drowned in the rush of emotion. His lips touched hers and the confusion and the pain of loss subsided. Not gone, but dwarfed by the conviction that this man loved her and she loved him. *Thank you, Gott.* The kiss ended, but Isaac's long arms wrapped around her, holding her close. She leaned her head against his chest. She could feel his heart pounding, a steady, sure sound that calmed her own heart. She never wanted to move again. "More." He raised her chin with two fingers. His eyes were so warm she wanted to wade into them. "Just a little more."

This time the kiss went on and on. She never wanted it to stop. She leaned into him, knowing they should stop. *Just a little more.*

"Isaac? Are you kissing a girl?"

At the sound of the boy's groggy, confused voice, Annie jumped back. Isaac laughed. Annie drew a shaky breath and managed a smile. Grinning, Isaac patted his brother's arm. "Not a girl, Seth, my future fraa."

Chapter 40

The note fluttered to the ground. Helen stared at the white, offending piece of paper as it settled in the grass at her feet. Not caring that it was damp from the rain, she sat down on the step on her front porch with a thump. Her legs didn't want to hold her anymore. Her only son had left her. Edmond had left her in a car driven by another woman who had left her faith. Catherine knew better. She knew the terrible cost. Yet she allowed this young boy to hitch a ride with her to the city. Helen lowered her face into her hands. It surprised her to find that her cheeks were wet. She closed her eyes and let the tears come. She'd failed. *I'm sorry, George. I'm sorry, Gott. I'm sorry.*

A hand touched her shoulder. She shrieked and stumbled to her feet.

"It's me. It's me, Gabriel." He towered over her, his battered face filled with concern. "What is it? You look so…sad."

"What are you doing here? You should be at the clinic."

"I'm fine." He didn't look fine. The bruises on his face had turned a purple so dark he looked like a raccoon. He had a bandage across his forehead, and he walked with a limp that said every step caused him pain. "At the clinic they said Ginny would be all right. I saw your brother. He said you'd come home."

"They're keeping her overnight because of the injury to her head."

Helen sagged back on the porch steps, relief mingled with a new aching sadness that made her legs weak. *Thank You, Gott, for sparing my children and for sparing Gabriel.* Blessings mixed with adversity. She'd come to expect that, but still, she sometimes faltered when the blows rained down. "I only came for a few things for Ginny."

"And Naomi and Betsy?"

"Bruises and bumps, that's all. What about Seth?"

"Broken arm. Broken leg. Concussion. A desk got him good. He'll be at the clinic for a few days, but the doctor says he'll be all right."

"I saw them take you away in the ambulance and I thought…"

"What did you think?"

"That I'd—that we'd lost you."

"And the thought pained you?"

More than he could imagine. "Why are you here, Gabriel?"

Wincing with the effort, he stooped and picked up the note. "What's this?"

His dark eyes studied the words on the page. His gaze came up and met hers. Neither of them moved, their gazes locked. He licked his lips, but he didn't say anything. After a few seconds, he eased onto the step next to her, his big body so close she could smell his soap and that scent of a man who worked to earn his keep. She inhaled it and closed her eyes, trying to hang on to the feeling of security it gave her.

His fingers, hard and callused, closed around her hand, resting on her knee. She swallowed, fighting the urge to sob. Beyond the occasional pat on the shoulder from her father, no man had touched her in seven years. Her chest ached where her heart had been wrenched from her body that spring day. The void filled.

"I'm sorry." Gabriel's voice sounded rusty, as if he hadn't used it in a while. Low and husky, with a hint of honey. "He's gone, then."

"Gone." She could manage only the one syllable.

"Do you want to go get him? He's sixteen. You're within your rights." His grip tightened. "I would go with you."

"He didn't finish his community service. I don't know what will happen to him if he doesn't come back, but he needs to do it of his own accord." She opened her eyes and focused on the horizon as if she would see him walking down the road, returning to her. "We accomplish nothing by dragging him back."

"You're a wise woman, Helen Crouch." Gabriel's thumb rubbed gently back and forth over hers. "And a good mudder."

"*Ach*, you're wrong." She swallowed back sobs and concentrated on the feel of his fingers on hers. "So wrong."

"He'll come back."

She studied his long, brown fingers covering her own smaller, whiter, plumper fingers. "I should've tried harder to keep your Daniel here," she whispered. "You must be thinking how I deserve this. I didn't keep your Daniel here and now my Edmond is gone. I'm a terrible parent. That's what you're thinking."

"I'm thinking how wrong I was to judge you. I'm thinking I know how you feel. I'm thinking the situation is different." He cleared his throat. "I'm thinking Daniel is a man. He went home to the woman who will be his fraa. I should never have forced him to come here. It's different with Edmond. He's young. He's running around. He'll come home."

"I don't know." She wiped at her face with her free hand. "You were right. You were right not to want Abigail to see him. I'm so sorry she'll be hurt."

"She's still a girl. If I were a lesser man, I'd see your son's leaving as a blessing for my girl. She'll get over him."

"But you don't see it as a blessing?"

"Your son's future in his community, his life with his family, his faith—all these things are at stake. I'm not the kind of man who puts himself ahead of that."

He didn't sound offended. He sounded almost surprised. He too had moments of insecurity, Helen realized. That surprised her too. "You don't think I'm a terrible parent?"

"Nee. I want you to be the mother of my children." His hand tightened on hers. "I trust you to be a good mother to my children."

The statement hung in the air between them. Helen tried to

comprehend them. What was he saying? They stared at each other. She couldn't find the words. He wanted her. Gabriel wanted her in his life, in his house.

"Helen." He sounded as if he were gathering his patience. "I'm staying here in Bliss Creek. I want you to stay too. Be my wife."

"You're staying?"

"We have to build a new schoolhouse, don't we? And they'll need a teacher until Bethel recovers. Abigail has a hankering to teach, and she's nearly old enough."

"Who'll take care of the little ones and the house?"

He pulled her hand from her lap to his. She forced herself to glance his way. His expression held a tenderness she'd never seen there. She tried to understand its meaning. Her heart hammered in her chest.

"Gabriel?" She watched as he raised her hand to his lips and kissed it. Surely, this was happening to someone else. The warmth of his touch said otherwise. Her mouth parted and her breath left her body. "Gabriel? What are you doing?"

"Don't you know?" He spoke in a gruff whisper. "I…I care…for you."

"I can tell from how easy it was for you to say that." A spurt of anger—Helen was sure it was anger—shot through her. She tugged her hand from his. "What do you take me for? A silly, lonely, old fool? You want me to take care of your children? I love your children. I love Rachel and Isabelle. But I won't settle for that. I want to be more than a mother to your children. I want to be more…"

She couldn't say it. Her face burned at how closely she'd come to saying it aloud. She wanted to be loved by Gabriel. Just as she loved him.

He bowed his head and sighed.

Her heart broke. He didn't love her like that. He needed a housekeeper. He didn't need Helen.

After a second he put his arm around her and pulled her into his chest. He grunted as if the pressure hurt, but he didn't let her go when she tried to pull away.

"Don't." She meant to say it louder, but the command became lost in the soft cotton of his faded work shirt as did her determination to pull away. His chest muscles were solid and rock hard. His heart pounded, steady and strong, like him. "You don't have to feel sorry…"

"I don't feel sorry for you." His beard rubbed against her cheek, tickling her. "You try my patience, woman. You truly try my patience."

His warm, soft lips covered hers. Helen's stomach dropped to her toes. Her hands slid up his chest and her arms wrapped themselves around his neck. She let herself go, let herself feel for the first time in years. Feel what it was like to be held and loved. He had wonderful lips. He kissed her like he meant it. Helen reveled in him.

When he lifted his head, she looked up at him, startled, embarrassed, uncertain, all over again.

"Don't." He shook his head. "Don't back down now."

"Are you sure?" Her voice trembled with emotions she didn't know she still had in her. "Of me. I'm not the most…I'm not very…I'm Helen Crouch."

"I've never kissed another woman besides my wife in my entire life." He brushed a finger across her cheek, sending a chill careening through her. "What do you think?"

She'd never kissed another man besides George. Not in her entire life. Now the lovely kiss Gabriel Gless had given her filled her mind to its brim, blotting out years of loneliness bereft of a man's touch. "I think I'd like to try that again. To make sure you know what you're doing and you mean what you say."

A smile broke across his face, like the sun coming up on a perfect, cool spring morning.

The second kiss told Helen the first had not been a dream. It went on long enough that she might faint from lack of air, but still it ended too soon.

He backed away, leaving a space between them wide enough to fit a half-grown child. Wise man. She tucked her hands in her lap to keep them from straying to his. "What now?" she asked, surprised at how calm her voice sounded. Inside, it felt as if a whole batch of puppies were playing rough and tumble in her stomach. "What next?"

"Now we tell the deacon we want to get married in November."

"We want to get married in November," she repeated.

"You do want to marry me, don't you, Helen?"

"I do," she said.

Epilogue

Helen lifted her head as the bishop's final words of prayer dissipated in the slight chill that hung in the air. Autumn might finally make an appearance, letting the hot summer take its leave. The newly rebuilt schoolhouse stood ready to receive its students. Fewer scholars would enter the doors when it reopened later in the day, and those who did would be greeted by a new teacher. Abigail Gless stood on the steps, hands clasped, looking all grown up. Bethel would make the trip to Missouri with Leah, where she could continue her convalescence under her sister's care.

The decision had been made to meet at the school so prayers could be lifted for a safe journey and goodbyes said in the comforting presence of the others who would stay behind. The white passenger vans lined the road, reminders that change awaited them all. Moving vans had gone ahead, taking with them the worldly goods that the departing families would need for their new start.

"God's plan." Smiling, Gabriel approached her, leaving behind the knot of men clustered a few yards away. "Remember that."

"I know." Helen forced herself to breathe. In the city, Edmond sought his new start. She prayed Catherine had the strength and wisdom to show a rebellious, confused boy the way. That they would both find their way home. "Always. I'll have a word with Annie about the bakery and say a few more goodbyes. Then I'll be ready to go."

"*Gut*. I'll talk to Josiah about the repairs he needs and meet you at the buggy."

She watched him stride away, unable to stop herself. She still marveled that this mountain of a man had chosen her. Smiling at the thought, she waited until Annie had had a chance to say her goodbyes to Emma and the little ones. When she moved on to Luke and Leah, Helen walked across the yard. Annie smiled and met her halfway.

"I'm so thankful we'll have each other." Helen gave her friend a quick hug and squeezed Noah's pudgy arm. The toddler favored her with a wide grin that sported two teeth in the middle. "I'm looking forward to helping you in the bakery."

"Until other duties take over." Annie grinned and cocked her head toward Gabriel. "I think you'll have your hands full come November."

"You too." Helen wagged her finger at her friend. "If I'm not mistaken."

"We'll see. I'm taking this one day at a time. We both are."

Helen nodded. That was all any of them could do. "I'm sorry about Catherine."

"Me too. I'm sorry she chose to take Edmond with her." Annie's smile faltered. "The letter she left me said she wouldn't publish the memoir after all. Or the photos. That she didn't need to do that, and that she could find her way on her own. She says she and her Englisch friend are engaged now."

"Engaged? I hope she really is finding her way. I hope Edmond finds his way too."

"He will and Catherine will help him. She won't abandon him in the big city." Annie sighed. "She sees someone who's searching, like she was, and she sees a way to make up for some of the hurt she caused."

"By taking my son away?"

"By letting him see what he will miss. He'll be back. I know he will."

"It's hard." Helen bit her lower lip, straining to keep the sobs at bay. "But I know you're right."

"He will. Noah, stop fussing. You can't get down. It's muddy." She adjusted her grip on the wiggling child, who began to cry. "I'd better get him home. He needs his breakfast and a nap before I take him to the bakery. I'm so glad Mary Beth has agreed to stay on and help with him. With Mark and Josiah working our farm and the shop, I'll need all the help I can get at the bakery. See you there later?"

"I wouldn't miss it." Helen felt contentment brush against her, like the wings of a butterfly beating against her skin, soft and quick. "I'm happy for Josiah. He finally gets to farm."

"Amazing how God's plan unfolds, isn't it?" Annie hugged Noah to her chest, her eyes luminous with unshed tears. "Isaac will get his chance at the blacksmith trade. Josiah will have income at the shop and still be able to try his hand at farming. We don't know if it will work out as we plan, but it will work out as Gott plans."

She turned and trotted away, one hand lifted in a wave. Helen remained where she stood, watching the myriad of goodbyes still being said. Six families faced a new future. Micah had chosen carefully. Families with children of marriageable age would grow the new district. He said the Bliss Creek district had become too large. Even without the oil and the drought, a change would've been necessary.

It didn't feel too large. It felt like family.

"Don't look so sad." Tugging his hat back, Thomas approached. The solemnity in his eyes matched the feeling in her heart. "God will see us on our way."

"That doesn't mean I won't…" She struggled for the right words. "You've been a good friend. You've been…family."

"You also." He raised his hand as if he would touch her arm, then let it drop. "To me and to my fraa and to her sister. I would ask a favor of you."

"Anything."

"Stay close to Annie. It grieves Emma so to leave her sister behind."

"Annie is like a sister to me. Emma needn't worry about that. And Annie will have Miriam and there's always Charisma. Although I'm not always sure if that is a good thing or a bad thing." Helen couldn't help but smile. "Anyway, I think Annie will be too busy to moon over the people she misses."

Thomas's gaze went to Isaac, who leaned against his buggy. The young man watched Annie as she tried to hold a squirming Noah on her hip and hug Mary and Lillie at the same time. "I reckon you're right about that." Thomas smiled back at Helen. "I reckon you'll be busy yourself."

Heat washed over Helen, but the joy that rushed through her couldn't be denied. She no longer felt clumsy or awkward or nervous. "Jah, very busy. I hope y'all will make it back for a visit, maybe in November."

"November it is." Thomas's normally taciturn face creased with a grin. "I'll mark the calendar when we get settled in our new home."

"And again at Christmas," she added, feeling she'd said too much. "We'll have much to visit about."

"I'll make sure of that." Gabriel strode toward them. He extended a hand to Thomas. "Blessed be all our new beginnings."

Blessed be. Helen repeated the words silently. Thank Gott for new beginnings.

Discussion Questions

1. As his mother, Helen feels responsible for Edmond's actions at the Fourth of July parade. Many times parents do all the right things and say all the right things, and yet their children still do bad things. Is Helen responsible for Edmond's behavior? Do you believe she was lacking as a parent? Does Edmond's behavior say more about him or about Helen? Have you ever felt guilty or responsible for someone else's failings?

2. When Catherine returns to Bliss Creek, she is met with silence from Luke, who insists that the *meidung*, or shunning, should be observed. The Amish believe shunning shows a person who has broken the Ordnung the consequences of their disobedience. It also keeps the family from being drawn into that worldly life. How would you feel about not being able to talk to a family member who breaks a church or community rule?

3. Is there a conflict between shunning and the Amish community's belief in absolute forgiveness? How can the two be practiced side-by-side? What is the Scriptural basis for the practice?

4. Do you think Catherine was right to agree to Edmond's request that she take him with her back to Wichita? Why or why not?

5. Annie and David chose to marry, knowing his illness might result in his death. Annie took her marriage vows as a leap of faith. Then her husband died. Were they wrong? How do you explain the fact that they had faith and yet their prayers were not answered in the way they had hoped? Have you ever had a prayer that wasn't answered the way you'd hoped? How did that affect your faith? Would you be afraid to take that leap of faith again if the opportunity presented itself?

6. Do you believe, as the Amish do, that God has a plan for you? How do the bad things that happen to you fit into that plan?

7. Gabriel, Helen, and Annie each are in different stages of dealing with their grief at the loss of a spouse. All three loved their spouses very much. The Amish expect members of their community who have lost a spouse to find a new one so that their families can be complete and flourish. How do you feel about the push for them to marry again in light of the vows they took with their first spouses? The vows say "until death do us part." How do you feel about taking that literally?

8. Aenti Louise is looking forward to tasting the earth on the tip of her tongue and putting her arms around warm earth, a very different view from the one most people have of cold dirt and death. Do you share the Amish view that death is simply the next step toward being closer to God? What does that view say about their faith and yours? Is being afraid to die a lack of faith?

9. Romans 5:3-5 urges us to glory in our suffering because it allows us to grow our character and our perseverance and our hope. Do you feel like that might be too much to ask? When you've faced difficult situations in your life, have you been angry with God? How did you reconcile those difficulties with the knowledge that God loves you and is with you in your suffering?

Kelly Irvin is a Kansas native and has been writing professionally for twenty-five years. She and her husband, Tim, make their home in Texas. They have two children, three cats, and a tankful of fish. A public relations professional, Kelly is also the author of two romantic suspense novels and writes short stories in her spare time.

To learn more about her work,
visit www.kellyirvin.com

To Love and to Cherish

In author Kelly Irvin's first installment in the Bliss Creek Amish series, readers will find a charming, romantic story of how God works even in the darkest moments.

It's been four years since Carl left. Four years since he left the safety of the small Amish community for the Englisch world. And in four years, Emma's heart has only begun to heal.

Now, with the unexpected death of her parents, Emma is plunged back into a world of despair and confusion. It's a confusion only compounded by Carl's return. She's supposed to be in love with him...so why can't she keep her mind off Thomas, the strong, quiet widower who always seems to be underfoot? Could the man she only knew as a friend be the one to help her to heal?

In a world that seems to be changing no matter how tightly she clings to the past, this one woman must see beyond her pain and open her heart to trust once again.

A Heart Made New

In the second novel of Kelly Irvin's Bliss Creek Amish series, readers will be delighted to return to a town and a family they've already come to love.

Annie Shirack is trying to fight her feelings for David Plank, a young Amish man who's struggling with an aggressive case of Hodgkin's lymphoma. David loves Annie too much to let her into his life, only, he fears, to leave her.

When a homeless young woman named Charisma and her two-year-old daughter, Gracie, show up in Bliss Creek, Annie welcomes them into the Shirack household and tries to help them establish a new life. But all the good deeds in the world can't change the ache in Annie's heart...or help her forget the man she loves.

The Bliss Creek Amish
An Interview with Author Kelly Irvin

How did you come up with the concept for the Bliss Creek Amish?

I'm not sure I actually came up with it at all! I was fascinated with the Amish folks' commitment to forgiveness. They practice what they preach, something I've found hard to do when it comes to forgiveness. That fascination grew into the story *To Love and to Cherish*. The second book, *A Heart Made New*, grew out of the first book as I wanted to see what happened to Josiah and his sister Annie. Again, the spiritual theme of learning to take on faith God's plan for our lives drove the story. Not knowing how our lives will turn out isn't important as long as we believe God will be there in the end—no matter when or how that end comes. The third book really came about because I felt bad for Helen—she's a widow who has a little crush on Thomas in *To Love and to Cherish*. She deserves her own true love. So that's how *Love's Journey Home* began.

Is any part of Bliss Creek Amish series true?

The characters are fictitious and so is the setting, but the challenges faced by Emma, Thomas, Annie, Josiah, David, Helen, and the other characters are drawn from real life. They're challenges we all face as human beings trying to deal with a broken world as Christians. As Plain folks, they work even harder than most of us because they choose to do it without modern technology and "basic necessities" like electricity. They face disease, the deaths of loved ones, broken hearts, and disagreements with family members…just as we do. I also drew some of these challenges from newspaper articles and media coverage about Plain folks dealing with disagreements with city officials over permitting, the fallout of finding oil on their land, the rising cost of farmland, and the difficulties of making small family farms profitable in today's economy.

Is Bliss Creek a real place?

No, it's totally a figment of my imagination, but it comes from having grown up in a small rural town in Kansas where farming is a mainstay. Bliss Creek is smaller than my hometown of Abilene, Kansas, which has about eight thousand residents, but it has many similarities. Small towns are wonderful because everyone knows everyone. They're great places to raise families. Small towns can also be painful places to live because everyone knows everyone—and their business!

Did you include any of your life experiences in the Bliss Creek Series?

I find that everything I write draws from the sum total of my experiences as a human being. My husband and I lost our first child before he was born, so when I wrote about Emma's miscarriage in *A Heart Made New* I called upon those memories and feelings and that sense of loss. Writing can be a painful, yet cathartic process, but I do believe those experiences contribute to the authenticity of an author's work. (Not that you have to experience the loss of a loved one to write about it—I have a good imagination and a copious amount of empathy when it comes to these things.) I just finished writing the first book in a new series for Harvest House in which I had to revisit the horrifying, unexpected death of a loved one in a boating accident. I found myself wondering how long it takes for a writer to incorporate these kinds of painful experiences into his or her writing without reliving them. Or if that's even possible.

Do you have a favorite character in the series? Why?

That is a tough question. I love them all. As I wrote each book, I became better acquainted with each character. Still, I'd have to say it's a tie between Josiah and Annie. Josiah, because he reminds me of myself with his rebelliousness and his desire to be his own person, even though it goes against everything he learned growing up. Annie, because she's the character I most want to emulate. She's so loving and so willing to put herself out there for the people she loves and the things she believes in. In *A Heart Made New*, she holds out for the man she loves even when he struggles to walk by faith. She takes a homeless woman and child into her home and helps Charisma get back on her feet. Annie puts her faith into action. I so admire her. Her struggles are not over, but she faces them with a lovely grace.

How much research did the series take?

Quite a bit. I'm still learning. The challenge is compounded by the fact that each Amish community has its own set of rules, or Ordnung. I want to be very careful and respectful of how I present their lives while constructing an interesting story that will hold readers' attention and make them think about their own faith and lives. I spent a great deal of time reading books and researching online before I began to write the first book. I'm still doing that, as well as reading *The Budget* newspaper to learn more about the rhythm of their daily lives, the little details that make the stories seem more real and authentic. This summer I had the opportunity to visit an Amish community in Missouri, which was really helpful in terms of the next series I'll be writing.

What was the most interesting fact that you learned while writing the Bliss Creek Amish?

I don't think there's one specific fact. It's all been enlightening and thought-provoking. Learning about the Amish way of life has forced me to examine my life, my priorities, and my faith. It's given me a renewed desire to simplify and to prioritize. I'm still learning and still struggling, but writing about the Amish has opened up that interior dialogue, where before I was too busy rushing around to make myself stop and think about it.

What are some of the challenges you face as an author?

Mostly, it's time. Time is a valuable commodity in my life. I work full-time in public relations. I'm married. My two children are adults now, but we're very close. Finding time to write is always a challenge. I write in the early morning before work, at lunch, and on the weekends. I also have to admit to a certain amount of envy when I see others spending their entire days writing. We all make choices and I'm blessed to have a great job that helps support my family. Balancing the two is critical.

What aspects of being a writer do you enjoy the most?

Losing myself in that fictitious world. Walking around the house while two characters are conversing in my head. Running to my desk from the shower or the treadmill to jot down the lines that suddenly appeared out of nowhere. I'm in the middle of a manuscript right now in which the words seem to pour out faster than I can write them down. It's the best feeling and it brings great joy to my life. It's a gift from God and I thank Him for it every day.

What is your writing style? (Do you outline? Write "by the seat of your pants?" Or somewhere in between?)

I'm totally an organic writer. Because I have so little time to write, I want to use it to get the story written. I find if I stop to outline I lose the momentum and the creative fire that feeds it. It's not any fun anymore—it's like a class assignment. I've written synopses for proposals in the past, but invariably the story veers off in another direction and I have to rewrite them afterwards. Being out there without a road map is half the fun—scary but exhilarating.

What other new projects do you have on the horizon?

I'm beginning a three-book spin-off series called the New Hope Amish. Readers will recognize some of the characters as several families from Bliss Creek will pick up and move to Missouri to make a new start. It's been so much fun because I still get to visit my Bliss Creek folks but also add some new characters and plop them down in a new setting.

What message would you like your readers to take from the Bliss Creek Amish series?

Don't lose faith. It would be easy to do in this broken world, but God is in control. Love each other. Help each other at the beginning, middle, and end of each day. Count your blessings.

What do you do to get away from it all?

Usually, my husband and I rent a condo in Port Aransas on the Gulf of Mexico for a few days in the summer, but next year, on February 14, we're celebrating our twenty-fifth wedding anniversary by taking a week-long trip to Hawaii. I'm counting the days!

Finally, my thanks to the folks at Harvest House for taking a chance on a new writer (especially Kim Moore, who offered me a contract for *To Love and to Cherish* before I finished writing it) and doing such a tremendous job producing and marketing these books. And my thanks to the readers who have responded with encouraging and kind notes. Writing these books and having them published is a dream come true, and I cherish it every day.

To learn more about books by Kelly Irvin or
to read sample chapters, log on to our website:

www.harvesthousepublishers.com

HARVEST HOUSE PUBLISHERS
EUGENE, OREGON